I0671311

A Demon's Quest
the Beginning of the
End
Volume III

Charles Carfagno Jr.

ISBN: 0692426205
ISBN-13: 978-0692426203

DEDICATION

For the final volume, I'd like to thank the following people. Andrea Cunningham for her outstanding edits and advice, my publisher Tameca Waid because without her my dream would've never come true. My brother Joe and his wife Michele for their continuous love and support, Ken and Leigh Frazier for their support and bought way too many copies. Jeff Farrington, who gets very excited about my book. Krystal and Joe McLaughlin for their support and years of training. And finally, to the rest of my friends and supporters on Facebook, who constantly encourage me with my writing.

Thanks everyone.

CONTENTS

Chapter 1: The Peril (Part II)   1

Chapter 2: Stand Together   30

Chapter 3: Quest for The Red Knight   54

Chapter 4: The Retaking of Redden   116

Chapter 5: A Child's Dream (Part II)   123

Chapter 6: Into the Depths   134

Chapter 7: The Truth   166

Chapter 8: A Spirit at Peace   199

Chapter 9: A Long Awaited Reunion   214

Chapter 10: An Old Nemeses   240

Chapter 11: Celthric -A Blade's Quest (Part II) 268

Chapter 1: The Peril (Part II)

It was mid-morning when Rustic arrived back at the camp. He hurried to Brim's tent where he saw Clay still caring for him.

"How is he?"

Clay didn't respond.

"Clay!" Rustic raised his voice. "How is he?"

Startled, Clay looked up. "I gave him the berries, but I think he is dying. Where's Broc?" Clay asked, realizing his friend wasn't with him.

"He's dead. I didn't find him in time." Rustic's tone was somber.

"What happened to him?"

"He was captured, tortured, and killed by a band of creatures known as Mangalers."

"Mangalers? I never heard of them."

"The foul beasts are a cross between a wolf and a human. They must have taken him by surprise," Rustic said. He was so angry that he wanted to hit something.

"I need to know the details." Clay stood up as if he were ready to run off and avenge him.

Rustic gripped his shoulders. "There's nothing you can do. Focus on Brim, he needs our help."

Over the next several hours, both men did their best to tend to his wounds. However, given the fact that neither of them had ever trained in the healing arts, Brim's chances for recovery were slim.

It was nearing mid-afternoon when Gilex and Utar arrived. They split up as Utar went to his tent to rest and Gilex walked to Brim's quarters to check on him.

Gilex was about to enter when Rustic, head down, came out and almost bumped into him. "Rustic how's Brim?" He asked.

Rustic stopped in his tracks and looked up at him.

"Is Brim okay?" Gilex sternly asked.

"Broc is dead." He said in a somber tone.

"What? How did it happen?"

"He needed herbs during the night and went off searching for them."

"Who found him?" Gilex was clearly irritated.

"I did, and avenged his death by killing all of those responsible."

"Excellent work, though I am saddened by the loss. He was a great person and a skilled healer."

"One of the best," Rustic added.

"What about Brim?"

"He's awake, but weak. Clay watched over him all night."

"I need the men ready in a couple of hours."

"I don't think Brim will be ready."

"This area isn't safe."

Rustic nodded and took two steps past his leader.

"Rustic!" Gilex said causing the big man to stop in his tracks. "Consider yourself promoted to second lieutenant."

Without responding, Rustic walked away. He knew that it was a hollow accomplishment, but thought that he still deserved it. He'd been, if anything, loyal to the group and a good sword when needed. He headed toward Utar's tent.

Gilex watched him leave, thinking about Broc again. Not about him as a person or for the remarkable skills he possessed, but for the sacrifice he would've become. Rustic arrived at Utar's tent a short time later and waited for the lieutenant to invite him in before entering.

"Did you find anything out about Gilex or our mission?" Rustic asked.

"Keep your voice down."

"Well?" Rustic whispered.

"No, everything is going to be fine." Utar replied calmly.

"What did you discuss?"

"We talked about various things: our mission, the men, and the future."

"Did he seem different?"

"No, not really." Utar shook his head and appeared evasive when answering.

"Is that it?"

"Look!" Utar snapped. "We agreed that when we find out more information, we'll share it with each other. Okay?"

"Fine, sorry to bother you."

Rustic turned and was about to leave when Utar spoke again. "I apologize that I snapped at you. I'm tired, and it's been a long night."

"Nothing is making sense," Rustic thought. *"Last night, Utar was acting very suspicious, and now he acts like nothing is wrong."*

"Go get ready." Utar said interrupting his thoughts.

Rustic left his tent thinking that maybe he needed to keep an eye on both of them.

****

The sky darkened ahead of the group as they headed west. Gilex and Utar led, followed by Rustic and Clay, then Perahn and Brim, who was tied to his saddle in such a way that it prevented him from falling and Kentra, bringing up the rear. Several hours later rain fell in heavy sheets as they entered a thick wooded area. What they didn't know was that an unseen enemy, shrouded within the trees, waited for them to pass before launching a volley of crude, but deadly arrows from the north and then south.

The first stream of arrows hit Perahn in the right leg, Brim in the throat and shoulder, and Rustic in the left arm. Gilex's armor protected him, and he remained unscathed. Gilex immediately yelled for his men to flee and then galloped away just as the second volley was launched. The next wave missed Gilex, Utar, and Rustic, but Perahn took an arrow in his left shoulder. The impact almost caused him to lose his grip on the horse's reins, but he held on to them and galloped away. He glanced back and saw Brim and his horse on the ground. Both weren't moving.

Meanwhile, Clay was hit a few times while escaping, but none of his injuries were serious or life threatening. His horse however, was hit several times, leaving the mare gravely wounded and bleeding profusely. Her strength failed a few hundred yards later and she stumbled to the ground, throwing Clay headfirst. Kentra never had a chance to flee because his horse was struck in the neck, causing the animal to rear up and throw him from the saddle.

Gilex, Rustic, Utar, and Perahn never broke stride until they were several hundred yards away from the attack, and then Gilex brought them to a full halt. "Where is everyone else?" he asked, looking at each of them in turn.

"I saw Brim get hit several times; as for Kentra and Clay, I don't know," Perahn answered.

"I'm going back for them," Utar shouted over the piercing thunder.

"We'll meet you further up ahead. Good luck," Gilex said.

Utar nodded and sped off.

Utar rode hard until he saw Clay. He was using his barb-hooked spear to keep several Mangalers at bay. Utar yelled his infamous battle cry, and then began hurling throwing axes at the enemy. The attack slew two Mangalers and distracted the others, leaving them exposed to Clay's weapon of death. The tall man made quick work of the others, and then took Utar's hand as he slowed his horse and helped Clay onto his mount.

"Are you okay?" Utar asked.

"A few scratches, that's all." Clay said and borrowed Utar's bow. "I got our backs. We need to move, there are many more around us."

"Do you know what happened to Kentra or Brim?"

"Brim was killed, and the last time I saw Kentra, he and his horse were shot multiple times."

"Where?"

An arrow then crossed in front of the horse.

"We can't go back for him," Clay stated.

Not knowing what happened to Kentra bothered Utar, but he knew they couldn't go back, so he spurred the horse on. They made it a few hundred yards when more wolf creatures, armed with swords, emerged from the forest. Clay quickly took aim and slew three on the right, followed by two waiting directly in their path. Utar never slowed and rode over another two.

As Utar and Clay rounded another bend, a small group of Mangalers, armed with bows, appeared in front of them and began firing. Clay was hit in the left leg and right arm. Utar was hit in his right shoulder, right leg, and one arrow skimmed off of his left ear. Utar struggled with the reins, but never lost control, because if he had the other dozen or so wolf creatures emerging from the foliage would have overwhelmed them.

Kentra knew he was alone and that escape was impossible after looking over at his dead mount. His breathing was heavy as a result of his wounds, and he conceded to the fact that nobody was coming back for him. There would be no great rescue or a hero to save the day. As the enemy approached from all sides, he looked skyward to enjoy the rain falling on his face. The cool water, coupled with several deep breaths, brought a sense of peace, and then he decided to meet death head-on and unsheathed his long sword one last time. He grinned all the while knowing that he was going to see his wife again on the shores of the afterlife. On this day, he fought with such skill and determination that it wasn't the number of his enemy that would be his downfall, but the loss of blood from the many arrows protruding from his armor. When the battle was finally through, at least twenty Mangalers were dead along with Kentra's body that was torn to pieces.

The leader of the wolf creatures walked over and picked up his decapitated head. "See what you get when you oppose us?" He shouted with a snarl. "Before this day is through, we will kill the rest of those pathetic humans. They are the ones who killed our brethren two nights ago, and they must pay."

The group of fifteen responded with shouts of delight.

"When we catch them, we'll eat their innards and let them watch us before we cut off their heads."

More shouts and grunts echoed over the thunder.

The leader tossed Kentra's head on the ground. "Come, my brothers." He said and ran off, with his men following closely behind.

****

Gilex, Rustic, and Perahn came to an abrupt halt after traveling for two miles, and hid within the shelter of the trees. As they waited for the rest of the group, Rustic removed the arrows from Perahn and dressed his wounds, while Gilex kept watch, staring out through the driving rain.

"If they're not here soon, we'll have to find proper shelter," Gilex said, wiping away the rain from his face and pushing aside his matted hair.

"Let's give them an hour and..." Rustic was saying just as they heard a horse galloping toward them.

When they recognized the riders, Gilex whistled and Utar stopped his mount.

"Rustic, help Clay." Utar said, then dismounted and limped his way over to Gilex. "They're still after us. We have to keep moving."

Gilex looked at his first lieutenant's leg, with the arrow protruding, and wondered how he was standing. "Who are they? Or better yet, what are they?" he asked.

"They're some kind of humanoid wolf creature," Utar said.

Rustic stopped what he was doing. "I think they must be from the same group that killed Broc. Maybe they're seeking revenge."

"I thought you said you killed them?" Gilex asked him.

"I did. Maybe this group was meant to join the ones I killed."

"We have to reach the caves before nightfall. I'm tired and don't want to fight anymore," Utar interrupted.

6

"What about your wounds?" Gilex asked.

Utar followed his eyes and, without responding, pulled the arrows out of his body, one at a time, wincing in pain with each one. "I'll be fine." He said, grabbed ointment and began rubbing it over his wounds.

"The cave isn't much further, so if we set some traps, that should slow them down long enough for us to reach it."

"I'll have Rustic give me a hand," Utar added.

After Gilex, Perahn, and Clay were on their way, Utar and Rustic began placing traps all around the area. Some of them were simple in design, while others were a bit more complicated. All of them were designed to slow down their enemy. They staggered the traps in such a way that when one went off, the unsuspecting enemy would be forced in a different direction that would set off another. By the time they finished arming the last trap, a mile from where they started, the first device went off, which was followed by another, and another, and then the screams of anguish began. Both men smiled at each other, mounted their horses, and raced off.

Midnight was approaching when they finally arrived at the cave. Utar dismounted and took notice of the strange footprints surrounding and leading into the depths below.

"I've never seen footprints of this nature before." He stated.

"Maybe there's another way in?" Clay asked.

"Hold on." Gilex said, dismounted, and began surveying the area.

Rustic looked over at Utar and noticed that he wasn't favoring his injured leg. "You're not limping anymore."

"The ointment I have works extremely fast," Utar quickly answered, not wanting to draw attention to his newly found healing powers.

"Did you get it from Broc?"

Before he could respond, Gilex said. "With the amount of foliage surrounding this area, it would take a long time, if ever, to find another entrance, so I think we should enter here." Gilex walked to the mouth of the cave, lit a glow rock, and peered inside.

Rustic dismounted and joined him. "See anything?"

"Set the horses free and light some torches. We're going in."

"Is that wise? Everyone is tired."

"If we camp outside, we run the risk of the Mangalers catching up with us, and we're in no condition to fight. We'll rest down below."

After Utar returned from releasing the horses, Gilex guided them down into the cold, dark depths below. Traveling cautiously and silently downward, they continued their spiraling descent until they reached a circular room four hundred feet below the surface. The room was thirty feet in diameter with another corridor at the far end.

"Let's stop here and rest," Gilex said.

"I'll scout ahead," Rustic added, pulled out his hefty ax, and then activated a glow rock. He was about to disappear down the hallway when Gilex stopped him and walked over.

"Don't go too far. We'll follow the map once everyone is ready," Gilex said.

"I'll make sure there's nothing hiding nearby," Rustic said and left.

Once he was gone, Utar placed a trap at the entrance, and the rest of the men began setting up camp. After they were finished, everyone, except for Gilex, went to sleep. Gilex, sitting with his back against the wall, stared at the flickering torchlight and began to reflect on the events from a couple of years ago. He knew in his heart that Togan was responsible for his demise, although he had no proof. The question was why? They were like brothers; both were well-respected and high-ranking officials. What could he have gained by getting rid of him? Was it money, power, or did someone else convince him otherwise? After he was exiled from Lindenmar, he returned a few months later to plead his case to the magistrate, but never got the chance because Togan and the elite guard intercepted him. Gilex thought about attacking him on the spot, but decided against it. It was a decision that he'd regretted since then. Staring into the dancing flames his eyes grew weary, and a few seconds later, they were closed and he drifted off into a rare and peaceful sleep.

He dreamt that he was in a courtyard of their family's citadel. His father and brother were with him, and it was a day in which both boys were honing their fighting skills. They sparred against their father, and each other, and when they were through their father led them to another area and began showing them different attack and defense formations.

After the lesson, Gilex's father picked up a spear and attacked him. Father and son fought back and forth with neither one able to gain the advantage over the other. That was until Gilex's father used unorthodox movements and began inflicting wounds all over his son's body. They were deep enough to pierce through his armor and draw blood. Gilex's father heckled him for his lack of skill and came at him. Time and time again, Gilex was stabbed and pricked. His blood ran down his body and pooled around his feet, becoming thick as molasses and binding him to the spot. His father stopped and laughed at his son when he was unable to move his feet.

"My son, you have failed me and the family," his father said and pulled back the spear, then plunged the weapon into Gilex's stomach, pushing the shaft forward until it passed through his back. His father smiled and lifted him high in the air. As the dying Gilex slid down the shaft, he looked at his father's face, and suddenly it morphed into the face of Togan. The dream was all too real for Gilex, and his body began convulsing uncontrollably while he slept.

****

The sloping passageway that Rustic was following leveled some fifteen feet later, and then went straight for another ten. He followed it until he came upon a corridor leading west, and he stopped. After listening for several minutes to the stillness, he moved into the passageway. The long corridor led to another on his right. Rustic decided to continue his investigation north. He soon came upon a crossroad and was faced with going east, west, or north. Instinct told him to go straight, which was the path he chose after marking the wall with an arrow pointing back toward camp.

Another fifty feet later, the corridor suddenly grew cold, then colder still with each step until Rustic was chilled to the bone and needed to turn around. When he reached the crossroad again, he heard a faint click or chirping sound coming from somewhere down the far end of the western corridor. He needed to make sure there wasn't any real danger then turned the corner, holding the glow rock higher now, and shining as much light as possible. The lengthy hallway was lined with medium-sized divots that were scattered throughout the entire length of the hallway; how deep they were, he did not know. Rustic hesitated and then heard the noise again and proceeded with the glow rock held face high and his ax, cocked, and ready to strike. He was halfway down the length, when a loud, frightening screech erupted from the far end. Rustic panicked, backed away, then lost his footing and fell, dropping the glow rock as he landed in a deep hole. The glass light shattered upon impact, and he was plunged into darkness. He remained motionless, staring, and waiting to discover if anything heard him.

Several long minutes of silence passed before Rustic rose to a squatting position and carefully began moving back toward the exit, using the wall to guide him and his ax - as a blind man would use his cane - to feel for the next divot. He'd just felt the corner of the wall when he heard the clicking sound again. This time it sounded like it was slowly moving up the same corridor. Rustic turned around, dagger in his left hand and ax in his right, poised and ready to strike. The strange clicking sound continued to draw closer, followed by heavy breathing, and a stench that permeated throughout the area. Despite the nauseating smell, he remained calm. Tense seconds passed while Rustic remained as still as a statue and ready to strike; he figured he'd have one, maybe two swings with his ax before employing the dagger. The creature moved a few feet closer, stopped, snorted in his general direction, and then went back down the corridor. Exhaling in relief, he waited for a full minute before standing up and following the wall until he saw the camp's fire, then he rushed forward.

As soon as Rustic entered the area, he saw a massive, gray-colored creature hunched over Gilex. The hairless monster stared down at his prey, then unraveled its forked tongue and began running it up and down his body. Rustic glanced over at the others and saw them motionless; he wasn't sure if they were dead or asleep. He needed to act. He threw a dagger, hitting the monster's left shoulder, grabbing its attention. The creature turned its large, narrow head in his direction and glared at him with black, soul-less eyes. The creature then retracted its maw, exposing rows of razor-sharp teeth, and let out a hideous screech, which sent chills up and down his spine. Rustic knew what was coming and gripped his ax so tight that his knuckles turned white. The beast dropped to all fours and charged at him with extraordinary speed and agility. In one instant, the creature was across the room, and in the next, it was directly in front of him, rising up on its hind legs, matching Rustic's height and ready to strike.

Rustic anticipated its attack and ducked under its sweeping arm, narrowly being missed by the monster's razor-sharp claws. The mighty paw slammed into the sidewall, tearing away solid earth and sending chunks of clay flying in all directions. The creature lashed out again, aiming for Rustic's head, but he ducked and moved past the beast while slicing its underbelly. The creature's tough leather-like skin slowed the ax long enough to allow the beast to turn and strike him with its left paw across his shoulder. The sharp claws tore through his armor, like it was parchment, and bit into his flesh, causing Rustic to scream in pain and drop his ax. The beast flicked its powerful paw, sending Rustic sailing through the air and then immediately dropped to all fours and charged after him. Rustic landed with a thud and despite banging his head, he had enough of his senses to bring his arms up defensively against the creature's attacks. His thick bracers gave way after a few swipes, followed by his leather jerkin shortly thereafter. Rustic blindly punched the creature square in the nose with his left hand and frantically reached for his dagger with his right. After the second punch, the creature paused for a brief second, and that's when Rustic plunged the dagger into its left eye. The creature moved backward in pain, frantically trying to dislodge the weapon.

Rustic was exhausted from blood loss. His left arm was useless and he struggled in a great deal of pain, trying to unsheathe his sword while regaining his footing. He freed the blade at the exact moment the creature removed the dagger, which still had its eyeball attached. The monster looked directly at him with its one good eye and began moving slowly, and methodically, toward him. Its maw was open as saliva dripped onto the ground. Rustic waved his blade in front of his body in a defensive manner. *"This is it,"* he thought.

As the beast was about to pounce on him, a spearhead ripped through its powerful chest. The beast thrashed back and forth for several long seconds before falling over and dying. Rustic's head swam in confusion; his vision blurred, and his legs finally gave way as he crumbled to the ground. The last thing he saw before passing out was Utar standing over the creature, pulling his weapon free.

Utar ordered Perahn and Clay to help Rustic and Gilex while he surveyed the area, trying to figure out where the beast came from. He followed the footprints until they ended against the wall opposite the entrance of the room. Puzzled, he got on his hands and knees and poked at the wall with his spear. Dirt began falling away in chunks, revealing a hole large enough to service the size of the creature. He was about to look further in when Clay appeared.

"Rustic is unconscious, and Gilex has some pretty bad wounds. That creature bit him in several places." Clay said.

Utar paused. "Give them the rose-colored vials. That should speed up the healing process."

Clay knelt down to see what he was doing. "What did you find?"

"I'm pretty sure it's the hole the creature used."

"I hope there isn't any more of those things."

"I'm going to find out. Tell Gilex when he wakes."

"Will do."

Activating a glow rock and placing a dagger into his mouth, Utar entered the hole and descended into the darkness. Gilex recovered faster than expected. He was up and walking around, surprising Clay and Perahn.

"Are you okay?" Perahn asked him.

"Yes, why?"

"You were wounded pretty badly."

"I feel fine. What did you give me?" Gilex rubbed his head.

Clay handed him the empty vial. "Utar said to give it to you."

Gilex looked at the label. "I remember Broc saying this would speed up the healing process tenfold. What happened?"

"That beast over there attacked us while we were sleeping. Rustic arrived and fought with the thing long enough for Utar to wake and kill it." Clay explained.

"Where is my second in command now?" Gilex glanced over at the dead beast.

"He found the hole the creature used and went down into it to investigate," Perahn answered.

"How long has he been gone?"

"A couple of minutes."

"We'll wait an hour. If he doesn't return, we're moving on. Make sure you leave markers for him, so that he can find us easily. Did anyone talk to Rustic before he fell unconscious?"

Clay and Perahn both answered in unison, "No."

****

Utar descended into the narrow hole quickly. He came to an opening that appeared to be much smaller than the creature, which made him wonder how the beast could have fit through. He listened carefully and when nothing stirred below, he extended the glow rock into the opening and looked around. The first thing he noticed was that he was at least nine feet from the floor of a room that was circular in shape and cluttered with boxes. The only other way out was an open doorway at the far end of the room.

After waiting a couple of minutes, Utar jumped down and scanned the room again. Feeling safe, he began quietly rummaging through the boxes. Most of the items were worthless except for six razor sharp, barb-tipped arrows, several low-grade red gems, and two self-igniting oil flasks. Although they were only half-filled, he thought they should still provide a nice, fiery surprise. He'd just finished placing the gems into his pouch when he heard a clicking noise coming from the corridor up ahead. He turned his attention toward the entranceway, then toward the hole, and then back at the boxes. He determined that he wouldn't be able to reach the hole, even if he stacked the boxes on top of each other. The noise grew louder and closer, leaving him with no other option than to stand and face whatever was coming his way.

He crouched, and while waiting, he remembered an effective tactic that might prove useful in such a situation. Quickly, he placed the activated glow rock behind several boxes near the hole and ran over and hid behind boxes near the entryway, where he waited with a dagger in one hand and a flask in the other. The clicking noise drew closer and then stopped just outside of the doorway. From where he was, he could hear the beast sniffing the air. Utar needed to draw it into the room, so he tossed his dagger, hilt first, into the boxes across the way.

A few seconds later, a creature, similar to the one from upstairs, entered the room. It noticed the light behind the boxes and shuffled toward it. Utar listened patiently as the clicking sound inched closer. He waited until the monster was close enough to the boxes before pushing on the plunger on the flask and igniting the oil. The flame danced on top of the liquid. Once the glass was warm, he took aim and threw the flask, hitting the creature in the back of the head, shattering the thin glass container and spraying the beast with oil. Immediately, fire raced up and down the creature's body. It howled in pain for several seconds before turning around and seeing Utar. The creature was about to charge when Utar pushed the plunger on the other flask and threw it directly at the creature's feet, shattering the glass and spraying it with even more oil, which added to the already intense flames. The beast burned, flailed and fell to the ground, trying to extinguish the flames. Utar grinned in delight as he watched the monster futilely thrash about until it was finally overwhelmed by the fire and stopped moving. He held the last flask in his hand and waited for several minutes before leaving.

****

Clay approached Gilex.

"Rustic isn't awake yet; it might be a while," he said to Gilex.

"We don't have much time. Did you give him the same healing vial you gave me?"

"No you had the last one. We did give him the blue one though."

"Give him another one and let's get going," Gilex said. "If he doesn't wake up, carry him."

"What about Utar?" Perahn asked.

"He'll find us."

The decision to move on was a difficult one for Gilex; Rustic was unconscious and Utar was off investigating where the creature came from. With their numbers dwindled down to three, they packed up, lit some torches, and descended further into the unknown. Gilex led the group, followed by Perahn, who carried Rustic over his shoulder, and Clay, guarding the rear. When they came across another corridor leading west, they stopped. Gilex sent both men to investigate to avoid anything sneaking up on them. They returned a short time later to report that the corridor came to a dead end. Clay checked on Rustic, who was beginning to wake.

"Where am I?" Rustic asked.

"Are you okay?"

"My head feels funny, but otherwise, I guess I am okay." He tried rising, but Clay held him fast.

"Take it easy." Clay forced him back down.

Gilex and Perahn joined them.

"It's good to see you awake, my friend, and thanks. I heard that if it wasn't for your bravery, we'd all be dead," Gilex said.

"Just doing what anyone else would have done."

"I'm guessing you want this back." Clay handed him his dagger.

"Where did you find it?"

"Next to the dead creature with an eyeball attached to it," Clay snickered.

"Where is Utar?"

"He followed the tunnel the beast used and hasn't returned."

"Gilex, there are more of those creatures down here." Rustic said.

"Hopefully Utar can find out where, and we can avoid them. Are you able to travel?"

"I think so."

Clay helped him up.

"Let's go. Keep an eye out for Utar and leave him some signs along the way."

They came to the same crossroad Rustic had found earlier. He warned them about the cold corridor ahead and the direction where he heard the clicking sound. Gilex took out the map and studied it by the torchlight.

"We need to go straight ahead, so hopefully we won't run into anymore of those creatures."

They were about to continue when they heard someone say, "Where's everyone going?"

Startled, the men turned with weapons at the ready.

"Relax, it's only me," Utar said as he came into the light.

"What did you find?" Gilex asked.

"Another one of those creatures."

"Where is it now?" Clay asked.

"Dead. Here take these arrows." Utar handed them to Clay, Perahn, and Rustic.

"Where did you find them?" Perahn asked.

"Where I killed the creature."

"Let's get going. We have a way to go," Gilex said

It didn't take them long to encounter the strange coldness that Rustic did. Gilex told his men to wave their torches back and forth in front of their bodies to help ward off the chilly effect. The passageway continued on for another five minutes before going upward slightly and then leveling off. The temperature grew warmer, and the men stopped waving their torches. The corridor eventually veered toward the left and then slightly to the right and left again. They'd just turned the corner and stopped immediately when they saw a group of cave wolves eating several unrecognizable carcasses. The big animals' feast was interrupted as they looked up in unison and stared at the intruders.

"What do you want to do?" Perahn asked.

"Back up," Utar ordered.

"There's no other way through." Gilex said.

"You don't want to mess with them. Their fur is said to be so thick that they can withstand numerous attacks and I heard they can unhinge their jaws wide enough to engulf a human's head. We need to regroup."

"Slowly move back." Gilex ordered.

As they did, Perahn, Rustic, and Clay kept their bows notched and pointed at them, while Gilex and Utar held their swords and torches out in front. They managed to take only three steps before the wolves snarled and attacked. Clay, Perahn, and Rustic fired in unison, killing three wolves. The barbed arrows were sharp enough to pierce through their heavy fur coats and find their marks. Utar hit the closest wolf in the head with his torch, stunning the creature. Then he stabbed it under its jaw and through its mouth, killing it.

Another wolf charged Gilex. He sidestepped its snapping jaws and hit the animal in the side with his sword as it passed. The blow did little to deter or slow the animal as it turned around and came at him again. This time, Gilex was too slow as the wolf clamped down hard on his sword arm, tearing through the leather bracer, biting into his flesh, and breaking bones with a loud crunching sound. Gilex grunted through clenched teeth and slammed the lit side of the torch against the wolf's enormous head. Instead of releasing his arm, the wolf clamped down harder and began shaking and twisting its head violently, knocking him off balance and yanking his right arm out of the socket. Gilex struggled to remain upright. He regained enough of his balance to hit the animal directly in the snout with the torch. The wolf released its grip, yipped and ran away.

Meanwhile, Clay went down under the weight of a wolf. As it was about to bite his face, Rustic shot the animal in the throat, killing it. Utar killed the last wolf, stabbing the inside of its mouth as the animal lunged for his throat. Rustic helped Gilex up.

"Are you hurt?" he asked, looking down at his bloody arm.

"My shoulder feels dislocated. I need you to put it back in place."

Rustic grabbed the limb with both hands. "Are you ready?"

Gilex nodded and Rustic pulled hard. Gilex felt excruciating pain then relief, as his arm went back into place.

"How's your wrist?"

"I'll be fine," he said and picked up his sword. He knew the bones were broken, but was surprised that he could flex his wrist. He contributed this to his newfound healing ability.

They ventured on through the twisting, turning corridors, always staying alert for pending danger. Eventually, they came to a dead end.

"Now what? The last turn we took was a mile back." Clay stated.

Gilex took out the map of the cave and studied it for several long moments. "Strange, this wall wasn't supposed to be..."

Human sized rat creatures, running upright, came rushing at them from behind. They wore armor, carried short swords and shields, and filled the corridor as far as the eye could see.

"Ambush!" Utar yelled.

For the next several rounds, Gilex and his men held their own, but they were losing ground and being pushed closer to the dead end. Gilex, knowing that it was only a matter of time before they'd be overwhelmed, yelled for his men to move out of the way and then went into a frenzy unlike any had ever witnessed. He was thrusting his spear with blinding speed and single-handedly drove the rat creatures back, allowing his men time to deploy their bows and kill more than three quarters of the group before they retreated. Gilex turned around, breathing heavy, and looked at his men, who stared at him in amazement.

"Don't ask," he said, then walked past them and searched the wall, while the rest retrieved most of their arrows and stood at the ready.

After searching, he found the latch that triggered a portion of the wall to rise upward, revealing a large, empty room with one door to the far right. They entered, used the lever on the other side, and closed the wall with a thud. Weary from battle, the men rested, while Gilex studied the map again. When they were ready, they opened the door and entered the corridor. It led them to another series of turns and ended at a junction going left and right. Gilex led them to the left until they were brought to a halt by a pair of giant-sized wooden doors. Clay walked up, listened, and when he was satisfied that nothing stirred beyond, opened one door and entered. The other men followed.

The room was big and appeared to be a large kitchen and eatery. There were shackles lining the eastern wall, an enormous table with chairs directly in the back, and a huge cooking pot hovering over an open flame with various cutting apparatuses and herbs placed on the table to the left.

"This must be someone's cooking chamber," Clay said, his voice almost a whisper.

"You think?" Rustic answered sarcastically.

"Get a load of the size of that cleaver," Utar said, pointing to the cutting tool on the table.

"I'd hate to meet the..." Clay was saying when they heard a light snapping noise somewhere in the room, indicating a trap was sprung. The door slammed shut, and the sound of a bar sliding into place followed. Perahn ran up to it, trying in vain to open the door. A few minutes later, they heard something on the other side.

****

It was only a matter of minutes before Mersdal the giant received the warning that someone or something entered his cooking area. He rose from his sizeable-padded wooden chair, called for his pet bear, and made haste to find out who had entered his room, hoping that it wasn't those stupid rat creatures again.

The giant was a mountain in comparison to the average human, standing nearly twelve feet tall, dressed in black furs, and carrying a very large spiked club that was at least as big as a human. All other creatures living within the cave, hid from him, and none dare challenged him. The giant arrived, along with the cave bear, to find the bar securely across the door handles. His trap had sprung just as it was supposed to do, which brought a wide smile to his bearded, dirty face. He walked to the door and listened, and when he heard human voices on the other side, he smiled in delight, exposing the three remaining teeth in his mouth.

"Tasty food, Bear, we have tasty food." He said to companion, and released the catch, opening the door.

A lone human, half his size with long, dark hair, stood before him, holding a spear. Preoccupied by the sight of him, the giant forgot that he'd heard other voices not longer than a minute before.

Tasty food." He announced. "Stay, Bear." He ordered, and walked into the room, while tapping his club against his free hand in a way that indicated he wanted to battle this intruder.

Gilex faced the giant, and waved his hand behind his back,

signaling to his men in hiding that something was in the room. He yelled at the big creature, "Come on and fight me, you coward."

"Hmm. Human food tastes the sweetest." The giant was more than happy to oblige the human by lunging forward, swinging his club in a side-to-side motion, and then attacking with it downwardly.

The attack was aimed for Gilex's head. He waited patiently until the very last moment before sidestepping the enormous club. What he didn't account for was the giant's strength. When the club slammed into the earth, the impact shook the foundation and almost knocked him off balance. The giant lifted his mighty club and swung downward. Gilex grabbed the spear with both hands and raised it over his head just in time to block the attack, but in doing so, his weapon was bent in half. The giant was about to attack again when several arrows, from different directions, pierced his body, causing him to stumble backward, roar in pain, and then call for the bear.

The Cave Bear raced into the room and was pelted with arrows, which caused the animal to change direction in mid-stride and attack the first human in sight, Perahn. Perahn was suddenly face-to-face with the bear. He was struck in his arm by one of its powerful claws and sent flying against the wall. The bear turned to Clay and was about to pounce on him when Utar raced over and rammed his spear into the animal's throat. Blood gushed forth from the wound. The bear reared back then fell over.

After the bear died, the giant turned to escape and was struck by another arrow from Clay, which staggered the big fellow. Despite his wounds and loss of blood, the mighty Mersdal—who prided himself as the toughest giant in all the land - ran. He was almost through the doors when he was finally brought down by a well-timed and accurate throw from Utar. His spear ripped through his left leg's quadriceps, dropping the giant to one knee. Mersdal fumbled with the weapon, trying to pull it free, but it was too late. Gilex stabbed him through the back with one of his scimitars and used the other to do a draw-cut across his neck, severing his artery. He watched with pleasure as the giant fell over dead.

After bandaging Perahn's bloodied and useless limb, they left the room and headed south, continuing on through the endless corridors until they entered a room that was almost caved in.

"This is getting ridiculous. Our path shouldn't have ended this soon." Gilex said in frustration.

"Could the map be wrong?" Rustic asked.

"Maybe or maybe it's some sort of door."

Clay searched the walls. He discovered a lever, buried deep within a recess of the wall, and pulled it down. The rubble on the left began to shift and split down the middle, causing the men to step back a few feet and wait for it to finish clearing. Another hallway emerged, and once they were safely through, Rustic used the lever on the other side, and the rubble closed again. The corridor went on for another hundred feet, turned sharply toward the right, where it led to another room and a lone door, at the far end, with a skull carved in the center.

"This is it. We made it," Gilex proudly announced.

Utar approached the door and searched for traps. When he didn't find any, he picked the lock and opened it. Bright light poured in from the outside, causing the men to squint their eyes against the light before stepping out and into a large field with hundreds of trees. The air had a crisp, clean smell to it - a nice change from the dank smell of the cave. After Clay sealed the exit, the group found a small grove of trees nearby and rested for several hours.

Birds chirped along the way, and the gentle sound of leaves rustling in the wind created a peaceful and tranquil atmosphere. Gilex continued to lead the group as they engaged in small talk to help pass the time. Only Rustic carried an unsheathed weapon, in case there were any unnecessary surprises. At one point, the men joked with him about the rumor of a killer rabbit roaming the region.

It was mid-afternoon when they arrived at the entrance to the Circle of Demise. Trees outlined the area, and a long stone path cut right down the middle. As they traveled through this part of the forest, the temperature grew increasingly warm and the men's spirits lifted even higher. Gilex brought them to a halt when they came upon a ten foot high stonewall, which stretched as far as the eye could see in both directions, and brass gates hanging loosely off their hinges.

"We're here. It should only be a few hundred yards away," Gilex simply stated. He opened the gates and led the men through.

"Treasure, gold, I can't wait," Perahn joyfully said.

"And more, my young friend," Gilex added.

When they reached the top of the hill, Gilex stopped them just short of entering to survey the area.

"It was just as the book described it." He thought.

Enormous trees adorned with blue and purple leaves created an outer circle. Forming an inner circle were seven waist-high white pillars with strange carvings etched up and down the length, and at the forefront was a massive altar carved out of black, shiny stone. Gilex was sure that if he was standing directly in front of it, he'd be able to see his own reflection.

"This is it? You bring us here to an altar? What are you going to do, sacrifice us?" Perahn's tone indicated he was a bit upset.

"Where's the treasure you promised, Gilex?" Rustic chimed in.

"It's here. I just need to uncover it," Gilex answered without turning his head.

"And how are you going to do that?"

"After everyone has taken their proper position in front of the pillars, I will read from the book, and the treasure will be revealed. Are you ready?"

"Let's get this over with," Clay answered.

Gilex instructed them to stand in front of a pillar and place their hands on top of it.

"No matter what happens, or what you see, do not move." He looked at each man before continuing. "Trust me, everything will be okay. In a few minutes, we'll have everything I promised."

Each man looked at the other, and then nodded in agreement. Gilex reached into his backpack and pulled out an ancient tome. He flipped through some pages and then began reading. *"I llac nopu eht nomed drol harehsa ot emoc htrof morf eht stip fo lleh."*

After hearing the strange words, everyone looked around, except for Utar, who appeared to be in some sort of trance. Gilex recited the words again, and mist began swirling all around the area. After a third time, the last two words spoken were clearly ***"of hell."*** The sky darkened, the wind started howling and blowing violently, and the tree branches began stretching and moving closer to each other until they entwined and trapped the group within the circle.

Rustic knew at once that something was wrong. He felt evil surging in and around the area, and no longer wanted any part of what was taking place. He tried to move his hands and his body, but some unimaginable force kept him rooted in place. Panic-stricken, he looked over at Clay and Perahn, who were also struggling. Gilex continued to read from the book, and this time, all who stood there, now understood his words: "I call upon the demon lord Asherah to come forth from the pits of hell."

"What is he doing, and why is he calling forth a demon?" Rustic shouted to anyone that could hear him above the howling wind.

Gilex raised his head, and Clay noticed that his brown eyes changed to black orbs as he continued staring at nothing in particular. Gilex called forth the demon again, without looking down at the book. Now the ground shook violently, and a large hole opened in front of the altar.

"What are you doing?" Clay shouted to Gilex, but he either ignored or didn't hear him.

Agonizing seconds passed until finally they heard the sound of something clawing its way upward from the cold darkness. The men continued to struggle against the invisible restraints, but stopped when they saw a pair of black-clawed hands, reaching out of the pit and grabbing hold of the edges. They watched in terror as the owner of the claws emerged. First, a pair of ram-shaped horns appeared, then a dark human-looking head with orange eyes, followed by his perfectly chiseled torso. Finally, his muscular tree trunk legs hoisted the creature out of the hole.

In its full stature, the being was at least eight feet tall and could easily weigh two or three horses. His skin was as dark as night, and his eyes glowed brighter than the fires of hell. Gilex smiled at the realization of what he'd done. Just as the book described it would happen; everything from the mist, the darkening sky, the tree limbs entwining, the hole in the center of the pillars, and now the demon Asherah himself.

"WHO SUMMONS ME FROM THE PIT?" the demon's voice boomed as his horns unwound and straightened to a length of four feet.

"I did, almighty Asherah," Gilex answered.

The demon turned, looked directly at him, and then lumbered over. "WHY DID YOU AWAKEN ME FROM MY SLUMBER, MORTAL?" The demon barked at him.

"I have use of the Blood Knights."

The demon grinned. "Are you aware of the sacrifice?"

"Yes, I am," Gilex bravely answered.

"Place your hands on top of the pillar."

Gilex did as he was told, and the demon looked around, studying the humans. "What are the names of you and your companions?"

"My name is Gilex and from my left to my right are Utar, Rustic, Perahn, and Clay."

"Sacrifices, what have you done?" Rustic shouted at Gilex as he continued to struggle.

The demon stepped back, spoke some words in an unknown tongue, and when he was finished, he waved his hand toward the hole. "Mortal, I will give you what you so desperately seek. Your souls will be mine, and once your mortal shell is destroyed, you will serve me for all of eternity."

"What?" Gilex exclaimed as his smile washed away from his face. "That's not what the book said, demon!"

The being laughed loudly for several seconds. "Think about it, mortal. If you would've known the book's true meaning, would you've come here to release my children and the hell they bring? You and your men are pawns for my enjoyment." The demon's eyes burned even brighter.

Gilex was ashamed, knowing he'd led his men straight to hell.

"What have you done? We trusted you, and this is how you repay us?" Rustic asked.

Gilex didn't answer and now struggled along with everyone else.

"If I ever get free, I will kill you." Clay threatened Gilex.

The demon smiled. "It's no use resisting, mortal. My powers are stronger than your will. Your soul and the souls of your companions belong to me now." The demon laughed and walked behind the altar. "I CALL UPON MY CHILDREN, MY CREATION AND MY EVOLUTION. COME FORTH, YOU'RE NEEDED AGAIN TO ROAM THIS PLANE OF EXISTENCE."

From somewhere deep within the pit, the sound of metal scraping against rock was heard and became louder until it sounded like something was clawing their way up the side of the hole. Many minutes passed until they saw a pair of black gauntleted hands appear at the rim of the pit and lift the rest of the armored knight out of the pit. The being from the underworld stood tall before moving in front of the altar. The black platemail was outlined with red trim and displayed a crest, which depicted Asherah slaying a much larger demon. Sheathed across the undead knight's back was a great two-handed sword, which - even though the ancient blade was covered - emitted a greenish hue that radiated pure evil. More clawing sounds came from below until five more knights, identical to the first in every aspect, walked in front of the altar.

Utar finally snapped out of his trance, while Perahn took notice of their beady red eyes, peering out at them from the top of their visors.

"Let me introduce you to my children. To my left is Gyleon. Next to him are Rantar, Umunis, Criptheon, and lastly, Prain." Asherah could barely contain his excitement.

The demon closed the pit with a wave of his hand and stepped out in front of the altar, raising his clawed hands to signify the beginning of the proceedings. Gilex was horrified at the realization of his and everyone else's fate. If he'd only known the book's true intention, he would've thrown it away and given up his quest for revenge. Silently he vowed that whatever happens this day, he would make amends to his men and never serve this demon for eternity.

"Criptheon, my child." The demon spoke the knight's official name. Upon hearing it, he turned his helmeted head to face his father. "Merge with the mortal named Clay."

The knight nodded, turned his attention toward Clay, and walked over to him. Clay struggled to break free, but it was futile. The knight grabbed hold of his left arm, lifting it free from the pillar with ease, and forced him to open the knight's visor. Fearful, Clay instinctively turned away from his gaze, but the knight grabbed his chin with his free hand, and forced him to look.

In the next instant, a bright light radiated from within his helmet and shined onto Clay's face. Clay screamed, which horrified the rest of the men as they could only imagine what he saw. His screams lasted several minutes until his heart gave out, and his body became limp and lifeless. The knight, known as Criptheon, lifted the carcass high into the air and discarded it into the center of the circle. Asherah produced a transparent square object and called for Criptheon. The Blood Knight walked over to his father, touched the cube, electricity sparked forth from his fingers, transferring something into the cube. The transferred mystery took the shape of a small, circular object and began moving inside of the box. One by one, the demon called forth the other knights to perform the same ritual. No matter how much Rustic resisted Rantar, and Perahn denied Prain, their fates were sealed. Utar almost broke free of his bonds from Umunis, but in the end, he gave in to the Blood

Knight's will.

"You will pay for this, demon!" Gilex said to Asherah.

"Mortal, accept your fate. You sought my help out." The demon snapped at him. "Don't worry; you will have the revenge you so desperately sought."

"All right, demon, get this over with!" Gilex said, no longer caring whether he lived or died.

Asherah grinned and ordered the last of his knights to merge with him. The knight marched over and took hold of his arm. Instead of resisting, Gilex freely lifted his visor and stared deeply into those beady little eyes. His hallucinations were by far the worst of them all. He saw gruesome images of wars, disasters, children being slaughtered, and monsters. Somehow, through it all, he knew that it wasn't real. Thus, a little part of his essence remained, and the battle began for dominance between Gilex and the knight known as Gyleon.

After Gilex's body was discarded, and the merging was finally completed, the mist dissipated and the trees transformed back to their original state. Asherah gazed upon his children, thinking about the last time they walked this plane; the one known to his kin as the Other. After they completed the quest for another greedy mortal, they encountered a group of knights known as the Pure Ones. They would've beaten them if it wasn't for their leader, a human named Realer. He used something called Pure Light, and his offspring were whisked back down to the lower planes and rooted by his side. How it worked still puzzled him to this day. But that was over a century ago and any remnants of Realer or his children should have died out by now.

His thoughts turned to mortals in general and how easy it was to trick them. All you needed was the right bait. For Gilex, his Book of Blood was a perfect instrument for his quest of revenge. He was enticed after reading the first few pages. The ones Asherah wrote, the ones that promised revenge and power but delivered the Entrapment Chant instead. The demon smiled, and his horns curled backward into the ram shape once again.

"Entrapment Chant," he said, snickering. "Such a useful tool. With some, it grants healing and fighting skills, while others receive levitation and telekinesis. All powers were designed to assist the reader with the ultimate task, and that's for them to venture forth to my circle and become my pawns."

Asherah suddenly became a proud demon. He was clever, strong, and knew that he was capable of ruling his world, and, someday, he would. The demon turned his attention back toward his offspring.

"My children," the demon began, "you're free to roam this plane." Each of the knights turned toward their father. "Gyleon, I want you to hide the book in the Cave of the Dead again, then fulfill the mortal's request by eliminating his enemies. After that, go forth and recover the Horn of Substance." Gyleon nodded. "Once you have it, bring the horn back here and release me, so that I can walk with you once more. Go now, my children."

Gyleon was the first to leave, followed by Rantar, Umunis, Criptheon, and lastly, Prain. After they were gone, he looked into the Cube of Entrapment and stared at the souls trapped within. He studied them for a while, wondering what they were thinking as they floated by for his amusement, then turned his attention toward the setting sun. His time was running short, and with a wave of his hand, the hole opened again. Excited by his new prospect, Asherah grinned and then descended toward the darkest place ever known to exist.

Chapter 2: Stand Together

Master Shoo walked briskly until he arrived at the Order of the Searing Blade. The school was larger than most of the other nearby buildings. Stationed in front was a lone man dressed in platemail and holding a spear.

He approached the knight. "I am Master Shoo Sin Yan from the Order of the Open Palm, and I am here to see your Lord."

The young man recognized the teacher by his hair and clothes, acknowledged his request with a nod, and allowed him to enter. Shoo was escorted by another knight to one of the private chambers. While he was there, he couldn't help but notice just how different their décor was from his own school. Instead of a peaceful environment with plants and flowers that would join the mind with the body, theirs was geared toward war.

Shoo strolled around the room looking at the display cases at the far end of the room. There was one with old and brittle weapons, another with maps from past wars, and finally one with of armor. He could tell they were remnants from battles of long ago by the number of small dents etched into the steel. A few minutes later, the door opened and in walked a young knight carrying a tray of food and wine.

"Sir Valden thought you'd like some refreshments." He offered and placed the items on the small table then left.

Shoo ate some of the food while thinking about what he wanted to say to Sir Valden. His plan was to be very direct and hope that he would be persuaded without much coxing.

A half-hour later, the same knight who allowed him access into their Order, entered the chamber and escorted him through the school. Along the way they passed several rooms. Some of them were decorated with weapons hanging on the walls, others had woven cloth tapestries of great battle scenes, and a few were casually adorned for socializing. Shoo was then led down several flights of stairs and into a large dining room. Seated at the far end of an enormous rectangular table was a lone person dressed in robes of royalty. His black beard and hair were cropped short, which made him appear younger than he actually was. Off to his left were two young boys. One held a jug of wine, and the other a tray with food. Master Shoo's escort asked him to take a seat and then left the room.

"Welcome to my Order Master Shoo. I am Sir Valden. Please have a seat. Would you like something to eat or sample some of my finest wine?"

"Do you have tea?"

Sir Valden commanded his servant to fetch some and then waited until it was in front of Shoo, before speaking.

"I was told me you wanted to see me. How can I help you?"

Master Shoo bowed his head slightly and then said. "Sir Valden we have pressing issues that involve the entire town. As you already know, Redden fell a few weeks ago and a couple of my students led a daring raid and rescued a handful of the prisoners."

"So why does this give you concern?"

"Because of their actions, I think the enemy will retaliate."

Sir Valden picked up his goblet. "Why did your students get involved in the first place?" He asked then took a long drink.

"They felt it was the right thing to do."

"Hmm, I see. Wouldn't it have been easier to leave well enough alone?"

Shoo didn't care for his comment, but kept his composure. "Sir Valden, doesn't it bother you that people were being raped and tortured?"

"It's not that, but if Redden fell so easily, despite being bigger and more fortified than our town, what chances do you think we'll have? We might end up being enslaved and tortured, and our women raped as well."

"Sir Valden, life has no meaning if it doesn't have a purpose, and if we are given an opportunity to do something good, then we should."

"And if your students would've minded their own business, then we wouldn't be having this conversation." Valden countered.

"They did what they thought was right and if their path allows them the opportunity to save some lives, then I back their decision."

"I agree with you about doing the right thing, but they should have thought things through when involving the entire town." Sir Valden was becoming increasingly agitated, because he didn't want any part of what might be coming.

"They had no way of knowing that." Master Shoo took a sip of his mint tea.

"I suppose you are right, but still, everything must be considered and because of what they did we'll need to act with haste. Who knows if we even have enough time?"

"Sir Valden, there's no changing what they did."

"I know. I need to think about it."

"Why would you have to think about it? It's your town too." Shoo stated.

"Since your students took it upon themselves to start this, then why am I obligated to assist? I just might leave this town."

Master Shoo had enough and rose to his feet. "If the time comes, I hope you find the courage to stand with us."

Sir Valden stood up, and his chair fell over. "Courage? You have no idea what hardships I've faced in my life, so don't insult me. If I was a weaker man, we would engage in arms, and you would regret your words. Now get out."

Shoo Sin Yan looked hard at the man and walked away.

Shoo's next attempt to unite the Orders brought him to the Order of the Slippery Hand. They touted their profession as simple thieves, but he knew differently. They were cutthroats and killers for hire. He had never had reason to associate with them and had only walked by their Order on one previous occasion. As he approached the area, he took note to his surroundings; from the thick bushes, to the oak trees, to the twelve-foot high smooth stone wall surrounding the complex, and the front gates.

He stopped just short of the entrance and said. "I need to enter your Order and speak with whoever is in charge." When there was no response, he turned his head towards his left. "It's a matter of great importance."

After several seconds, a tall figure stepped out of hiding. He was dressed in garments that were the same color as the bushes, held a loaded crossbow, and carried a long sword strapped across his back.

"You're good old man," he began, "no one, not even our highest ranking student, would have detected me. Why do you need to enter?"

"My name is Shoo Sin Yan from the Order of the Open Palm. There is a threat coming to our town, and I need to talk to the leader of your sect."

"I know who you are and your reputation as an honest man, so I'll allow you access." The thief said as he walked over to the gates, unlocked the locks with sleight of hand, and then swung them open. "When you arrive at the door tell them Killswitch gave you passage."

Shoo bowed slightly and walked through the gates, which were then closed and locked behind him. Halfway up to the walkway, he paused and studied the pathway before him. He easily detected many traps placed directly and indirectly in his way and thought back on his life.

Before joining the Order of the Open Palm, he was a very good thief and learned a great deal of skills during his training. One, in particular, was detecting and disarming traps. In fact, he was so good that a master thief bet him a thousand pieces of gold; he couldn't avoid or deactivate one of his traps. Shoo took the bet and won. Grinning, he moved on towards the building without setting them off.

Back at the gates, Killswitch watched, and admired the monk as he skillfully avoided the traps. Before hiding in the bushes again, he wondered how tough it would be to kill the old man.

Shoo Sin arrived at the unmanned front doors and after closely examining them, he then selected the only area that wouldn't trigger a trap and knocked. A piece of the wooden door slid open, revealing a pair of eyes. "Who are you and state your purpose?" A deep voice asked.

"My name is Shoo Sin Yan from the Order of the Open Palm, and I am here to speak whoever is in command. Furthermore, Killswitch gave me passage."

"Hold on."

The small window slammed shut.

A few minutes later, the door was opened and there stood a female with short dark hair, dressed in a thief's garb with an assortment of weapons draped across her body.

"You may enter." She said, allowed him to do so and then led him down the hallway.

Shoo scanned the corridor without turning his head and could sense many thieves hiding in the shadows, poised to attack.

"So many men armed and hiding; is this how you treat all guests?" Shoo said to the woman.

"We are always ready." She answered flatly.

Shoo also noticed the Order was much different from the Searing Blade. Instead of being warm and inviting, it was cold and sordid looking. Every corner posed a threat to the untrained eye and every threat was real and deadly. The young lady led him through many rooms and then down several flights of stairs to a large, dimly lit, rectangular, room with a table towards the back. Men and women sat around the table and a handful more, holding loaded crossbows, stood somewhere just out of sight. They were good at hiding but not good enough to avoid Shoo's detection.

"So what brings the Master of the Open Palm to our Order?" The man with the scarred face asked.

"My name is Shoo Sin Yan. Are you the leader?"

"Yes. My name is Tef."

Tef unsheathed a dagger from his belt and used it to cut an apple.

"The town is in danger."

"From what?"

Master Shoo walked over in front of the table and explained the reason for his visit. When he was finished, he was met with criticism over allowing his students to get involved.

"I see there is no use in talking to you about this matter. I just hope you fight when the time comes or like Redden, this town will fall as well."

"What about the other Orders. Will they fight?"

"We will see, won't we?"

Tef didn't really care about why Shoo was there. He only had one thing on his mind. "Old man, are you as skillful as they say?" He asked and then chomped on a slice of apple.

"Why?"

"I'll tell you what. If you best some of my men, then I will help you."

"It doesn't matter if you do or not, I am here to warn you of the danger this threat poses."

Shoo heard a very faint click of a crossbow from somewhere behind Tef. It was a sound that no one should have heard from where he stood. "Tell the owner of that weapon to stand down or this woman by my side will be the target of his bolt."

The leader waved off his man. "You'll have my answer soon enough." He said.

Shoo turned and found several men blocking his way with weapons in their hands.

"Have it your way." Shoo stated.

The fight was over before it even started. Shoo grabbed the closest thief by the throat and ripped out his larynx using the praying mantis style. He ended another man's life when he kicked him in the head and crushed his skull. The other two attacked, but it was of no use.

Master Shoo's reflexes were far superior to theirs, and he crushed almost every bone in their bodies when he used the deadly bone breaking technique. Their bodies crumpled to the floor in a heap because there was nothing left to support the weight. Crossbows suddenly fired and Master Shoo grabbed the woman, just like he said, and used her as a shield. She was struck in the throat, chest, and head. When her body went limp Shoo threw it onto the table.

Tef clapped. "Excellent, you are as good as they say and have proven yourself to me. We will fight by your side."

Shoo didn't respond and began walking away.

"By the way Master Shoo, why did you kill my men? I thought you would have just knocked them out."

Shoo stopped just short of the door. "An attack with intent is never taken lightly, remember that for the future." He said and left without further incident.

After he left the thief's guild, Master Shoo went to the western part of town to the Order of the Holy Hammer. Of all the Orders in this town, this was the one he had highest hopes for. Upon arriving, he noticed several female and male students walking around the perimeter and when they saw him, they stopped and bowed out of respect.

"Master Shoo." One of the male students straightened and said. "It's a pleasure to see you. What brings you to our humble place of worship?"

"I need to speak to High Priest Hamond."

The student nodded and led him up the ramp to the modest, yet beautiful building, carved out of stone and marble. After entering through the steel doors, master Shin Shoo was asked to wait in the foyer while the student went to find priest Hamond. Shin had only been there once before, and besides his school, this was the one he admired the most. The inside of the building housed stone statues with such detail that they looked like they could come to life at any moment. One, in particular, off to the left, was so lifelike that Shoo thought it was someone standing guard.

His wait wasn't long as the young priest returned and then escorted him to their main chamber. Along the way, they passed several chambers used for prayer and he could hear voices chanting from within.

"We pray at least three times a day to appease our god and receive special knowledge to heal the sick and injured." The student commented as they passed the rooms.

"We too pray daily." Shoo added.

They continued making small talk until they arrived at the room where priest Hamond waited. The smiling, big-bellied priest was of medium height and dressed in purple and blue robes.

"Master Shoo it's a pleasure to see you again. It's been... several months I believe."

Shoo bowed and greeted the man.

"Please sit while young Ures brings us something to drink." The student left and both men sat down at the table built for four. "How are you?"

Shoo smiled. "We can exchange pleasantries a little later. Right now, I have a more pressing issue, so I will be direct. A day ago, some of my students entered the town of Redden and rescued some prisoners. I'm afraid their actions might have provoked a forthcoming attack on our town."

"How did your students accomplish such a feat? I heard the town was well fortified."

"They entered through a secret entrance and raided their makeshift prisons under the cover of darkness."

"Impressive to say the least." Hamond shifted his weight to help ease the discomfort of his ailing back. "Your students are indeed brave; I just wish they would have stopped by here first, because some of my students would have gladly gone with them."

Just then, Ures walked in carrying a tray with two steeping kettles on top. He poured tea for both men.

"I thought you were a wine man?" Shoo asked.

Hamond smiled. "In honor of your visit I am drinking tea."

Shoo bowed his head slightly at the hospitality.

"So why do you think they'll attack the town? Hamond continued.

"I believe they'll attack us because they might think we sent them."

"I see. Did you speak to the Magistrate or the other Orders yet?"

"The magistrate is a coward and never believes anyone. I'll send word telling him that we will not defend the town without his support."

"Do you think he'll listen?"

"I'm hoping he's foolish enough to believe my words." Shoo took a sip of his tea before continuing. "Of the Orders, I spoke with Sir Valden from the Order of the Searing Blade and as of right now I don't think he'll support us. Tef from the Order of the Slippery Hand will stand with us."

"He will? I thought he was only concerned about his Order and not the town."

"He just needed some convincing." Master Shoo couldn't help but chuckle.

"How did you do that?" Hamond had to ask.

"Let's just say he lost some students today."

The priest laughed loudly and his belly jiggled. "Do you have a plan?"

"Not yet. I'll send word to the Orders where we could meet at a mutual place and discuss the best course of action. I believe we have at least a few days to prepare and from what my students told me, their army consisted of giants, war beetles, and many goat and boarmen."

The priest looked down and swallowed hard. "It doesn't sound good for our town."

"I know, but if we don't fight, then all will be lost. The townspeople will end up being tortured and raped and whatever else they impose. Can I count on you?"

Hamond simply nodded.

"I'll send word when the meeting is set."

Shoo finished his tea and left.

Master Shoo returned to his school and entered his private chambers, without saying a single word to his students, and prayed for guidance. When he was through, he went downstairs and instructed four students to visit the Magistrate and the other Orders to inform them that he wanted to have a meeting at the Inn of the Unholy Cow, to discuss battle tactics.

Master Shoo and his top three students arrived at the inn ahead of the others and selected a table in the far back. Next to arrive was High Priest Hamond. He was dressed in chainmail and had a mace secured to his belt.

Sir Valden followed him a few minutes later. He looked like he was ready for a fight, wearing platemail and a large sword sheathed at his side. Finally, Tef entered wearing leather and carrying a short sword scabbard on his left, and a row of daggers strapped across his chest. Each party was escorted by several of their students. After they were seated and drinks were poured, Master Shoo broke the ice and was the first to speak. "I would like to thank all of you for attending. We have many things to discuss."

"Where's the Magistrate?" Sir Valden interrupted.

"He was given the same instructions to meet us here."

Tef smiled then spoke. "You mean the one who's supposed to protect us and make all of the decisions regarding this town? I've known him since he was a child and never once has he ever shown an ounce of courage or accountability. If you ask me, the only reason why he's the magistrate is because of his father."

Tef, like everyone else was displeased with the magistrate and the way he conducted business.

"Let's forget about him for the moment, and discuss what is needed to survive this ordeal." High Priest Hamond calmly said.

"Does anyone sitting here really think our three Orders can

withstand an attack from a large army? Most of my men are off on adventures and honing their skills." Sir Valden stated.

"Truthfully? I don't think so, but maybe we could frustrate them enough that they'll leave." Shoo said.

"Master Shoo, is that what Redden believed as well? I don't think so. They have a wall and still they fell within a day. Reports confirm that the army has war beetles and giants." Sir Valden was clearly disgusted.

"The war will come to us, so what do you suggest we do? Run and leave the townspeople to those savages?" High Priest Hamond answered before Master Shoo could.

"Maybe we could evacuate the people?" Tef suggested.

"Do you know how long that would take? Do you think they won't track us down if we leave?" Sir Valden snapped at the thief.

"Sir Valden, please deliver your words in a positive manner or leave." Master Shoo said.

Valden's blue eyes turned to hatred, and his escorts drew their weapons, causing Shoo's students to stand up as well. Nearby patrons got up and moved away.

"If we had more time, I'd show you just how I conduct myself." Sir Valden barked at him.

Master Shoo waved off his students, who were gathering around him in a protective manner, before replying. "If you would like, then how about we wait until this is over and test our skills?"

"Enough of this, we're not getting anything accomplished." Tef stated.

Valden held his tongue and told his men to sheath their blades.

Priest Hamond spoke. "Sir Valden, what do you suggest?"

The warrior leaned back in his chair. "This town will fall if we're the only ones trying to defend it. I say we force that coward of a Magistrate to help."

Shoo then spoke. "You're most likely right about the town; however, before we go and convince him, we should come up with a plan first. Maybe after he hears our strategy he'll come to his senses."

Master Shoo looked directly at Sir Valden. "Since you're the most skilled at the art of war; what do you think we should do?"

Sir Valden was caught off guard, and somewhat surprised by the compliment. "As everyone already knows, there are only two ways into and out of this town. I think for this reason, the enemy will split their forces into three parts and..."

"Why three?" Tef interrupted.

"One at each end of town, and another waiting to cut off those who try to escape."

"Good point." Tef added.

Valden continued. "I think they'll most likely attack one end first trying to draw our main forces to them, and then they'll attack our flank, which they believe will be weaker. In all of my studies of war, I've come to realize that both sides of their forces will not be equally divided, and the stronger force will be attacking our rear. I suggest we fight the initial force with little resistance, in order to draw them into the town, and then hit them with almost everyone and kill them all."

Tef was about to say something when Master Shoo waved him off to allow Sir Valden to finish.

"Once they're dead, we'll engage the enemy waiting for us to escape. I'm sure their leader will be among them, and after we kill him, the others will become fearful and retreat to the safety of Redden."

"Interesting, what about the army entering from the rear?" Priest Hamond asked.

"We'll still need to keep them busy for a while."

"And how are we supposed to do that?" Tef asked.

Sir Valden looked directly at the thief and spoke calmly. "My plan is just an overview; I still need to know how many men we have and what type of weapons they're proficient with. We'll need scouts to feed us information and captains to lead the smaller groups."

"Do you think it will work?" Hamond asked.

Valden smirked. "What we're doing here isn't easy, in fact, we might all die."

"Tef, do you care to weigh in?" Master Shoo turned to the thief.

"I'm not as schooled at the art of war as Sir Valden, so I suggest we hide the bulk of our forces outside of town, flank their position, and then attack them before they even arrive. Once we do..."

"You mean like a coward would?" Valden interrupted.

Tef smirked. "Sir Valden, why not disrupt their forces before they even get a chance to place troops outside of our town? We could also spread oil leading here and set it ablaze as they pass through, while raining arrows down upon them from a safe distance. Maybe they'll become discouraged enough to give up their cause."

"Thank you Tef. Hamond?" Shoo said.

"Both men make some really good points, so I suggest we combine the two, and..."

"We don't have that many men." Sir Valden interrupted.

"I wasn't finished, so stop interrupting." Hamond raised his voice. "We need to create enough mayhem in order to lower their morale if we want to have any chance of success. I also agree about allowing their weaker forces in, but instead of attacking them directly we should set some traps in place like the oil idea and..."

"And what, set the town ablaze?" Valden interrupted again.

"If we have to, yes, but it will only be a small portion of town. We can rebuild any structures, but return lives, we can't."

After a long pause, Master Shoo spoke. "All of your ideas are very good and like Sir Valden, I also feel we don't have enough men, so I suggest we do this in stages. First, we should line the area coming to the town with oil and have Tef and Sir Valden's men hiding further out. As soon as half of their forces pass over the oil, we'll ignite it. That should cause their troops to split and then simultaneously, we'll attack them so they won't have time to surround the town."

"Sounds good, but what about our beloved Magistrate?" Tef asked.

"If we convince him to fight, then we'll split his forces among ours, and hope for the best."

"Okay, it sounds like we have some really good ideas." Sir Valden said.

After they fine-tuned their battle tactics, they left the inn and walked to the magistrate's building. Along the way, Master Shoo felt better knowing that at least the Orders were united, and they were all going to stand and fight. Silently, he vowed to severely beat the magistrate if he refused to help them.

They arrived at the Magistrate's building and were surprised to find it heavily guarded, with at least fifty men walking around the perimeter and another twenty on the rooftop armed with bows and crossbows.

"Now what?" Tef whispered as they slowed in front of the building.

"I'll show you what." Sir Valden stated and walked straight up to the closest guard.

"Hold your position." One of them ordered.

Sir Valden did so. Scanning the guards, his eyes came to rest on one, in particular, and he grinned.

"What do you want?" Another guard asked as he was approaching the owner of the Searing Blade.

"We need to see the magistrate to discuss the future of this town, especially over the next few days."

"He's not seeing anyone at this time. However, if you wait until morning maybe he'll change his mind."

"Morning? We don't have that long. Either way I, I mean we, will be seeing him tonight."

"I'm afraid that won't be possible." The guard then peered upwards, and the men raised their weapons."

Master Shoo stepped closer towards Sir Valden, but before he reached him, Valden stormed over in the direction of the man he recognized and seized the young lad by the throat.

"Let him go." The first guard command.

Sir Valden turned around and held his prisoner as you would a shield. "I don't think so. Now tell your men to lower their weapons or the Magistrate's nephew will no longer be in possession of his throat."

"You will die if you do."

"What do I care? This town, like Redden, will fall in the next day or so."

"What do you mean?"

High Priest Hamond stepped forward and said. "The enemy from Redden is poised to strike at this town and if the Magistrate doesn't join with us, then there is no way we can hold them off."

The guard was taken aback. "Where are they now?"

"They gather their forces and will march on us within a few days."

The guard knew of Priest Hamond by the services he attended, so when he spoke he heeded his warning and waved off his men. "Sir Valden, if you release the Magistrate's nephew, I'll allow you access."

"I'll do so when I feel like it. We'll call it insurance."

"Fine, just don't hurt the boy. I am only permitting the leaders of the Orders to enter." The guard said and escorted them inside the building.

Once inside, the guard instructed Sir Valden, Master Shoo, Tef, and Priest Hamond to wait in the vestibule while he walked upstairs.

"I think you got his attention." Tef said to Sir Valden after he was gone.

"Without a doubt." Hamond added. "Should you release the boy's throat?"

Valden nodded and let it go.

The guard returned, told them the Magistrate would see them shortly, and then escorted them down the hallway to a room filled with chairs and a large round table. Once seated, Sir Valden ordered the boy to stay put. The Magistrate entered the room a few minutes later. He was escorted by at least a dozen armed men who then stood around him after he was seated. He looked at each of his unexpected guests then spoke. "What do you people want? What gives you the right to barge in here and demand an audience with me in the middle of the night?" The Magistrate looked over at his nephew. "And you have some nerve to threaten me by holding my nephew."

"Drastic times call for extreme measures." Sir Valden said.

"Magistrate," Shoo began, "we needed to speak with you tonight. It's urgent."

The magistrate looked at him. "Why?" His tone clearly indicated how annoyed he was.

"The army from Redden threatens our town."

"How could you possibly know this? They've made no indication of doing so."

"Several of my students led a daring rescue attempt and saved many townspeople, but in doing so put our town at risk."

"Who gave them the order to go blindly into the town and do so?" The Magistrate snapped.

"We are here to come up with a solution to our situation, not to be berated by you." Tef responded.

"You will if you want my help, thief." He barked at him.

"No one told them to, they took it upon themselves to do the right thing even if you wouldn't." Shoo said.

"What do you mean, wouldn't?"

"Don't lie to us. We know for a fact that they asked you for help, and you turned them down."

"Prove it." The Magistrate countered.

"It doesn't matter anymore. What matters is what will happen if you don't lend your support." Priest Hamond said, trying to calm the ever-growing tensions.

The Magistrate rolled his eyes and Sir Valden's patience finally gave way. He slammed his fist on the table and said. "If you don't help us, then I will personally hold you accountable if anyone dies."

Some of the guards drew their weapons and the Magistrate raised his hand, indicating for them to hold their ground. "Don't threaten me or I'll have you and your Order exiled from this town, and every nearby town! Don't think I can't do it either."

"Enough!" Tef snapped.

"Oh great, the thief will now speak again." The Magistrate said.

"Magistrate, if you don't stand with us, then I don't think I want to risk my men on a cause that will fail."

"That's if they attack, thief."

Tef looked around the table at his companions. "Gentlemen I think we're done." He stood up. "I've changed my mind." He left the table, ignoring priest Hamond's protests to stay.

Sir Valden waited until the door closed behind Tef before speaking. "Here's something else to ponder; without our Orders, this town will falter financially as well. You have no idea how much revenue it accumulates just from our annual events." He also stood up.

"You should think of the town's well-being for once." Hamond added as he too got up and was ready to leave.

The Magistrate frowned and a humbling look finally was etched across his face. "Alright, I'll lend my support."

Valden and Hamond looked at each other and sat back down.

"Do you have a plan at least?" The Magistrate asked.

They told him what they wanted to do, and he listened intently without resistance. Eventually, he called in his top advisors to add their opinions as well. They spoke well into the morning hours and after the meeting ended they went back to their respective Orders and prepared for the inevitable.

****

Meanwhile, a few nights prior to Master Shoo's meeting, a man leading a small group of Chatar and Hurnol creatures was camped thirty miles northwest of the town of Redden. He was tall and lean, wore special black leather armor that enabled him to move as freely as if he was wearing thin clothes, and extraordinary boots that allowed him to move stealthily. The only weapon he carried was a five-foot spear draped across his back.

He walked around the area speaking with his two human

bodyguards. They were taller by several inches, dressed in traditional studded leather, and carried sheathed scimitars. They were halfway around the camp when a boarman with razor-sharp tusks came running over. The creature was clearly winded.

"Master Yang...up ahead there is a group of...travelers with lots and lots of stuff." He huffed and snorted.

"Why are you so tired? Lose some weight you pathetic creature." The bodyguard on the left said in obvious disgust.

The boarman didn't look at him, and the bodyguard kicked him for not doing so, sending him sprawling to the ground. The others laughed loudly. The boarman got up, brushed off the dirt from his hide armor, and apologized. The man carrying the spear was amused and said almost jokingly. "You were saying?"

"A small caravan with many items is camped to the west."

"How many people?" Yang asked.

"Not many." He snorted.

"You are dismissed."

The Chatar bowed and left.

"Shall we have some fun?" Yang asked his bodyguards.

"You stay here; we'll go." The guard to his right said.

"And miss the fun? I need the exercise and it's been awhile since I killed something." Yang paused. "Unless, you want to be my training partner Vex?" His tone was serious.

The other bodyguard snickered, and Yang looked at him with a deadpan expression. "You think it's funny? How about you Jyre, do you want a lesson?"

When Jyre's smile faded, Yang laughed at him and walked away, leaving them to ponder if he was serious or not.

Under the cover of darkness, Yang and his two companions walked through the forest until they came upon the merchant's caravan. Around the fire, they saw seven armed men, most likely hired to protect the merchant and his wares. Yang studied them, quickly determined their worth and entered. Those seated, although surprised by the sudden emergence of the strangers, remained where they were and continued to drink. Yang, Jyre, and Vex stopped a few feet away.

"Good evening gentlemen. Can we see the merchant?" Yang said to them.

"Go away, the merchant isn't selling anything this evening." The man who spoke to them was far older in years, wore a chainmail shirt, and had his unsheathed long sword within reach.

"We're not here to buy anything old man." Yang calmly replied.

"Oh, then why are you here? Surely not to get warm by our fire or drink our mead."

"Nope, not that either."

"Then state your purpose before I get angry."

Yang grinned. "We want the merchant's wares."

"I told you he wasn't selling anything tonight. Are you deaf?" He raised his voice.

"Oh, I'm not deaf. You must be, because I told you we're not here to buy anything."

"Well if you're not here to buy anything, then you must be here to steal his stuff and if that's the case, you have a problem."

"Good deduction, took you long enough." Yang coolly replied.

"I'll give you one more chance to leave before I get up, whelp."

The other men around the fire laughed at Yang, who then causally glanced over his shoulder.

"When will people know when they're outmatched?" He said to his bodyguards but loud enough for the others to hear.

One of the mercenaries stood up and withdrew his sword. "I think he's serious about his intentions." He stated to the others.

"Don't care if he is, there are only three of them and seven of us." Another mercenary added.

"You should heed my boss' warning and leave before you die." Vex said.

The mercenaries had enough of the intruders and began standing up one by one and unsheathing their weapons.

"Tough words, we'll see about that." The older mercenary countered, and he began moving towards them with his men following closely behind.

Yang, Vex, and Jyre did not move nor indicate that they were going to defend themselves until the mercenaries were within striking distance. They then took out their weapons and attacked.

It was over before the mercenaries knew what had happened. Yang used several feints to draw his opponent out of position enough to strike him in the stomach and throat, while Vex and Jyre made small work of the others, except for the old man, who they disarmed and kicked to the ground.

Yang walked over to join them. "As you were saying, you were going to do what?" Yang said.

"Please spare me, we didn't mean to..."

The trio laughed at him, and then the merchant emerged from one of the wagons.

"What do you men want?" He asked Yang after seeing the carnage all about.

"We'll deal with you in a second." Yang held up his hand toward the merchant and silenced him. "Now pick him up." He said to his bodyguards.

They took hold of his arms and roughly picked him up.

"You're going to love this." Yang said to the mercenary and patted his cheek several times and then walked back at least eight feet away.

The old man didn't know what he was going to do, but had a feeling his life was about to end. With blinding speed, Yang twirled his spear around his body, over his head, behind his back, and then abruptly stopped the weapon in front of body and held it firmly with both hands. He smiled and said. "Now watch this." He tensed his muscles, and the spear's shaft lengthened until it tore through the man's armor, abdomen, and out of his back carrying his innards along with it. The old man's eyes widen in shock as he died. After the weapon retracted back to its original length, Yang looked over at the terrified merchant.

"Please take what you want just let us live." The merchant pleaded.

"Oh we will, and since I am a man of my words then..." Yang's words trailed off as he threw his spear at the merchant. The weapon plunged into his stomach and pinned his dying body next to the door. Fearful screamed then erupted from within the wagon.

"Good, he has some daughters." He announced to his men, and they entered the wagon and that's when the screams really started.

****

A few days after Yang and his men left the area, a holy fighter named Tracs stumbled upon the merchant's camp. He saw dead bodies right away and quietly dismounted his gray mare. After placing his horned helmet on of his head and unsheathing his broad sword, he entered the encampment. Pots and other crockery were strewn about along with the bodies of men, woman, and children. He gazed upon their lifeless bodies, and was saddened and angry all at once by the slaughter. He was preoccupied determining who or what did this atrocity, when he heard a faint noise coming from within the wagon. He climbed the stairs and stopped just short of entering and listened for several minutes. What he heard from within was sporadic movement and not enough for someone who'd be stealing.

He stepped back from the door and said. "Who's in there?"

At first, there was no reply then he heard a female's voice crying out for help.

"Are you alone?"

"Yes." She coughed in reply.

Tracs looked around once more and entered. Inside the dimly lit wagon, he saw the outline of a naked body towards the back and

50

approached.

"Please don't hurt me." The women pleaded.

"I'm not here to hurt you. I want to help." Tracs removed his gauntlets and helmet and knelt down.

The woman had multiple stab and slash wounds in her chest, face, arms, and legs and her blood stained the wooden floor. He was surprised that she still lived at all.

"Are my children..." she coughed several times, "alive?"

"I'm sorry but no one is."

The woman cried, and Tracs grabbed a nearby blanket and covered her with it. He went through his pouch producing a rose-colored vial and held it up to her lips.

"Drink this." He said and poured the liquid down her throat.

She drank about a third of the vile and began coughing violently and spit up the liquid all over his hand and blanket.

"Do you know who did this to you?" He asked.

"Three strangers."

"Where did they go?"

"I don't know. I passed out before they left..." She coughed again.

"Is there anything you could tell me about them that I would recognize them by?"

The woman's eyes fluttered, and she lost consciousness. Tracs quickly reached into his pouch, grabbed a yellow vile, and poured the contents down her throat. A few seconds, the woman stirred. He felt bad bringing her awake, but needed to know who did this crime.

"Can you tell me anything else about these men?"

"I can't feel my legs." She whispered.

"Please tell me if you remember anything."

Her breathing became labored. "There's a necklace... over there." She pointed to her left.

Tracs saw a necklace with a pendant attached to it and grabbed it. Engraved on the medallion was a person's face with its eyes closed, hands holding its head and wavy horizontal lines above it. The waves reminded him of someone thinking. He studied it for a few more minutes then asked.

"Where did you get this?"

When she didn't respond, he looked over and noticed she had finally succumbed to her wounds. Saddened, he placed the necklace into his pouch and vowed to make those responsible pay for their actions. By nightfall, Tracks buried the last of the dead and finished gathering enough clues to determine the ones responsible went southward toward the town of Redden. He mounted his mare and rode off into the darkness.

When Yang arrived in the town of Redden, he found the general in the dining hall of the mayor's elaborate mansion enjoying a meal. The Red Knight rose after he entered unannounced.

"Paven, how are you faring in your new role?" Yang asked and sat down at the table.

The servants quickly filled a goblet with wine and placed it in front of him.

"Very well." Paven responded and sat back down.

Yang took a long swig and said. "That's good, now well me everything that's happened since you overtook the town."

Yang listened patiently until the general spoke of a group of strangers who infiltrated the town and became agitated.

"Who were these people?" Yang demanded.

"They were looking for someone named Torhan."

"Torhan? Was he, the mayor or someone of importance?"

"No idea."

"How did you come across that piece of information?"

"We captured one of them, and he told us everything."

"Where is he now? I'd like to ask him a few questions." Yang took on a sinister look.

"We sent him on a special mission."

"I don't have time for a guessing game, so what does that mean, special mission?"

"I transformed him into my own image, and I sent him after his friends. Of course, The Lord of the Mind had his influence on him beforehand."

"You're not as useless as you appear." Yang said in a condescending tone.

"So what brings you to Redden?" Paven asked.

"The master wanted me to make sure you did as you were instructed. I am pleased with your work. He will be as well. Furthermore, I am to let you know we'll be leaving Redden in a few weeks."

"Why?"

"It was not his intentions for us to occupy this town for too long, just to send a message to the surrounding towns that we are coming. Do you understand?"

Paven nodded in response.

"Good, now, how about a tour of the town?"

Chapter 3: Quest for The Red Knight

Captain Strom and a clutch of his men entered the inn looking for Konafar and Tonles, figuring that's where they'd be.

"There they are captain," one of the men said while pointing towards the last table in the back of the room.

Strom excused him with a nod and approached the table, gazing at Konafar and Tonles with their heads down, obliviously passed out drunk.

"Konafar!" Strom called.

The big man stirred, and Strom shook his head smiling.

"Wake up you lazy bum."

Konafar lifted his head, looked around sheepishly and then placed his head back down.

"You need to leave the inn or at least go upstairs and sleep it off."

"We'll be fine, we're just resting." Konafar replied through barely separated lips.

Strom reached for Carnage and instinctively, Konafar grabbed his wrist. "Don't touch my blade. We're getting up." He rose, stretched, and shook Tonles awake. "I'm glad you're here captain. We were coming to see you today anyway."

Strom noticed traces of splattered blood on his armor. "I see by your appearance that you took care of business."

"We sure did." Tonles said stretching. "You'll find him in his room."

"What is it that you wanted to see me about?" Strom asked and sat down.

"We're leaving in a day or so, and we'll need some men."

"For what?" Strom replied.

"We owe one of our comrades some revenge. Have you ever heard of someone who goes by the title of the Red Knight?" Tonles asked.

"I haven't heard of anyone going by that name, who is he?"

"He tortured one of our classmates and turned him into something horrible. He will feel our wrath."

"If he's only one man, then why do you need assistance?" Strom was a bit puzzled given the fact that he didn't think any one man could actually stand against these two.

"He has an army and we need to get inside of Redden, so I was thinking we'll need some help." Konafar explained while rubbing his head, trying to clear away the cobwebs from the long night of drinking.

"How many men are you looking for?"

Tonles and Konafar looked at each other and then back at Strom.

"I'm guessing twelve." Tonles stated.

"It sounds like a suicide mission. I'll see what I can do. Will you be paying them or will you promise them glory?" Strom chuckled.

"We'll pay them handsomely if they're willing." Konafar said.

"Okay, eat something and I'll be back with whoever is willing to go."

Strom got up and clasped their arms in turn, then left.

It was around midday when Strom, and his most trusted men, returned to the Inn of the Wolf. When they entered, Konafar and Tonles were still gorging on several plates of food but stopped eating when the captain and his men walked over.

"Is this it?" Konafar asked looking over the guards.

"Yes, but I have an idea." Captain Strom sat down without being asked to, and after introducing his men, he motioned for them to go somewhere else.

"And what would that be?" Tonles asked and then quickly went back to eating.

"I had an idea as to how you can get some more men, without even paying them."

"Can they fight?" Konafar asked.

"They are some of the most hardened men I've ever met."

Konafar placed the roasted pheasant's leg on his plate and leaned closer. "Go on, you've got my attention."

"In my prison we have several criminals who are awaiting

execution, but because of some people in high offices, we are having a degree of difficulty putting anyone to death nowadays." Strom leaned slightly back in his chair disgusted, prompting the wood to creak beneath his weight.

"It just seems," he continued, "if you commit a crime all you have to do is stay in prison, eat for free, and wait to be released. If I were the Magistrate, I'd change the law."

"So what can we do if they are locked away?" Konafar said looking over at Tonles, who was paying more attention to his food than to what Strom was saying.

"I was thinking that if you took them with you, you could do society a favor and kill them after they use up their usefulness."

"What are you going to offer them in return?"

"I'll promise them freedom if they help you."

"How many men are you proposing?" Tonles chimed in without lifting his head.

"Three total."

"So that will give us twelve. Do you think that is enough?" Konafar asked Tonles.

The big man lifted his head, stew dripped down his beard staining it brown in certain parts. "I like the idea of having some expendable men."

One of the guards overheard Tonles and shot him a look.

Tonles noticed his gaze. "I didn't mean you, so calm down." He said and turned his attention back to the men at his table.

"Tell us about them." Konafar said.

"One goes by the name of Burner. Another is called the Butcher, and the third is an archer, named Cord."

Tonles' arched his left brow. "What are their crimes?"

"Burner burnt down a school full of children because they threw trash at his house and called him names. The one that goes by the name of Butcher was convicted of murder after he hacked apart his family because they didn't like his girlfriend. He's a bit crazy because he kept repeating that the voices made him do it after we captured him. As far as the archer; he was an upstanding citizen until one day, during an archery demonstration, someone made the mistake of taunting him after he missed splitting an arrow by a few inches. That mistake proved costly, because he snapped and killed everyone who was watching."

"Sounds like they could be useful. How will you get them released?"

"I'm going to tell the sergeant that you're from Wistful and need to take prisoners there so they can stand trial for crimes they committed."

"Will he believe you?" Konafar asked.

"I think so, but if he doesn't I know what will persuade him."

On horseback, Strom, Konafar, Tonles and the guards rode east for several miles until they came upon a structure buried halfway in the sand. Two guards, wearing light leather armor and holding heavy crossbows, were posted directly at the stairs leading downward into the prison. After dismounting, Strom greeted the men and they in turn moved aside and allowed the group to traverse the stairway below.

They went down for several flights and ended at a steel gated door with a lone guard. His short red hair was worn in a similar manner to Strom's, and his features resembled the captain's to the point that they could have passed for brothers. His black chainmail glimmered under the poor lighting, and his ax appeared to be razor sharp. He recognized captain Strom at once, and after saluting him, he turned around and banged in a rhythmic pattern on the gate using a metal object. In response, the gate lifted, allowing them to enter.

Strom led them down a long, empty hallway until they entered a medium-sized room, with a large, thick wooden door to the east and several guards sitting around a table.

"Captain Strom, what are you doing here?" an officer of medium stature, dressed in dingy chainmail said after seeing him enter.

"Jusid, it's a glorious day. I'd like you to meet Tonles and Konafar." The captain replied.

Jusid nodded slightly in their direction.

"They're from Wistful on official business and will be escorting Burner, Butcher, and Cord there to stand trial."

"For what?" Jusid quickly responded.

"Crimes they committed before we arrested them."

"Oh? Did the Magistrate approve of this?" Jusid said, giving Tonles and Konafar a suspicious glance.

"Sergeant let's talk privately."

They walked out of the room and stopped when they were far enough away where they wouldn't be overheard.

"Jusid we finally have a chance to rid our society of these foul people once and for all, and you know with our laws its damn near impossible to put them to death." Strom said.

"How will you explain it to the Magistrate?"

"I'll take care of him."

"Captain, with all due respect, he will question me."

"No he won't. I'll have paperwork to back up my claim."

"I don't feel right doing this." Jusid said. He knew Strom was putting him in an awkward position.

"How about this, if you go along with me, then I'll see that you get reassigned to Mirkin instead of this place. You'll be able to see your wife and kids every day. Would you like that?"

"You would do that?"

"Yes. And I'll get you a raise as well."

"Are you sure the Magistrate will never find out?"

"It's my neck too."

Jusid grinned. "Okay I'm in."

They returned to the room and escorted Tonles and Konafar deeper down into the prison. Eventually they came to the main hallway where the prisoners were kept. The on duty guard opened the door and allowed them to enter.

"When you're finished, come back upstairs." Jusid said and left.

The hallway beyond was long, dimly lit, and cells were on both sides. The prisoners watched Captain Strom and the others pass by. They did so in silence, fearing the two strangers might be executioners, and that they might die.

Strom stopped when they were halfway down and looked into the cage to his left. "This is Burner." He announced and then beckoned the prisoner forward.

The tall slender man, with wiry black hair, got off of his cot and walked over to the bars.

"Captain Strom, it's good to see you. How are the children?" His sarcastic tone irritated the captain and he tensed up.

Captain Strom wanted to open the cell and rip his head off, but held his composure knowing that this lunatic would die soon enough. "Burner, I have a deal for you." He offered.

"For me? What is it?"

"If you accompany these men on their journey, and live up to your end of the bargain, I will grant you your freedom."

Burner was curious. "What is it that you want me to do?"

"Go with them and do whatever they need you to do. Once you're finished you can walk away."

"That's it?"

"That and agree never to return to Mirkin."

"So why do they need me?" He suspiciously asked.

"I heard you like to set things ablaze." Konafar stepped forward and said.

"I do. I like to burn things. Burn everything. Ignite things that can't be burned." He replied in a sick manner.

"Good. You will get your chance to do just that.

"That's all I have to do?"

Konafar nodded.

"Do we have a deal?" Strom asked.

Burner nodded and was then handed a piece of rolled-up parchment from the captain's satchel.

"Sign it." Strom ordered.

Burner unrolled the writ, read it carefully, signed it, and then handed it back to Strom, who overlooked his signature.

"When do we leave?" Burner asked. They ignored him and walked further down the hall.

"Make sure he dies." Strom reminded them.

They stopped at a cell on the right.

"Butcher." Strom called and a short stocky man with long, unkempt black hair, stepped forward.

"Captain Strom, it's been a while. Is my family coming to see me today?"

"Butcher, don't you remember that you killed them?"

Butcher looked puzzled and then sad. "Oh ya, they made me do it." He said.

"I know, but you still have to pay for your crimes."

"But it's not fair."

"Do you want to redeem yourself?"

Butcher's eyes lit up. "Do you think if I do the voices will stop?"

"They might."

"Then I agree."

"You must do whatever these men want, okay?"

Butcher nodded, and Strom handed him a rolled-up writ. Butcher signed it without even reading it and then handed it back to the captain.

They walked down to the very last cell on the left, and Strom called for the archer. Cord stepped forward towards the bars. He was slender in build, a couple of inches shorter than Konafar, and wore his blond hair in a ponytail.

"What do you want?" Cord asked.

"How would like to be set free?" Strom simply asked.

"I'm listening."

"My two associates have need of your skill. All you have to do is help them, and once you're finished you can go your own way."

"What's the mission?" Cord asked while looking at Konafar.

Konafar stepped closer. "A few weeks ago, an army invaded and took over the town of Redden. We need to get inside and kill their leader."

Cord looked at the man like he was insane. "You want us to invade a town and kill someone? Just the three of us?"

"Fifteen to be exact." Tonles added.

"Are you insane?" Cord countered. "I'd rather stay in here and live."

"You do know you're never going to see the light of day?" Strom interjected.

"Why me?" Cord asked.

"I've never seen anyone as skilled as you are with a bow, and they need an archer." Strom answered.

"Is this a full pardon?"

Strom nodded. "You must also agree never to step inside the walls of Mirkin again."

Cord was highly intelligent, and knew the captain well enough to know that his freedom was a lie. However, he did not want to stay behind bars for the rest of his life, and agreed to sign the writ as soon as the document was handed to him.

After they left the cell area, Captain Strom took out the three writs and tore them to shreds.

"Why did you do that?" Tonles asked.

"They were written by me and would never hold up in our courts, plus after your mission, they're dead men anyway." Strom looked proud. "I'm thirsty, so let's have a drink with the men upstairs."

"Strom," Konafar began, "I need to talk to the prisoners alone."

"Why?"

"I have to find out what supplies they'll need and gain their trust."

Strom nodded, allowed Konafar back inside and then went upstairs with Tonles.

Konafar revisited the archer first. "Cord is your name right?" He asked.

Cord walked to the bars. "It is."

"I'll be leading this mission, so what do you need?"

"I'll need a composite bow, a few scores of arrows, and some daggers. Get the arrows that have rows of sharp edges."

"Why them?"

"I'm guessing you're not a true archer?"

"I'm pretty good with a bow."

"Good with a bow and a true archer are two different things. The tips that I want are nearly impossible to remove, and even if they are, death is almost certain."

"Anything else?"

"I need a black cloak, leather armor, and the softest boots you can find."

"If you keep to the mission and do not try anything funny you will have your freedom." Konafar reassured him.

"I will as long as you keep your word."

Konafar grinned and then walked to Butcher's cell and called out his name.

Butcher responded immediately and walked up to the bars.

"My name is Konafar and I'll be leading this mission."

"Who's your companion?"

"His name is Tonles."

"That's a good name, do you hear voices?"

"I do not, so what do they tell you?" Konafar asked curiously.

"They tell me what is right and what is wrong. There was a time when a group of kids picked on me, and the voices told me if I stabbed them; they would stop." His face took on a serious look.

"Did you stab them?"

Butcher nodded.

"What do the voices say about me and my friend?" Konafar wanted to gauge whether this man was going to be a high risk or not.

"They said that you would come and set me free and that my name will live on for all of eternity."

"What supplies do you need?"

"I like to chop things."

"So you want an ax then?"

"No. I like to play with small cleavers."

"Ok, I'll be back later when we're ready to leave."

Konafar walked away and went to Burner's cell. Burner was already waiting for him.

"I know you're Konafar and your friend is Tonles, so let's cut to the chase. I'll take at least twenty flasks of oil, a girdle to hold them, tinder, a knife, a small hammer, and a long black robe."

"Is that all?"

"Are you writing all of this down?"

"Cut the attitude."

"Or what? I'm not afraid of you." Burner snapped in response.

"I'll rip your throat out. That's what."

Konafar suddenly reached in and grabbed him by the throat and began choking him. Burner's arms flailed. Konafar released him and shoved him backwards.

"Anything else?"

Burner rubbed his neck and was shaking his head.

"Just remember if you do as we ask, then you'll be free within a week or so."

Konafar walked away without saying another word and went upstairs to join Strom and Tonles.

After he was seated, Strom was eager to get his opinion. "How did it go?" He asked.

"The only one that might be an issue is Burner, so we'll need to keep an eye on him." Konafar said and then started scribbling something down on a piece of parchment.

"What are you doing?" Tonles asked him.

"They'll need supplies." Konafar handed the list to Strom.

Strom looked it over. "You're going to give them everything they want?"

"I need them to carry out the mission to a tee, and if they don't have their tools, then they are useless. Who can handle this request?"

"I'll give it to one of my men. I'll be right back." Strom said and left.

"What do you really think of the prisoners?" Tonles asked him.

"We'll need to watch our backs for sure. I think the one called the Butcher will be okay. Burner and Cord I'm not sure about. Cord seems intelligent and Burner is just plain crazy." He paused and then continued. "I also think that we shouldn't kill them unless we have to. I don't care what we told Strom."

"I was thinking the same thing. We've been associated with far worse and ended up becoming good friends with them."

"I'm glad we are on the same page."

It was nearing dusk when the guard returned from his trip to Mirkin. In his hands, he carried three backpacks. "Here are the supplies you asked for." He said to Konafar.

"What's your name?" Konafar asked.

"My name is Pierce."

"Please wait with them outside Pierce, we'll be leaving soon."

The guard nodded and left.

Strom walked into the room as Pierce exited.

"When do we leave?" Tonles asked the captain.

"Are you ready?"

They nodded.

"Let's go get them now."

After shackling the prisoners, they were escorted to the outside and given over to Tonles, Konafar and the elite guards of Mirkin. Only a couple of prison guards asked Jusid where the prisoners were going. After he told them it was official business they didn't' say anything further.

Konafar and his company rode west for about a mile and stopped abruptly. He dismounted, grabbed the three backpacks, and asked Cord, Burner, and Butcher to walk with him so they could speak privately.

"If you want your freedom then do everything that I ask, and you'll have it. I will also pay you handsomely if everything goes smoothly."

"Sounds simple enough." Burner said.

"However, if you don't live up to your obligation, I will cut you down. This agreement is between you three, Tonles, and me. Do you have any questions?"

"Have you thought about how we are going to enter the town?" Cord asked.

"I have an idea, but the details haven't been fully worked out just yet."

"When will you know, after we get there?" Burner asked.

The question seemed simple enough, but it was his tone that irked Konafar. "Just do as you're told alright?"

Burner reminded Konafar of Gunther's personality, and then he grinned, reflecting on the way his eyes looked after his head was cut down the middle.

"Continue please." Cord said, sensing tension.

"Can I count on you?"

"You have my word." Cord said.

"Mine too." Butcher added.

"Mine as well." Burner said.

"Good." Konafar said, removed the chains and handed them a backpack each. "When we break for camp, then you can equip your wares."

Around mid-evening, Konafar and the others came upon the Harazon Forest and made camp outside of it. Around the campfire,

Burner, Butcher, and Cord exchanged their prison garb for armor, boots, and cloaks. Butcher tested the sharpness of his cleavers against a nearby log, while Cord tightened the string of his new bow and inspected the arrow tips. Meanwhile, Burner placed the girdle around his chest, and then took the hammer and dagger out and began scoring each flask. When he finished the first one, an elite guard named Hue asked him what he was doing.

"By scoring the glass, they break easier and my victims are sure to burn." Burner looked intensely at the man.

"Just make sure you burn the enemy and not any of us." Hue replied and walked away.

Standing a few yards away, Tonles and Konafar eyed the looming forest.

"Do we go through?" Tonles finally asked him.

"Not unless we have to."

"It's going to cost us a few more days to go around."

"I don't want to risk another encounter with that beast. We couldn't best it before, even with the help of Din and his kinsmen, and with this crew..." He paused and looked over at the men, "I doubt we could now."

"I'd like to get my hands on that ax that Din was using and have another go at it."

"You're crazy my friend." Konafar said.

"Maybe so, but what a test that creature poses." Tonles had that challenging look in his eyes.

"I'm going to sleep, so don't get any bright ideas about going in there alone." He said as if reading Tonles' mind, and then walked back to the campfire to join the others.

After his friend was gone, Tonles stared into the thick dense woods and wondered if the creature was looking back at him wanting, and hoping, he would enter. He stayed there for a few minutes more before joining the others, most of which were already asleep. Before turning in, he made sure to tell some of the guards to keep a watchful eye on

Burner, Cord, and Butcher while they slept. Light rain mixed with a cold wind ushered in the morning as the group rose from their slumber. Konafar had already made up his mind that they would go south, around the woods.

By mid-afternoon, they came upon a wagon, and two large tents camped just inside of a cluster of trees. There was a sign above the wagon that read "Trankle's Wares." Konafar halted the group, dismounted and proceeded to the middle-aged merchant.

"Good day sir, welcome to Trankle's Wares. I'm Trankle." The fat bellied man, wearing traveling clothes and a straw hat said when Konafar was close enough.

"I'd like to see what you have." Konafar replied.

"Carissa!" The man called.

From inside of the tent on the left, a dainty woman came walking out.

Konafar looked at the teenage girl and thought she looked homely, but did have a sensuous appeal about her. He liked the way her tightly fitted garb hugged her curves, and the way her long dark hair was draped down her back.

"Show the man our wares." Trankle said.

Carissa smiled at Konafar and led him to the tent on the right. It was filled with rows of tables with weapons, armor, and other items stacked neatly on top.

"What are you looking for?" She asked.

"I have one of the best blades throughout the land, so maybe some armor to go with it."

"Right this way."

She led him towards the tables in the far back. He liked following her because he could admire her ass from behind.

"So where are you headed?" The merchant said to Tonles and the others.

"To Redden." Tonles replied.

"Redden!" the merchant sounded shocked.

"That town fell a few weeks ago. I wouldn't go there if I were you."

"That's why you're not me. We have some unfinished business with the new residents."

Trankle was surprised as he gazed at the men. "Just your group? What are you crazy?"

Tonles grinned. "You'd be surprised what determination can do." He walked away and joined Konafar in the tent.

Tonles entered and walked over to Konafar and the girl. "Did you find anything?" He asked him.

"Nothing much, other than a tough hide leather vest and armbands, however, there's a two-handed mace over there that might interest you."

"Oh! Where?" Tonles asked, looking around.

"Come with me." Carissa interjected and led him to a table off to the side and near the front.

Tonles quickly spotted the weapon right away. It was blackened steel with gold embedded throughout the obsidian color. He'd never seen such a weapon before and marveled at it. "I haven't seen anything like it in all my travels." He said.

"My father calls it a Gothic Flanged mace, and it's great against plate armor because it will tear into the metal with ease. If you can lift it."

Tonles picked up the weapon by the handle. The mace was almost as long as Ripper, and the head was a third bigger than most flanged maces, which brought a wide smile to his bearded face. He tested the weight with several swings and was surprised at how light and balanced the weapon felt. While debating if he wanted to buy it, something strange happened. He began feeling a tingling sensation coursing up and down his arms and then through the rest of his body. He actually felt stronger. His muscles flexed and tightened on their own accord for several long seconds. He gave it few more swings and discovered the weapon felt even lighter.

"Where did you get it?" He asked.

"We found it a few days ago after we stumbled upon a group of dead men to the east."

Tonles swung the weapon a few more times. "How much did you want?"

"My father knows the price."

Konafar walked over to them while holding several pieces of armor. "Are you ready?"

Tonles nodded, and they left the tent.

After paying a few thousand gold pieces for their items, Konafar discarded his old chainmail and brigandine armor in favor of the new one he'd just bought. First, he donned the crimson-colored gambeson onto his bulky frame and then fastened a tough-hide leather vest on top of that. After a few minor adjustments by one of the guards, he put on matching leather wristbands and shoulder pads. When he was satisfied with the feel and movement, he took out Carnage and began swinging the blade to ensure that there would be no limitations when the time came.

Meanwhile, Tonles studied his new weapon and took a special interest in the strange symbols on each of the flange heads, which he hadn't noticed earlier. He then ran his left thumb along the edge of each flange and could feel that they were extremely sharp. Satisfied, he raised the weapon high into the air and made an announcement, "I'll call you Justice," and took a few hearty swings.

"Congratulations my friend, may you slew many foes." Konafar said to him.

Tonles smiled then walked over and tied his trusty ax to the horse. He felt a sense of loss putting his friend away, because Ripper had been his weapon of choice for several years. He could always rely on it in the heat of battle.

"If you need to buy anything, do it now. We need to leave soon."

Konafar announced to the others.

By the time dusk settled in, the rain dissipated and the end of the forest was in sight. Konafar halted them for the evening and gave everyone a specific task. Some gathered wood, while others took part in setting up the camp and cooking the food.

After Tonles finished eating, he sat on a log and studied the strange markings on the flanges, drawing Cord's attention as he passed by.

"Do you know what those runes mean?" Cord asked him and then sat next to him.

Tonles shook his head.

"May I have a look?"

Tonles handed him the weapon and Cord struggled against its weight and almost dropped the mace. "This is heavier than I expected."

"It is?" Tonles was puzzled because it felt very light to him. "Wait here, I'll be right back."

Tonles got up, retrieved Ripper, and then offered his great ax to Cord upon his return.

"Is my ax heavier?"

Cord took the weapon and said that it wasn't.

Tonles took a weapon in each hand and held them forth. "This is very strange to me, because they feel like they weigh the same."

"I'd like to study the runes some more, can I have the mace back?"

Tonles handed it to him.

Cord laid it onto his lap and began studying each of the flange's heads one at a time. "Interesting." He said on more than one occasion. "If you start over here," he pointed to one of the flanges, "and follow them in order, they spell out what this weapon does for the wielder."

"Oh!" Tonles exclaimed.

Cord took out a piece of parchment and began writing down his interpretation of what the symbols meant. When he was finished, he smiled and gave it to Tonles. "Read this."

"So what you're saying is that if the wielder is strong enough, then the weapon will deliver devastating damage." He paused and continued scanning the next paragraph. "Am I reading this correctly?"

Cord smiled at him. "You are."

"You mean to tell me that this blunt weapon can rip and break apart almost any solid object?"

"And don't forget about the owner becoming stronger." Cord added. "How much did you pay for it?"

"A thousand gold pieces."

"Given its value, I'd say you got a good deal."

Tonles' smile broadened.

"You should go try it out." Cord handed him back the weapon.

Tonles walked around until he found suitable redwood for his test and hoisted the weapon high into the air, took aim, and swung Justice with intent. When the mace struck the tree, the flanges sunk so deep into the wood, it became buried all the way up to the shaft. He removed the weapon with ease, struck the surface two more times and had the same results. Satisfied, he tried his weapon on a nearby boulder. The weapon tore away chunks of the stone with each swing, until the boulder cracked down the middle.

His test got the attention, and curiosity, of just about everyone in camp. Hue, walked over to him. "Can I try it?" He asked.

Tonles smiled and handed the skinny man the weapon, and to his delight, he immediately dropped it. The others laughed as he struggled to hoist the weapon. Hue eventually gave up when it fell from his grasp for the third time. Tonles laughed out loud with others. Another guard tried and just like the last man, had the similar difficulties. Konafar, who was amused by everyone's failed attempts, came over and lifted the weapon with ease, and felt the same tingling sensation Tonles did, running up and down his arms and felt stronger.

"Did anyone else feel a tingling sensation after touching the weapon?" He asked.

Everyone, except for Tonles, shook their heads no.

"This is some find, my friend. I feel stronger." Konafar announced and unsheathed Carnage. He held the sword in one hand and the mace in the other and hit the tree with alternating strikes between the weapons.

The onlookers stared in awe, because no man alive should be able to wield two, two-handed, weapons in each hand with such power. When he was finished, he gave Justice back to Tonles. The tingling sensation ceased a few seconds later, and his strength returned to normal.

"It's interesting that the mace gave Tonles and me more strength. I wonder why no one else benefitted from it." Konafar stated.

Cord joined them. "Maybe the wielder needs to be strong enough to wield it in the first place." He began. "I've been thinking the reason why the merchant probably sold it cheap was because to him; it felt unbalanced and too heavy to swing."

A very muscular man, who went by the name of Yon, stepped forward. "May I try?" He was a little smaller than Tonles, but looked every bit as strong.

Tonles handed him the weapon.

Yon grasped the mace with both hands and was met with the same sensation of strength as Konafar and Tonles felt. The muscles in his forearms and biceps tightened, and he felt the powerful as he hefted the weapon. "You are right criminal," he looked at Cord, "you do need to be as strong as I am."

Konafar took note to his comment, but kept quiet because he knew how it would end for him if he got angry.

Yon walked over to another tree and went to work, hitting it several times. When he was finished, the tree collapsed and fell with a thud.

"You're making too much noise. Why don't you give the weapon back to Tonles?" Konafar suddenly said.

Yon paused and looked over. There was something disturbing in his eyes. "I'll give you two thousand gold pieces for the weapon." He offered.

"I already named it, so the weapon is not for sale." Tonles stated.

"Come on, you'd make twice the amount of money. Who cares that you named it?" Yon faced the group with the mace held across his body, as if he was ready for a confrontation.

"You'd better give my weapon back." Tonles said, growing angrier by the moment.

"Or what?" Yon snapped at him.

"You're going to lose your life." Konafar added.

Yon smirked and grew more confident. "I never had something like this before."

Cord sensed what was about to happen and stepped away towards the camp without anyone really noticing.

"This is your last chance." Konafar added.

"Come on Yon, give it back." Pierce said.

"Two against one wouldn't be a fair fight. So how about this, I challenge one of you to take the weapon away from me, and if you do, then it's yours. If not, I keep it." Yon said.

"I'll handle this." Tonles said to his friend, and Konafar handed him Ripper.

"Last chance?" Konafar asked.

"I'm even going to call it Justice." Yon said.

Tonles shook his head and motioned toward him. Everyone backed away to give them enough room.

The swirling wind embraced both men as they circled each other for a couple of minutes. Yon studied Tonles for an opening and Tonles smirked condescendingly back at him, and then the fight began. Yon led off with a downward strike, which Tonles easily sidestepped and butted him in the face with the ax handle, breaking his nose and sending him reeling with his face covered in blood. Tonles advanced on him and swung Ripper downwardly. Yon blocked the attack, pushed aside his weapon and countered with a side strike. Tonles parried the blow and came around with the ax and would have lopped Yon's head off if he didn't jerk it away in time. Tonles' follow up strike was interrupted, because Yon unexpectedly swung Justice at his knee, which made Tonles bring up his ax to block the attack. Yon was about to strike him in the face, but Tonles slammed his elbow into his jaw knocking him sideways.

The onlookers thought the fight would end when Tonles brought Ripper about, but they were wrong. Yon recovered in time and blocked the ax, thus binding both weapons against each other. Yon seized the opportunity and grabbed Ripper, and as he was about to hit him with the flange part of the mace, Tonles then did something unexpected, let go of his weapon, grabbed Yon by his shoulders and kneed him in the stomach.

Yon felt the air leave his lungs, but immediately lowered his elbow to stifle another knee attack and shove Tonles back. Tonles moved in, and Yon swung the mace. Tonles ducked under the attack and punched him in the jaw, then kicked him in the stomach, grabbed his arm and flipped him over his shoulder. Despite landing hard onto his back, Yon held firmly onto the mace and hit Tonles in the stomach with the flange, as he was reaching in for him. Tonles stumbled backwards acting like he was more hurt then he was until he smacked into a tree. Yon was on his feet and advanced. When he was close enough, he swung Justice with the intent of concaving his opponent's head in, but the mighty Tonles ducked out of the way and the mace crashed into the tree and became lodged into the trunk. Tonles punched him in the ribs and face and then ran over to pick up Ripper.

By the time Yon freed Justice and turned around, Tonles was standing in front of him, poised with Ripper's deadly spike pointed at his stomach. Yon flinched more out of fear, but Tonles thought he was going to attack and rammed the ax into his midsection tearing open his stomach. Yon grunted and let go of the mace as he sank down to his knees. Tonles pulled the weapon free, and blood oozed from Yon's mouth. Even though the fight was over, Tonles stayed where he was, watching him in case he had more fight left in him.

Yon coughed up more blood. "Please let... me..." He coughed, "live."

"Would you have shown me the same mercy?" Tonles barked at him.

"I would...have..."

The man's pleas and obvious pain brought a smile to Tonles' face. "Do you promise never to do this again?"

"I do...I do."

Tonles turned around as if he was going to walk away and then spun around bringing Ripper down onto Yon's head, splitting his skull apart like a ripe melon. The bystanders cringed and stared in shock at his brutality.

"Does anyone else want my mace? Or have an issue with what I've done?" Tonles said looking at everyone.

No one responded.

"I didn't think so."

Konafar picked up the mace and handed it to him. "Come with me." He said, and they walked away to speak privately.

"Nicely done." Konafar said once they were away from the others.

"Thanks."

"I was beginning to get worried until I saw you move against the tree, and then I knew what you were doing." Konafar added.

"My uncle taught me that move. He said that if you present an opening to your opponent, then he will always fall for it."

"Your uncle was a wise man."

"That he was." Tonles laughed.

"I'm glad that you didn't spare his life."

"There were a couple of reasons why. He wouldn't have done so for me, and I'm sure he would have made another attempt for the weapon. Plus I never leave my enemy alive."

"I've always liked your thought process. By the way, I think the archer can be trusted."

Tonles was puzzled. "How so?"

"During your fight, he retrieved his bow and was ready to strike down your opponent if need be."

"Are you sure he wasn't going to strike me down instead."

"You're still alive aren't you?"

"Good point."

They laughed together.

"Let's get some rest as we have a big day tomorrow." Konafar gripped his friend's shoulder, and they went back to camp to join the others.

When Butcher saw them coming, he got up off his log. "I like your handiwork." He said to Tonles as they were passing.

Tonles and Konafar ignored him, and Butcher looked confused and sat back down.

Shortly before dawn, Burner woke Cord and asked to speak with him secretly. He agreed, and they walked away from camp and hid behind a few trees.

"Do you think they'll let us go?" Burner asked.

"Truthfully," he paused, "no. Strom wanted us dead so why did he have a sudden change of heart and allow us to go off with his friends?"

Burner peered around the trees to make sure everyone was still sleeping and then back at Cord. "Do you think they'll kill us?"

"If they do, it will be after we're finished."

"That's what I was just thinking too. So what are you going to do?"

"I'm not sure yet."

Burner grinned. "We could kill them right now and be done with it."

"We could, but I'm not going to. These men didn't do anything to me."

"You may not get another chance." Burner insisted.

"I'm not killing anyone without cause; if they attack me, then I'll defend myself."

"If I get the feeling that my life is in danger at any point, then I am going to take action."

"You do what you have to do, just make sure you don't kill me by accident."

"I think you're a fool." Burner spat.

"Maybe I am, but either way, I don't kill without cause." Cord turned away and started walking back.

"Cause, did you have one when you killed those people?"

"That was a long time ago." Cord took a few steps.

"You know that you had the perfect opportunity last night when Tonles was fighting." Burner simply stated.

The archer paused. "I know." He replied and walked away.

After everyone else woke up, Konafar addressed the group.

"We should arrive at Redden by nightfall. Our mission is simple. We get in, look for someone called the Red Knight, and kill him."

"And how do you plan on doing that?" Hue asked.

"There's a secret passageway that leads under the city."

"Have you used it before?" Pierce asked.

"We did. The passageway will take us to an old abandoned house. From there we'll..."

"You said that you used it before right?" Burner interrupted.

"We did."

"Do they know that you did?"

"No." Konafar decided not to tell them that they did and continued. "Anyway, after we enter the town, we'll create a few distractions and seek him out. Do you have any questions?"

"What are we up against?" Cord asked.

"Mostly there will be boar and goatmen, a few giants, and maybe a war beetle or two."

Some of the men grumbled.

"You're crazy if you think you can kill him." Burner interjected.

Butcher was off playing with his cleavers and looked up when he heard the word crazy.

"Think what you want, but it will be done." Konafar said.

"Why do you want to kill him so bad?" Burner asked.

"He will die for what he did to my friend."

"You see, there's nothing more important to us then friendship." Tonles added.

"I'm organizing our group based on your skills, and then we'll decide the best approach after we enter the city. I need everyone to tell me about yourself and what skills you possess." Konafar said.

The men told him and after they were finished, Tonles and Konafar devised a plan and then led them away.

It was around midday, and shortly after clearing the forest, when a gusting wind, ice, and snow pelted the weary travelers prompting them to seek shelter inside of a cluster of trees. When the storm finally abated, it was nearing nightfall, which the group decided was too late for travel.

While the others slept, Tonles kept watch. As he stared at the flames of the fire, he decided to take out the figurine of the winged snake. Tracing his hand over the wood gave him an idea. He recited a few words to the object and like magic, the statue grew and took the fleshy form of a living snake with wings. He then gave it a few instructions, and his scout flew westward to survey the area. The snake returned a couple of hours later, hovered around his ear, and began hissing. When it was through, Tonles said a few words, and the snake returned to its original form and was placed back into his pouch for safe keeping. After Hue relieved him of his duty, Tonles grabbed a torch, said he needed to do something, and left without further explanation.

Less than a mile away, Tonles came upon the campsite that his snake figurine told him about and saw a lone person sitting on a log, drinking a cup of streaming liquid near the fire. To his left was his mare, tethered to a tree with a banner of a knight riding out into battle. There was no mistaking that this man seated before him was from the Order of the Blessed Knight.

Tonles was about to encroach further in when the knight suddenly said. "If you're a friend, please enter. If not, then you would be better off leaving." His words caught Tonles off guard.

"My name is Tonles, may I join you, Knight from the Blessed Order?"

The knight beckoned him in further after he didn't sense evil radiating from the stranger. "Well met Tonles. My name is Tracs. I'm assuming that the winged messenger was yours and relayed my whereabouts?"

Tonles nodded. "How did you know?"

"I've seen such familiars as those before." Tracs took another goblet out from his bag. "Would you like some hot ale?"

Tonles nodded.

While Tracs removed the kettle from the fire, Tonles thought he had the look of an experienced warrior, despite his youthful appearance.

After he was handed the mug, Tonles gladly accepted his offering and tasted the honeyed nectar. "Delicious." He said.

"I'm glad you like it. Tonles you recognized my Order, which one do you belong to?" Tracs asked.

"I belong to the Order of the Dragon." He answered and then took another sip.

"That's a good Order, filled with mighty warriors. That was my first selection when I entered manhood."

"First selection?"

"I felt your Order wasn't pure of heart, so I picked the Blessed Knight Order instead."

Tonles grinned. "We're not for everyone."

"Are you traveling alone?" Tracs asked.

"No, my camp is less than a mile away. What are you doing out here?"

"I was on a quest from my Order, and now I am on a mission of righteousness."

Tracs refilled their cups.

"Righteousness? Where are you headed?"

Tracs reached into his pouch and took out a necklace. "To find the owner of this." He showed it to Tonles. "Have you seen this before?"

Tonles thought of Runit and how he had a similar one around his neck. "Can I look at it more closely?"

Tracs handed it over.

"Where did you get it?" Tonles curiously asked while holding the medallion closer to the fire.

"I came upon a few wagons a few miles back. There was a survivor and before she died, she gave it to me." Tracs noticed the look of recognition on his face. "You've seen this symbol before, haven't you?"

"Once, a friend of mine wore a similar necklace."

Tracs looked at him square in the face and started moving his hand towards his sword. "Is that so?"

"Hear me out before drawing your blade."

Tracs paused, but kept his hand within reach of his sword.

"A few weeks ago, we entered Redden attempting to find someone who was there before it fell. Our plan was simple, get in and get out, but plans always don't go that way. My friend got captured, tortured, and turned into something hideous by a person called the Red Knight."

"Never heard of this Red Knight, where is your friend now?" Tracs asked.

"Dead. We were forced to kill him after the Red Knight sent him after us."

"Forced?"

"Yes. He pleaded for us to end his life, so he couldn't harm anyone else." Tonles paused and reflected.

"That must have been tough for you."

"You have no idea. I've known him for years."

"Well if your friend had one of these pendants then the owner of this one must be hiding in Redden as well."

"You should join us and together we'll make them pay!" Tonles said.

Tracs was about to say something when he spotted Justice strapped to his back. "Where did you get your weapon?"

"I just picked it up today, why?"

"That thing was created in the demon world."

"What?"

"My Order studies demonology and that material comes from their world."

"Are you sure?"

"Yes."

"Good because it's very powerful and it's the right weapon to use against the Red Knight. It should make it that much easier to kill him." Tonles said.

"Just be careful because the longer you own it the greater the chances are that you'll lose your soul."

"I don't understand."

"People never do. Just get rid of it before it corrupts you." Tracs hated the fact that weapons like this actually existed.

"Tracs I must be getting back to my camp. Do you want to come along with us?"

"Give me until the morning to decide. I must pray for guidance."

Tonles got up. "We'll stop by in the morning." He bid the knight farewell and left.

Tonles announced his arrival into camp so the new watchman on duty wouldn't be alarmed. He'd forgotten his name, so instead of greeting him by name; he merely nodded as he passed him by. The guard smiled back and took note to where he was going to lay down. The guard has been plotting Tonles death the moment his best friend was killed and now was his opportunity. He was pretty sure his forth coming actions would properly cost him his life, but he didn't care because Yon was like a brother and didn't deserve to die the way he did, beat up yes, but killed, no.

He waited another hour to make sure he was asleep before taking out a stiletto and holding the blade tightly against his forearm, so that it was barely noticeable as he walked silently across the camp. After he reached Tonles, he knelt down and grinned. He was so preoccupied with his own agenda that he failed to notice Cord was missing and when he raised the dagger to end Tonles' life, an arrow flew through the night and pierced his left eye, killing him instantly. Tonles woke abruptly when the body fell on top of him. He tossed it off and was on his feet with Justice in his hands within seconds.

Cord emerged from the shadows and walked over. "He was going to kill you." He said.

"Did you know this beforehand?" Tonles asked.

"After you killed Yon, I noticed his reaction and figured they were friends."

"Do you think anyone else is plotting my death?"

"You should be okay."

"Thanks for your help, I owe you one."

"Actually it's two." Cord said and walked away.

Tonles picked up the body, threw it into the bushes and woke almost everybody up, by doing so. Tonles faced them with anger in his eyes. "Let this be a warning to anyone else that is having thoughts about my demise. If you want to kill me, then do it like a man and not like that coward." He said and then walked away to sleep.

When morning arrived, Tonles told Konafar about the assassination attempt and what Cord did for him.

"After we eat, I'll talk to him and give him some incentive to watch our backs." Konafar said.

"Sounds like a good idea. There's something else. I sent my figurine out looking for anything that might pose a threat, and it discovered a man from the Order of the Blessed Knight.

Konafar lowered his goblet. "A knight from the Order of the

Blessed Knight, they're well trained fighters, almost as good as ours. We could use a man of his talents."

"It looks like he might be going to Redden as well. He came upon a few wagons, and he found the same type of necklace Runit had, among the dead."

"That's interesting and fortunate for us. Maybe he'll join us."

"I already asked him and he said for us to stop by today, and he'd let me know."

After they finished breakfast, Tonles approached Cord who was in the process of restringing his bow.

"I wanted to thank you again for saving my life."

"Don't mention it." Cord responded without looking up.

"If you continue watching our backs, we will reward you handsomely."

Cord looked up. "It's not necessary. Do you know why I helped you?"

"Honestly I don't."

"I don't like bullies and cowards."

"Then we have something else in common. I don't either."

Cord was about to tell him about Burner, but decided not to at that point.

Konafar and Tonles left within the hour and entered Tracs' camp while he was eating his morning meal.

"Tracs this is my friend Konafar." Tonles said.

Tracs put down his plate, stood up offering his arm in greeting; they clasped arms. "Nice to meet you."

"Tracs, have you thought about coming with us?" Tonles asked him directly.

"I did and I can't join you."

"Why not?"

"I am pure of heart and going with others that aren't is ill advised by my Order."

"I can respect that. So what's your plan?" Konafar asked.

"Since my enemy most likely hides inside of Redden that's where I am going. I'll stand before the gates and challenge the ones who laid waste to the caravan."

"Noble cause, but you can't expect them to answer your call fairly." Konafar replied.

"It doesn't matter how they answer my call, as long as they do."

"You might die."

"Maybe so, but it will be for a good cause."

"That's why your Order puzzles me," Konafar began, "Some of your quests are noble and just while others are..." He paused looking for the right word to say.

"Others are what?" Tracs cut him off.

"Pointless. Take your approach, for instance. You're going to stand before the gates of Redden and challenge anyone to a fight. Do you know how they're going to respond? They will shoot you with arrows and your death will be meaningless."

"Stay your tongue about me and my Order." Tracs snapped back at him.

"All I am saying is that you should come with us, together we can accomplish the same objective."

"I stand by my code of ethics. I will put my trust in my god and his higher calling." Tracs calmly said.

"Let's go." Konafar abruptly said to Tonles and walked away.

"Try to reconsider." Tonles said to him and left.

As they were walking back to camp Tonles paused. "We can't let Tracs do this by himself. They'll kill him."

"I know, but he's stubborn so what do you recommend?"

"We ride out and help him fight."

"Are you sure that's what you want to do?" Konafar asked even though he knew his answer.

"I am."

"What about the Red Knight? He's never going to come out, and I think we'll lose our opportunity to take him by surprise."

"We can take our revenge anytime we want to. It doesn't have to be today."

Konafar paused and then came up with an idea. "How about we hide near the city gates and when they open, you can help Tracs while I take a few men inside and seek out the Red Knight? I think the distraction will benefit our cause."

"That might work. Who will you take?"

"Burner, Cord, and a few of the guards."

"Sounds like a plan."

****

After they were gone, Tracs considered their offer again for several minutes before deciding against it. His biggest fear was they'd get in his way and somehow cost him his life by interfering. He finished his breakfast, dressed in his plate armor, and secured his sword and dagger in the belt hanging loosely around his waist. He picked up his most treasured weapon, Recur, and made sure the side chamber of the crossbow had a full complement of bolts stored inside. The weapon was designed in such a way that once he fired a round, another bolt would quickly fall into place permitting him to shoot it in rapid succession. He thought back to the day his father gave him the weapon and said that if he practiced with it long enough, he'd become a marksman able to score direct hits by using the best angles possible. How right his father was, Tracs realized. Gazing skyward, he took a deep breath, allowing the cold air to settle into his lungs, and then placed his helmet on his head. He was ready for this he told himself as he mounted his horse and rode off toward Redden.

Tonles and Konafar arrived back at the camp, and quickly called the others.

Konafar looked at them and spoke. "There's been a change of plans..."

"Are we still going to Redden?" Burner interrupted him.

"You interrupt me again and I will strike you down. Got it?"

Instead of responding, Burner held his tongue and fantasized about throwing a lit flask at his face and watching his skin melt away.

"As I was saying, there has been a change of plans. There's a man named Tracs from the Order of the Blessed Knight, and he is on his way to Redden to seek his own justice. He recently came upon a horrific scene and wants those responsible to pay for their crimes. His quest will also aid us as well, because if they respond to his challenge, then we'll use this distraction to sneak into the town."

"What a waste he'll die." Hue stated.

"I think you're right, unless we tip the scales when they least expect it."

"What do you mean?" Pierce asked.

"I want some of us to help him, while the rest enter the town with me."

"Why are we helping him?"

"I think it's the right thing to do." Tonles said.

"I agree." Cord said. "Who is going with you into the town?"

"I want you, Burner and a few others."

Burner was surprised to hear his name and looked at Konafar with interest.

"You know, helping the knight might be suicide." Hue stated.

"It might be suicide whichever path we take." Konafar paused. "We'll be hiding near the gates, so once they're opened, Tonles and the others will wait until they pass before attacking their flank."

"What if there are too many?" Pierce asked.

"Then I want you to attack them, break off, and run into the woods. I'm betting they'll pursue, and that will give Tracs his best chance. Does everyone understand their part?"

They each nodded.

"Good. By midday, we should be positioned near the gates. Let's go."

Tonles, Konafar, and the others arrived ahead of Tracs and hid behind boulders and trees near the city walls to wait for things to unfold.

****

It was shortly before dusk when the holy knight rode into position in front of the gates. Tracs dismounted, held his large shield in one hand and the crossbow in the other and addressed the boar creatures walking the battlements.

"I demand to see the owner of a pendant I am carrying." He shouted.

They responded to his request with snorting laughter.

Tracs remained calm. "I'll ask again. I want the person who owns this necklace to step forth and answer my challenge."

This time, his request was answered with several arrows. Tracs blocked the projectiles with his shield, then mounted his horse and began rifling through his sack until he found three dark flasks and lit them.

"Have it your way!" He said to them and rode directly toward the gates.

The guards, for the most part, watched him with a strange fascination as he charged the gates. They were pretty sure the three bottles of flammable liquid couldn't do anything against the doors, until he threw the first one and it exploded against the doors with a deafening thud. The explosion shook the walls so violently that it knocked most of the guards to the ground. Before they could retaliate, Tracs threw the other two containers at the gates, and they set them on fire. He rode back to his original position, turned, and was delighted to see the gates burning.

Inside the town, Tracs' actions caught the attention of one of Yang's bodyguards as he was coming out of the tavern. His first reaction was that they were under attack. He ran over and climbed to the top of the battlements and pushed past a few frightened boarmen. Through the fire and smoke, he saw a lone warrior sitting atop a horse, holding a shield.

"What is the meaning of this?" Vex demanded.

A Chatar looked at him. "He attacked the gates, sir." He snorted.

"He did what?"

"He came here demanding to see someone who owns something he's carrying, and then he rode up and attacked the gates."

"With what?"

"A bottle of something."

The bodyguard stiffened and then turned his attention below. "Who are you?" Vex shouted down to the man on the horse.

Tracs smirked in satisfaction because he finally got someone's attention. "My name is not significant. What's important is that I want the owner of this pendant to come out and fight me." He held up the necklace.

Vex's eyes widened as he reached into his tunic searching frantically for his pendant. Tracs picked up on his reaction.

"I see that I've found the owner, so why don't you come down here and fight. You are accused of murder, rape, and theft."

Vex realized at once that he must have dropped his most treasured possession while they were butchering the merchant and his family and there was nothing he could do about it now. "On whose behalf do you come here knight, the dead merchant and his family? If so, tell their spirits to get in line because my family is first." Vex menacingly replied.

"So you admit to your crimes, and now you will face your judge, jury, and more importantly your executioner. I'll give you until morning to prepare, and if you fail to face me," he paused, "I'm coming in."

"No need to wait for me that long knight. I'll be out shortly to reclaim what's mine. Get those gates open NOW!" He demanded and then left the battlements.

After Vex was gone, Tracs tied his mare to a tree, said a quick prayer, grabbed his weapons, and waited.

****

Vex was seething as he climbed down the ladder. He wanted nothing more than to kill this knight. He walked hurriedly through the streets and when he reached his quarters, he retrieved his weapons and leather armor. He was in the process of fastening the remaining straps on the armor when his friend, and fellow bodyguard, entered the room.

"What's going on?" Jyre asked after he closed the door.

"It appears someone has come to our town looking for us because of what we did to that merchant a few nights ago."

"So, why are you going out there?"

"He has my pendant and I want it back before Yang finds out."

"Does he look tough?"

"He must be, or he's crazy to come here and challenge us."

"I say we have some fun and send a giant or some of those worthless boarmen out there to see just how tough he is." Jyre smiled.

"I don't need them to defeat him."

"I know I was just stacking the odds in your favor." Jyre said.

"Good point."

Jyre walked over, grabbed his armor, and began putting it on.

"What are you doing?" Vex asked him.

"Do you really think I'm letting you go out there alone? These are tough times brother and there's no honor in dying. We will defeat him together."

Jyre finished dressing, and both men did their ritual of pounding their fists several times on the shoulders of each other's armor. It was a ritual they liked doing before every battle to inspire victory.

"He's brave; I'll give him that." Cord stated looking at Tracs in the open field.

"It looks like Tracs got his wish, so when that guy comes out I'm going in once the battle commences." Konafar said. "Tonles are you ready?"

"Always." He grinned and tightened his grip on Justice.

Two hours passed before the smoldering gates were finally opened wide enough to allow a very large Northern Rock Giant to step forward. He was followed by several boarmen and two humans on horseback dressed in leather. Tracs held his loaded crossbow downward until they were within range and then emptied the entire chamber into the giant's head, throat, and stomach. The mighty creature fell backwards onto a few boarmen and crushed them underneath his weight. Vex ordered the boarmen to attack, and they too were cut down after Tracs reloaded and fired. Vex and Jyre stopped their mounts after Tracs reloaded a second time and trained his weapon on them.

"So, which one of you owns this pendant?" Tracs said and threw the necklace on the ground.

"Why did you kill my men? I came out here to fight you alone." Vex said.

"I figured that since you killed a helpless merchant and his family that you must be a pathetic, sniveling, little coward who can't fight his own battles. I just wanted to level the playing field and make sure there was no outside interference."

"I see." Vex replied and dismounted.

"Are you going to put that weapon away and fight him fairly?" Jyre asked.

"As soon as you turn around and leave."

Jyre looked at Vex, who nodded for him to do so.

"Wait a second. Do you have a similar necklace as well? Because if you do, you're next."

"Knight, you do want to die today don't you?" Jyre's words were more of a statement than a question.

"Before we begin our fight, tell me why you killed the merchant and his family in cold blood."

"Well," Jyre paused and smiled, "it's easy he…"

Jyre's next action was so fast that Tracs did not see his dagger until it was painfully sticking out of his right shoulder. Tracs grunted and lowered the crossbow. Jyre knew he missed his target because he would've disabled his arm.

Vex charged after Tracs who raised the crossbow and fired, catching him in his chest and left arm, sending him stumbling away. Jyre unsheathed his sword, jumped down off of his horse, and was hit by several arrows in the back, killing him instantly. Tracs didn't have time to ponder about who shot him, because Vex was on his feet and charging after him with his broad sword held high. When he was close enough, Vex swung his weapon at his head and Tracs deflected it away with the crossbow, he moved in and kneed him in the midsection, knocking the air from his lungs. Tracs then butted him in the head with the stock of the crossbow and sent him reeling, when Vex tripped and fell over Jyre's lifeless body. Tracs discarded his crossbow and removed the dagger from his shoulder with a quick jerk. He unsheathed his sword and waited for his opponent to get up. Vex looked over at his dead friend and saw arrows, not bolts, protruding out of his body.

"So you do have help. Where are they?" Vex said as he rose to his feet, holding his sword waist high and pointed at Tracs. He looked around nervously, but couldn't see anyone else. "You called me a coward. You're the coward." He stated.

Like Vex, Tracs did not know who shot Jyre, but he didn't want him to know. "Your friend's death is from my god passing judgment on you, so accept it."

Vex was in serious pain, his head, arm, and chest hurt, and he was about to run, when he heard the sound of a horse galloping up from behind him. He smiled. "It appears you're going to die."

Tracs saw a man dressed in dark leather, and carrying a spear, riding out of the town with several goat and boarmen.

"Maybe I will, but so will you." Tracs said and suddenly dashed forward, swinging his sword.

Vex blocked the attack, grabbed the blade of his own sword with his left hand, and hit Tracs in the head with the hilt, denting his helmet and knocking him to the side. Vex was about to hit him again when Tracs pointed his weapon directly at his face and halted his advance. Just then, Yang arrived and dismounted. Tracs looked frantically for his crossbow and spotted it several yards away.

Yang followed his gaze. "That's not going to help you. Who are you stranger?" He asked, even though he had a good idea which Order he represented.

Tracs pointed to Vex. "This man killed a merchant and his family, and I am here on their behalf to serve justice."

Yang chuckled.

"Master Yang he has help." Vex said.

"Oh! Where?" Yang looked around casually.

"Stay out of this or you'll die as well." Tracs threatened him.

Yang turned his attention back to him. "Silly fool. They work for me, so who do you think was with them when the merchant was slaughtered?" He paused. "We did have fun with his daughters and wife, didn't we Vex?"

Vex smiled while remembering.

Tracs grew angry. "Then I'll kill you as well, pig!"

Yang laughed at him.

From out of the town, two giants and a score of goat and boarmen marched out.

"I don't think so, knight from the Order of the Blessed, you will die for coming here by my spear Dominance." Yang's facial expression changed to a more sinister look.

****

After Yang left the city, Konafar whispered to Tonles. "I've been thinking. Are you sure you want to do this? The odds are growing against Tracs and I fear he won't last much longer."

"Go kill the Red Knight for what he did."

"There will be more men and creatures coming out of the town soon, you can count on it."

"Good, I need the practice." Tonles chuckled.

"Okay. I changed my mind about who's coming with me. I want Burner, Cord, and five others to stay with Tonles. Butcher and the rest, you're with me." He looked at Tonles again. "Good luck."

"Good luck to you as well. I'll meet you a couple of miles to the north after we're finished."

After both men clasped arms, Konafar left with his group.

"I didn't sign up for this." Hue finally admitted as soon as they were gone.

"A man is standing up for what he believes in and doing it all by himself, doesn't that inspire you?" Tonles asked him.

"It does, but I'm afraid to die."

"We all have to die, whether it's now, tomorrow, or ten years later. I'd rather die for glory, and you might not get another chance that you are being given on this day. Stay close to me and we'll get through this, alright? "

Hue nodded his head in agreement. Tonles faced forward and kept his eyes on the ever-approaching spearman riding out to greet Tracs.

"Here's the plan. Burner, you will go first and set them all ablaze. Cord, I want you to follow him while unleashing hell on them. Everyone else, follow me and we will attack them from the west. Once we kill them, we'll retreat into the woods to the north and wait."

"What about Konafar? Don't you want to go in after him?" Cord asked.

"He's on his own." Tonles answered and prepared himself mentally for what he was about to do.

With all the activity going on outside of Redden, and the ever growing darkness, it was easy for Konafar and the others to slip into the town unnoticed. Konafar figured the Red Knight would be at the

Magistrate's house, if he was going to be anywhere, and that's the direction he led them in. They were careful to avoid the guards along the way and arrived at the house, taking up residence along the side. Pierce left them, surveyed the area and returned a short time later.

"I counted five guards." He said.

"Can you kill them by yourself?" Konafar asked.

"I'm pretty sure I can." Pierce notched an arrow.

"Okay. Once we take care of them, we'll enter the house and kill everyone inside. Pierce, are you ready?"

He nodded and ran around to the front, killing the first three guards before they saw him and the other two as they were trying to flee. They quickly hid the bodies.

Konafar gathered them close. "There are only two floors, so we'll move through the rooms on the first floor and then meet back at the front door. No one gets left behind. I mean no one." He emphasized his last statement.

They entered the mansion and began running through the lower-level, killing everyone in sight. It was a brutal display of death and slaughter as Konafar led the charge through each room, hacking and slicing his way through his victims.

When they were finished with the first floor, Pierce looked over at Konafar, who was staring downward with his sword lowered. "Are you ok?" He asked.

Konafar looked up. Blood and gore coated his body. His breathing was labored, and his eyes indicated that something was wrong. "Just resting...for a second...did we lose anyone?"

"Kitner fell."

Movement abruptly roused from the floor above, indicating that someone was awake and prompting them to advance up the stairs to complete what they came to do.

****

They waited for the enemy to march out of Redden, before Burner and Cord left the confines of their concealment and circled behind the group. Cord began firing arrows, while Burner started throwing lit flasks into the masses, striking a good portion of the group and spraying them with the hot oily fire. Screams and howls erupted as they continued their assault.

From somewhere near the front, a large rock came hurling at them. Cord saw the boulder, broke off his attack and ran. However, Burner wasn't so lucky and was struck in the chest and sent sailing through the air. After he landed, the lit glass container, he held slipped out of his hand and shattered on the ground, setting the area ablaze as well as the bag containing the rest of his arsenal. His dying screams blended in nicely with the others who were already on fire. Through the haze and smoke, the giant saw the little bowman running for his life. After taking careful aim, he threw the last of his projectiles and missed hitting him. Angered, he growled, gripped his massive club and gave chase.

Yang, Vex, and the others heard the screams coming from their flank and turned around. They stared in horror as most of their troops were set ablaze. Yang was about to say something, when out of the corner of his eye, he caught a glimpse of a big stout man leading several others directly at them. Spear in hand, he raced past his subjects and met the charging man with the two-handed black mace.

As soon as Tonles charged at Yang, Tracs grabbed his crossbow and headed off towards the woods. His injury was the reason why, and he figured he could kill his opposition from afar. Meanwhile, Vex ordered the others to meet the new threat and then caught a glimpse of the knight fading off into the woods. He followed, knowing Yang would've wanted him to do so.

When Tonles reached Yang, both men swung their weapons simultaneously and blocked each other's attack, as they passed, and turned around to face one another. Tonles went on the offensive and swung Justice with an overhead strike, at his head, which was followed by several random attacks. Yang deflected the first strike and avoided the rest by twisting and turning his body out of the way. Tonles pressed him further, and Yang met his weapon with full force, and then stepped backwards with his front leg and thrust Dominance with just one hand. Tonles sidestepped the attack and swung the mace at his ribs, a strike that would've definitely shattered his insides if not for the bodyguard's quick reaction. He planted his weapon firmly into the ground and stopped the attack. Tonles swung Justice to the other side of Yang, and as soon as he felt the weapon leave his spear; he rolled safely away and was on his feet again, spear at the ready. Tonles paused his advance and that's when Yang glanced around and realized the knight and Vex were both missing.

"You fight well; we could always use a man of your talents." Yang said to Tonles.

"Join you and your pack of degenerates? I'd rather die." Tonles replied.

Yang smiled. "That can be arranged. However, before you die answer me this. Why did you attack us?"

"For what your leader did to my friend Runit."

Yang thought for a few seconds and then remembered Paven's experiment and his toy that he called the Green Knight.

"So that was your friend? Now everything makes sense. You must be one of the people who came to Redden and rescued some of the prisoners. Last I checked your friend was sent out to kill you. What befell him?"

"You and your leader will die for what you did to him." Tonles firmly stated.

"First off, off let's get something straight. He's not my leader; he's just a servant to a higher being. Second, I don't see how you're going to do so. You'll have to get past me, and that's not going to be easy, then there's the army that waits for you in Redden and on top of that, you stand alone. If I was you," he paused, "I'd leave and forget about the whole thing."

Tonles hefted the mace. "Let's see if you can stop me." He said.
The two men engaged each other once again.

Vex cautiously walked toward the forest and felt something strange coming from within the wooded area. The sensations radiated somewhere off to the right and grew stronger the closer he walked. He paused, contemplating his next action and was suddenly overwhelmed by fear, which became so intense his arms and legs started shaking, and he was unable to move. He'd never been this scared in all his life and when he heard branches snapping, and bushes shaking, he tried to run, but his legs still wouldn't respond. He began praying to a god he no longer believed in.

From afar, Tracs pointed his crossbow at Vex and was about to pull the trigger and end his miserable life, when he sensed something evil, with a singular purpose, approaching from the west. He turned and spotted a figure walking towards Vex. Something told him that this being was here for revenge, so he lowered the crossbow and watched.

Leaves crunched under the weight of the creature as it came closer toward the entrance of the forest. Vex was unable to do anything but watch as this being walked out and stopped directly in front of him. Vex recognized the creature with the gaping hole in his stomach and yellow eyes that appeared to be glowing.
"No, it can't be. We killed you!" He exclaimed.
The being opened its mouth and screamed silently at him, thus paralyzing him further, and then walked over and grabbed him by the arms. As Vex's limbs were being torn away from their sockets, he screamed so loudly that anyone within a mile could've heard him. Tracs did not interfere as the creature tore the rest of his body apart and then continued toward Redden. He was left wondering what Vex meant when he said he'd killed him before.

Tonles and Yang had just finished another series of attacks when they heard someone screaming from the woods, causing them to pause and look in that direction.

"Looks like your man got what he deserved." Tonles happily stated.

Yang was about to reply when he caught a glimpse of something emerging from the forest with glowing eyes. As a child, he'd heard tales that it was possible for someone who died violently to come back as a Revenant and seek revenge against those responsible. Now he knew those stories to be true, because walking towards him was the merchant they'd killed a few nights ago. He didn't know how or if there was a way to kill such a being, so he ordered his remaining companions to attack the dead man.

As the Revenant marched straight toward his murderer with his arms extended, Tonles and Hue backed away to allow it to pass. The Revenant didn't acknowledge the advancing goatman until he stabbed it in the chest and then the creature turned its attention on him by grabbing his throat and squeezing.

The boarman looked over one last time at Yang, hoping he didn't have to fight the creature, but after seeing the look on his face, he knew he had to. The Revenant was still strangling the goatman when his fellow soldier took a mighty swing with his ax and cleaved the creature's arm off below the elbow, sending the goatman to the ground with the merchant's hand still strangling him until he died. The Revenant turned and looked deeply into the boarman's eyes, instantly paralyzed him with fear, and then tore him apart.

When the last of Yang's servants died, the creature refocused its attention back on him and that's when Yang attacked. He kept his distance while plunging his spear into the creature's stomach. His final thrust, which he thought should have stopped the being, ripped through its back and sent organs, and whatever else lived inside the corpse, exploding out of its back.

The Revenant did not die, nor slow down, and frantically reached for its target. Yang didn't know what to do, so he disengaged his spear and quickly mounted his horse. He took one last look at Tonles and then sped off toward Redden with the Revenant following after him.

The giant pursued Cord until he disappeared into the woods and stopped just short of entering. He wasn't very bright; he knew, but the one thing he was good at was sneaking up on an enemy and pounding them into the ground. With gritty determination, he entered the woods and began stalking his adversary.

Meanwhile, Cord ran through the woods and changed direction several times to throw the giant off, and then hid behind an oak tree. He knew a well-placed arrow was his best chance to slay the giant and knowing their kind; he liked his odds. They were big, clumsy, and stupid, so when he peered around the tree, he was surprised that he didn't see him anywhere. He was sure it was right behind him before he entered. He remained where he was, waiting for the giant to enter.

After several long minutes, he was about to leave and hunt down the giant, then heard a branch snap directly behind him. His mind raced as he tried to comprehend what to do next, and then he heard a snicker, wheeled about and was hit by a large club in his side that sent him to the ground. The giant quickly came over and placed a foot on Cord's back, pinning him to the ground.

"You humans are so stupid. Always thinking giants are dumb and easy to kill." The giant said.

Cord tried moving and the giant stomped on his back, breaking several ribs in the process.

Cord's breathing was labored. "Tell me giant..." he coughed several times. "How did you get..." he coughed again, "behind me?" He asked while reaching for a dagger in his belt.

The giant smiled, relaxed his grip on his hefty weapon, and lifted his left leg in the air. "My boots, they allow me to walk without a sound. You are stupid..."

While he was talking, Cord reached up and plunged the dagger into his foot. The giant screamed and hopped a few times on one leg trying to grab the blade's hilt. Cord quickly got up, stepped on the giant's planted foot, lifted his other leg further into the air and toppled the giant. Instead of running toward freedom, Cord decided to end the giant's life and whipped out another dagger and jumped on top of the big creature. Together they wrestled and grappled and even though the giant was bigger and stronger, he could not pin Cord down and eventually lost track of Cord's dagger. The fight and the giant's life ended when Cord stabbed him in the throat.

After the giant took his last breath, Cord removed his boots to get a closer inspection of how they were constructed, thinking maybe he would uncover their secret of moving silently. While looking at the soles, the boots began shrinking until they were the same size as his boot, and the hole left behind from the dagger closed, making them appear new again.

"Interesting!" He exclaimed and exchanged his boots for the giant's, then stood up.

The first thing he noticed was that they were more comfortable than his and it felt like he was walking on air. He walked a few paces and did not hear his footsteps. He then ran a few feet straight into a pile of leaves and was rewarded with silence.

"This is great." He said knowing that he could be the finest thief in the world, or more importantly, the best assassin, if he chose to go back to that lifestyle.

Cord continued to test his new find and when he was satisfied, he left the forest.

After the creature left, Tracs walked over and stared down at the unrecognizable form of Vex. The horrific scene made the knight gag despite what he'd seen many times on the battlefield. Vex was simply torn to shreds, his ribcage was split apart so far that his organs were outside of his body. His legs and arms were broken and torn away from his torso, and his head was smashed into fragments. Pieces of his skull lay in several different places. Tracs knew he got what he deserved, but still blessed his soul anyway. He was about leave when he noticed the gauntlets around Vex's arms glowing slightly.

He knew right away they contained unusual properties, so he removed them from the dead man's arms, wiped off the gore and tied them around his forearms. Immediately, he felt a tingling sensation race up and down his limbs until they settled into his hands. The last time he felt similar sensations was when his cousin let him try on his Boots of Velocity. Tracs wondered if the gauntlets held the same properties, so he waved his left hand in front of his face and when it became a blur, he tried the right and had identical results. Next he swung his sword to the side, downward, and finally upwards and after each strike, his arm and the weapon moved faster. He was even more ready to end the life of the spearman; he thought, and left.

****

"Did you see that thing?" Hue asked Tonles, who was still staring after the Revenant.

"I wonder what it is."

"I don't know. I never saw anything like it."

"Me either." Tonles scratched his head.

"What should we do now?"

Tonles was about to answer when Tracs came out of the woods and walked up to them.

"Why did you go into the woods and hide? We came to your aid." Tonles asked him point blank.

"My shoulder was injured and I decided to attack them from afar."

"You should have stayed and fought with us, because we were risking our necks for you."

"I didn't ask for your help did I? So don't question my tactics."

Tonles knew he was right. "What happened in there?"

"I was followed into the woods by the one called Vex, and that creature appeared and killed him. I'm not sure what it was, but it's evil and had a singular purpose, and that was to kill him. Did you see where it went?"

"Redden, after the guy with the spear."

"His name is Yang and he is also responsible for the merchant's death as well, but after what I saw the creature do; I wouldn't want to be him."

"I think it's some kind of undead being." Hue began, "I saw one of the boarmen chop off its arm and the spearman kept stabbing it repeatedly, and it didn't even slow the creature down."

"Tonles where is Konafar?" Tracs suddenly asked after realizing he weren't there.

"Redden." Hue interjected.

"Should we go after him?"

Tonles rubbed his chin contemplating. "I don't know if we'll be able to get in there with all the commotion going on. Konafar is very resourceful, so I'm sure he'll be fine." Even though he said it, he wasn't confident that he believed it. "Tracs what are you going to do?"

"As soon as Yang is dead I'll be on my way. What about you?"

"After the Red Knight falls, I'm not sure what we'll do, maybe we'll raise an army and take back Redden."

Suddenly, and without making a sound, Cord appeared behind them. "Where are the bad guys?" His voice startled the group and they turned around, weapons at the ready.

"Where did you come from? I didn't even hear you." Hue said.

"Isn't it great?"

"What's great?" Tracs asked.

"That you didn't hear me? These boots make it so."

"You didn't have them when we started, so where did you get

them?" Tonles asked.

"The giant I killed was wearing them."

"You killed a giant?" Hue interposed.

Cord smiled and shook his head.

"What happened to Burner?"

"He died shortly after we attacked."

"How did you kill the giant?" Tracs asked.

"They're so stupid, it wasn't that hard."

"Why did you return? You could've left, and we'd be none the wiser." Tonles asked him.

"Despite whatever Captain Strom told you about me, I would never do that."

"You're definitely showing me your true worth." Tonles added.

"I see Konafar hasn't returned yet, do you want me to go in there and see if I can find him? After all, I do have my new toy and in my former life, I was a pretty good thief."

Tonles thought about it. "Okay. Start at the Magistrate's house, that's where I think the Red Knight will be." He said.

"Alright I'll start there."

Cord was about to leave when Tracs said. "Take these gauntlets. They're special." He removed them from his arms and handed them to him.

Cord placed them on and felt a surge run up and down his spine. He knew right away what they were. "Gauntlets of Quickness." He said without even realizing it. "Thanks, I'm sure I can put them to good use." He said and left.

"Where did you get them?" Hue asked.

"That guy Vex had them on his arms."

"Great, all I get is useless weapons from the creatures I killed." Hue stated.

"Let's move back near the woods and wait." Tonles added.

****

Konafar led Butcher and Pierce up the stairs and fell upon three unarmed boarmen, just as they were coming out of their rooms. Butcher was swift, and brutal, as he hacked one of them to pieces, Pierce was deadly in his own right with his blade, and Konafar ran another through with Carnage. There were several closed doors down the long corridor.

Konafar pulled them close. "Let's split up because I fear if they hear us, there will too many, and we'll get overwhelmed. Be swift, quiet, and leave no one alive. Butcher you start over on the left and Pierce on the right. I'm going for the double door. Okay?"

They nodded.

The first three rooms Butcher entered housed a variety of goat and boarmen, all of which were fast asleep and were easily chopped to pieces without uttering a sound. His blood lust led him through several more rooms, until he encountered a very large boarman just as he awoke from his nightmares. Butcher ran over and swung at the creature, but the boarman quickly sat up, grabbed both of his arms, and flung him hard against the wall thus allowing him enough time to leave the bed.

****

After Pierce entered the last of the rooms on the right, he encountered a clean-shaven human, with short-cropped hair, sitting at a round table reading a thick book. A candle to his right provided enough illumination to read and nothing more.

He looked up after Pierce entered. "Oh I have a guest. And who are you?" He calmly asked.

"Are you the Red Knight?"

"Me? No. My name is Grop"

Pierce moved closer, sword arm outstretched.

"What's your name stranger?"

"My name doesn't matter, but your death will." Pierce said as he advanced.

Grop chuckled and then stood up holding his left hand outward, causing Pierce to stop in his tracks.

"No stranger, it is you who will die and feed my soul." His voice took on a deeper tone, and his eyes narrowed and turned blood red, paralyzing Pierce.

Pierce tried moving, but found his legs and arms unresponsive and his sword arm hung downward in a non-threatening manner. Grop smiled, then his body suddenly convulsed. His muscles began twitching and growing until they tore through his skin, exposing raw flesh, tendons, and veins. The only thing Pierce could do was watch in horror as Grop's arms and legs elongated, and his torso expanded so rapidly that his clothes ripped apart.

After the transformation was completed, Grop straightened his twisted form to a stout seven feet tall and then spoke. "I guess you never met my kind before have you, human?"

Pierce somehow willed his legs, and they began moving slowly toward the door. Grop quickly maneuvered his way behind him.

"Human, there isn't any escape for you." Grop's eyes narrowed as he reached out, taking hold of Pierce's shoulders and picking him up with ease.

Pierce kicked him in the midsection, but the attack did nothing to lessen his hold.

"I am known as a Turner." He whispered and turned him around, looking deeply into his eyes while sending a wave of fear into his mind. He paralyzed his prey to the point that he could no longer move at all.

Pierce had never heard of their kind, and shortly before Grop sunk his teeth into his face, he'd wished that he was anywhere else but here. Those final thoughts lasted a few more seconds before darkness overtook him, and he thought no more.

After Grop finished his meal, he rose, wiping away the strands of flesh that were still dangling from his mouth, and then took his normal form again. He dressed in fresh attire, sat down, and went back to reading.

Konafar entered the room and was wrong in his assumption. Instead of finding the Red Knight, he discovered a dozen guards sleeping in their beds. As Konafar slowly closed the door, in anticipation of the slaughter, one of the guards woke up.

"Who disturbs my rest?" The distinct tone of the guard's voice sounded like a cross between a human and a goat and was coming from the center of the room. Konafar knew that any type of answer would give him away, so he casually walked toward his bed.

The goatman sat up slightly and gauged that the interloper was neither boar, nor goat, and it didn't sound like he was wearing plate, so that ruled out his master. The Hurnol was about to say something when Konafar drove Carnage into his chest and straight through the bed frame. The goatman began choking violently on his blood, which in turn, woke some of the others, who then began reaching for their weapons. Instead of attacking them, Konafar singled out the ones that were either sleeping or just coming awake. His first victim was in the next bed. In one motion, he removed the blade from the dead body and swung the massive weapon down upon the boarman's head, splitting his skull apart. Nimbly, he moved to the next bed and chopped the head off of a goatman who'd just sat up.

Meanwhile towards the door, a boarman began yelling that there was an intruder, and the rest of them began waking up and grabbing their weapons. By the time they were armed and out of their beds, Konafar had hacked apart three more goatmen and faced the rest of the guards blocking the door.

"There's no escaping human." One of the boarmen snorted at him in hatred.

"You're going to taste my steel," snorted another.

"Sounds good, but who wants to be the first to die by my blade?" Konafar taunted them, and they moved in.

The closest Chatar lunged at him with his sword, and Konafar easily pushed aside the weapon with his, and gutted him. Another tried to chop his extended arm, but Konafar anticipated his move, retracted his blade, and brought the weapon around and across the guard's exposed neck, separating his head from his shoulders. A goatman dashed forward, and Konafar sidestepped his advance and brought the hilt of Carnage down upon the back of his head, cracking his skull wide open and killing him.

The three remaining boarmen paused and began having second thoughts about fighting the intruder, but Konafar sensed their uncertainty and jerked his body forward like he was going to advance. Each Chatar reacted differently. The first, swung high and missed and was rewarded when Carnage was driven downward into his right shoulder; cleaving muscle, bone, and tissue. Another boarman tried to stab him in the head, but missed when Konafar ducked under his attack, used the false edge of his sword and chopped off his leg with a quick swipe.

The remaining Chatar waited for his opportunity and when it became available, he plunged his spear into Konafar's side and began pushing his body forward. Konafar dropped Carnage, gripped the shaft with both hands, overpowered the boarman and toppled him to the ground. The guard was about to get up, when Konafar slammed his foot into his throat and crushed his wind pipe, and then began stomping on his head until he died. Intense pain from the spear, coupled with dizziness, prompted Konafar to pull the weapon out with a quick jerk. What he didn't expect was his weakening legs and the ensuing darkness that followed a few seconds later.

****

The boarman was on top of Butcher before he had a chance to regain his footing, and began kicking him in the stomach and face. When he grew tired of beating him, he picked him up and tossed him into the table and chairs. The boarman grinned with delight and ran over and beat him some more, and then picked him up and peered into Butcher's vacant eyes.

"You humans are weak and pathetic." He said and then spat into his face.

The Chatar lifted him higher, slammed him into the wall, and then threw him across the room. The boarman followed to continue the fun. Despite the abuse Butcher took for next several minutes, he never lost consciousness and managed to hold onto one of his cleavers, which somehow went undetected by the boarman. When the boarman finally grew tired of beating the human to a bloody mess, he walked over and unsheathed his long sword to finish the job.

"I will eat the flesh from your bones on this day." He snorted in delighted.

Butcher looked at the creature walking toward him and then someone spoke to him inside of his head. *"He's just like the rest of those bullies and must die. KILL HIM! KILL HIM! KILL HIM!"* The voice shouted. The boarman stood directly above him, and after he lifted his sword above his head, Butcher reached up and sliced his inner thigh, cutting through his pants, severing the femoral artery and spraying Butcher and the floor with thick blood. The Chatar stumbled backwards and fell to a knee. The voice inside of Butcher's head screamed at him to kill the creature, and he obeyed. He hacked the dying boarman into tiny, unrecognizable pieces.

****

After Paven finished sharpening his weapons and mending his armor, he left the cellar for a good night's rest. He entered the dining room and discovered several dead guards. He knew something was wrong and hurried back downstairs to put on his armor and grab a sword. He returned to the same room and listened to the eerier silence for several minutes before proceeding further in. More bodies decorated the area, prompting him to unsheathe his weapon and cautiously ascended the stairs hoping to catch the culprits.

When he reached the landing, more dead guards littered the hallway and only three doors remained closed. The one to the far back was where the bulk of his guards slept, and the others housed Grop and

Vlasta. Cautiously, he opened Grop's door and after seeing him sitting in the high backed chair, he entered.

"What's going on?" Paven asked, and then stopped dead in his tracks when he realized that he was walking through someone's gore, and a body was torn to shreds a few feet away.

Grop smiled upon seeing him. "Oh that," he began, "well, while you were playing with your weapons someone broke into our house and had the misfortune of entering my room."

"Was he the only one?" Paven asked in disgust.

"I'm not sure, but no one else came into my room."

"Did you check? Is Vlasta alive?" Paven asked angrily.

"It's not my affair."

"You're useless. Stay here, I will deal with you when I get back."

"I am looking forward to it." Grop said, turning his attention back to his book.

Paven turned in disgust and left the room.

The hallway was still deserted, and the other two doors remained closed, which gave him a bad feeling. For a brief second, he thought about going back into the room and forcing Grop to come with him, but he was so disgusted by the mere sight of him that he would rather face whatever was there alone.

He was still having a hard time imagining that one person broke into his house and killed all of his guards, especially Vlasta, who was by far his toughest. Paven decided to check on him first and slowly opened the door. In the dim light, he could see the room was in a shambles with broken tables and chairs. He entered and heard the sound of chopping coming from somewhere further in. He silently traversed the room with both hands gripping his blade tightly. He thought about calling out for Vlasta, but deep down inside he knew the Chatar was already dead.

He finally came upon someone kneeling over a body and repeatedly swinging two sharp cleavers into him. Paven's thoughts raced regarding how to handle this situation. *"Should he attack and kill the intruder or find out who he is? If he decided to do the latter, then he too could end up like Vlasta.*" He decided that it wasn't worth the chance and moved closer with his sword in the high guard.

The voice inside of Butcher's head continued to tell him to hack apart the boarman until Paven was in position, and then they forewarned him that someone was in the room and told him to move out of the way just as Paven swung downward. Paven's attack wasn't even close as Butcher rolled out of the way and was on his feet facing him with both cleavers. Paven no longer cared who he was or why he entered his home and went on the offensive, swinging repeatedly at the intruder. The short, stocky fellow surprised Paven with his speed and agility, as he either moved out of the way or deflected the attacks.

Paven's onslaught continued until Butcher crossed both cleavers above his head and caught the sword long enough to step forward and pushed the blade out of the way. The maneuver gave Butcher time to move in and use both cleavers simultaneously, hitting Paven on both sides of his armor, denting the plate and breaking a few ribs. The sudden pain caused Paven to grunt loudly and he dropped his weapon.

Butcher then heard the voice once again. *"HE MEANS TO HURT YOU!, KILL HIM! KILL HIM! KILL HIM!"*

Butcher listened, and in one fluid motion attacked Paven's left shoulder with both cleavers and broke his collarbone. Paven dropped to his knees and tried to move away, but Butcher was on top of him at once and continued to attack his armor with the fury of a madman. Some strikes deflected off of the platemail, while others dented and split apart the metal, sinking deep into his flesh and bringing fresh screams and blood from the General.

Paven fought through the pain, trying frantically to grab his booted dagger with his good arm, and as he grasped the hilt Butcher severed off his left arm and then stopped when he saw the limb was bone and leather straps instead of flesh. The voices immediately commanded Butcher to continue chopping apart his enemy, and just as he turned his attention back to his task, Paven reached up, with what little strength he had left, and thrust the dagger into his throat. Butcher choked on his blood for several long seconds before falling over. Before he died, the voice told him he was finally coming home. Paven rose to his feet feeling dizzy from the pain and loss of blood. He gazed over at his limb, and for once was glad his arm no longer held flesh and tendons. Paven grabbed his weapon and stumbled out into the hallway. On shaky legs, he staggered toward the stairs until a feeling of nausea, coupled with stars dancing before his eyes, forced him to his knees. Before giving in to the darkness, he saw a lone figure ascending the stairs, holding a bow and looking all too human.

Cord reached the top of the stairs just as someone in red armor fell over. When he made no attempt to get up, Cord walked over and kicked his sword away. He could tell by the glistening wetness covering the armor, and blood pooling on the floor, that the armored warrior had to be unconscious. Turning his attention down the dimly lit corridor, Cord continued on with his senses heightened. He checked several rooms before coming to the one that housed Butcher's dead body. The crazed man was slumped on the floor with a smile on his face. He actually looked happy, Cord thought, making him wonder what he could have been thinking during the final moments of his life.

A door creaked open from the hallway, drawing Cord's attention away from Butcher's body. He moved toward the entrance of the room and peered out ever so slightly. He saw a humanoid figure dragging a big person wearing armor. Cord was pretty sure it was Konafar being dragged, and drew the bowstring back. The person dragging the body suddenly stopped.

"Whoever you are; I'd leave before you become my next meal."

"And if I were you, I'd back away and let him go." Cord said and kept the bow pointed at his back.

"Those are brave words coming from someone pointing a bow at my back."

Cord took aim and fired the arrow. Grop dodged the arrow,

retreated into his room and slammed the door shut. Cord notched another arrow and kept watch. When it didn't open, he took out a long dagger and walked forward, never taking his eyes off of the door.

When he reached Konafar, he placed his hand under his nose and was relieved to find him still breathing. Konafar was far too heavy to drag, so he quickly took out a vial and poured it down his throat. A few seconds later, his eyes snapped open and Cord immediately placed one hand over his mouth and used the other to point to the closed door. Konafar acknowledged his signal, and Cord removed his hand. Konafar gestured that his sword was in the other room, and Cord handed him a spare dagger and then walked backwards into the room.

A few seconds later, Grop's door slowly opened and Konafar closed his eyes to little slits and acted like he was unconscious. Grop, in his hideous form, waited just inside the doorway, looking down at the comatose human and wanting badly to taste his blood and flesh. He slowly gazed out into the hallway and a few seconds later; he heard the sound of metal being lifted off of the floor in the back room and smiled. He savored the hunt and his mouth watered in anticipation as he crept forward to the room.

As soon as he passed Konafar, he was stabbed in the calf, thigh, and then his lower back; the last of which severed his nerves and caused him to lose control over his legs and fall over, screaming in pain. Konafar pulled himself onto his back while viciously stabbing him repeatedly, until he reached the top of the spinal cord and severed his brain stem, killing him. Cord came out of the room after hearing Grop's screams and cringed when he saw Konafar stabbing him too many times to count. He waited until he was finished before helping him up.

"Did you see Butcher or Pierce?" Konafar asked.

"I found Butcher's body in one of the rooms and I didn't see Pierce." Cord gazed down at Grop. "What is that thing?"

Konafar turned over the body and then said. "I've seen their kind before, they're called Turners, and I am glad you showed up because they live off of the flesh and blood of others."

"There's someone wearing red armor at the top of the stairs, and he's unconscious." Cord said suddenly remembering.

"That's the Red Knight. Help me up."

Cord handed him his sword once he was on his feet. Paven was still where Cord found him, and Konafar propped him upright against the wall.

"Do you have anything that we can give to him so that he wakes up?" Konafar asked.

Cord reached into his pouch and produced a dark vial. "This is all I have." He handed it to him. "It's potent and depending on his wounds; he should stay awake for at least a few minutes."

Konafar nodded and then poured the liquid down his throat. Paven stirred awake.

"Who are you?" Paven whispered after seeing both men staring at him.

"My name if Konafar and that's all you need to know."

"What do you want with me?"

"Answers."

"Answers? You broke into my house, killed my men and all you want is answers?"

Konafar punched him square in the nose and broke it. "I had a very close friend by the name of Runit, does his name sound familiar?" Konafar paused for a few seconds and continued. "Let me remind you. First you changed him into something horrible, and then you sent him after me along with a pathetic army of misfits. That was a bad move."

"So you must be the ones who entered my town."

Konafar punched him in the mouth, and Paven spit up blood. "That is another issue entirely. Why did you do that to my friend?"

"Wouldn't you like to know?" Paven taunted.

Konafar backhanded him so hard in the mouth it left Paven dazed for a few seconds. "Answer me or I am going to pluck your eyes out one at a time."

"Alright I'll tell you. Look at me! Like your friend, I was turned into something horrible!"

"So what are you saying?" Konafar barked at him.

"I did not have a choice, because I answer to a higher calling." Paven said.

"Who is this person you answer to?" Cord asked.

"The one you should seek vengeance upon goes by the name of Repan."

"Never heard of him." Konafar said looking over at Cord who shrugged.

While he was distracted, Paven reached for a dagger sheathed behind his back. "He lives up north and goes by the title of Lord of the..." his words trailed off as he tried to jab the dagger into Konafar's head.

Konafar instinctually raised his arm and blocked the attack with his left and punched him in the eye with the right. He hit it so hard that he broke the socket and popped his eyeball out. Paven screamed and dropped the weapon. Konafar picked it up.

"Tell me everything you know about him, and I promise to make it quick, otherwise I have no problem cutting you into tiny pieces and keeping you alive while doing so." Konafar threatened.

Paven told them everything he knew about Repan and where he could find him. When he was finished Konafar, of course, did not hold up to his words like he promised and savagely cut into his chest, removing his left lung and then part of his intestines. He then presented both to Paven.

As Paven was dying and gasping for breath, he thought back to the pain he experienced at the hands of the Lord of the Mind and found it was nothing compared to what Konafar put him through.

As soon as Yang entered the town, he commanded anyone nearby to stop the Revenant and then rode off to his room to make his final stand. The Revenant entered the town a short time later and killed many boar and goatmen along with several giants before finding Yang's quarters. The creature's single purpose of revenge was coming to fruition as it smashed the door and entered the house. It paused long enough to detect its killer hiding in the lower level and then proceeded through the maze of rooms and down several flights of stairs.

Yang waited for the creature on the bottom floor with his bow, flasks of oil on the small table, and his spear within reach. He knew that no matter where he went, or hid this being would find him, so he was prepared for the inevitable by lighting the flasks and notching his bow. He always imagined his death would be on a battlefield with Ying by his side and the thought of dying from something not of this world irritated him to no end.

He was still in mid-thought when he heard someone pounding on the door as if they wanted to break it down. Even though the wood was very thick, the Revenant broke through and entered. Yang shot his arrows until the entire quiver was emptied, and when that didn't kill the creature he threw the flasks and set the creature, along with the basement, on fire.

He gripped his spear as the vengeful creature ambled toward him with outstretched arms and eyes glowing yellow. Yang met its gaze and became so stricken with fear that he was helpless to the Revenant's fiery embrace, and was engulfed in flames.

The fire engulfing Yang's house caused all kinds of confusion within the town, allowing Konafar and Cord to escape quite easily. A few boar and goatmen tried to enter the building to save Yang, but the intensity of the fire prevented them from doing so. Eventually, they were able to enter the house and found his charred remains still clutching his spear.

To the north side of town, others discovered the Red Knight and his elite warriors dead as well. With no one to lead them, it didn't take long for tensions to build and chaos to form, sending the town into a civil war for control. In the aftermath, the giants were the first to fall under the combined strength of the boar and goatmen and then the boarmen fell to the much more skilled, and intelligent, goatmen. The war lasted for three days and nights. In the weeks that followed, boredom ensued and the goatmen did nothing but drink and fight among themselves, thus further decimating their numbers.

****

By the time Konafar and Cord met the others just inside of the forest, heavy snow began to fall. They sat by the fire, and while Konafar worked on his wound, he told them what befell the Red Knight.

Tracs waited until he was finished before asking about Yang. "Do you know what happened to Yang the Spearman?"

"Who?" Konafar responded.

"You don't know about him because you had already entered the town." Cord said to Konafar.

"We did not see a guy running around with a spear, if that's what you're asking." Konafar said.

"I need to know if he's dead." Tracs stated.

"It's suicide to go back in there."

"The family will never be at rest until he is."

"That undead thing following Yang looked pretty unstoppable, so maybe it took care of him for you." Hue said.

Tracs nodded in agreement.

"What thing?" Konafar asked.

"I'll tell you about it over a tankard of ale sometime." Tonles said.

"With the Red Knight dead, what are you going to do now?" Tracs asked Konafar.

"The plot thickens," Konafar began, "the Red Knight spoke of someone else who is responsible for the invasion of the town and what happened to Runit."

"Who?" Tonles' eyes narrowed.

"His name is Repan and calls himself the Lord of the..." He paused.

"Mind." Tracs finished his sentence.

"Well if he's responsible for what happened to Runit, then we should go pay him a visit." Tonles said.

"What do you know about him?" Konafar asked Tracs.

"Let's just say he has gotten my Order's attention."

"Can you elaborate?"

"I think we need to find better shelter for the evening first." Hue suddenly said after looking up into the dark sky.

"He's right." Tonles added.

They left the area, found a nearby cave and made camp by a roaring fire. Tracs told them everything he knew about Repan and why he was kept under a watchful eye by his Order. When he was through, Konafar definitely wanted to meet Repan and put an end to his life. Hue and Tracs agreed to go and so did Cord, even though he had his freedom.

Chapter 4: The Retaking of Redden

Master Shoo, Sir Valden, Tef, Priest Hamond, and the Magistrate gathered their forces and waited several weeks for a battle that would never come.

It was nearing nightfall of the sixth day of the fourth week when Shoo's student Yushi, returned and raced up to his master's chambers to give him his scouting report.

"Master, the troops are not making any attempt to attack."

Master Shoo put his tea cup down. "Yushi, I've made a decision. I am going to ask the other Orders to march on the city; maybe we can harass them enough so that they leave."

"Do you think that will work?"

"Truthfully, I don't know, but I'm tired of feeling like a sheep waiting to be slaughtered."

"What about the other Orders, do you think they'll lend you their support?"

"High Priest Hamond will. The others, I'm not sure about."

"What if they won't go with us?"

"Then we'll go anyway."

"Master its suicide."

Shoo stood up, placed his hand on his student's shoulder and looked into his eyes. "Yushi, maybe our sacrifices will teach other people that if you unite, then this sort of injustice will never prevail."

"But I'm scared and don't want to die."

"Neither do I, but we all have to someday. I just can't live with myself knowing that those people died and justice wasn't served. I've made up my mind, so go tell the other students."

Yushi bowed and did as he was instructed.

Master Shoo left the school and presented his cause to the other Orders and the Magistrate. It took some convincing, but when all was said and done, they agreed to support him. It was decided that a certain number of students from each school would be left behind, along with the bulk of the Magistrate's force, to guard the town. While they were preparing for their departure, the last of the scouts returned and came running up to Sir Valden. They reported that the gates were in ruins and guards were no longer walking the battlements. The news took him by surprise, and he made haste to meet with the other leaders.

Together, they changed their battle plans and came up with following. Priest Hamond, Sir Valden, and Master Shoo would lead two-thirds of their men into the city and kill anyone in sight. Anyone they missed or left wounded, would be dealt with by Tef and the remaining forces. They finished preparing and left that very night to take up position in the forest to the north of town. Tef sent in a few scouts to assess their strengths and weaknesses. When the two thieves returned, they found him sitting on a fallen oak tree.

"Sir." The scout on the left said and waited until their leader finished what he was doing before speaking again. "We scoured through the town and found only a fraction of the army that we thought was there."

"What?" The unexpected news took Tef by surprise. "How many?"

"From our estimate we think maybe two or three hundred."

Tef smlled.

"There's more good news." The other scout offered.

Tef stood up. "Go on."

"Apparently, they suffered major casualties of their own by either an invading army or had a civil war."

"What do you mean?"

"There are dead bodies everywhere."

"Did you see any giants?"

"We found them among the dead." The first scout said.

"What's left?"

"We only saw the goat creatures. They were either roaming the streets drunk or sitting in the tavern drinking heavily.

"This must be some sort of trap."

"It's not. I am telling you they are only interested in drinking and gambling."

"Good work. That will be all."

Tef finished with the scouts and walked over to Sir Valden, Master Shoo, and Priest Hamond.

"It appears our enemy is ripe for the picking." Tef stated.

"What do you mean?" Sir Valden asked.

"My men tell me there are only goatmen roaming the city."

"And their numbers?"

"Around two to three hundred."

"What?" Hamond exclaimed.

"Where are the giants?" Master Shoo asked.

"Dead."

"Are you sure?" Valden asked.

"Yes. They found them among the dead, scattered throughout the city." Tef grinned

"I wonder what happened there." Valden simply said.

"My men think there was a civil war or another army invaded the town."

"I think we should start with the taverns and inns and then work our way through the city." Priest Hamond said.

"Good. Let's move on them when the moon is at its highest and put an end to this." Shoo said.

After dividing their men into three parts, they began their assault to take back Redden. Sir Valden led the first wave of troops throughout the city, overwhelming and slaughtering any non-human creature, and clearing the path to the taverns.

Master Shoo and Priest Hamond led the second charge and did

their part by setting the four taverns ablaze, killing all inside, while Tef led his men behind the others and finished off the last of the goatmen.

It was nearing morning when Priest Hamond and his men discovered a cavern to the north. The smell of something rotten preceded its discovery. What they found inside was so horrific and disturbing, it would definitely haunt them for many years to come. Festering, unrecognizable corpses in various stages of decay were piled on top of each other and stretched as far as they could see.

"What do you want to do with them?" An acolyte asked Hamond.

"Get some oil and burn the bodies." Hamond replied with great sadness, knowing that they were discarded to rot inside of this hollowed out grave.

After emptying several jugs of oil on the bodies, Priest Hamond said a few prayers and then lit them. All present watched the flames engulf the dead in one massive fireball. They were about to turn away, when something towards the back of the cave made a hideous screeching sound. In the next instant, the pile began shifting and moving until the flaming bodies were thrown out of the way, and a war beetle charged out of the cave. Priest Hamond and a few others moved out of the way just in time, but others weren't so lucky and were trampled under the beetle's enormous body. The creature turned around while hissing and attacked with its large mandibles snapping and tearing apart three others.

High Priest Hamond retreated to the side of the cave and began working his hands frantically into the air while chanting words of summoning. The carnage of death continued a few yards away as the men fought ineffectively against the beetle's tough shell, and were either quickly cut down or trampled upon.

At one point, the beetle parted its shell and began flapping both halves, causing a loud screeching sound and forcing everyone in its path to cover their ears. Priest Hamond finished his chant and when he saw the soldiers trapped between the beetle and the fire in the cave, he panicked and commanded the Air Tirip to attack. He realized his mistake too late, as the Air Tirip, not knowing friend from foe, attacked everything in its path, starting with the soldiers. It was over quickly for them, as the Air protector swirled counterclockwise and drew the very air from their lungs until they fell over and died.

Next, it sent swirling wind tunnels at the beetle, lifting its massive body into the air and threw the bug into the fiery inferno, roasting it alive. When it was over, Priest Hamond slumped to the ground, shaking and crying over his mistake and then praying for the dead and their forgiveness.

By mid-morning, Master Shoo, Tef, and Sir Valden met near the town square to discuss the future of Redden and how they would rebuild the town.

"We have a large task before us." Master Shoo began. "So where do we begin?"

"First we need to have a strong presence and more importantly keep order." Sire Valden stated.

"That's a start." Tef added. "What about the stores and the riches they contain? I think we should have first crack at everything before we let anyone else enter the town, in fact, maybe we should keep everything."

"Spoken like a true thief." Valden sneered.

"We earned it, don't you think?"

"I agree with you; we should take what we want, but not everything!"

"I hate to say it, but I think we'll need the Magistrate's input on how to rebuild the town. He has a mind for that sort of thing." Shoo added.

"Rebuild the town yes, to run it no."

"Then what should we do Sir Valden?"

"Run this place until we elect a new Magistrate. From there we..."

He was about to say something more when Priest Hamond

rounded the corner. The grave look on his face gave everyone pause.

"Are you okay?" Tef asked him.

"I found the rest of the townspeople." He simply stated.

"Where are they?"

"They were all dead and stuffed into a cavern to the north. It was disgusting. Their bodies were just left there to feed the war beetles."

"Please join us we're discussing the future of the town."

"Not right now, I need to lie down." Hamond said as he walked away.

"That was strange. I wonder what's wrong with him? He only found dead bodies." Tef asked after he was gone.

"I guess we should be grateful that we didn't find what he found." Master Shoo said. "When we're done we'll send word to the Magistrate to join us."

"I don't think he should get any of the spoils." Tef said while looking directly at Shoo.

"He's entitled to some of the profit. After all, he did lend us some of his men." Sir Valden said to the thief.

"I guess you're right."

"You know; I might move my Order to this town. There's room to grow and I could recruit more men. What about you, Master Shoo?"

"I think that I like the simplicities of the smaller towns."

"Tef?"

"I haven't decided yet. Let's meet again in a couple of hours when Priest Hamond can join us."

"Do we agree that we'll oversee the entire operation, and the Magistrate will just offer us guidance?" Valden asked, wanting a clear answer. The others nodded, and he continued. "We'll gather all the wealth, take out just a share, and then store it in one centralized place. Make sure you tell your men to keep the looting down to a minimum." Sir Valden looked at the thief and smiled.

They continued their discussion and a few hours later Priest Hamond joined them and they talked well into the night. By the next morning, they sent word to the Magistrate and then set out to start rebuilding the town.

Chapter 5: A Child's Dream (Part II)

Shortly after midday, they left the woods and entered the surrounding area. The sky was clear; the snow had stopped altogether, and towards the north stood anther forest.

"I guess that's where Fefantor lives." Katara decided.

"I think we can make it there by nightfall." Torhan added.

They began walking.

"I was wondering if your god can protect us against those undead creatures."

"In what way?" Katara curiously asked.

"Does she give you blessings against them?"

Katara shook her head. "She does, but I'm not sure how much she can do against reanimated corpses, if that's what they are. I've been meaning to ask you, do you believe?"

"In what gods?"

"Yes."

"I used to."

"What happened to change your mind?"

"When I was young boy, my mother was attacked by an animal and was injured. The healer said it was minor and told us to pray for her. We did and when her condition worsened, he said to pray harder, so we spent every waking hour in the church, and you know what? She died anyway, so what's the point of praylng?"

"I'm sorry she died, but you have to remember, gods don't answer every prayer."

"It just seems like a waste of time when you ask for something, and it doesn't get answered."

"Believe me, it's not a waste of time."

"He was so sure she would get better." Torhan was getting angry over the memory of losing his mother.

"It doesn't matter what he said, when it's your time, it's your time."

"I don't want to talk about this anymore."

Katara let the matter drop, and they walked along in silence.

It was nightfall when they arrived at the forest. After lighting some glow rocks, they entered the dense woods.

"I think we should look for the house and then camp. What do you think?" Torhan asked.

"I'm tired, but I can keep going."

They walked in a straight line, for the most part, and left markers every time they changed direction. A few hours later, they came upon fresh footprints leading north and followed the trail until they saw tiny lights coming off in the distance. Katara insisted they get a closer look. Another mile or so brought them to a two-story mansion which was down an embankment. The enormously large house had one visible entrance and many windows on both floors. Each windowsill had a lit candle, and from their position, they could see someone sitting in a chair by the closest widow on the second floor.

As they continued studying the structure and the person inside, Katara caught sight of a cloaked individual walking outside carrying a lantern. He or she walked from the far end of the building toward the front. They deactivated their glow rocks so that they would not draw any attention, and watched the figure walk around.

"Do you think that's one of the creatures?" Torhan asked.

"No. Whoever that is they are walking normal and carrying a lantern. Now be quiet."

They watched the figure pass the door and continue towards the other end of the building and then around the back. When the person disappeared from sight, another emerged from the other side and walked in the same direction. They watched the guards walk in this pattern for many rotations until Katara grew cold and said she wanted to leave. Torhan didn't object, because he was feeling the same way.

They made camp a half-mile away, built a small fire and placed the

Ring of Warmth next to it so that it could recharge itself. After they were situated, Katara, exhausted from the day's events, covered herself in furs and fell asleep within seconds, leaving Torhan to take first watch. Torhan grabbed the rest of the furs and sat down with his back against a tree. He used them like a blanket, placed his spear across his lap and left his sword within reach. He figured that if he was going to keep watch, then why not be warm. What he didn't take into account was the warmth of the furs coupled with his weariness would eventually cause him to fall asleep.

Morning arrived, and Katara was the first to wake. She looked around, realizing at once that she never took watch and upon seeing her companion, she knew why. He was sleeping. Getting up she walked over and was about to shake him awake when she noticed a trail of blood and large paw prints leading away from camp. Something got close to them while they were sleeping, and it sent shivers up and down her spine. Taking out her mace, she nudged Torhan awake with her foot. Seeing her standing there with her mace in hand, he got up, quickly gripping his spear.

"What's going on?" He whispered.

"Look at the ground." She said and continued scanning the area.

"Blood!" He exclaimed.

"Looks like something paid us a visit after you fell asleep."

Torhan gazed at his scabbard, and it wasn't glowing. "Whatever it was, it's gone."

"How do you know?"

"My scabbard isn't glowing." He then removed his dagger from the scabbard and saw that it was covered with blood. "It looks like my dagger must have fought with it." He showed it to her.

She relaxed a bit. "How could you fall asleep? Next time, if you're tired tell me, and I'll take first watch. I don't want to end up as a meal."

"Look, I'm sorry and..."

Katara held up her hand, cutting off the rest of his words. "You should be, just don't let it happen again." She started picking up her things. "Let's get moving and we'll eat later."

"Look I'm sorry."

"Save it."

Katara was so furious that she didn't talk to him until they reached the manor and were in position behind several trees to study the building. They didn't see anyone walking around or inside like they did last night.

"We should go around back to see if there's another way in." She said.

"And if there isn't?"

"We'll knock." She got up, and he followed.

They gave wide berth and stayed inside the trees. As soon as they were around back, Torhan noticed a door at the base of the building that normally led to the cellar.

"We have another way in." He said.

"I thought there would be one. Let's take up position over there." She pointed further back into the woods. "I need to pray for protection and construct a guardian. I need you to gather enough wood so that I can create him and then keep watch until I'm finished."

"When do you want to enter the building?"

"When it's dark of course."

"I have to ask you something."

"What is it?" Katara looked at him with concern.

"If we have to kill someone innocent are you okay with it? Because if you're not; then I'll do this alone. We don't even know if the guy in the house is a bad person or not."

"Well if he's stealing dead people, then chances are he's not a good person and the people working for him are guilty by association. So, to answer your question, I'm good with it."

"Okay." Torhan smiled at her and was glad he got that off of his chest.

After Torhan gathered enough wood required for Katara to construct one of her guardians, he took up position on top of the hill and studied the mansion. By midday, heavy snow began falling and the first of the guards appeared from around the building. Torhan watched him walk from one end of the house to the other, and as soon as he turned the corner another one emerged and did the same thing. By the time Katara finished with her prayers and animating the wooden sentinel; Torhan knew exactly how long it would take the guards to complete their rotation around the building.

As the day faded into night, Katara and Torhan removed their furs to allow for extra movement, filled her pouch with vials of healing liquids, and took a few weapons. They waited until the guards were in mid-rotation before running down the hill and over to the door. Torhan found it locked and instructed Katara to keep watch for the guards while he picked the lock. She moved to the end of the building, flattened herself against the wall and waited with her mace in hand. While Torhan worked feverishly on the mechanism, Katara heard footfalls crunching in the snow. She looked over at Torhan, saw that he wasn't finished and knew what she had to do.

When the guard rounded the corner, she swung her mace with purpose and struck him in the side of the head, caving in his skull. She hit him again to make sure she finished the job and then dragged his body over to where Torhan was.

"He's dead. We need to hurry or I'll have to kill the other one."

"Do you think we should? I mean it's going to be nearly impossible to cover up all that blood and hide our tracks."

She looked over at the blood covering the snow and house. "You're right." She said and took up her position again.

Katara killed the next guard just as easy and on some level, she was glad she surprised him. It seemed more humane that way. Torhan finally unlocked the door, and after they dragged the dead bodies down with them, he closed it. They descended the stairs and when they reached the bottom, they came to another closed door and were met by the stench of rotting flesh permeating from the other side. It was so powerful they had to cover their mouths so that they wouldn't gag. Torhan tested the knob, found the door unlocked and pressed his ear against it to listen.

"I think there's someone inside." He said quietly. "I'm going to open the door and take a look. If we can't surprise whoever it is, we'll rush in and attack."

She nodded and Torhan slowly opened the creaky door and peered inside. The room was dimly lit and stretched the length of the manor. He saw shackled tables down the center of the room, wooden barrels in each corner, pointy instruments hanging on the walls, and a couple of closed doors on both sides of the room. It reminded him of a very large healer's room, but darker and more sinister looking.

His gaze came to rest upon a lone figure, dressed in a hooded robe, toward the front. His back was to them, and he appeared to be preoccupied at one of the far tables. He signaled to Katara and they squatted down and entered the room, closing the door once they both were inside. When they were sure they didn't draw any unwanted attention from the person at the far end, they crept closer to the front, moving in and around the tables.

When they were halfway there, Torhan switched from his spear to his bow and notched an arrow, training the weapon on his back, and then motioned Katara forward with a slight nod. She moved and when she was about ten feet away, the robed figure stopped what he was doing and remained motionless, as if sensing their presence. Katara stopped advancing and hid behind one of the tables, while Torhan drew the bowstring back further and waited to see what he was going to do. The robed figure quickly turned around, holding a limb and headless torso. Torhan fired and hit the fleshy shield, which was followed by laughter from the man behind it.

He peered around his meaty shield. "I see that I have unwelcome guests." He paused. "I'm glad you volunteered to become one of my projects."

"Not on your life." Torhan answered.

"You can tell your friend to stop hiding behind my table and come out. I think that I'll use her to satisfy my needs before turning her into one of my followers." He chuckled.

Katara stood up. "Let's see if my mace can change your mind." She challenged.

"Well if you feel that way, step forward."

Katara moved away from the table and Torhan fired an arrow, notched another, hesitated slightly, and fired again. The pause in his attack worked perfectly, because the robed figure blocked the first arrow with his shield but because he didn't anticipate the second, he lowered his shield and was struck in his right arm, causing him to drop the one side of the shield. Katara charged him and in a panic, the robed figure flung the torso and hit her square in the chest, knocking her to the ground. Torhan let loose another arrow and missed because his target went after Katara with a knife he had hidden behind his back. Before he could land on top of her and drive his knife into her throat, Katara kicked him in the groin and sent him reeling away in pain.

Torhan discarded the bow, grabbed his spear, and rushed him. The robed figure saw him coming and threw his dagger at Torhan and missed. Unfortunately, for him, his actions prompted Torhan's now glowing scabbard, to reciprocate and defend its master by launching the dagger. When Torhan saw the weapon fly after him, he stopped and allowed the knife to do its job. The robed man waved his arms, frantically trying to protect himself from the knife, and received several slashes across his hands, legs, and face.

Katara was back on her feet and joined Torhan. Together they watched him fight helplessly as the knife ended his life. With the threat neutralized, the dagger returned to the scabbard, and the scabbard stopped glowing.

"Now I really don't feel bad if we kill everyone in this house." Katara said.

"Me too, do you think he was Fefantor?" Torhan gazed down at the dead man.

"I guess we should have asked him before we attacked."

Torhan pulled back his hood. "He's not. Unless Tole was wrong, and he cut his hair short."

Katara walked over to one of the barrels and peered inside. The stench quickly overpowered her senses and made her stomach churn to the point that she retched and almost vomited. Holding her mouth, she looked again and saw arms, legs, innards, and other unrecognizable body parts.

Torhan joined her. "What is it?" He said as he looked inside and gagged as well.

"Body parts."

"Let's check the doors."

The doors were locked, so they searched the robed figure and found a key, which opened them. The door on the left led upstairs and was illuminated by glow rocks embedded within the walls. The one on the right was also illuminated the same way and led downstairs.

"Which way do you want to go?" Katara asked.

"I think we should check downstairs first."

"Why?"

"Less of a chance of encountering someone, plus if I was to hide my valuables, that's where I'd place them."

"Makes sense. What about him? Should we hide the body?" She pointed to the dead man.

"Yes."

After shoving him underneath a table, Katara locked the door leading up, and then they went downstairs. The spiraling staircase led them to a landing and another closed door. Torhan pressed his ear against the wood and when he couldn't hear anything on the other side, he tested the handle and found it unlocked. He looked at Katara to see if she was ready, and after she nodded, he slowly opened the door and peered inside.

Hanging braziers were positioned all around the room, and illuminated the area enough so that he could see the room was about thirty feet long and ten feet wide. A few chests were stacked neatly against the back wall. Off to the side was a lone figure squatting down and facing them. Because the figure didn't react to the door opening and remained perfectly still, Torhan wasn't sure if it was a statue or a real person. He held up a finger to inform Katara of how many people occupied the room, and she placed a reassuring hand on his shoulder, indicating that she was ready.

Spear in hand, Torhan stepped inside with Katara right behind him and proceeded to the front of the room. Torhan kept a watchful eye on the figure wearing tattered clothes and when he noticed it was breathing; it was apparent that it was made of flesh and blood. Now he wasn't sure if it was asleep or waiting for them to get closer. Torhan looked nervously at his scabbard, and even though it remained unchanged, he was having second thoughts about moving any further.

Katara saw his hesitation and paused. "That thing is alive isn't it?"

"Yes and look it has four arms."

"That must be one of his experiments." She whispered.

"Maybe we should leave it alone."

"That would be wise."

As they started backing up, the creature rose to a hunched position and then growled at them, which caused the scabbard to glow intensely.

"It's going to attack." Torhan warned.

Katara separated herself from him. "Keep moving toward the door." She said.

They were almost to the door when the creature raised its arms and charged. Torhan braced himself and pointed the spear directly at the creature, while Katara suddenly advanced on it. Before she could hit the creature, it slapped her aside in one motion and sent her stumbling into the wall. The powerful blow left her dazed and unsure of herself after she hit the ground. The monster went after Torhan, and his scabbard responded by sending the dagger after the creature. The blade sliced the monster deeply across the chest and then stabbed it a few times. It delivered wounds that should have killed, or at least slowed it, but for some reason, they didn't.

When the creature was close enough, Torhan stabbed it through the stomach, and before he could retract the weapon and stab it again;

the beast grabbed the shaft with its hands, flung him off of his feet, then jumped on top of him and began pummeling him. It would've been over for Torhan if it wasn't for his dagger's continuous attacks, one of which stabbed the creature in the neck. When the beast gripped its throat and began choking on its own blood, Torhan reached up and used the spear to push the dying monster off of him.

Katara was on her feet again, rubbing her head. "We need to get out of here. That thing almost killed us." She said looking down at the monster.

"Let me check the chest first."

"Hurry up."

Torhan squatted in front of the chest furthest on his left, took his lock pick and began probing the lock. He quickly discovered a needle towards the back of the mechanism, and knew that it was designed to spring forth if anyone opened the chest. He moved off to the side and used the pick to trigger the needle and then went to work on the locking mechanism. A few clicks later, the lock opened. Thinking the chest could have another trap inside he took his dagger and traced it along the seam of the lid. When there wasn't any resistance, he opened the chest and to his disappointment, it was empty. He went to work on the next chest, didn't find it armed with a trap and picked the lock rather easily. *"Too easy,"* he thought as he was tracing the seam with the dagger.

When he was halfway around, he met some resistance and stopped. Figuring there was a trap, but not really knowing what kind, he stood off to the side and slowly lifted the lid. When it almost fully opened, he heard a click, which was followed by a hiss. Torhan dropped the lid and began running toward the door. Katara followed him. A few seconds later, a cloud of green smoke seeped out of the lid and covered a ten-foot area. After the cloud dissipated, Katara stayed where she was, while Torhan went over and opened the lid. Inside, the chest was filled halfway to the top with gold and silver, a few potions, gems, a diamond necklace, and buried a few inches down, was a circular amulet just like Tole had described.

Torhan knew right away that was what he was looking for and

when he grabbed the silver medallion and lifted it, he heard another click inside the chest and one coming from the wall directly in front of him. He panicked and accidentally tripped backwards and fell onto his back, just as a small panel opened and flames shot out of the hole and over his head. He could feel the intense flames licking at his face, knowing that if he didn't fall, he would have been roasted alive.

When Katara saw him fall and the flames coming from the wall in front of him, she ran to the front of the room and to her relief, he wasn't on fire. After the flames ceased, Torhan scooted away from the chest and was helped up by Katara.

"Let's get out of here." He said.

"I agree. Did you find the amulet?"

He showed it to her, and as they were walking toward the door, they heard something that sounded like a part of a wall sliding open near the chests. Turning, they saw two misshapen figures step into the room. They began looking around until their eyes came to rest on them. The scabbard began glowing.

"Move." Katara said.

The creatures gave chase.

Torhan and Katara made it through the door, slammed it shut, and quickly began ascending the stairs. As they reached the top, they heard pounding on the door below with such ferocity and determination that the wood began splintering apart. They made haste and left the mansion.

They ran up the hill, grabbed their belongings, and stopped at the wooden guardian. Katara told it to "Protect" and the sentry moved toward the mansion.

"We'll go that way first," he pointed to the north, "and then backtrack to Tole's grove, that should throw off anyone that follows."

Chapter 6: Into the Depths

It was nearing dawn when they arrived at the grove. The woods appeared darker and quieter than before, which made them feel a bit uneasy. After walking for a while, two large black cats with long protruding fangs suddenly appeared and snarled at them, causing them to stop dead in their tracks.

Torhan glanced at his scabbard and noticed that it was glowing faintly, indicating that the animals were unsure of their intentions. He held the spear in front, and Katara was ready with her mace. The animals slowly walked toward them and paused to sniff the air. After several long, heart-pounding minutes the cats turned around and left. They waited until the scabbard stopped glowing before continuing.

By midday, they entered the inner grove and saw Tole sitting on a log, cross-legged and smoking a pipe, with two big black cats lying at his feet. "I see that you've returned." He said, smiling.

"Somehow, I think that you already knew that." Torhan answered.

"And how was your visit to Fefantor's manor? Did you get the amulet or were you too scared to enter his house?"

"We got it." Katara snapped, clearly not amused by his sarcastic tone.

"Where is it?" Tole asked as the smile left his face.

"You'll have your precious ornament after we have ours."

"That wasn't our deal. You were to retrieve my amulet, and I would tell you the location of yours."

"Things have changed, we really don't trust you."

Tole stood up. "You know I could release my cats and you would be torn to pieces, and then I can take the amulet off of your dead bodies."

"Do that and you'll never know where it is." Katara said.

Tole took out a gray gem, and it started glowing. "Let me tell you something about the amulet. There are five unique stones that belong to it and when the amulet is near them, they begin glowing. Now, given the fact my gem is one of the stones, I'm willing to bet that one of you has my relic."

His pets rose again after they heard the tone of his voice and started pacing in front of their master. Katara's bluff failed, but she had a knack for thinking on her feet.

"Well it appears that we have a situation." She said.

"Just give me the amulet before I lose my patience!"

Torhan's scabbard started glowing as the tension grew. Katara took out the amulet and held it in front of her, bringing a wide smile to the hermit's face. He looked like a child who was waiting for a birthday present. Tole stepped forward with his cats in tow and stopped in front of them.

"Where is the amulet of REM?" Katara demanded.

Tole's smile faded. "The thing you desire is hidden in an old cemetery some ten miles southwest of here. The amulet is buried, along with its owner, inside a crypt that has sunk almost all the way down into the earth."

"How do we enter if it's buried?" Torhan asked.

Tole never took his eyes away from the amulet. "That's not my problem."

"It will be if you want this." Katara waved the amulet back and forth irritating the hermit.

"Alright then, I'll tell you. Near the crypt, there is a mechanism that will raise the mausoleum high enough for you to enter. How you get the doors to open; I don't know."

"What does the mechanism look like?" Torhan asked.

Tole looked disgusted. "It looks like a tree stump, and if you push it over, then the structure will rise. That's all I know, now give me the amulet."

Katara glanced over at Torhan, and he knew from the way she looked at him that she was going to do something risky. She turned back to Tole and offered him the amulet. As he reached for it, she grabbed his arm and spun him around, so that his back was against her chest, and gripped his throat tightly.

"Stay your pets or I'll rip your throat out." She said.

Tole said something in a strange language, and his pets walked back to the log and sat down.

"You won't get away with this." He said.

"We're not trying to get away with anything. You will have your amulet in a few seconds."

Katara nodded to Torhan and he realized what she wanted him to do. He grabbed the hermit's hand, forced his palm open and took the glowing stone. She released Tole and handed him the amulet.

Tole was furious. "I should release my cats on you."

"Do that and you'll be dead before they even pounce on us. Now here's the deal, take us to the crypt, and as soon as we recover the amulet we'll give you back the stone and be on our way. You have our word on it."

Tole thought about it. "I will go only if I get to take one of my pets with us."

Torhan and Katara thought it was a fair offer, agreed, and left.

Their journey from Tole's grove to where the crypt was took them until nightfall. It was too dark to do anything further, so they camped. The panther took to the forest in search of food, while the others built a small fire and ate. Tole feasted on figs, nuts, and dried beef, while Katara and Torhan ate bread, berries, and cheese. Their conversation was light until Torhan wanted to know more about the hermit.

"Tole, so why did you leave the monastery in search of solitude?" He asked.

"Boy, I don't see the point in you getting to know me, because by tomorrow we'll be parting ways."

"He's just making conversation to pass the time." Katara said.

"Its people like him, that's the reason why I sought solitude."

"Have it your way." Torhan said.

"I'm going to sleep." Tole said as he got up and made his bed a few yards away.

When the hour grew late, they covered themselves in furs and settled down to sleep. Torhan made sure Tole's back was to him and slipped the stone into his boot. He fell asleep shortly after that.

Katara lay there thinking about her new partner and was surprised that she was actually growing fond of him. This rarely happened to her, and the last time it did; she was a teenager. "A teenager," she whispered. "Where did the time go?" To her, it seemed like only yesterday that she was playing in the orchard with her friends. Her mother used to say that life went by so fast, and by the time you realized it; you were old.

Maybe someday soon, she would take a lesser role in the Order, settle down, and start a family. After all, at the age of twenty four she wasn't getting any younger. She glanced at Torhan and smiled. Less than ten minutes later, sleep claimed her unexpectedly, and she dreamt of the life she now wanted.

Torhan dreamt that he was standing next to Katara in an open field, holding a bloodied ax. Like the weapon, he was covered in gore. She said something and led him to a cemetery where they came upon a large monolith with the following words etched on the door.

"Your journey ends here. Push the recessed button to the right and enter if you dare."

Torhan walked over and found something that felt like an indentation and pushed it. The stone door opened revealing a flight of stairs going down.

"Here is where you find your true calling my love." Katara said to him and then pushed him down the stairs into the darkness below.

After he landed at the bottom, the door closed above, leaving him in total darkness. He was on his feet, and while searching for the stairs that suddenly disappeared, a light from an unknown source revealed a steel door directly to his right. He approached, opened the door, and entered a circular room with four stone sarcophagi neatly placed against the wall. He proceeded to the coffin on the right and opened the casket. Inside was the corpse of a young woman in chainmail; she appeared to be recently deceased. He recognized her, but at the same time did not. He opened the next coffin and inside was a man wearing leather armor and holding a sword; he also looked recently deceased. He gazed at the man and again sort of recognized him, but couldn't place him. The last two coffins contained two little boys holding freshly cut flowers and they too looked strangely familiar.

Torhan was about to leave the room when the door slammed shut, all four corpses rose at the same time and started moaning. He backed up as the cadavers climbed out of their boxes and walked over to him.

"You will join us soon." The older man said, and the others began chanting. "Join us, join us."

Torhan grew fearful and backed away until he bumped against the door, and then turned around pushed on it with all his might. The door wouldn't budge.

The corpses continued chanting. "Join us, join us."

Torhan panicked and pushed harder as they raised their voices. With one final push, the door opened and on the other side, Tole was standing there holding a pitchfork in front of his body. He was about to say something to the hermit, when Tole viciously plunged the weapon into his stomach, which tore his belly open.

Torhan gazed down to watch his intestines spill slowly out onto the floor. The hermit started laughing. When he looked up again, the dead corpses grabbed him and dragged him back into the room. Tole slammed the door shut.

****

When Torhan's eyes opened, he was greeted by the sound of a crackling fire and the smell of meat cooking. Remembering the stone, he reached into his boot and was relieved that it was still there. He put it back into his pouch and sat up. Tole and his cat were by the fire with their backs to him, and Katara was still sleeping. He got up and walked over to Katara and squatted down. She looked so peaceful that he hated waking her, but did anyway. A few nudges later and she opened her eyes and smiled.

"Time to get up." He said.

"I see that our friend didn't try to kill us." She whispered.

"No I didn't." Tole said surprising them both that he overheard her. "Let's eat and get this day over with; I have better things to do."

While they were enjoying their meal, Torhan noticed that Tole was wearing the amulet. "Tole what exactly does the amulet do?" He asked.

After swallowing his tasty morsel, he answered. "The amulet is nothing special. However, the stones are, well at least to my family."

"What do you mean?"

"Each stone holds information regarding my family's ancestors." Tole took another bite.

"Why is it called insight?" Katara asked.

"It has nothing to do with anything insightful. It's just a name my family gave it."

"Do you think Fefantor has the other stones?"

"No. He probably sold them, the greedy bastard."

"Why did he steal the amulet in the first place?"

Tole paused. "I don't want to talk about it."

Torhan knew there was more to the story, but didn't press the issue. "Can you show us how it works?"

"I need the other four stones." He said flatly, lowered his head, and went back to eating.

Torhan looked over at Katara, and they both silently agreed that he was lying.

They finished eating, packed up their belongings about an hour later and left.

Along the way, Katara began noticing that the sounds of birds and small creatures alike was missing, and the normal sounds related to the forest were gone as well. The forest suddenly became eerie.

"I wonder why it's so quiet." Torhan stated.

"It is a bit odd." Katara added.

"Tole, you know the area, do you have any idea?" Torhan asked the hermit.

His cat was also pacing around nervously. "The crypt we're traveling to holds the evil spirits of the dead, and the animals and bugs alike, must sense this."

"What do you mean evil spirits, how do you know?"

Tole smirked. "A long time ago, when someone was convicted of a crime, dependent upon how serious it was, the criminal would be thrown down inside of the crypt."

"Why?"

"The townspeople wanted them to suffer during their last days."

"That's cruel." Katara said.

"Cruel, yes, but well deserved."

What else do you know about the crypt?"

"You don't want to be near it after dark."

"Why is that?" She asked.

"Legend has it; the evil spirits come out at night and drag anyone they find down below."

"And you believe such stories?" Torhan asked.

"Me? No."

Shortly after midday, they reached a deserted village. Most of the structures, although still standing, were either burnt out or in such bad shape that they looked like they could fall down at any moment. They didn't linger very long and followed the hermit northward until they reached a cemetery.

The desolated area was overrun with weeds and vines, and the walls were crumbling apart in many places. Beyond the walls, the statues, headstones and crypts were in different stages of decay; some of which, although weathered, were in near perfect condition, while others were cracked in half, or broken.

"Somewhere in the middle is the crypt you're looking for." Tole said and entered through the rusted gates.

They were halfway across the field when Tole stopped suddenly. "There it is." He announced.

"Where?" Katara asked looking around.

"See the statue of the man holding the staff?" He said with excitement.

"You mean the one down the hill?"

"Yes, that's it."

The crypt was buried deep within the earth. The top of the structure and the statue were the only things visible. A stagnant pool of black sludge surrounded the building, making it appear like the ground would swallow it up one day. Tole started walking away.

"Where are you going?" Katara asked.

"To sit down."

"Aren't you going to help us open it?"

"My job is done. The rest is up to you."

"Where is the stump?" Torhan demanded.

Tole scanned the area until his eyes fell upon one in particular. "It's the one over there with the strange markings inscribed on it." He pointed to it and then sat down on a nearby log. "You need to move it until it falls over, that should trigger the mechanism and raise the crypt."

"Sounds easy enough." Torhan said.

"Do you need help?" Katara asked.

"No. Wait here."

Torhan walked over to the three-foot stump, grabbed it with both hands and began pushing. At first, it didn't budge, and then suddenly; it gave way and fell.

A few seconds later, they heard a loud rumbling from the crypt as the building began rising from the muddy water. They watched the mausoleum until it was fully erected, and the door was accessible.

Torhan signaled to Katara to join him. "I want you to wait here while I go down." He said.

"You're not going down there alone." She looked concerned.

"He might lock us down there if you do."

"He won't because you still have the stone."

"He could just wait for us to starve and then get it himself."

"Good point. I could always summon a Water Tirip from the pond to protect us." She offered.

Torhan looked over at the water, considering the possibility. "Will it be the same alignment as yours, given the evil of the area?"

"Hmm, you might be right, it could change."

"What happens if it does?"

"I'd rather not say." The look on her face told him all he needed to know.

"Watch your back." He said and placed reassuring hand on her shoulder.

She nodded and started fishing through her backpack. "Here take these." She handed him a few small torches, flint, two flasks of oil, and the Ring of Warmth. She hugged him and said. "Be careful."

After their embrace, Torhan walked over to Tole. "As soon as I get back you'll have your precious stone." He stated.

"Please be safe, because I don't feel like going down there to recover my stone." He answered, sounding annoyed.

Torhan entered the sludgy water, and his feet sank into the mud and then deeper with each step after that. Eventually, the water spilled over the rim of his boots and pooled around the soles of his feet, numbing them instantly. By the time he reached the steps leading up to the doorway, his entire body was cold and his feet felt numb. He sat down on the wet steps, placed the Ring of Warmth on his finger, and then removed his boots. His feet were irritated and itchy.

"Are you alright?" Katara asked.

"Yes. Don't walk into the water unless you have to, it irritated my skin."

After using water from his waterskin to rinse his feet and the inside of his boots, he dried them both, put the boots back on and stood up to face the building. The rusty, bronze, door lacked a handle and a keyhole, so he didn't think it would just open, but pushed on it anyway. The door remained firmly in place. He searched for a hidden button or something that would trigger the door, and when his search proved futile, he took a step back to study the structure. The statue was definitely too high and lacked any real footholds to climb up it, so he was pretty sure the trigger wouldn't be up there. His gaze fell upon the word "SEMADTONS" underneath the statue's feet.

"Tole, do you know what the word SEMADTONS means?" He shouted.

After the hermit lit his pipe, he answered. "The name doesn't hold any meaning, so maybe it's the name of the family who owned the crypt."

"You said the townspeople dumped the bodies of those they deemed evil down there, so no single family would own it."

"You're right. I guess it means something else then."

"Do you think you need to do something with the letters above the door?" Katara offered.

"Like what?" Torhan asked.

"I don't know, try pushing one of them."

Torhan took her advice and used a small indentation on the right to climb up and grab the ledge just below the raised letters. After his body stopped swaying, he released his left hand and pushed the first letter on his left. It didn't move, so he tried the next one and still nothing. When he reached the letter "D" it moved until it became flush and clicked into place.

Torhan tried the rest of the letters and couldn't get them to move, so he jumped down and pushed on the door. To his disappointment, it still didn't move.

"Any luck?" Katara asked.

"The letter "D" moved, but none of the others."

"Maybe they do, but in a certain order. Did you try pushing the ones you already did after the letter "D" moved?"

"No." He said and climbed back up and started pushing the letters again. This time the letter "E" clicked into place, which was followed by "M," "O," "N," and "S." Shortly after the last letter fell into place the door creaked open, and he dropped to the ground.

"Nice job, what did it spell." Tole shouted to him.

"Demons!" He responded.

"How appropriate." Tole commented.

Torhan lit a torch, looked back one last time at Katara and entered.

Nothing but silence greeted him below, and red algae covered the dirt walls and stone steps. He knew that he'd have to be mindful of his footing and took the first of many steps downward. The stairs ended in a ten-foot square room, with a closed gate directly ahead of him. Off to the left side of the entrance was a plaque. He walked over and read the sign.

"Beyond this door lays the most vile, and evil people to have ever walked the face of the earth. Their deeds are the results of their entrapment. Those who enter, be warned that a similar fate will follow you into the afterlife."

Torhan scoffed at the warning and turned his attention to the rusty lock. He leaned the torch against the bars and went about picking the mechanism. After a few tries, it clicked open.

He removed his furs, picked up the torch, opened the door outwardly and entered. He followed the narrow corridor through a series of turns until he was standing in a large room. From where he stood, he could tell the room was circular, but spanned too far to see the end. He followed the wall to the right and came upon a brazier, which was just above eye level and suspended from the ceiling. He reached up with his torch, traced it above the rim and a few seconds later the brazier ignited and illuminated a portion of the area.

The room was large, circular, had several braziers scattered throughout and five steel doors in a row, with a sign above each of them. Torhan lit the other braziers, approached the doors, and began reading the signs from left to right.

"Beyond this door lays the first of the traitors named Ruder, his crimes are as follows. Stealing, rape, treason, and murder; may his soul remain behind this locked door."

"Beyond this door lays the second of the traitors named Trusten, her crimes are as follows. Stealing, treason, and murder; may her soul remain behind this locked door."

"Beyond this door lays the ring leader of the traitors named Shoel, his crimes are as follows. Stealing, rape, treason, murder, and leading the retched band of fools; may his soul remain behind this locked door."

"Beyond this door lays the third of the traitors named Binder, his crimes are as follows. Stealing, treason, and murder; may his soul remain behind this locked door."

"Beyond this door lays the fourth of the traitors named Aplone, her crimes are as follows. Stealing, treason, and murder; may her soul remain behind this locked door."

"Tole made it sound like there were a lot of criminals buried down here. I guess he doesn't know there're only five." Torhan said.

He took note that the criminals had exactly the same charges on their plaques, indicating that they were a group of outlaws. He thought about which door he wanted to enter first and decided that if the amulet was down here, then it would be buried with the leader Shoel.

The lock on his door was strange; it consisted of raised numbers from zero to nine, with no visible means to pick it. He pushed down the number one, and the digit stayed in place. He had the same result with the numbers two and three. *"Maybe it is this simple."* He thought.

Grinning, he pressed number four and the number popped back up. He turned the handle, and the door remained locked. "Maybe it's not that simple." He said and went about trying various combinations of numbers. Each time the fourth digit was pressed, no matter which one it was; the numbers popped up, and the door remained locked. Several attempts later, left him frustrated, so he gave up and went to the door on the far left, which housed the criminal named Ruder.

The lock was traditional in style and easily picked within minutes. He was proud of himself for getting good at picking locks and again, silently thanked Grappin for allowing him to use his library. The corridor beyond was dark and musty, and as soon as he entered, he was met by gusting wind that almost blew the torch out. He held the torch off to the side and walked straight ahead. After thirty feet, the wind abruptly stopped, like someone closed a door, and he started feeling uneasy. He took two more steps, and the scabbard suddenly glowed, causing him to stop. He held the torch further outward, and listened intently.

Cautiously, he continued. Several yards later, the scabbard's glow intensified and the dagger left its home and sailed off into the blackness beyond. It didn't take long before the first of many non-humanoid shrieks echoed off of the walls. He thought it sounded like an animal of some sort, so he backed away. The battle between dagger and creature lasted for a few minutes and then stopped. He was about to proceed, when the screeches abruptly started again.

Knowing there was at least one more, he crouched with his torch arm extended and sword pulled back so that he could deliver a devastating blow from his sword. It was a basic move, but if applied correctly, should slay whatever it was, or at least wound it enough to drive it away. Poised with his senses heightened, his dagger fought the monster, and then his worst fears came true when he heard more hissing directly in front of him. A few seconds later, a big furry creature that looked like a badger came creeping out of the darkness, with its mouth opened and razor-sharp teeth exposed.

When the animal was within range, Torhan hit it in the maw with his torch and then followed through in a slicing motion with his sword that cut the creature's throat and spilled its blood on the cold earth. The animal took a few steps back ad fell over. Torhan stabbed it a few times to make sure it would die. When the fight between animal and knife ended, the dagger returned to the scabbard, and the scabbard's glow diminished. Relieved, he moved ahead and found another four badgers dead. He proceeded down the corridor straight ahead. After ten feet it turned left, right after another twenty, and then left again thirty feet later. As soon as he rounded the bend, the scabbard glowed, and he stopped. From where he was, he could see a hole on the right side of the wall, at least a foot in circumference, and a badger staring at him. It appeared to be guarding the entrance to his burrow and remained motionless. If it wasn't for the scabbard, the animal might have gotten to him.

With his back to the opposite wall, he extended the torch and approached the hole. He didn't want to fight the creature, so when he was close enough he waved the torch back and forth aggressively, sending the animal scurrying downward into its dwelling. For good measure, he lit and threw a flask of oil after the animal.

Once he was safely away from the hole, he continued along the passageway until it ended in a large circular room with a square hole directly in the middle and four stone pillars at each corner. Before moving ahead, he held the torch aloft and carefully scanned the room for any sign of hidden danger. With the scabbard remaining unchanged, he crept closer toward the hole and felt something was amiss with the room. It was like a presence, but nothing tangible, which frightened him to the point that he halted his progress to look around several times.

After he reached the hole, he held the torch closer to the opening and saw the skeletal remains of a humanoid creature, wearing tattered leather armor and a metal helm strapped to his head. A pouch tied to the corpse's belt, enticed him enough to climb down into the shallow grave and investigate further. As he reached for the pouch, a bright light suddenly appeared on his left and took the shape of a male figure, which floated in his direction. The entity radiated cold that struck Torhan with dread, and he was unable to move.

"Shoel is that you?" The entity said in an ethereal voice.

Torhan could not respond.

"Shoel I've been hiding and waiting for you." The ghost moved closer and then realized Torhan wasn't Shoel. "You're not Shoel."

The spirit reached out and touched Torhan's left shoulder, sending painful chills deep throughout his body.

"Who are you?" The ghost demanded, causing the scabbard to glow.

Torhan somehow managed to overcome his fears, climbed out of the hole, and started running towards the exit. The spirit followed for a few feet and shouted. "WHERE'S SHOEL?"

Torhan ran as fast as he could until he reached the main room and slammed the door shut. He stood there, rooted, until the feeling of dread finally left him.

Hoping to have better luck with the next room, he went to Trusten's door and went to work on the lock. After the tumblers fell into place and the door opened inwardly, he entered the corridor and just like the last, it twisted and turned until it ended in a circular room with a hole directly in the middle. The only difference with this one was that the hole was round and there was a lone pillar several feet beyond it.

He scanned the room and when he felt safe, he walked toward the center. The closer he moved to the hole, the colder it felt. It was a different feeling then the coldness Ruder projected. It felt like the coldest day winter had to offer. After reaching the opening, he peered down and saw the remains of a humanoid skeleton, dressed in tattered red traveling clothes and laying in the fetal position. In the skeleton's bony left hand, he saw a pouch snuggled inside, prompting him to climb down. As he reached for the bag, a female voice moaned loudly, startling him and causing him to look up to see an ethereal form of a female in a dress floating over to him.

The entity emitted a chilling effect that prevented his legs and arms from moving.

"Rhold is that you my love? I miss you very much. Where have you been?" She asked and moved into the hole, floating directly in front of him.

Torhan could not respond, and the specter stared at him waiting for an answer.

Trusten held his gaze for several seconds before speaking. *"Rhold, please answer me."*

Torhan took a deep breath, steadied himself and then found his voice. "I'm not Rhold."

The ghost's eyes lowered. *"Stop lying to me. You're my beloved Rhold. I love you more than life itself."* The spirit reached out and touched Torhan's chest, causing him to feel her anguish. So great was the emotion that he fell to a knee and started crying. *"Rhold I love you."*

"I'm sorry, but I'm not him." Torhan said, sobbing.

Trusten's facial expression suddenly changed to one of anger. *"IF YOU'RE NOT RHOLD THEN WHO ARE YOU? GET OUT!"* She boomed at him and then shoved Torhan to the ground, causing the scabbard to glow and the dagger to attack her.

Torhan scooted away, clawed his way out of the hole, and ran out of the room, leaving behind the torch. With only the glow of the scabbard to lead him, he ran with his hands out in front to help navigate his way back to the main room. As soon as he entered, the feeling of despair left him and the dagger returned to the scabbard, and stopped glowing. It occurred to him that the spirits might be bestow their feelings on him if they were enraged, so he would be cautious if he encountered another spirit in the next chamber.

The lock housing the room of the thief named Binder opened fairly easily, and after the door was opened, he lit another torch and entered. The corridor eventually ended in another circular room with a square hole in the middle and nine candlesticks surrounding it. He studied the area, and it dawned on him that maybe the four pillars in the first room, the one in the second, and the nine candlesticks in this one, might be the numbers to the combination on Shoel's lock.

Seeing no reason to go any further, he walked back to the main room, picked the lock on the fourth door and entered. This corridor ended in a rectangular room with a square hole in the middle of the room and nothing else. Because there wasn't anything visible to indicate a number, he approached the hole and peered down. Inside, there were the remains of a humanoid skeleton wearing chainmail and a small bag. He was about to jump down and grab the bag when a white cloud materialized. It took the shape of a female warrior wearing armor and held a very dangerous looking sword in her left hand.

"Get away from my grave, or I will kill you, living one." Her voice was like winter wind whispering through dried leaves and gave Torhan the impression that, in life, she was someone in command. Torhan's scabbard glowed and he took two steps away from the hole, heeding the entity's wishes.

"Why do you disturb my rest mortal?" She stopped a few feet away, holding her weapon in a threatening fashion.

Torhan was leery of this spirit, because he wasn't sure if she could hurt him, so he chose his words carefully.

"Spirit, I apologize for disturbing your rest. I only seek something called an amulet of REM."

"REST. You call this rest. Leave here before I decide to kill you and trap your soul with mine forever."

"Do you know where the amulet is?" He pressed.

"Living one, I don't care what you need. My time has passed, and the affairs of the living are no longer my business." She started emitting rage, causing the scabbard's glow to intensify.

"Please Aplone, help me." Torhan addressed her by name hoping it would make a difference.

She raised her weapon and poised to strike him. *"Leave now."*

Torhan obliged her wishes and did so.

On his way back to the room, he thought about the combination lock to Shoel's door. He was pretty sure the pillars and candlesticks made up the first three numbers, but the fourth room didn't have anything except for the hole. He moved over to Shoel's door and pushed the digits on the lock in the following order; four, one, and nine. The last number would have to be a guess, so he started with zero, and as soon as he heard the lock click and the door open; he knew that he guessed correctly. Proud of himself for figuring it out, he entered the passageway and followed it until it ended in a small square room with a large circular hole in the middle.

He did his routine of scanning the area before walking over. At the bottom of the hole was a skeleton in rusted armor holding a small metal chest. He thought about the other rooms and how the ghosts usually appeared when he tried to take whatever was in the hole, but he climbed down anyway.

The small coffer had a number pad with twice as many numbers as the door. He knew the combination would be far too great to guess, so he decided to steal it instead and have Katara help him open it. Placing both hands on the chest, he lifted, and couldn't budge it. After several more failed attempts, he studied the chest. Even though he couldn't find anything holding it in place, he knew there had to be something that was hidden from his sight. He tried using his sword and moved only slightly. As he was trying again, an entity materialized and floated over.

"YOU WILL NEVER TAKE MY CHEST MORTAL" The spirit boomed.

Startled, Torhan looked up and saw a very tall man wearing platemail and carrying a long sword strapped across his back. Torhan felt rage emanating from this entity and backed away, tripping over the skeleton and falling down. His scabbard glowed, and he was again stricken with fear and unable to move.

The ghost entered the hole and hovered slightly above him. *"MANY HAVE TRIED AND FAILED TO TAKE WHAT'S MINE. YOU WILL BE NO DIFFERENT THIEF. BEFORE YOU DIE, TELL ME WHY YOU HAVE COME TO MY TOMB AND DISTURBED MY REST?"*

Torhan was unable to speak, and the ghost grew angrier.

"FEEL MY WRAITH AND KNOW THAT YOU WILL BE TRAPPED HERE WITH ME FOREVER IN MY WORLD." The entity unsheathed his weapon and held it high over its head poised to strike.

The glow from Torhan's scabbard intensified and sent forth the dagger to protect its master. As the blade sailed through the ghost's body, the entity paused and looked rather amused as he watched the dagger pass through him.

Torhan found his voice and spoke. "I'm not here to disturb your rest."

The ghost, still entertained by the dagger, did not respond.

"Shoel I am not here to steal your treasure."

The spirit looked at Torhan again. *"IT SURE LOOKS THAT WAY TO ME, THIEF."*

"I only need to borrow the amulet of REM, not steal it. I promise to return it when I am finished."

The spirit lowered its sword and calmed its voice. *"Why do you need my amulet?"*

"A child named Sybil fell into a deep sleep, and I was charged with bringing her out of it."

The scabbard's glow began to diminish, and the dagger returned to its home.

The spirit of Shoel hovered silently for several moments before speaking. *"Mortal if you allow me to read your thoughts and only if your intentions are as you say, I might consider your request."*

Torhan wasn't sure if wanted him to do so, but considering he didn't have a choice; he agreed.

"Open your thoughts to me."

Torhan did and Shoel probed his mind and saw everything he had experienced over the last few weeks.

"I see that you had dealings with the demon kind, and your intentions are as you say regarding the child, but much is hidden from you. Mortal, you are so easily led by material things that you can't see what people are using you for." He paused to allow his words to settle and then continued. *"A long time ago, I was led the same way you are, and eventually it resulted in my death and entrapment here in this tomb. Tread lightly and watch anyone you come in contact with, or you too may end up as I have."*

"What am I supposed to do to prevent this?"

"Do? Your choices define who you are, so be warned that if you help certain people, they might harm you for their greater gain. Just like the demons walking around in your world who will stop at nothing to achieve their ultimate goals."

Torhan reflected on his words.

"I need you to do something for me mortal. You have already met my spirit brothers and sisters. If you can free their souls from this place, I will look very favorably upon you and give you the combination to the chest."

"How am I supposed to do that?"

"You need to convince them they don't belong here any longer."

"And if I can't?"

"You already know the answer." And with that said, Shoel vaporized, leaving Torhan alone again.

Torhan walked back to the main room thinking about the ghosts, their plights and what he must do in order to put them to rest. "Ruder appears to be waiting for Shoel. Maybe he thinks they were separated during one of their missions. I could convince him that Shoel is dead and won't be coming for him. Trusten misses her husband, so I think that I'll to convince her that he did come back, and she is the one who died. It appears Aplone is aware of what she has become, so I need to think about her situation." Torhan decided that Ruder would be the easiest to deal with first.

He walked down the hallway, passed the badger's home without incident, entered Ruder's chamber and climbed into the hole. He reached for the pouch and a few seconds later; a light materialized, took the shape of Ruder and then floated over.

"Shoel is that you?" The ghost asked.

"Ruder, I'm here to deliver a message to you. Shoel isn't coming."

"What do you mean not coming? I've been waiting for him for a long time. He told me to wait right here until things settled down."

"Tell me what happened and I'll try to explain." Torhan said, knowing he was onto something.

The ghost bowed his head. *"We were searching for a child, and… and… I can't remember anything else."* The spirit raised his head and looked around frantically. *"Where's Shoel?"*

"Ruder, you died."

"Dead? I don't believe you. You lie."

"Look around, do you recognize this place?"

Ruder did so. *"We were just in the woods searching for…"* The ghost paused. *"Where am I?"*

"You are in your final resting place, and this is your body." Torhan pointed to the skeleton.

"Am I really dead?" He asked sounding so sad.

"I'm afraid so."

"What am I supposed to do?"

"Let go of this world, and you'll find peace."

"But my family needs me."

"You can't go to them any longer. You need to wait for them on the other side."

"Will they come to me?"

"When it's their time, I'm sure of it."

Ruder closed his eyes and vaporized. With his disappearance, the room took on a different feel, and Torhan knew that he was finally gone. Before leaving, Torhan searched the skeleton and found a diamond encrusted dagger sheathed at his side and a black onyx ring on one of his bony fingers. The pouch contained several gold pieces and a red ruby gem.

After pocketing his find, he walked back to the main room and entered Trusten's chamber. After climbing down into the hole, he thought about what he was going to say, and then reached for the pouch. The spirit materialized off to the right and then floated over.

"Rhold is that you my love? I miss you very much. Where have you been?" She said and entered the hole. Once again, he could feel her chilling emotions radiating from her ethereal form and they grew stronger the closer she came.

"It is me Trusten." Torhan answered.

"What took you so long to come back?"

"I'm afraid that you have passed on into the afterlife, and it took me a long time to find your spirit."

"I don't understand."

"You had a terrible accident and died."

"I couldn't have. I'm right here in front of you."

"Look around. Is this our home?"

She looked around in obvious confusion. *"Where am I?"*

"You were lost to me a few years ago and somehow your spirit is bound to this place."

"I want to be with you again."

"And I want to be with you too, but we can't right now."

"Why not? Tell me this is a dream"

"I wish that it was."

"Where were you when it happened? Why didn't you save me?" She sounded sad and scared.

He looked at her intently. "I was away when it happened, and I'm sorry that I couldn't have saved you."

"I miss you. You are my one true love."

"I need you to find peace and let go, so that when it's my time I can join you. I'm afraid that if you don't we won't be together in the hereafter."

She looked even sadder. *"How my love?"*

"Let go of this world and be at peace."

"Promise me you'll come for me when it's your time."

"I will."

She hovered, staring at him for a few minutes. *"I will be waiting for you on the other side."*

"I look forward to that day."

She smiled and dissipated.

Torhan waited a few minutes before taking the pouch. Inside he found a few gold pieces and a blue ruby stone. On his way back, he decided that one day he would find her husband and let him know what had happened to her.

He entered Aplone's eternal prison and entered her grave. The entity appeared, floated over, and said. *"Mortal why have you returned? I told you that I would take your life if you did."* She unsheathed her blade and Torhan's scabbard glowed.

"I am here to help you find peace."

"Find peace? You're an odd one, living one. How do you plan to do that?"

"I spoke to Shoel and he said that as long as I help his friends find rest; he will give me what I need."

"Shoel is a fool. He's the reason why I'm in this mess in the first place."

"Nonetheless, I am here to help you. You shouldn't be trapped in the world of the living any longer."

Aplone held her position. *"How do you propose on doing that?"*

"Not sure. Tell me what happened to you?"

"There isn't much to tell. The last thing that I remember was Shoel leading us on a quest to find something that I no longer recall, and the next moment; I was down here guarding my remains."

"Do you know who killed you?"

"I only remember the beast that did. A strange-looking creature with the upper body of an ape and the lower half of a horse."

"I know of such a beast and who might be responsible for your death."

"Who?"

"Was it a hermit named Tole?"

"The name is familiar. Yes, I remember him. He was the one that sent us on the quest and when we returned he attacked our group."

"Do you think if I bring him to justice you might find rest?"

"I don't know, but knowing he was; I might find some peace. Would you avenge my death living one?"

"I will."

"Thank you. You may take my pouch if that helps you bring him to justice."

Torhan did and left. On his way back, he opened the pouch and found several platinum coins and a green emerald gem, which he figured must be worth a few thousand gold pieces.

He returned to Binder's room and stopped at the edge of the hole. His gaze fell upon a twisted and broken skeleton wearing leather armor and boots. A bulky pouch was tied around his waist, and his jaw was set in a position which could have indicated that he must have died in some horrible fashion. When he was through studying the remains, he jumped down. As soon as he reached for the pouch, a spirit appeared in the shape of an overweight man wearing robes. The ghost groaned in a painful wail and stopped directly overhead, staring down at him.

"Mortal why I am here? I don't recognize this place." He looked around. "I should have found rest after I died, so why am I here?"

"Binder if you tell me what happened I might be able to figure out why you're still here."

"The last thing I remember was that I was with Shoel and the others, we came upon a grove and were attacked by this creature that was a cross between a horse and an ape."

"I know of such a beast and the one who is responsible for your death."

"You do?"

"He's a hermit named Tole. Aplone is bound to another room, and I think that if I bring him to justice you will both be able to find rest."

"Aplone is here? What about the others; Ruder, Trusten, and Shoel?"

"They are. Ruder and Trusten have already found peace."

"Why them and not us?"

"I'm not sure, but I think they never realized they were already dead, so I convinced them to find rest. On the other hand, you, Aplone, and Shoel are all aware that you have died."

"Help me please. I hate this place."

"I will do my best." Torhan said, and Binder faded away.

Torhan reentered Shoel's chamber, and the room felt colder and looked darker than before, despite the glow of the torch. He ignored his discomfort and walked straight up to the grave and called the spirit by his name. The entity appeared within seconds and floated over.

"Mortal I sense that you have not completed what I asked of you."

"Ruder and Trusten have found peace."

"What about Binder and Aplone?"

"Like you, they are aware of their existence, so I don't know how."

"Then I cannot allow you to have the amulet."

"Shoel, did a hermit named Tole kill you?"

"He was one of them. How did you know?"

"I figured it out after speaking to Aplone and Binder. Who are the..."

Just then they heard a low rumble come from somewhere above and then stop a few minutes later.

"What was that?" Torhan asked.

"It appears someone has closed the entrance to the tomb, and you will now be trapped here with me for all of eternity."

Torhan's face turned white at the thought of being trapped down there. "Is there another way out?"

"Why should I help you mortal? You failed my task."

"Tole is up above and I think if he dies you might find peace."

"You might be right mortal. Do I have your word that you will bring him here, alive or dead?"

"Yes."

"There's a small lever at the far end of the chamber. It will reveal a passageway that will take you to the outside."

"You will have him before this day ends."

Torhan ran over to the wall, found and pulled the lever, and quickly ran up the passageway. His path abruptly ended at another wall with a lever on his left, which he pushed down, causing the stone façade to slide open, revealing the outside world.

****

Shortly after Torhan descended below, Tole began plotting the death of Katara. He studied her intently while she was looking away, and every time she suspected something; he would quickly turn his head in another direction. He was pretty sure she was some sort of low level healer and the only problem he foresaw was from that mace of hers. His plan was simple. Conjure a Water Tirip from the black sludge and have it attack her. If she tried to stop him, she would have to deal with his pet. After she was dead, he would move the stump back into place and lock Torhan below and then wait for him to die of starvation. In time, he would send another fool to collect the stone off of his lifeless body.

After catching Tole eyeing her suspiciously on several occasions, Katara devised a plan of her own. She knew that she could kill him with her mace, but she wasn't sure about the cat. She needed to even the odds, and since she couldn't risk conjuring a Water Tirip, she began walking around looking for a few fallen logs to summon a Wooden Tirip. When she found the materials needed to raise her protector, she unhooked her mace and began chanting. She was almost through, when the big cat suddenly appeared ten-feet away.

His ears were pinned back and he hissed in warning at her, both were signs that he might attack. Her heart raced as she sped up the chant and then out of the corner of her eye the cat leapt at her. It happened so fast that the only thing she could do was whip her right arm upward, catch the cat in the side of the head and crack its skull. The lethal blow, however, did nothing to stop the cat's momentum as it crashed into her, sending her tumbling to the ground. It took a few minutes for her head to clear, and once it did, she looked over at the wood and began chanting again.

Before the cat decided to attack Katara, Tole moved closer to the water and began summoning the Water Tirip. It was taking longer than he expected, but he knew that it would be worth it. He loved seeing the faces of his enemies as water filled their lungs and body parts were shattered and broken apart from the force of the spirit's blows. The mad hermit smiled with each spoken word and when he was finished, the guardian took shape from the pool of stagnant water and looked at its owner, awaiting his command.

Tole spoke only one final word to it. "Kill."

The Tirip rose to its full height of eight-feet, scanned the area until it saw its victim, and then sent a few water balls at Katara. The dense water would've hit her, but she was positioned in such a way, they hit a log instead.

She finished her own chant and when her guardian stood erect, she uttered the command of protection. Instinctively, the Water Tirip recognized its mortal enemy and advanced. Katara crawled behind her protector to the sound of Tole's curses for not conjuring the right spirit. If he had summoned an Air Tirip instead, it would've made short work of her puny protector. Disgusted, Tole walked over to the stump and pushed it in the opposite direction. With a mighty rumble, the crypt moaned and lowered into the earth, sealing Torhan below.

The battle raged on a few yards away as the Tirips clashed with each other. Every time the Water Tirip attacked, the Wooden Tirip blocked and countered with massive swings from its thick arms, splitting the water creature apart and damaging the spirit.

Katara scampered further away and watched her guardian slowly winning the battle, but something strange was happening as well. The Wooden Tirip, on several occasions, turned towards her and started advancing, but as soon as it did, it was struck by the Water Tirip and turned around again to embrace its enemy. Her worst fears were taking shape, and she was sure that if it wasn't for the Water Tirip, her own guardian would have turned on her by now. Katara began backing away while digging around in her backpack for her flasks of oil, just in case it happened.

Tole knew what the outcome would be, and walked away until he found an open area with a large ditch and did the unthinkable. He was warned early in his training that conjuring another Tirip while one was already under his control could be disastrous, but he was so mad that he didn't care and began chanting once again. Once he finished, a massive swirling wind appeared out of nothing and formed a deadly Air Tirip. The creature blinked its two small dots that were eyes and as soon as Tole gave the command to seek, the Water Tirip disengaged its assault against the Wooden Tirip, and began rolling back towards Tole with hatred for being summoned into this plane.

After the Water Tirip left, the Wooden Tirip fought hard against the constant pull of its alignment changing, until the draw was too strong, and it now saw Katara as an enemy and advanced on her. When Katara lost control, she was left with two choices. Destroy the Tirip or pledge her loyalty to evil and change her alignment. On one hand if she destroyed her protector, she'd be too weak to conjure another one, and pledging evil would be even more disastrous, especially if she conjured another Tirip, and wasn't true to her new alignment. The Wooden Tirip closed in, and she made up her mind.

Meanwhile, the Air Tirip swirled past the Water Tirip, on its way to kill Katara, while the Water spirit rolled towards its former master. Tole saw it coming straight for him and when the Water spirit was close enough, it sent a wave of water after Tole. Fortunately, for him, he was positioned in front of a deep trench and shortly after, the wave poured harmlessly into the ditch. The Water Tirip followed and became trapped. Tole still possessed enough control over the spirit to stay its water balls and easily walked past the helpless entity, knowing that the spirit's host would eventually dry up and dissipate.

Except for the flasks of oil, Katara was defenseless against the Wooden Tirip. She knew that her mace would serve no purpose against its hard bark, so she lit the flask and threw it at its trunk. It shattered against the surface and ignited the tree. She added another flask to make sure it would die and then caught a glimpse of something swirling in her direction.

****

Torhan entered the forest, quickly figured out where the crypt was and ran in that direction. When he came upon the area, he saw Tole and ducked behind a tree. He couldn't believe what was happening. There was a Tirip on fire, another lapping helplessly against a ditch, trying to reach for Tole, and something that looked like a pair of eyes, suspended in midair and swirling toward Katara. He had to do something about the hermit. He took the bow from around his shoulder and notched an arrow. Taking aim, he fired. Tole sensed Torhan's presence too late and when he turned around, the arrow pierced his throat. Before the fateful impact, he uttered only one word, "Impossible," and then fell over, clutching the gaping wound until he died.

While Katara frantically ran looking for some place to contain the Air Tirip, she was hit in her back with a gust of air that sent her to the ground in pain. The Air Tirip took up position just above her head, swirled counter clockwise and began drawing the air from her lungs. Katara began gasping for air, and her lungs began burning like the fires of hell, until she couldn't breathe any longer and passed out. The Tirip continued to swirl, and as it was in the process of removing the last bit of air from her lungs, Tole died, causing it to dissipate.

Torhan found her unconscious and was relieved that she was uninjured. He lightly slapped her on the face until she opened her eyes.

"Where's Tole?" She asked, almost in a panic.

"Dead." He replied and helped her to a sitting position.

He told her what had happened in the crypt and how Tole was responsible for the deaths of the spirits. She was amazed at what he'd accomplished. After he helped Katara to her feet, they retrieved the amulet off of Tole's lifeless body and carried him down into the crypt below. Torhan told her what to expect from the spirit and for her not to be afraid. Despite his words of caution, she still prayed to her god for good measure.

After entering Shoel's room, Torhan dropped Tole's body into the shallow grave next to Shoel's skeleton. A few minutes later, Shoel materialized and moved closer.

"I never thought that I would see him again." Shoel said and floated around Tole's body, inspecting the corpse. *"Torhan you have done well."*

"Did Aplone and Binder find rest?" Torhan asked.

Shoel paused and then said. *"They have, because the one that killed them is dead."*

"What about you, will you find rest?"

"No."

"Why not?" Katara asked.

"Because he wasn't the only one that took my life."

"Who was the other?"

"I cannot say."

"Why not?" She pressed.

"The laws that bind me here do not allow it."

Katara had an idea how find out who did or to at least get a clue. "Shoel, will you tell us what happened to you and how you ended up here?"

The spirit looked at her and then spoke. *"Many years ago when I, along with my brothers and sisters, roamed your plane of existence; we were trackers. We traveled to many towns offering our services and help right what was wrong. One day, we came to the town of Snowdrift and were hired to capture a suspect and bring him to justice. We found him and his accomplice, Tole, inside of a grove and together they murdered us and placed our bodies down here behind the locked doors."*

"Shoel what did he look like?" Katara asked

"I'm sorry living one, I cannot say."

"Shoel was it a priest?" Torhan asked.

"Torhan you are wise, but no."

"Shoel we will figure out who did this, and you will find peace." Torhan stated firmly.

"Torhan the just, if you should eliminate those who did this to me, I will be eternally grateful. Now for your reward. The combination to the chest is as follows. Press the numbers six, five, four, and then press the letters A, P, and L, and finally the number two."

"Shoel I have one more question. How did you come to guard this chest?"

"I don't know, but after I died, the chest was in my grave, and I was bound to protect it."

Torhan climbed down and pressed the numbers and letters in the order Shoel suggested and opened the chest. There was only one item inside, a silver amulet with a medallion. Etched on the round circle was the image of a male human's face with his eyes closed. Without even thinking, he placed it around his neck, felt dizzy right away and passed out.

Upon seeing him fall; Katara jumped down and removed the

necklace from around his neck. A few seconds later, Torhan woke up.

"What happened?" He asked.

"I don't know."

Shoel floated closer. *"It appears your mind is too weak to wear the amulet."*

"Let me try." Katara said.

Before Torhan could stop her, she placed it around her neck. Instead of succumbing to the same effect Torhan went through, her mind began filling up with images of life and death, visions so strong that she fell to one knee. Torhan was about to remove the item when she waved him off, indicating that she was okay and stood up. "I'm fine. We should go."

"What happened?"

"I don't want to talk about it." She took off the amulet and put it away.

"Shoel, we will do our best." Torhan said.

"Good luck Torhan."

After they were gone, Shoel said an ancient chant. The room filled with smoke and a foul poison that would fell any mortal exposed to it. The smoke shifted and eventually took the shape of a person wearing a robe.

"Tole my old friend it's nice to see you again. Please take your rightful place."

Tole's spirit floated and hovered towards the entity and then screamed at the realization of what was happening.

"Did you really think that you would ever own that amulet again? You made a wise choice in picking those two; he's clever, and she has the mental capacity to don the item."

Tole's spirit just floated and was unable to speak.

"Now you will remain here with me." Shoel began to laugh, and Tole's spirit was sent to one of the other chambers to stay there for eternity.

Chapter 7: The Truth

By the time they left the crypt and were headed back to town, the sky was dark, the weather colder, and a light snow began falling. They were each lost in their own thoughts when Katara suddenly spoke.

"Did you think a few months ago that you would have done something like that?" She asked.

"What do you mean?"

"Speaking with the dead."

"Before this journey, I never really believed in the hereafter; let alone, ghosts."

Katara smirked. "Keep the faith because there's more to life than what we are."

"What do you think the amulet of Insight does? I'm sure it doesn't have anything to do with Tole's family history."

"Given his lies, I agree. I think it might contain some sort of power."

"I wonder what though. Should we test it out?"

"Maybe later after we make camp. Where are your furs?" Katara asked realizing for the first time since they left the crypt that he wasn't wearing any.

Torhan stopped and looked back in the direction from where they'd come. "I think that I left them inside of the crypt."

"Do you want to go back we're not that far?"

"I should be fine as long as the ring stays active."

"Are you sure?"

Torhan nodded, and they continued.

It was around mid-evening when they stopped and lit a small fire. The temperature grew even colder and Torhan felt a slight chill. He knew that the ring was losing its charge. Upon seeing him shiver, Katara opened her coat and sat close to him, wrapping her furs around the both of them.

"You're going to get cold." She said.

"I'll be fine, as long as we huddle closer together for warmth." Torhan smiled at her.

"I should keep my furs to myself." She smiled back.

"And let me freeze?"

"I'm not the one who left his stuff behind."

"I'll buy you dinner the next time we eat."

"I'm holding you to that."

Torhan removed the ring and placed it near the fire, and then sat down again. "That fortune teller was right about some of the cards."

"Really? Which ones?"

"I think the one with the gravestone and burnt tree meant Fefantor, and the one of the mouth and pair of eyes was about the spirits in the crypt."

"You might be right, but don't forget most fortune tellers just make up stuff in order to get your money." Katara opened her backpack and took out some food.

Torhan opened his pack. "Look at what I found." He proudly stated and handed a gem to her.

Katara's eyes lit up. "It's beautiful." She simply said and held it to the light of the fire. By the way the light reflected in the stone, she could tell it was worth a small fortune. "Can I have it?"

"Sure, I have another. Here take this ring."

"You don't want it either?"

Torhan shook his head.

The black onyx stone was flawless, and the silver band had strange markings etched around the circumference. "I wonder if it's magical." She put it on and waited. When nothing happened, she frowned and took it off. "Well at least it will fetch a nice price." She said and slipped it into her pouch.

Torhan took out Tole's amulet and the stone. Immediately, the rock glowed in response to being near the amulet, and like an attraction born of desire, he could feel them pulling closer to each other. He positioned the stone inside one of the five slots, and it locked into place by itself. Surprising them both,

"Are you going to put it on?" She asked.

He nodded and did so.

At first nothing happened then he found himself drifting upwards, high above their camp. He looked down and saw himself and Katara sitting together on the log and quickly realized that he wasn't physically floating in the air, but his mind was projecting that he was. He turned his gaze upward again and hovered there, looking far out into the distance and then suddenly; he thought about Jacko and took flight. He flew through the air at unheard of speeds until he arrived inside of a forest, which looked strangely familiar to him. He came upon two people tied to a tree facing each other. The person on his left had his head down and appeared to be unconscious. He looked to be the same build as Jacko. Torhan moved closer, and his worst fears were confirmed; it was him. The other person on his right was a tall, thin man, with a long beard, wearing dark-green robes soaked in blood. Torhan figured by the way he was dressed it was either a classmate or possibly a teacher.

He waited for something to happen and a short time later it did, when three figures, escorted by a dozen boarmen, entered the area. One was from the fox race; another was from the goat race, and the last was a human. All were armed and dressed in different manners of occupations.

They walked over to their prisoners, checked their restraints, and then spoke to one another. Torhan realized that he must be invisible to them and moved closer to eavesdrop. To his surprise, he was unable to hear them as well. They spoke for some time until finally the goatman walked over and slapped Jacko in the face until he stirred, and then the human took his place.

He began asking him questions, and Torhan could tell his friend was replying adamantly. The human pointed to Jacko's classmate, and his companions laughed. More words were exchanged between the captors, and the fox creature took out a handgun-crossbow and showed it to the others. The human grabbed the gun and presented it to Jacko. After a brief exchange of words, the human backhanded him in the face and then mouthed something to the fox, who left with the boarmen. Jacko taunted his captors further, and this time; the goatman exchanged words with him and raised his pike in a throwing way. Torhan couldn't understand what his friend was trying to accomplish until his classmate, now free of his bonds, killed the goatman and then fell on the human, striking him with several powerful blows. After he was dead, Jacko was freed of his restraints and sent on his way. The scene ended, and Torhan was whisked back to the campfire.

"Are you okay?" Katara asked staring at Jacko's blank facial expression.

"How long was I away?" He replied blinking a few times.

"Away? You were here the entire time. What happened?"

Torhan was about to answer, when a trickle of blood suddenly ran down from his nose, and he swayed back and forth. Katara steadied him and wiped the blood away with a piece of cloth.

"Are you alright?" She asked.

"I don't feel good. I'm really tired."

Katara cleared a small area and then escorted her friend over and wrapped him snugly in her furs.

"Better?" She asked.

"Thanks."

"Can you tell me what you experienced?"

He nodded and told her what he saw in the vision.

"Do you think your friend is alright?" She asked when he was through.

"I think so. I'm pretty sure the events happened a few weeks ago before I left Redden."

"How do you know that?"

"He was going for a promotion, and the other person looked like a teacher. I'm really tired."

"I'll be over there." She said and returned to the log.

Katara gazed into the crackling fire and thought about her life and the man who slept a few feet away. He was a good person with the ability to make her feel safe. She wondered if she could ever love once again after the way her last lover had treated her. The physical and mental abuse he caused was so bad that she vowed if anyone did that again to her, they would find themselves a cripple or worse.

Her thoughts changed to her family and how she missed them, especially her father who died many years ago. He was not only her father, but her mentor and biggest supporter. Her yearning to see him again, or just to relive a day in the past, gave her the idea to try Tole's amulet. Maybe it could do that for her, after all, Torhan believed he was reliving the past when he'd used it.

She took out the amulet, studied the relic and then began tracing her fingers over the item. She wanted to have an experience like Torhan did and placed it around her neck and thought hard about her father. At first, nothing happened, and then suddenly; she was lifted high above the camp. The sensation of floating in the air felt so real to her; she actually believed she was flying. She looked around and saw the lights from the town of Snowdrift several miles away. She thought about her father again, and suddenly she was sailing through the air until she arrived at her childhood home.

The place, as always, was warm and inviting in the spring, with the flowers in full bloom and the vines creeping their way up and down the sides of the cottage. She was a bit puzzled as to why she did not hear birds chirping, the sounds that bugs make while mating or the fact that she couldn't smell anything either.

While pondering this abnormality, the front door opened and her father dressed in field clothes and carrying a small scythe in one hand and a bucket in the other, came walking out. He stopped and turned around, as if someone called to him from within the cottage, and then mouthed something back and smiled just as a little girl, with long curly, blonde, hair and worker clothes, ran and jumped into his arms.

Katara realized right away it was her as a child, and it brought tears to her eyes. The hug between father and daughter lasted for a long time and after a short exchange of words, they walked off toward the fields with grown-up Katara following. Younger Katara and her father stopped when they reached the wheat fields and after a brief exchange of words, she moved out of the way so that her father could work. His technique was effortless as he used the scythe to cut through the wheat stalks.

After mowing down a few yards, he stopped to speak with his daughter. They smiled and laughed, and then younger Katara ran over and hugged him again. Older Katara's heart filled with love and happiness, and she smiled and said silent words telling her father that she loved him very dearly. The simple, yet, enjoyable scene played on until the day turned into dusk, and her father gathered the crops and walked back to the cottage.

In the next instant, the vision was over, and she awoke with a start. She found herself still sitting upright on the log and felt a trickle of blood running down from her nose and into her mouth. A small headache, fatigue, and a feeling of being bone weary followed a few seconds later. After wiping away the blood and removing the amulet, she got up, lay down next to Torhan and wrapped herself in the same furs he was using. He stirred briefly, but did not wake, and after she was situated, she fell asleep within minutes.

They woke up shortly after daybreak to the sound of the birds chirping in nearby trees. Both were feeling fine after their ordeals and hungry. While they were eating, Katara shared her experiences with him and Torhan, although happy for her, didn't like the idea that she used it without him watching over her. She acknowledged his discomfort and agreed not to do that again without him.

"I am starting to understand why this amulet was so important to Tole." Torhan stated.

"How so?"

"If this stone allows you to see the past, I think the others might enable you to foresee the future."

"You might be right and if you are, then this is one powerful relic and should be locked away or destroyed."

"I think Priest Piersum and Molech are the others responsible for Shoel's death."

"I think so too, but we need to be sure. I don't want to accuse the priest if we don't know for sure."

"We'll question him after we wake Sybil."

"We need to be careful. We're dealing with another priest, and we don't want the townspeople turning on us." Torhan paused. "So I think if he is involved, then we sneak him out, bring him to Shoel and let him deal with him."

"How do you want to do that? If anyone sees us then they'll grow suspicious."

"We'll visit him tonight."

"Sounds like a plan; let's hope it works, because I'd really hate to be wanted in two towns."

They finished eating, collected their belongings, and walked back to Snowdrift at a slower than normal pace. Along the way, they rehearsed their plan and arrived at the town just as the sun was setting. When nightfall was upon them, they had drawn their hoods tightly around their heads and used the pathway behind the houses until they arrived at Priest Piersum's house. After checking the front to make sure no one saw them, they knocked on the door.

A few minutes later, the door swung open and Priest Piersum was standing there with a surprised look on his face. "My friends, you've returned." He said smiling.

Torhan could tell his smile was a fake one.

"Please come in you must be cold." Piersum said and led them to the dining room table. "Would you like some tea?"

"That would be great." Katara answered for the both of them.

"You have to tell me everything." Piersum said as he was pouring the tea.

"We found Tole and you were right he was a bit crazed. We convinced him to help our cause, and after he led us to a crypt, we retrieved the amulet."

Priest Piersum's facial expression changed. "Just like that? It was that easy?"

"You sound surprised." Katara said.

"I just thought it would've been dangerous."

"We're not saying It wasn't, but we'll keep the details to ourselves."

"Where's the amulet of REM?"

Katara took it out and showed it to him.

The priest's eyes lit up. "Can I hold it?"

She handed it to him.

"I'd never thought that I would see this day. Hopefully, it will work." Piersum stated.

"Now what?" Torhan asked.

"Someone needs to wear it and enter her mind."

"How does it work?"

"I'm not sure." Priest Piersum flatly said.

"Do you want to use it?" Katara asked Piersum.

"Sadly, I can't. My beliefs do not permit me to wear such a device." He handed the amulet back to her.

"Are you ready?" Katara said to Torhan.

He stood up and said. "Let's go save a child."

They followed the priest to Sybil's room. Piersum sat down in a chair directly across from the bed, while Katara and Torhan knelt beside the bed.

They exchanged looks. "I'll do it." Katara said.

"Are you sure about this?"

She nodded and placed the amulet around her neck.

"If something goes wrong, I'll remove the amulet. Okay?"

"Make sure you do." She said and turned her attention toward Sybil and began concentrating on helping her.

At first, nothing happened, and then all at once; the amulet glowed; the room began to spin and darken, and the feeling of everything closing in on her began.

In a blink of an eye, Katara found herself standing alone in an open field. Everything from the sky to the flowers and trees were bathed in dull grayness. Just ahead there was a small Keep surrounded by many trees. She walked toward the building, and by the time she was halfway there, lightning ripped across the sky, and thunder boomed loudly. Instinctively, she looked around and when she turned back toward the Keep, a demon-like creature of medium size was standing a few yards away from her. Its sudden appearance startled her.

"What are you doing in my domain?" The monster hissed and waved its elongated arms at her.

"I'm here for Sybil." She answered.

The creature cocked its head from side to side. "She is in my care now, so leave." He said grinning.

Katara went to grab her mace and realized that she was weaponless.

"I SAID LEAVE." The creature barked.

The being terrified her. She was about to back up, when a voice whispered in her mind and told her to stay put. Finding the courage she did and said. "I'm not leaving while you are still here."

The creature raised his arms, waved them in a pattern, and from out of thin air, daggers, too many to count, appeared and were pointed directly at her. He hissed and sent them. The same voice, whispered the word "shield". Katara thought of one and an invisible force field rose up and deflected the daggers away.

Frustrated, the creature conjured up a small swirling whirlwind and sent that at her. The voice whispered the word "redirect" and when she thought of pushing it away, the wind tunnel was cast aside.

"You will fail." The demon said and disappeared.

With the amulet protecting her, Katara felt as though she could save the child and continued. The closer she got to the building; the more lightning lit up the landscape and thunder rumbled overhead. As she neared the open gates, a child's scream erupted from somewhere ahead. She was pretty sure it was a trap, but didn't care and ran toward the castle with grit and determination. After passing through the gates, she entered the courtyard and stopped to look around.

The interior of the courtyard was void of windows and doors and the only thing accessible was a flight of stairs hugging the left side of the building, leading up and disappearing around the back. Screams, even more shrilling then the last, sounded from the top of the stairs. Enraged, Katara ran toward the noise, and just as she was about to step on the first step, vines shot up from the dry earth and quickly wrapped snugly around her legs and immobilized her. She reached down trying to remove the vines, but they were wound so tightly around her limbs; she was unable to get her fingers in between them.

Preoccupied, she did not notice the demon-like creature slinking down the stairs and holding a child's hand until they were standing a few steps away. It was fascinated with her struggling against her bonds. Katara looked up at them and knew right away that the child was Sybil.

"What are you doing here miss?" Sybil asked.

"Sybil, I'm here to save you from him."

"Save me? I don't know what you mean. He's my friend."

"Let her go whatever you are." Katara said directly to the creature.

The creature's eyes never left Katara's. "Let her go? I'm here to protect her against beings like you." The demon looked down at the girl. "Sybil do you remember what I said. Evil monsters can appear in many different shapes and sizes, including nice old ladies or small boys. Do you remember?"

The child nodded.

"Sybil he is the one who is here to harm you. He keeps you locked away in that prison." Katara said, still struggling with the vines.

The demon smirked, thus irritating Katara further. "Prison? Sybil tell her why you like being here." The creature said.

"My guardian lets me play all day, and I get to eat anything I want. I don't have to do yucky chores."

"Sybil he is not your guardian. He has you trapped here. Don't you remember playing with other children and your mom and dad?"

"Children are mean to me, and my mommy and daddy make me do things that I don't like to do. He lets me play."

"That's right Sybil. I'm your best friend, and I would never hurt you." The creature delightfully said. "After she leaves, we'll go inside and play, and you can eat all the candy you want. Now tell her to leave." The demon said with glowing eyes.

Sybil looked at Katara. "I want to play miss, so please leave."

The demon grinned from ear to ear.

Katara tried again to move, but was unable to do so.

"We'll be going now. I hope you enjoy your... accommodations." The creature said, relishing in contentment. He waved his left hand and created a swirling tunnel of wind that began swirling around Katara, in case she got free, and left with Sybil.

"You're not going to get away with this. Sybil he's a demon." Katara shouted to them as they began ascending the stairs. If the child heard her, she made no indication.

****

"Torhan where's Tole now? I'd like to see him again." Priest Piersum asked as soon as Katara was in her trance.

"We left him inside the Grove." Torhan responded without even turning around.

"Why don't you tell me how you were able to get the amulet?"

"I'd rather not say."

"Why?" Piersum insisted.

"Because, it's better that you don't know."

"Tell me, because I'd like to know how you got past the guardian that guarded the relic."

Torhan looked over at him. "That's interesting."

"What is?"

"How did you know about the guardian?"

Priest Piersum realized he'd made a mistake and quickly said. "I told you about him before you left."

"That's funny, you only mentioned that Tole knew the whereabouts of the amulet and said nothing about whom, or what, was guarding it."

Piersum's face turned ashen, and he stood up to leave.

"Sit back down and don't move." Torhan barked at him, and the priest complied.

After Torhan turned his gaze back toward Katara and Sybil, Priest Piersum began quietly chanting and within a few seconds, Torhan's scabbard glowed in warning, catching his attention.

"If I were you, I would stop chanting, or else you will die before you finish." Torhan threatened.

The priest heeded his warning and did so.

****

Every time Katara tried to remove the vines, and get free of her ensnarement; the small whirlwind drew closer, threatening to hit her. When she left them alone, it moved away. Katara thought about how to deflect the whirlwind, but nothing happened, and now she wasn't sure what to do. Obviously, she couldn't stay where she was, but wondered what would happen if she'd died in this place. She mentally asked for help, and a voice whispered for her to relax and think of something that could unravel. She listened, and calmly thought of a length of rope unraveling and like magic, the vines did the same thing from around her legs and released their hold.

Free to move, she took a few steps backwards and when the whirlwind attacked, the voice whispered to deflect and with a mere thought from Katara, it was sent high into the sky and disappeared. The voice reassured her, that as long as she wore the amulet, she was safe from any type of harm the creature could bestow. Fully trusting the source, she walked up the stairs and around back where the steps ended on a landing with a wooden door. Quietly, she opened it and entered.

The room was large and filled with toys the likes of which Katara had never witnessed. Towards the center, Sybil was sitting and playing with several strange toys. The demon stood nearby, eyeing her protectively. They didn't notice her enter.

"Sybil, listen to me. He is here to harm you." Katara said.

Both demon and child turned their gazes toward her and were equally surprised by her appearance.

"I see that you have escaped my vines." The demon was clearly annoyed. "You have no business being here."

"And neither do you. So leave or I will destroy you."

The demon bared his teeth, raised his hands, and created icicles above his head and then sent them forth. The voice whispered "shield" to her, and Katara thought of one and a split-second later a force field was erected in front of her and deflected the sharp projectiles away.

Katara looked directly into the creature's eyes and said. "I told you, you couldn't hurt me."

The demon sent forth fire and ice balls and just like the sickles; they bounced away. In retaliation, the voice told her to think about a powerful force and when she did the demon was blasted across the room and knocked unconscious after it hit the wall.

Sybil screamed. "Why did you hurt him? You're a bad person. Get out and leave us alone." She said as tears streamed down from her eyes.

"Sybil you need to come with me right now before he wakes up." Katara inched closer to her.

The child looked over at her captor and back at her. "He's my friend and you hurt him."

"He's an ugly, evil, creature and this place is bad."

"He's a nice old man. How could you say that?"

"Nice old man. Maybe she was under some sort of illusion." Katara thought. "What does he look like to you?"

Sybil described the demon as an elderly bearded man wearing multi-colored garb. Katara now knew she did not see the creature's true nature.

"He is not a nice old man, but an evil creature keeping you captive here." Katara stated.

Sybil looked puzzled.

The demon regained consciousness.

"Sybil," the demon whispered caching her attention, "look at what she did to me. She hurt me." He moaned.

Sybil cried anew.

"Sybil, don't believe him. He is keeping you a prisoner."

The demon groaned in pain and Sybil looked over at him and then back at Katara. "You're mean." She said to Katara.

The demon climbed to his feet grinning, careful to kep Sybil from seeing the delight on his face. "Sybil, tell her to leave before she hurts you like she did me."

"Leave." The girl ordered.

"Now think of her outside of the room." The creature commanded.

Sybil did and before Katara could do anything, she was teleported outside of the room.

Katara faced the door deciding what to do. She knew the creature couldn't hurt her, but didn't know if Sybil could. She was running out of options. Behind the door, she heard them laughing and having a good time. Maybe she was going about it all wrong, and the direct approach wasn't the best option. She decided to create her own illusion and thought about Sybil and her family. Images suddenly appeared and coursed through Katara's mind that could only have been from Sybil's memories. When she was ready, she entered the room again. Both Sybil and the creature looked up.

"Not you again." The demon said.

"Mommy?" Sybil said, and her eyes lit up.

"That's not your mommy." The creature said trying to dissuade her.

"It is. It is." Sybil got up excited and ran over and hugged Katara around her waist. The creature rose up in a furious manner.

"Let's go home Sybil." Katara told her.

The child looked up at her mother with tear streaked eyes and nodded.

The creature began waving its hands in the air. "GIVE HER BACK TO ME OR FEEL MY WRATH." He shouted at Katara.

Katara shook her head in a mocking manor, and the infuriated creature summoned daggers above its head and sent them directly at her. Katara concentrated her thoughts, erecting a wall between them, and the daggers bounced away. The voice whispered the word "reality" in her mind.

"Sybil, look at him now." Katara said and projected how she saw the creature into the little girl's mind.

Sybil screamed when she saw the creature's true form. "Mommy, save me!" She cried.

Katara picked up her up and turned.

"You may have won this day, but know this; my Lord Avalos will hunt you down in the material world, Katara from the Order of the Hallowed." The creature laughed.

Hearing her name sent shivers up and down her spine, and she suddenly wondered how he knew it.

After leaving the room, Katara took her to the place where she appeared and stopped. She wasn't sure how to leave and then the voice spoke to her. It said for her to remove the illusion and to convince the child to wake.

Katara looked down at Sybil and removed her façade.

"What did you do with my mommy?" Sybil asked. She was clearly upset.

Katara knelt down and placed her hands on the child's shoulders. "Sybil, I came here to rescue you from this place."

"Where's my mommy?"

"Truthfully, I don't know."

"Then I am not leaving."

"Do you want to be trapped here with that creature?"

Sybil remembered what she saw. "No."

"I don't think we can leave this place unless you want us to."

"Why did you lie to me and look like my mommy?"

"It was the only way to get that creature to reveal itself." Katara paused and stared into her eyes. "Do you understand?"

Sybil shook her head.

The voice whispered "return" in her mind.

"Hold my hands." Katara said and reached out taking the child's hands in hers. "I want you to think about sleeping in a bed." Katara instructed and then said "return".

The area darkened, and they disappeared from the dreary area.

Back in the bedroom, Katara lifted her head and met Sybil's

blinking eyes.

"Welcome back." She said to the girl.

Sybil smiled.

"You did well." Torhan said to Katara after noticing they were both awake.

Katara turned her head to look at him, and her smile faded when she noticed his scabbard glowing and the priest standing over him poised, and ready to stab him with a knife. Before she could warn him, Torhan's dagger left the scabbard and intercepted the priest as he was about to strike him.

Priest Piersum only had seconds to defend himself. In his former days, before he repented and joined the holy order, he used to be a cut-throat thief and avid knife fighter often terrifying the locals of his town for money. So when Torhan's dagger attacked him, his skills that were dormant for many years, kicked in and allowed him to parry the blade while moving away. Katara stayed close to Sybil, while Torhan got to his feet and unsheathed his sword.

Despite how well he fought off the knife, Priest Piersum's arms grew weary, and he was cut and slashed in his arms, chest, and legs. Torhan debated whether to allow the priest to die, but decided he wanted answers instead and told him to drop his weapon and remove any thoughts of aggression toward him, or he would surely die. The priest half-heartedly did so, and the dagger returned to the scabbard. The glow dwindled to a light shade of green.

"That was foolish. I told you not to do anything stupid." Torhan said.

The bloodied priest dropped to his knees begging for forgiveness and asking to be allowed to live.

"You will have our forgiveness after you answer a few questions. Now sit in the chair."

Piersum complied. Torhan bound his hands and feet to the chair and asked Katara to take Sybil out of the room. When they were gone, he picked up Piersum's knife and stood in front of the priest.

"Let's start at the beginning, shall we? I want to know the real story behind your relationship with Tole." Torhan moved the rusty dagger near his left cheek, indicating his intention if he found that he was lying.

The priest glanced at the dagger and then spoke. "The part about me and Tole belonging to the same Order was true, and yes, we did become good friends while serving there. Every year, the head priest asks his students to go on a pilgrimage and retrieve certain items like herbs, amulets, necklaces, goblets, and other trinkets to help our cause. A few years ago, Tole and I were given the task of finding an item called the Chalice of Plenty, and we weren't supposed to return until we found it."

"What did it do?" Torhan interrupted.

"The chalice was supposed to refill itself on its own and satisfy your thirst, no matter how parched your throat became. After a few discouraging weeks of searching, we stopped at a small village and met a stranger named Molech at one of the inns."

Torhan did not react when he heard the assassin's name.

Piersum continued. "After a few tankards of ale, we found out he was a forager, by trade, and he asked if we thought about a different career path, one of fame and riches instead of being errand boys. Tole was already tired of our Order's lifestyle and was easily persuaded, but not me. Several hours later we left the inn and went to our rooms to rest. We left the town the next morning and—"

"What happened to Molech?" Torhan interrupted.

"Here's where it gets a bit strange. A few days later, while we were camped for the evening, he shows up with two young males that were obviously twins. They were identical in every way; from their looks, to the way they wore their hair, their mannerisms, and how they finished each other's sentences. I asked him how he found us and Molech said something about they were scavenging in the area and saw a campfire. I had my suspicions about him. Tole, on the other hand, was delighted to see him and asked them to join us. While we were talking, I noticed something a little strange about the twins, it was something in their eyes, but I couldn't put my finger on it at the time. Eventually, the conversation turned to riches and fame and by morning, they had convinced me to join up with them, and so I did."

"I thought that you said you didn't want to leave your Order?"

"I didn't, but I don't remember how they convinced me otherwise."

"Was your faith that weak?"

"I guess it was." Piersum said sadly, looking down.

"What happened next?"

"The twins promised to pay us a fortune if we were to travel to the town Snowdrift and watch over a child named Sybil, and her family, until she was a teenager. They also wanted us to establish a foothold in the town's church and gave us a lot of gold."

"That's it, no strings attached?"

"That's all we had to do."

"So that's how you became the priest of Snowdrift?" Torhan flatly said. "After you left what happened to Molech?"

"Every now and then, he would show up and give us gold, ask about the child's wellbeing, and leave."

"And the twins, did they visit you as well?"

He shook his head no.

"What happened after that?"

"A year later, during one of Molech's visits, he wanted Tole to take up residence inside of the grove. We questioned his motives, and he said that is what the twins wanted and implied a small threat if he didn't comply. Tole left the following day, and I was instructed not to stay within the town.

Molech made a few more visits over the next six months and when I asked about Tole, he said he was fine, and I should keep to my task and not to ask again. I could tell his demeanor had changed. I grew concerned for my friend, and after he was gone, I left the town to go see him."

"Weren't you afraid Molech might find out?"

"Yes, but I didn't care. When I arrived at the grove I found him speaking with the twins. As I approached them, the twins saw me and told me to wait where I was and continued speaking with Tole for a few more minutes. Afterwards, they approached me. I noticed right away they looked older and less alike then I remembered. They asked me why I was there, and I told them that I was worried about Tole. They insisted that I turn around and leave. I called Tole's name and when he didn't respond, I made an attempt to walk over to him. They barred my way and said that I should leave and not return until I was instructed to, so I did."

"Did you go to the authorities?"

"I was too scared. After another month, I went back to the grove at night and found Tole sitting alone by the fire. Without turning around, he said that he was expecting me and for me to sit down so we could talk. I could tell right away that something had changed the man that I had once known. We spoke for several hours and all he wanted to talk about was our task and money. I finally grew fed up with him and threatened to leave Snowdrift, and that's when the twins and Molech suddenly appeared. I knew they overheard me talking to Tole. Molech told me I might want to rethink my plans, and then the twins' shapes changed into these black hideous creatures with red glowing eyes. They told me they were demons and said that if I didn't continue to do what I was asked to do, they would torture me until I died and take my soul down into their world and torment me for all of eternity."

"You were a priest, couldn't you do anything?"

"Against them? I didn't have the skills." Piersum continued. "It took Molech two years before he returned to Snowdrift. He posed as Sybil's long lost uncle, went to her birthday party, and presented her with the two gifts for her birthday. A nightgown and a teddy bear."

"Let's backup. Why was everyone interested in Sybil in the first place?"

"She has a special gift that allows her to commune with animals."

"How would that serve the demons?"

"That I don't know. Anyway, after the party, Molech left the town and everything was okay until Sybil fell into a deep sleep a few nights later."

"Was she supposed to?"

"I don't think so. I heard about what had happened and how the parents suspected Molech, so I went to the grove and told Tole. When I returned to the town, I found out Sybil's parents already went to the authorities and when they weren't going to do anything, they hired a tracker named Shoel to find, and bring Molech back for questioning. Shoel and his band of mercenaries, tracked Molech down to the grove. What they didn't know was that he and Tole were already waiting for them along with this creature Tole called a Rime Lord. They killed Shoel, his group and dumped their bodies in a nearby crypt, locking each corpse behind a separate door.

Tole always believed that if you murdered someone, then you needed to bury their body in a shallow grave and bind their spirit to some sort of trinket, so that their spirit would remain rooted where it was. After Tole finished binding their souls, they left the crypt and summoned me to the grove and told me what they did to Shoel.

At that point, we didn't know what to do with Sybil, so we contacted the demons and explained what befell her. They ordered us to bring her out of her slumber, and said that we would need the amulet of REM to do so. They even told us where it was and how to use it."

"You knew where it was, so why didn't you go get it yourselves?"

"Unfortunately for us, the amulet was buried in the same room where they dumped Shoel's body. When we went down there to retrieve it, the amulet was locked inside of a metal box, and Shoel's spirit was guarding it. The ghost told us to leave and when Molech ignored his warning, Shoel almost took his life."

"Did Shoel remember you?"

"Lucky for us, he didn't, and allowed us to leave. A few weeks later, Molech came up with the idea to send the family down into the crypt and retrieve it for us. After I convinced them there was a way to wake Sybil, they went into the crypt and never returned."

"You're a disgrace. How many people did you send down there to their deaths?" Torhan got angry and reached over, holding the blade against his throat and pressed the edge tight enough to draw a bead of blood. "I should kill you for what you did."

The priest grunted in discomfort. "Please spare me." He pleaded. "I never wanted this life. I am a good man. The demons are to blame."

Torhan relaxed his grip a few seconds later. "I'll be right back. If you get free or try to escape, you're a dead man." He gagged the priest, stormed out of the room and went downstairs.

Katara and Sybil were sitting at the table. Torhan entered the room and motioned for Katara to join him in the other room.

"You didn't hurt him too badly did you?" She asked once they were safely away from Sybil.

"No, but I wanted to kill him. I'm so angry right now. Everything Clodovea said was right; Molech coming to town and giving Sybil the gown and teddy bear, her parents going down into the crypt, and Shoel and his group. He claims Molech introduced them to a pair of demons, and they were manipulated into helping them."

"What did they want with Sybil?"

"It has something to do with her ability to commune with animals, but he doesn't know why the demons are so interested in her."

"Did her parents know Molech?"

"I'm not sure."

"What caused Sybil to fall into the deep sleep?"

"I think it was the gown."

"And where did they get the gown?" Katara was quickly putting the pieces into place.

"He said the demons gave it to them."

"So the gown must have special powers."

"I believe so."

"I wonder how long Molech has been dealing with demons. I need to speak with Piersum; watch Sybil."

"Don't tell him we killed Tole."

She entered the room, walked over to the priest, and removed his gag.

"Are you a man of the cloth?" She asked directly.

He looked puzzled.

"Are you?" She demanded.

"I am."

"Then how could you do what you did? You are solely responsible for the deaths of Sybil's family and anyone else you sent down into that crypt."

"You don't understand. I was trapped. They forced me into helping them, or they would have killed me."

"Forced?" Katara was getting angrier. "No one is forced. You had a choice before you met Molech, and after you met the demons, so don't give me that."

"I thought that I could make things right after we..."

Katara backhanded him across the face. "You should have stood up to them. You sent people to their deaths, you are a bastard!"

Blood trickled out of the corner of his mouth. "Please, I didn't mean to. Give me a chance to make it right."

"Make it right. MAKE IT RIGHT!" Katara was so angry; she gritted her teeth and then punched him square in the face, breaking his nose. Piersum was dazed for a few seconds. His eyes watered as blood flowed down from his nose, into his mouth, and then all over his clothes. "Have you ever heard of someone named Avalos?"

He shook his head, regaining his senses. "Are you going to stop hitting me?"

She nodded.

"I have heard the name before."

"Tell me what you know of him."

"I don't know anything about him. I only heard the demons speak his name on several occasions."

"Are you lying to me?" Katara took out her mace.

Piersum became very fearful. "I don't know him; I swear."

She stared into his eyes. "Describe the demons to me."

Piersum went into great details. First, he described them in their human form and then their true hideous shape. "What's going to happen to me?" He asked when he was finished.

"Do you feel remorse for what you did?"

Piersum shook his head.

"Since you cooperated and feel remorseful, we will allow you to live, but in exile."

"Where?"

"With Tole of course, but you must make a vow never to return to this town."

Piersum nodded in agreement. Katara gagged him and then left the room.

"We are leaving tonight when it's dark." She said to Torhan after she entered the room.

"What about Sybil?"

"Where are my mommy and daddy?" Sybil suddenly asked.

Katara walked over, bent down, and looked into her eyes. "I'm sorry sweetie but they are in a better place."

"Better place?" Sybil started crying and hyperventilating.

"They're safe from harm."

"I want to see them." Tears streamed down her face.

"You will someday."

Katara and Torhan spent many minutes to calm her down.

"Where's Rodle?" Sybil asked.

"We don't know where your brother is." Torhan answered.

"Do you want to live with Clodovea?" Katara asked.

Sybil nodded her head.

"After I come back we'll deliver the priest to Shoel." Katara said, took Sybil by the hand, and left.

After they were gone, Torhan went upstairs and had mixed emotions when he saw the blood all over Piersum's face and clothes.

"I see you made her angry." Torhan commented, taking out his knife and walking over to the bed.

Piersum eyed him carefully as Torhan cut the sheets into several pieces of cloth.

"I can't leave you bleeding all over the place." Torhan said and shoved one into each of his nostril to stifle the flow. Satisfied, he grabbed a chair, sat by the window, and looked at the falling snow.

Katara arrived at Clodovea's cottage and knocked lightly on the door. A few seconds later a voice on the other side answered. "Who is it?"

"It's Katara and I have a surprise for you."

The door opened, and Clodovea's eyes widened upon seeing Sybil. "How did you do it?" She asked.

"Can we come in?"

"Please do."

Once inside, Clodovea grabbed Sybil and hugged her so tight that Katara thought she would never let her go. It made her heart full of joy watching the caretaker and child reunited. When Clodovea was finished, she led them to the table and poured tea for them.

"I can't believe you saved her." Clodovea said excitedly.

"It wasn't easy." Katara said and took a sip of tea. Putting down the cup, she went on to tell Clodovea how they revived Sybil and about Priest Piersum. Clodovea was shocked to hear about him and was relieved when Katara said he would be leaving tonight and would never return.

The conversation turned to the future and well-being of Sybil.

"Clodovea where's her brother?"

"After she fell asleep, Mr. Lockington asked me to take him to his sister's village so that she could look after him until," she paused and looked down, "they returned."

"Can you care for Sybil?"

The woman's eyes lit up. "Of course, I can. I love the girl like she's my own."

"Good. I think you should take her to her aunt's village just to be safe. Can you do that?"

Clodovea nodded.

"I must be going." Katara said and got up.

Sybil came over and hugged her with tears in her eyes.

"Sybil, you're a brave child." The child hugged her tighter. "Good luck and please keep her safe." Katara said to Clodovea.

"You gave me a purpose in life, and we can't thank you and Torhan enough. Tell him thanks for me."

While Katara was walking away from the cottage, she paused to take one last look at Clodovea's home and saw two winter wolves walking up to the porch. The animals laid down in front of the door, and she realized they were there to watch over the girl.

When Torhan saw Katara walking toward the house, he got up and untied the priest from the chair, leaving his hands bound, and mouth gagged and led him downstairs. Katara walked through the door.

"Did you take care of Sybil?" Torhan said to her.

"She'll be fine just like we discussed."

"Are there a lot of people walking around?"

"Not many."

Torhan placed furs on himself and Piersum, while Katara packed food and water into their backpacks. When they were ready, they left through the backdoor.

It was shortly after midnight when they made camp inside a small cluster of trees a few miles from the town. Torhan untied Piersum and removed his gag, while Katara lit a fire to help ward off the bitter cold.

"I've noticed that we're not going toward Tole's Grove." Piersum stated.

"We're not." Katara answered and handed him bread, dried beef, and a waterskin.

"I thought that you said I was going to be exiled with him?"

"You are. We've relocated him to another location that both of you will find peaceful and quiet, and you can live out the rest of your lives."

"Where?"

"We'll be there tomorrow, so you'll have to wait and see." She smiled at him, and they started eating.

When they were finished, Torhan tied Piersum to a tree and took first watch while Katara slept. About an hour later, he grew tired and despite shifting his body constantly and occupying his thoughts of their task ahead, his eyes grew heavy, and he fell asleep. Maybe it was some sixth sense, or he heard them, but something woke Torhan just in time to see the three strangers entering camp. They were wearing gray traveling cloaks with their hoods pulled tightly around their heads, dark clothes, so they blended in with their surroundings, and carried long stilettos in their hands.

He watched them with his eyes barely opened. One of the thieves began waving his hands in a circular motion and grayness came forth and began engulfing the area. He recognized who they were and what was happening when the snowflakes froze in place in the air.

They were Chromos Lords, and he wasn't sure if they were looking for him. He had his answer a few seconds later when one of the strangers took out a red gem from his pouch and held it aloft. It glowed and so did something on Katara, which Torhan quickly realized was the amulet of Insight. He watched them while inching his right hand over to the hilt of his sword.

"How did this end up in her hands? It was supposed to be with someone who lives in a mansion." The one with the gem said.

"It doesn't matter who has it. Just get it." The one to his left said.

"It's like stealing candy from a baby." The third commented and began walking toward Katara.

The intruders were so preoccupied with their tasks, and confidence in their abilities; they did not see Torhan get up until it was too late. Torhan bull rushed the one holding the gem, and ran him through with his sword and then proceeded to the one who created the time stopping grayness.

The Chromos Lords, upon hearing their comrade die, turned around together, but it was too late for the one that stopped time, and he was beheaded while taking out his sword. Time resumed, and Torhan faced the remaining Chromos Lord with his long knife pointed directly at Torhan. Torhan's scabbard glowed in response to the threat.

"How do you walk freely, when others can't?" The Chromos Lord asked.

"That seems to be the mystery your race can't figure out." Torhan smirked. "What do you want with the amulet?"

The Chromos Lord knew he was clearly at a disadvantage with his skills and smaller weapon. "I'd rather die than tell you."

Their conversation woke Katara and when she saw the stranger, with his back to her; she took hold of her mace, knelt up, and struck his right forearm. The impact shattered his bone in three different places causing him to scream, drop his weapon, and then fall to his knees while gripping his arm with his other hand. Torhan walked over and kicked him in the shoulder, sending him tumbling backward.

Katara was on her feet. "What the hell happened?" She asked, noticing the other two dead men.

"They were after the amulet of Insight."

Priest Piersum was now awake.

"How did they enter our camp so easily?" Katara was clearly upset.

"Remember when I told you about the race called Chromos Lords?" She nodded. "Here are three more of them. They entered our camp, stopped time and were about to take the amulet from you. The scabbard is immune to their abilities, and I was able to surprise them."

The Chromos Lord turned his head when he overheard Torhan talking about the scabbard. He thought that if he could only get the item away from him, then he could stop time and kill them. He got to his knees and was about to lunge after Torhan when the scabbard glowed again drawing Katara's attention. She hit the Chromos Lord in the left shoulder with the mace and shattered his collar bone, rendering the limb useless, and sending him to the ground reeling in pain. The scabbard's glow ceased.

"Kill me." The Chromos Lord begged through gritted teeth.

"Not yet. You have some questions to answer first." Torhan said and dragged him over to a nearby tree, propping him up against the trunk and then tying him up.

"You don't have to kill him." Piersum said.

"Is that what you thought about when you sent Sybil's family to their deaths?" Katara barked at him. "If you don't mind your business, then you'll be next."

"You're no better than Molech, or the demons."

His comment struck a nerve with her, and she walked over and punched him in the face, and then grabbed him by the front of his furs and pulled him closer to her face. "We are different than you or them." She then punched him in the face again, knocking him out.

"Now for you." Torhan said to the Chromos Lord. "What does this amulet do?"

When he didn't answer Torhan removed the dagger from the scabbard and cut him across the left cheek. The Chromos Lord winced in pain and tried to show a brave face. Torhan opened his cloak and cut through his shirt.

"We have all day for you to get acquainted with this dagger." He said and cut the man across the chest very slowly causing him to scream. "Let's start over, what does the amulet do?"

The pain was too much for him to bear, so he decided to talk. "The amulet itself is useless, but when you add the stones it allows the owner to see the past and future of people, places, and events. So the more stones you insert, the further you can see, meaning specific days, weeks, months, and even years and that is why we seek it."

"Is that all it does?"

"Yes."

"Why does your Order want it?" Torhan pressed.

"To be able to see the future is an advantage my master would like to own." Suddenly, the Chromos Lord remembered a conversation he had with one of his brethren a few weeks ago. "You're the one my brothers spoke about. The one from the cave, aren't you?"

"It is me." Torhan boasted proudly. "If you continue to cooperate, I might allow you to leave and deliver a message to your kind."

"And what would that be?"

"To stay clear of me, or I will kill them if they ever cross my path."

Katara approached, and Torhan noticed something was on her mind. "Are you okay?" He asked.

She looked over at the unconscious priest. "I'll feel better after we drop him off. What did you find out about the amulet?"

"He says the amulet will allow the user to see the past and future of people and places."

"So what do the other stones do?" She asked the Chromos Lord.

"They serve a unique function once they're added to the amulet."

"How did you hear about the amulet?" Torhan asked.

"We possess a book, written in an ancient language that talked about items of great power scattered throughout the land, and this is one that we wanted. Did you know about the amulet's powers?"

"No."

"Then why were you in the cave if you weren't looking for the stone?"

Torhan ignored his question. "How are you able to stop time?"

"I'm not telling you our Order's secret." The Chromos Lord said it out of instinct. "I'd rather die."

"Well I'll tell you one thing for sure. If you don't answer our questions, you will, and it will be very excruciating."

"Fine. I'll tell you what I know if you let me leave." He bargained.

Torhan and Katara looked at each other and nodded their agreement.

"So, how are you able to stop time?" Katara asked him again.

"It's really hard to explain, but I'll try. We don't stop time; we manipulate and bend the very fabric, so that it appears that we do."

"But how?" Katara asked.

"Like I said it's really difficult to explain if you've never studied our skills."

"Where is your Order located?"

"We are not from your world."

"World!" Torhan exclaimed.

"Maybe world is too strong of a description it's more like another plane somewhere in the folds of time itself."

"How many are in your Order?"

"Our numbers are down to fifty. You alone are responsible for the deaths of several top students."

"Well it was either me or them, so don't fault me."

"If your skills are so special, how do you recruit other students?" Katara asked.

"Once a year, we visit the towns across the continent and search for special children possessing the abilities needed to do what we do. Our skills are so rare that we might find only two children a year and when we do, we take them to our plane and teach them our art."

"So you kidnap them?"

"I guess we do. Anyway, after the child enters our domain, they are given special stones that allow them to harness and absorb our abilities. In time, and with many years of practice, they won't need them anymore and will be able to manipulate time by themselves."

"I have one more question for you. Besides me, who else can resist your powers?"

"We have encountered many races, and except for the demons, no one can."

Torhan turned to Katara. "Do you have any other questions for him?" He asked.

"I'm done." She answered.

"Untie me now so that I can leave." The Chromos Lord said.

"We haven't decided yet." Torhan said, and they walked away.

"But we had a deal."

"What do you think?" Katara said after they were away from him.

"If we let him go, he'll definitely tell his people about the scabbard, and if they know they'll hunt me down."

"I think so too, but I don't think we should kill him."

Torhan rubbed his chin. "Then what should we do with him, leave it up to fate?"

She liked the idea and Torhan began gathering their items, while Katara went over to Piersum.

"Are you going to set me free like you said?" The Chromos Lord asked when he saw them gathering their stuff.

"No, but we're not going to kill you either." Torhan responded coldly and picked up the red gem off of the dead man.

"That wasn't the deal."

"Would you rather die or take your chances?"

"My arm and shoulder are broken." He pleaded.

"Yes they are." Torhan smirked in satisfaction.

Katara slapped Piersum until he woke up, untied him, and then helped him up.

He looked at the Chromos Lord. "You can't leave him like that."

"If you don't shut your trap, you'll join him." She replied sternly.

"The animals will eat him." Piersum stated.

Katara had enough of his mouth, gagged him and then tied his hands behind his back.

Torhan added several more logs to the fire to keep the animals away. "That should help." He said.

****

In the early hours of the morning, the Chromos Lord finally got one of his limbs free, despite the unbearable pain. After the pain subsided, he took the knife from his boot and cut away the rest of his restraints. His right arm was swollen and irritated, and his left shoulder felt even worse. He felt feverish and sick to his stomach and knew that if he didn't find a healer soon, he would lose the limb if not his life. Before leaving, he tried to use his powers and found that he couldn't make the proper hand motion to complete the task, leaving him vulnerable and defenseless. He knew there was a town close by and started walking in that direction.

By mid-morning, Snowdrift came into view, and he quickened his pace. Thoughts of revenge, relief from the pain, and a hot meal quickly faded when he heard buzzing directly behind him. Turning around, he came face-to-face with a six-foot dragonfly hovering a few yards away, beating its multi-colored wings in a hypnotic pattern. They were beating so fast, he was unable to move. The dragonfly swooped in and wrapped its legs around his body while stabbing him with its stinger. After the paralyzing toxin took effect, the dragonfly soared away with its meal.

Chapter 8: A Spirit At Peace

Katara, Torhan, and their prisoner arrived at the crypt shortly after dusk. Priest Piersum mumbled something through the gag as soon as he recognized the area.

Torhan removed the cloth from his mouth. "Well my friend it's time that you know the truth. Your fate along with Tole and Molech's are linked to each other."

"You're not sending me down there. Are you?" Piersum panicked.

"I'm afraid so."

"You lied to me."

"No we didn't." Katara added.

"You said Tole and I would be quietly living together."

"You will. Tole is already down in the crypt waiting for you and so will Molech when the time comes."

"You won't get away with this." The priest threatened.

"Get away with what? Having you spend a little time with the people you murdered?" Torhan answered.

"What do you mean?"

"Shoel is waiting for you too." Torhan said and gagged him again.

Katara pushed the stump over, and the crypt began rising again. Piersum pulled away, and ran. Torhan found it almost laughable, and gave chase. When he eventually caught up to him, he shoved him hard to the ground.

"You're not going anywhere." Torhan said and bent down to pick him up.

Piersum rolled onto his back and kicked him in the stomach, which made Torhan fall on top of him and punch him once in the face, knocking him unconscious. The attack was done so swiftly that when the dagger left the scabbard to protect him, the threat was already neutralized, and it returned to its home, leaving the priest unscathed. Torhan picked him up, slung him over his shoulder, and carried him back to the crypt.

Katara activated a glow rock and handed it to him. "Do you want me to come with you?" She asked.

"No. I'm not sure how the spirit will act." He answered and went down into the depths below.

After reaching Shoel's room, he entered the chamber and placed the priest into the shallow grave. He removed the gag and loosened his restraints. Piersum stirred awake.

"Any last words before we proceed?" Torhan offered.

"I will haunt you from the afterlife."

"Good luck with that." He said and climbed out of the grave. "Shoel, it is Torhan and you have a special visitor."

The spirit materialized and floated over. *"Well, well, well, what do we have here?"* The spirit gazed upon the man in the grave, sending shivers up and down his spine.

"No, it can't be?" Piersum said as he began backing away.

"Ah Priest Piersum." The spirit looked delighted. *"We're going to have so much fun."* The spirit turned his attention to Torhan. *"Torhan of the mortal realm. How can I ever thank you for this gift?"*

"Don't thank me yet Shoel. I have one more person to bring to you."

"You're a man of your word. Did you save the girl?"

"We did thanks to you. I'll be back in a day or so with the other killer."

"Day, week, month, year. It doesn't matter to me. I have all of eternity." The spirit smiled at the priest.

"Please don't leave me here." Piersum pleaded staring at Torhan.

Torhan looked long and hard at him. "You need to atone for your actions." He said and left.

After Torhan was gone, Piersum climbed out of the grave and fled. Shoel was delighted with his attempt and waited until he was near the door, before closing it and throwing him against the wall with a mere thought. Piersum banged his head and was knocked senseless.

Shoel floated over. *"Piersum you will serve me for all of eternity."* The spirit said and began chanting.

The room filled with foul smelling smoke that blinded and choked the former priest, just as he got to his knees and began reaching for the door handle.

"Breathe deep my pet." Shoel said with delight, watching his new prisoner grasp at the locked door handle until he slumped to the floor. The rancid poison filled Piersum's lungs and stopped his heart a few seconds later. His spirit was separated from his mortal body and floated over to its master.

"Piersum I've made you a private room, but feel free to visit your friend Tole whenever you want. Now be gone."

Priest Piersum's spirit and body were then cast away into another room.

"One more and I will be free." Shoel said and dissipated.

****

"Is it done?" Katara asked Torhan, as soon as he reemerged from the crypt.

He nodded.

"Are you ready to face Molech?"

"He's not going to be easy." Torhan said.

"I've been thinking. Maybe we can surprise him."

Torhan was intrigued. "How so?"

"While you were down there, I thought about how we could. He doesn't know me, so while you're talking with him, I could conjure up a Tirip and ambush him."

"He's a crafty assassin, so I am guessing he'll have some sort of surprise for me."

"Can we just avoid him altogether?" Katara finally asked.

"No. He'll track me down sooner or later." He looked defeated. "I feel like I am at a major disadvantage."

"What do you mean?"

"He knows all about me, from my fighting style to the scabbard. I'm so mad at myself for allowing him to manipulate me."

Katara touched his hand. "We'll get through this, have faith."

Her words did nothing to ease his feelings. He was really nervous and then something dawned on him.

"I want to use the amulet again."

"We don't know what the other stone does and what effect it will have on you." Katara said, trying to discourage him.

Torhan was more afraid of Molech then the effects of the amulet. "I'm willing to take the chance in order to get an advantage over him."

Reluctantly, she gave in and handed him the red gem and amulet. Torhan placed the stone into another slot of the amulet, and it locked into place.

"Ready?" She asked.

He nodded and placed the amulet around his neck and sat down. Closing his eyes he thought about meeting Molech and within a few seconds, something in the recesses of his mind told him to either think about the past, present, or future. After choosing the future, he was lifted high into the air and hovered above Katara and himself for a few seconds, before being whisked away.

Torhan found himself standing outside of a cave and observed his surroundings, taking in as much detail as possible. He looked for the obvious places where traps could be positioned, and while doing so, Molech walked out of the cave and stopped a few feet away. He appeared to be looking for someone. Torhan loathed the man, and yet was thankful for him turning his life upside down, because without him, he would've never met Katara, saved Sybil, and brought Tole and Piersum to justice.

Growing impatient, Molech took out a sleeve of throwing knives and began tossing them at the wall directly behind Torhan. When he was finished, he retrieved the daggers and reentered the cave. Torhan followed him in and stopped once he was inside. Molech's campfire gave off enough light to allow Torhan to see the cave's dimensions. The ceiling was some twenty feet high, and the width of the cave was about the same. He couldn't see the back and when the thief walked in that direction, he followed. Molech stopped in front of some bushes and began fidgeting with something behind them. Torhan crept closer. Behind the shrubbery was a rack full of spears that were pointed directly at the entrance. Molech adjusted the spears and something at the bottom of the device, and then connected a long string to the side of the wood. The trap was hard to detect, and he wondered if Molech intended on killing him, or if it was just a precaution in case their encounter didn't go as he planned.

He continued following the thief around the cave and watched him position loaded crossbows towards the entrance and at different angles. His final trap was by far the deadliest of them all. Molech tied several spears across his back, scaled up the left side of the wall, and across the ceiling until he was positioned above the entrance. He began fastening the weapons to the ceiling, and after he was finished, he let go and landed lightly on the ground. Moving off to the side, he set the trip wire and tested his trap by tugging on a thinly connected string. The spears fell from above and plunged deeply into the earth. Torhan realized that if he was standing under them he would die horribly, there was no question about that.

Molech reset the trap and then sat down in the corner of the cave and waited. Eventually, he got up and walked outside. Torhan followed him and saw Katara and himself walking up the road. Molech greeted them with a wave and walked toward Torhan, indicating that he was about to clasp arms with him in greeting.

As Torhan was about to take his arm, Molech quickly removed the dagger from Torhan's scabbard and backed away several feet while grinning. The maneuver happened so fast that neither Torhan nor Katara reacted until it was over, which they did by taking out their weapons. Molech held up his hand, mouthing something, and Katara and Torhan relaxed a bit and lowered their weapons. Molech continued speaking with them. They spoke for a long time, and it appeared that everything was going well, until Molech became animated, and Torhan's scabbard began glowing.

Upon noticing the warning, Molech relaxed and by doing so caused the glowing to cease. The thief smiled sinisterly at them, and Katara knew that things were about to go awry, so she nudged Torhan away, but he wouldn't go and kept talking to Molech. Katara suddenly interrupted their conversation, and Molech said something to her, causing her to grow angry and threaten him with her mace. Molech smiled and said something again and this time Katara lost her composure and when she charged him, she was hit by several crossbow bolts and toppled to the ground. The thief disappeared into the cave grinning. Torhan ran over, fell to his knees, and took her hand. They exchanged words until she passed away. Torhan stood up with tears in his eyes, sword in his hand and ran inside the cave.

Dream state Torhan followed, knowing how this was going to end. In the back of the cave, the thief sprung the trap of spears as soon as Torhan entered and hit him with three of the projectiles, causing him to stumble over the tripwire and release the spears above, skewering him where he stood. Dream state Torhan looked on in horror, as his mortal self, stood erect, with a spear jutting from out of the top of his head, through his groin, and planted firmly into the ground. Molech walked over, removed the scabbard, took whatever else he wanted from their corpses and then left the cave. Dream state Torhan looked at their lifeless bodies and was so grateful that it was not real and only a vision of things to come. A few seconds later, his eyes snapped opened and wet tears flowed down his cheeks.

"What did you see?" Katara asked.

Torhan was about to answer, when his nose began bleeding, slow at first, then like a floodgate opening, and it couldn't be stopped.

Alarmed, Katara sat him up, placed a cloth on his nose, told him to pinch the bridge, and said to breathe through his mouth. Torhan did as he was instructed. She reached into her pack and took out several items, which included strips of cloth, a small rose colored vial, and a container of black paste. After rubbing the strips in the paste, she shoved them up each of his nostrils and handed him the vial. She told him to drink it and hold his head back. A few seconds later the blood slowed.

"You gave me a scare. I didn't think that I would be able to stop it." She paused when she saw the somber look on his face. "What is it? What did you see?" She asked.

"I saw us die."

"What? How?"

"After I put the amulet on and thought of Molech, I was given a choice by the amulet to see the past, present, or future of him, which was different from the last time that I used it."

"It sounds like the amulet offers more options when there are additional stones added. Interesting, I wonder what happens when we have all five."

"I'm not sure I want to find out." Torhan said.

"So what happened when you thought about Molech?"

"I appeared at the entrance of a cave and found him setting traps both inside and outside. I think he was preparing in case something went wrong with our meeting and decided to kill us outright.

A short while later, we arrived, and as we were talking to him, he said something to get you angry enough to attack, and then everything fell apart and we ended up dying."

"What about the Tirip?" Katara was mad, not at Torhan, but at herself for dying.

"The Tirip wasn't in the vision, so I don't know."

"And your scabbard, didn't that warn us? How about the dagger?" She asked, growing impatient.

"He's clever. Here's what he did. We were about to clasp arms in greeting, and he quickly removed my dagger from the scabbard."

"Why?"

"Because he knows what the item does. Remember, he was the one who gave it to me."

"Tell me exactly how we died." Her mind was racing.

"You charged him and were shot by some crossbows."

"Where were they?"

"Hidden in the bushes and crevices, just outside of the cave's entrance. After you died, I ran after him and triggered his other traps."

"Which were?"

"He had some contraption that launched spears from the back of the cave, javelins above the entrance, and more hidden crossbows."

"Let's revise our plan and I'm using the amulet to see if it works." Katara said firmly.

"I'm not sure if you'll be able to use it."

"What do you mean?" She got agitated.

"You never met him."

"You're right."

"I'm going to use it again." Torhan insisted.

They spent the next few hours scheming exactly what they were going to do and modifying their plan in case something went wrong. When they were finished, and felt like they had every cause and effect covered, Katara plugged his nose with a few strips of cloth covered in black paste, and he placed the amulet around her neck.

"Here goes." He said and thought of Molech.

When he returned from his experience, he told her what he saw and said that as long as they followed their plan exactly, they should survive. They gathered their belongings and left.

It was around dusk when they arrived near the cave. Torhan found a place to light a fire and spread out their sleeping beds, while Katara searched for a small pond, which she found a half-mile away. After she conjured a Water Tirip and took full control of the entity, she returned, and they rehearsed their plan one last time, before she left with the

Water Tirip. When she arrived at the cave, it was exactly like Torhan had described it. She stopped near the entrance and called the thief's name. A few seconds later, Molech emerged from within and looked at her and then at the Water Tirip.

"Who are you?" He said, gripping the hilt of the sword.

"My name is Katara and I am here to escort you to where Torhan is waiting."

"Waiting? He's supposed to meet me here."

"He was injured on his way here and can hardly walk, so he wants you to come to him."

"I see. Did you manage to save young Sybil?"

"I don't know who Sybil is."

"Aren't you traveling companions?"

Katara shook her head. "I met him yesterday and was hired as an escort."

"Where is he now?"

"Not far."

"I'll be right back." Molech disappeared into the cave.

"Does he really believe that I'll fall for this pathetic trap?" Molech said when he was inside. "It's all the same. He's going to die and so will she."

He stopped in front of his weapon cache and grabbed a girdle of daggers, a wicked looking barbed spear, a rare double shot crossbow, a little box, and his cloak. After securing the girdle around his chest and placing the box inside of a concealed pocket, he walked out of the cave.

"I'm ready. Make sure you keep that thing away from me." He said.

"He's insurance in case you do anything against me."

"I know what they're used for." Molech sneered.

Katara led the way, followed by Molech, and the Tirip. The Tirip was instructed to protect her, so she wasn't all that concerned about Molech walking behind her. It didn't take the thief long to say something.

"So how does an escort learn how to conjure up a spirit?"

The question caught her a little off guard. "Before I became a guide, I used to be a healer."

"I see. And why did you leave that profession?"

"I don't know you, so I do not want to share my personal life." She sounded a bit annoyed.

"Just trying to make conversation that's all. You don't have to be rude." He said, knowing that he would get a reaction out of her.

Katara wheeled about and found his spear pointing at her throat and the Water Tirip gone. Her facial expression changed.

"I know all about you and Torhan."

She looked around for her protector.

"Your guardian has taken a permanent leave of absence." He smiled and showed her the cube. "Do you like it? A friend of mine gave it to me, in case I should ever encounter hostile spirits."

"What did you do with the Tirip?"

"I don't see any harm in telling you. This little box sucks them in and destroys their very existence. I love it." He paused. "You look a bit puzzled as to how I know you, so I'll tell you. Shortly after you left for the amulet of Insight, Tole told me everything. I almost killed the fool for sending you after his amulet. He almost ruined everything for his stupid heirloom." Molech was clearly aggravated.

"*He doesn't know what the amulet of Insight does.*" Katara thought.

"I'm assuming you found it and then went looking for the amulet of REM?"

She nodded.

"I was wondering. How did you get by the spirit of Shoel?"

"You'll have to ask Torhan."

"I guess it doesn't matter. Would you be so kind as to place your mace on the ground and step away?"

Hesitant, she did as she was instructed and Molech picked up the weapon and looked at the details.

"Nice weapon, it looks very dangerous." He looked at her with an evil grin.

She regretted relinquishing her weapon, but knew the alternative if she attacked and failed to kill him.

"I was thinking that I will spare the both of you if you agree to accompany me on my travels and, of course, service me whenever I want."

At that moment, she wanted to drive a knife through his throat.

"You can decide later. Let's get moving." He ordered.

They entered the camp just as nightfall approached, and Torhan stood up upon seeing them. Katara nodded in warning that something was wrong. He limped towards them.

"I didn't think I would ever see you again." Molech said sarcastically and pointed the loaded crossbow at him.

The scabbard glowed. "What's the meaning if this?" Torhan demanded.

"Let's see. You didn't meet me in the cave like I asked, made me walk here, and your friend lied to me."

"I'm injured."

"It does appear that you are, but of course, we'll test that injured leg shortly. I see you still possess the scabbard, so why is it empty?"

"The dagger was lost in my last fight, and I haven't had the time to get a new one."

"And how did that happen? The dagger would've returned to the scabbard."

"What does it matter?" Torhan responded sternly.

"I guess you're right. Katara go sit over there." He pointed toward a log close to Torhan, and she walked over and sat down. "Torhan, kindly remove your weapons and place them over there," he pointed toward a spot a few feet from him, "and then go sit next to her."

Things were not going as they had planned, and after he placed his weapons on the ground and was seated next to Katara, the thief spoke.

"Why don't we start after your first meeting with Tole?" Molech trained the crossbow at Torhan. "And please, don't leave out any details."

Torhan told him about the amulet of Insight and their trip to the manor. He was about to say something about the amulet of REM when Molech interrupted him.

"You know; it really aggravates me when Tole puts his own agenda ahead mine. I can't wait to see him again." He regained his composure. "Tell me how you recovered the amulet of REM."

"There's not much to tell. I went down into the crypt and recovered the amulet from Shoel."

"Just like that?" Molech asked doubtfully.

"Well I had to convince him to allow me to have it."

"You convinced Shoel? How did you do that?"

Torhan was about to answer when they heard footsteps moving through the bushes nearby.

"More help!" Molech said and then turned his attention, and the crossbow, towards the noise.

"Was this supposed to happen?" Katara whispered to Torhan.

"What?"

"Whatever is out there?"

He shook his head. While Molech was distracted, Torhan took the hidden dagger from his boot and placed it into the glowing scabbard.

"We need our weapons." Katara said to Molech.

"Stay put or I'll shoot you in the head. Who's out there?" Molech barked at Torhan.

"I don't know."

"Are they with you?"

"No, because if they were my scabbard wouldn't be glowing; think about..."

Before Torhan could finish his statement, two greenish colored creatures with four arms each, stormed into the camp.

Molech took aim with his crossbow at the closest creature and pulled the trigger. The first bolt pierced its left eye, and the second went straight through its opened mouth and killed the monster.

Molech quickly dropped his weapon, grabbed the spear, and stabbed the second abomination in the midsection. It was a perfect thrust that should have stopped the monster, but instead, the creature grabbed the shaft and began pushing the weapon through its body, while moving hungrily toward him. The thief jerked the weapon to the side, toppled the creature and then fell on top of it with a dagger he'd grabbed from his girdle.

At the exact same time, the initial creatures entered the camp; two more came at them from the other side. One went straight for Torhan, which prompted his dagger to take flight and defend its master, while the other focused on Katara. Torhan told her to get their weapons and bravely intercepted the creature running straight for her. When the creature saw Torhan, it paused long enough to knock him aside and then continue unimpeded toward his quarry. By the time the monster neared Katara, she had her mace in hand and struck the beast with a well time uppercut that knocked it to the ground. She then clubbed the creature in the head until its skull cracked open.

The remaining monster, wounded severely, ran from the area. Once the creature's aggression was stopped, the dagger returned to Torhan's scabbard, and the sheath ceased glowing.

"What the hell are they?" Molech asked.

"There's a lunatic not too far from here that breeds them." Torhan answered.

"How do you..." Molech's body suddenly went limp, and he fell down.

Torhan heard more noise nearby. "Run." He said and as he turned, he was struck in the lower back by a needle, causing his legs to go numb, and he tumbled to the ground. He tried rising, but his limbs wouldn't respond. Katara was about to help when she saw two more creatures and four men holding blow guns, coming their way.

Torhan glanced over his shoulder and then back at her. "Get help!"

He said.

A few needles whizzed by her head and as much as she hated leaving him, she ran.

The four men stopped several yards away from Torhan. One of them ordered a monster to get Katara, while another loaded his blowpipe with a dart and raised his weapon. Just as he was about to blow into it, and shoot Torhan; Torhan's dagger left the scabbard and stabbed him repeatedly. It happened so fast, and surprisingly; the others couldn't do anything about it, except look on in awe at the weapon that needed no owner to wield. The knife returned to the scabbard after the man was dead.

"What sort of magic is this?" The man on the far right with the white beard exclaimed.

"Come closer and find out?" Torhan said to them.

"Take him. The master wants him alive." The one on the left said to his companion.

"But the knife?" The man in the middle replied.

"There are three of us and only one dagger." The bearded man pointed out.

"Forget what the master wants. This guy is dangerous." The man in the middle said as he unhooked his crossbow and loaded it.

His actions proved fatal when he made his intentions clear. Before he had a chance to aim his weapon and pull the trigger, the dagger responded, flew over, and sliced his throat.

After the dagger returned to the scabbard, the guy with the white beard realized how the blade protected its master and stopped his companion from advancing. "I have an idea." He said and ordered the monster to pick up Torhan.

The creature lumbered over and when the dagger ignored it, his assumptions were correct.

"It looks like the dagger protects him if he's threatened." He explained.

After Torhan was hoisted over the monster's shoulder, the guy with the white beard carefully removed the dagger from the scabbard.

****

Katara ran as fast as she could through the darkness until she tripped over a thick tree root and stumbled into a thicket full of thorny bushes. She came to rest somewhere in the middle. Long prickly thorns stabbed her legs, face, and hands, and if she wasn't careful, they would have cut her in many places. She was in the process of removing the vines when someone came running past the bush, causing her to freeze. She waited that way until she was sure her pursuer wouldn't return, then untangled herself and hobbled her way back to town.

When the creature returned empty handed Torhan smiled, and both captors looked at each other in bewilderment.

"Can't they do anything right?" The bearded man stated.

"Should we go after her?"

"No it's too dark. We'll hunt her down later or maybe…" He paused. "One of her friends will do that for us in a few days."

Both men laughed, and Torhan knew right away what horrors were waiting for them at the mansion.

"Bind their hands and feet and blindfold them, we need to go, Fefantor is waiting."

After they were secured, the other creature picked up Molech, and they left.

Chapter 9: A Long Awaited Reunion

It was midday when Jacko, Sun, and Breen left Mirkin and followed the road northwest toward Snowdrift. The snow fell in thick sheets and was dense enough to hinder their progress and slow their mounts down to a canter. Their heavy cloaks, despite being wrapped tightly around their bodies, and hoods pulled close about their heads, did little to ward off the chill from the whipping wind and snow.

An hour later, Jacko slowed his steed and Breen pulled up next to him.

"What's wrong?" She asked him.

"Something isn't right; my saddle keeps shifting." Jacko dismounted and began checking the straps.

"Hurry up. I don't like being out here in the open." Sun said, while scanning the dense forest on both sides of the road. He had a sneaky feeling something was watching them and as a precaution, he put on his studded gloves.

Preoccupied, Sun did not see the horned snow leopard sneaking up behind him. The cat's white fur made it blend in perfectly with the surroundings, and the animal's stealthy movements made it impossible for the humans to hear.

When the cat was close enough, he leapt up and knocked Sun from his horse, then pounced on him and began tearing at his cloak with its sharp claws. Sun instinctively punched the cat with his right hand, while protecting his face with the other. Jacko and Breen turned their heads simultaneously when they heard Sun hit the ground. Jacko ran over to help him, while Breen dismounted and unsheathed her sword. By the time they scared the cat off, Sun's chest had suffered multiple deep wounds, and he was gored in the stomach.

Sun gazed up at them looking pale. "That animal really hurt me." He said, wincing in obvious pain.

"We need to stop the bleeding, or he'll die." Breen stated and ran to her horse.

"Hurry!" Jacko shouted.

By the time she grabbed her bag and returned Sun was already unconscious.

"We need to work fast. Here take this cloth and apply pressure on the wound." She said and handed it to him.

Jacko did as he was told, while she reached into the bag and took out a black and a white powder, a mortar and pestle, water, a fish hook, string, more cloth, and big green leaves. She poured the black powder and water into the mortar, quickly made a paste, smeared it on the leaves and placed them within reach. Next, she threaded the hook.

She looked at Jacko. "Listen carefully. I need you to remove the cloak and cut his shirt open. I'll pour the white powder all over the wound and use another piece of cloth to apply pressure. Do you understand?"

"What's after that?" He asked.

"You'll remove the cloth, and we'll do the same thing again. Hopefully, the blood will be slow enough for me to stitch the wound. If not, we'll keep doing it until it does. Are you ready?"

He nodded and picked up another piece of cloth.

"Here we go." She said.

Breen removed the blood-soaked rag. Jacko used his knife to cut his shirt open, and she poured a generous amount of the white powder all over his stomach, swiftly grabbed the cloth and pressed down on the wound. A few minutes later, she indicated that she was ready to do it once more. Jacko removed the bloody cloth, while she poured even more powder over the wound and applied pressure again.

After a third time of doing this, the blood finally slowed enough for her to stitch the wound. When she was through, she placed the paste covered leaves on top of the stitches, added another piece of cloth, and then tied everything in place.

"We still need to get him to Snowdrift right away." She said.

After securing Sun in his saddle, they trotted off to Snowdrift and arrived shortly before nightfall. They quickly found the healer's house and after dropping Sun off for further treatment, they took to the streets to find out anything they could about Torhan.

While they were walking, Breen noticed the worried look on his face. "He'll be fine." She said reassuringly.

"I hope so. I would have a tough time dealing with it if anything happened to him."

She smiled at him. "Don't worry I promise he'll be okay. Now where should we start?"

"I think the tavern would be as good a place as any." Jacko replied.

They came upon the Snowdrift Inn a little ways down the road and entered. The room was crowded with local patrons and a few weary travelers. Jacko led Breen straight up to the barkeeper and addressed him.

"Excuse me." He said.

The barkeep, with his back turned, ignored him and continued filling a tankard with sweet mead.

"Excuse me." Jacko said again.

"Hold on." The barkeep grumbled. When he was finished, he turned around. "Mead?"

"Have you seen..."

"Can I get you a tankard of mead?" He said cutting off Jacko.

Jacko looked at Breen, and she nodded. "Two please."

"Coming right up." The barkeep turned around, poured two ales and placed them in front of them. "I'm busy, so what do you want?"

"I'm looking for a friend of mine. He's a little shorter than me with brown hair and most likely wearing armor. He would have arrived here a few days ago."

"A guy wearing armor. Hmm... let me think... Do you know how many people come into this inn wearing armor?" The barkeep snapped.

"Please sir it's really important. His name is Torhan, and he might have been traveling with a female healer." Jacko said.

The barkeep looked at him. "I don't know your friend. Kiala might. She was working over the past few days."

"Where is she?" Breen asked.

"You want a lot; don't you?"

Breen handed him some coins. He grabbed the silver and called to her. The serving wench across the room looked up when she heard her name and came over. "Can I help you?" She asked.

"I'm looking for a friend of mine named Torhan. He would've arrived a few days ago and most likely would have been traveling with a healer named Katara." Jacko said.

The young girl thought about it, and then her eyes lit up. "I do remember a man and woman stopping by."

"You do? Do you know where they went?"

"That I don't know."

"Did they stay long?"

"They caused a ruckus with two of our locals."

"What did they do?" Breen asked.

"I think that they were asking too many questions, and it upset them."

"We really need to find my friend. Can we talk to the people they upset?"

Kiala hesitated. "Only if you promise not to upset them like your friends did. They're kind of old."

"We'll do our best not to." Jacko answered.

"They're over there in the corner." She said and pointed.

Jacko saw the two men she was referring to and gave her twenty silver pieces.

"What's this for?"

"A round of mead for the table and for your time." He said, and they walked over.

"Excuse me can we join you?" Jacko asked them.

They stopped talking and looked up at them.

"Why?" The man on the left asked.

"We have a few questions to ask you?"

"Well if you're buying you can." The man on right added.

Jacko smiled, and they sat down. Kiala was there in the next instant and placed ale in front of each one. Jacko ordered two more for them.

"My name is Jacko and this is Breen."

"Well met strangers. My name is Kipt and this, here is Erea." Both men picked up their fresh tankards in delight, smacked them together, and then took a long swig. "What brings you to our little town?" Kipt asked.

"We're looking for friends of mine that stopped by a few days ago."

Erea lowered his mug. "Why talk to us?" He asked.

"Because they were seen speaking with you."

Kipt looked a bit uncomfortable. "I don't think we want to talk to you."

"If you answer some of our questions I'll give you enough coin so that you both can drink yourselves into a stupor for at least a week." Jacko placed a handful of coins on the table.

"Okay, what do you want to know?"

"What did you talk about?"

"They asked about the town and the stores."

Jacko could tell he was hiding the truth. "Did they mention a child named Sybil?"

"Why are you people so interested in the child? She's cursed." Erea said.

"I just need to find my friends; they're in danger. Do you know where they went?"

"We haven't seen them after they left the inn."

"What did you tell them about Sybil?" Breen asked.

"Nothing because the girl lied to us."

"What did she say?"

"She said that she was a family member, and we knew she was lying." Kipt said and took another swig.

"If you don't know where they are can you tell us where to find Sybil?" Jacko asked.

"No." Erea firmly said.

"Just tell us and we'll be on our way." Breen said.

Kipt looked at them. "I'd suggest you go see either Priest Piersum or the former caretaker, Clodovea."

"Where do they live?"

"Clodovea lives down the street in an old cottage, with a wraparound porch, and Priest Piersum lives in the house next to the temple."

Jacko gave them another ten gold pieces and bid them farewell. They first went to see the priest and when he didn't answer, they went to Clodovea's house and knocked.

"Who is it?" A female voice from the other side of the door asked.

"Are you Clodovea?" Jacko asked.

"Who wants to know?"

"My name is Jacko and I'm with someone named Breen. We're looking for our friends, Torhan and Katara, and we heard that they might have visited you."

"If you're his friend, then tell me why he would've talked to me?"

"He most likely spoke with you about a child named Sybil."

"What was wrong with Sybil?"

"She was in a deep sleep and the only way to bring her out of it was by using a special amulet called ROM, RAM, or something like that."

Clodovea opened the door. "If you're lying to me, these wolves will attack you." She stated.

Standing next to her were two very large wolves and behind the wolves was a child.

"Do you understand?"

"Yes." Jacko said.

Clodovea nodded to the girl, and she bent down close to the animals and whispered something to them. The wolves parted enough to allow the strangers to enter. Clodovea introduced Sybil to them, and she was asked to go upstairs. The largest of the wolves followed her.

"Please come this way." Clodovea said and led them to the formal seating area. The other wolf followed her closely.

"Thanks for allowing us to enter your home." Jacko said after he was seated.

"I see they succeeded in waking her." Breen said.

"They did."

"Do you know if they left town?" Jacko asked.

Clodovea looked at them still uncertain if they were friend or foe.

"Please help us." Jacko pleaded with her.

"They did."

"Do you know where?"

"After Katara dropped Sybil off, she told me Priest Piersum was partially responsible for what had happened to her, and they were taking him away. That's all I know."

Someone knocked on the door.

"Are you expecting other visitors?" Breen asked.

Clodovea shook her head.

Jacko placed the finger knives securely around his fingers and Breen unsheathed her sword.

More knocking and then someone said. "Clodovea are you in there? It's Katara, and I need your help."

Suddenly, Sybil came running down the stairs. "Katara." She said and opened the door.

Katara entered. Her many cuts and bruises from the thorns made her appear like she'd been through a war.

Clodovea came rushing over. "What happened to you?" She asked.

Katara was about to answer when she noticed the two strangers with weapons drawn. "Who are you?" She asked them and took out her mace.

"Don't you know them? They're friends of Torhan's." Clodovea said. She was clearly puzzled.

Breen sheathed her weapon.

"My name is Jacko and this is Breen. Where is he?"

Katara looked at them suspiciously. "How do I know you are who you say you are?"

"Ask me anything you want." He replied.

"Did you have a promotion a few weeks ago?"

"How do you know?"

"Well?"

"I did." Perplexed, Jacko answered.

"Tell me what happened to your friend."

"He was my teacher and met an unfortunate end."

"By who?"

"By a fox name Slyantom."

"Was there anyone else with him?"

"A human and a goatman. How do you know this?"

"I believe who you are, and I'll explain later. Right now, Torhan is in trouble, and I can use your assistance."

"What happened?"

"He's been captured by a lunatic, and we need to rescue him tonight." She said.

"What?" Clodovea exclaimed.

"I'll do whatever is needed." Jacko said.

"You look like you're in bad shape. Are you going to be okay?" Breen said to Katara.

"Not really, but it doesn't matter, we need to go now."

"Drink this." She said and handed Katara a yellow vile.

"What do you want to do, kill me? That's for unconscious people. Do you have a blue one?"

Breen searched through her pack until she found one and handed it to her.

Katara drank it in one gulp and felt better a few seconds later. "Clodovea, you have to leave before dawn and stick to our plan."

Clodovea nodded.

"Let's go. Goodbye Sybil you be good." Katara said, and the girl smiled.

Once outside, Jacko stepped in front of Katara. "Tell me where we are going?"

"The person who has him lives a few miles to the north of here."

"Why was he captured?" Jacko pressed.

"We stole something from him, and he finally caught up to us."

"Torhan's not a thief."

"Well he's not a killer either, but try to convince someone of that in Mirkin." She quickly answered and walked past him.

Jacko turned to Breen. "Stay here with Sun and tell him where we went after he wakes up. I'll mark the trees along the way so that you can find us."

"Are you sure about this?"

He nodded, and Breen went into her pack and handed him the flask of dissolving liquid and then hugged him. "Be careful." She said and walked away.

Jacko watched her for a few seconds and then caught up to Katara, who was about to enter the woods.

****

Torhan, groggy from the toxins that coursed through his body, passed out several times during their trek to the manor despite being jostled around. In between the haze-like dreams, he thought about Katara, Jacko, Sybil, Molech, and the demons. Some visions were peaceful, while others were violent and mysterious and didn't make much sense. He came fully awake, by the time they reached the mansion and when heard someone walking toward them, he wished his blindfold was gone.

"Where's the female?" A male asked.

"She got away, but we'll send that one over there when he's ready."

Torhan knew that they were talking about him.

"What happened to our other pets?"

"They were killed trying to capture them."

"Really? They don't seem all that tough."

Torhan heard footsteps walking over and then someone grabbed his chin and lifted his head.

"He'll do fine; the master will be pleased." The same man from the mansion said and pushed his head forcefully away.

"What's this?"

"It glows and if you do anything violent toward him. This dagger will respond and attack you all by itself."

"How is that possible?"

"No idea."

"Did you throw it away?"

"I did, but it comes right back."

"Interesting. Take them upstairs to the far room. The master wants to speak with them."

Torhan and Molech were taken inside, up the stairs, and dropped into a room. The guards removed the blindfolds, placed metal cuffs on their arms and legs, and removed the ropes.

"You're going to love it here." His captor said and left, locking the door behind them.

The room was large, empty of furniture, and dimly lit.

"Congratulations, you managed to get us both killed." Molech said to him.

"No I didn't. You did by getting me involved with your scheme when I met you in Redden." Torhan snapped at him.

"I did? Don't give me that! You benefitted as well?"

"From what? Being turned into one of those creatures?"

Molech laughed. "So dramatic." He said and moved his arms until they responded. "I think the toxin is wearing off, try to move your limbs."

Torhan did and they responded slightly. "What do you think these cuffs are for? They're not attached to chains."

"Don't know." Molech tried getting up, but his legs were still too weak. He looked at Torhan and saw he looked defeated. "Don't worry we'll get out of this. I've been in tougher situations."

"And after we get free, what about us?"

"We'll settle our little matter, or maybe just part ways." Molech continued moving his limbs back and forth, trying to regain their circulation. By the time he was able to stand on his shaky legs, footfalls approached from outside the door. He produced two knives. "Here take this, but wait for my lead." He handed him one of the daggers and Torhan placed it out of sight instead of in the scabbard.

The door unlocked, opened inwardly, and in stepped two cloaked men carrying staffs and a middle-aged person. Torhan knew at once that he was Fefantor by Tole's description.

"I see the poison is wearing off." Fefantor said when he saw both of his prisoners standing up.

"Why are we here?" Torhan demanded.

"Let me think about that one. You entered my house unwelcomed, killed some of my men and my pets, and stole an item from me. Is that reason enough for you? Now let's have a brief introduction. My name is Fefantor, and you are?"

"My name is—"

"Don't say your name." Molech interrupted.

"Come now thief, why be so rude?" Fefantor replied.

"If he doesn't know our names, then how can he find us after we escape?"

Fefantor laughed. "Escape? You are going to serve me until your body rots away."

"Old man, you are going to die." Molech said and pulled out his dagger.

Torhan did the same.

"Didn't you search them?" Fefantor barked at his men.

"We did sir." The one on his left answered.

"I'd advise you both to lay down your weapons."

"Come get them." Molech challenged.

Fefantor snapped his fingers three times and suddenly the daggers flew from their grasps. Their metal cuffs around their hands and feet began pulling them backward until they were pinned against the wall and unable to move.

"Do you like that? I call it magnetism." Fefantor said in a gleeful voice.

Molech and Torhan tried pulling away from the wall, but their invisible restraints held them in place. Fefantor watched them struggle with delight until they conceded.

"I'm going to start over, and every time you don't answer my questions my men will administer some cleansing. What are your names?"

"Don't tell him." Molech said in defiance.

"That's the wrong answer fool." Fefantor nodded to one of his followers, and he walked over and whacked Molech in the stomach with his staff until his ribs cracked, causing the thief to cringe in pain. Fefantor then looked at Torhan directly. "Do you want the same cleansing or will you answer?"

Torhan didn't respond.

Fefantor nodded to the other guard and as he approached. Torhan's scabbard glowed In response, catching Fefantor's attention. Fefantor held up his hand, and his servant stopped.

"That's the toy my men told me about. I want to know how it works." Fefantor demanded.

Torhan remained silent.

"Have it your way." Fefantor said and nodded to his man.

The guard sternly hit him several times on his side until he heard bones crack, and then stopped.

"We can do this all day long if you like. I've dissected the human body many times and believe it or not, there are two hundred and six bones that we can break. I can also mend them, and we can break them all over again. I'm going to let you ponder this for a few minutes." Fefantor stated and walked out of the room along with his men.

"Do not give him your real name. I've dealt with his kind before, and he'll find you again." Molech said after the door was closed and began twisting his right hand back and forth.

"Hopefully Katara will return with help." Torhan said and then paused to watch the thief trying to free his hand from the metal ring. "What are you doing?"

Molech didn't answer and continued twisting, pulling, and pushing his hand back and forth until something snapped, and he was able to free it from the cuff. "Dislocated joints are the least of my worries." The thief said and snapped his wrist back into place. "See, good as new."

"Nice trick."

"Trick nothing, it was painful." Molech did the same thing with his other hand, and as he was about to start on his legs, the door opened.

Fefantor applauded the thief by clapping his hands. "Very good. I can use a man of your skills."

"I'll never work for you, old man."

"You will, after I teach you obedience."

Two of Fefantor's men walked over and beat on him until he lost consciousness.

"Take him below, chain him up, and begin the process." Fefantor commanded.

His men removed the metal cuffs from Molech's legs and dragged him out of the room.

Now alone, Fefantor stood in front of Torhan. "Your friend is either stupid or very brave; I'm guessing a little of both. Now for you, are you going to corporate?"

Torhan nodded.

"Good. Now what's your name?"

"My name is Danter." Torhan said, using the name on the note he recovered from the cave of ants.

"Now was that so hard? Who is your friend?"

"His name is Molech." Torhan didn't care what happened to the thief, so that's why he used his real name.

Fefantor smiled. "We're making progress. Why did you come here?"

"Friends of mine were being threatened, and if I didn't steal his amulet back they would have been killed."

"By who?" Fefantor was clearly aggravated.

"Will you let me go if I tell you?"

"We can do this one of two ways. You can tell me everything I want to know, and I might consider your request, or I will extract the information one painful second at a time."

"It seems that I have only one option. A hermit named Tole captured my friends and—"

"Tole, I've heard that name before." Fefantor said interrupting. "Tole..." he said the name again while rubbing his chin, and then he snapped his fingers. "I remember him. Does he have my amulet now?"

Torhan nodded.

"Did the thief help you steal it?"

Torhan chose his words carefully before answering. "No. After we gave the amulet to Tole, he sent Molech to kill us, so that the amulet couldn't be traced back to him."

"That makes sense." said Fefantor. "Who's the girl?"

"You leave her out of this."

"It doesn't work that way. You stole something from me, so if you don't want her hurt, I recommend that you tell me."

Just then one of Fefantor's men returned.

"Master?"

"What is it?" Fefantor asked without turning around.

"All connected sir. Do you want me to take this one down there as well?"

"Not yet."

"Very good." The man bowed and left closing the door behind him.

"You have no intention of letting me go, do you?"

"Again, it all depends on you. Who's the woman?" Fefantor was losing his patience and Torhan could tell.

"She's innocent."

"I'll make it easy for you. If you tell me her name, I'll let you go, and if you don't, I'll turn you into one of my servants." Fefantor paused. "I'll let you think about it." He said and walked out of the room knowing that he had a win-win situation.

Torhan was left alone for well over an hour to contemplate his decision. There was no way he was going to give Katara's name to him. He was lost in his thoughts, when the door opened, and instead of seeing Fefantor, it was two of his men. They walked up and stopped several feet away.

The one on the left spoke. "The boss wants to know your decision."

"Tell him that I will never give him her name."

"He knew that you would say that."

The one on the right took out a dart and walked back to the door. "I bet I can hit him in the throat." He said and threw it at Torhan, hitting him right where he said he would. Before losing consciousness, Torhan heard him gloating. "I told you so."

****

Along the way, Katara told Jacko everything she knew about Fefantor's mansion; from the layout, to where they might be keeping Torhan, to the guards walking along the perimeter, and finally, his horrid creations. She also mentioned Molech, and how he fit into the equation, just in case they had to deal with him. After they found the area where Torhan and Molech were captured, they picked up the backpacks and continued. They arrived at the mansion just as the sun peeked over the horizon.

Katara led them to the same area both, she and Torhan, plotted during their first visit. She had all but forgotten about her Wooden Tirip, until she spotted the charred remains scattered about.

"Why would someone start a fire with logs and then scatter them?" Jacko asked.

"That's because the logs weren't used for a fire. The last time we were here I created a wooden guardian to help us escape, so they must have destroyed him."

"You can do that?"

She nodded.

"Do you think you should create another one?"

"We don't have time. After the guard passes, we'll enter through the door down there."

Jacko looked through Torhan's backpack. "We have three flasks of oil, so we'll use them if there's trouble we can't handle."

"Don't use them unless you have to. I don't want the house to burn down while we're in there."

"I'll try not to. Are you ready to go save our friend?" Jacko asked.

****

Torhan woke up in searing pain and screamed.

"Calm down and breathe deeply, the initial pain is the worst." A shallow voice said to his left.

Torhan looked over and saw Molech not more than a few feet away. He was chained to the wall by his arms, legs, and waist and was wearing tattered clothes. His entire body from his face down to his feet had a yellowish tint. Torhan glanced left and then right and saw long needles, with clear tubes filled with yellow liquid, protruding from his shoulders. "What are they doing to us?" He asked after the pain subsided somewhat.

Molech took a couple of deep breaths before speaking. "I think they are turning us into those creatures.

Torhan was dressed and chained just like he was. All of his items, including his scabbard were gone. He began pulling against his restraints.

"It's useless; these chains are..." Molech was in midsentence when he suddenly fainted.

Torhan looked around and recognized the room at once. It was the same one they killed the guy in before entering the basement. Just then the door to the far end opened and Fefantor, along with two creatures, entered.

"I see that you're finally awake Torhan," Fefantor paused, "that is your real name, is it not?"

Torhan looked over at Molech.

"Don't blame him he really didn't have a choice." Fefantor continued walking over until he stood directly in from of him. "You will make a nice addition to my collection." Fefantor grabbed his face. "Last chance, what's the female's name?"

"I won't tell you."

Fefantor released his grip. "That's okay I already know." He smirked. "I just wanted to see if you were going to tell me. Her name is Katara. And guess what? You'll be hunting her down for me in a few days. I would like you to meet your new brothers, K and L." He gestured to his creations. "Your brand new name will be M, and the thief will be known as N. Before you ask me why I used only one letter; it's because I got tired of coming up with new names."

Fefantor laughed like the madman he was and walked over to this strange-looking contraption against the wall. "Ready for another dose? I want you to feel every ounce of fluid as it fills your body." He pressed a button, releasing more yellowish liquid into the tubes that were connected to his shoulders.

"You'll never get away with this." Torhan said and felt a hot burning sensation as the liquid entered his body. He screamed.

"That's what everyone says. Now I must go upstairs and rest. I'll see you in a few days, and together we'll rule the world." Fefantor laughed insanely and left.

A few minutes later, Torhan's legs began burning so intensely he thought they would melt away. Before the darkness claimed him, he wished that he would never wake again.

Katara and Jacko waited until the guard turned the corner at the far end of the building, before making their way down the hill. She did her best to cover as many of the footprints as she could, while Jacko went over to the door. He nearly tripped over a wire at the bottom of the steps and figured it was a trap. He couldn't determine how to disarm it and went back up the steps to Katara.

"We need to go around the front." He said.

"Why?"

"The door has a trap, and I can't disarm it."

"We'll have to kill the guards." She said coldly. "Hopefully, they'll have a key to the front door."

They retreated down the stairs and waited. A few minutes later, they heard the sound of snow crunching beneath someone's feet. Patiently, they waited for the guard to pass the steps before rushing out and killing him. So swift was their attack, the guard never knew what happened. They moved the body further away from where they were, left him in a kneeling position and then retreated back down the steps.

They heard someone else turn the corner, walk a few feet and then stop.

"Hensny!" He shouted and began moving quickly toward them.

Katara knew their diversion worked and as soon as she saw his leg, she hit it with her mace and sent him stumbling to the ground screaming. Jacko ran over and covered his mouth, and then placed his finger-knives against his throat.

"What are you doing?" Katara said.

"I have some questions for him." He said and looked into the guard's eyes. "If you remain quiet and answer my questions, we'll let you live. Do you understand?"

He nodded and Jacko slowly removed his hand away.

"Where do they keep the prisoners?"

"In the lower level."

"What are they doing with them?"

The guard was hesitant to answer, so Jacko pressed the blades tighter against his throat.

"My master turns them into his servants."

"He means those things." Katara said.

"I don't have anything to do with this. I'm just a guard who walks the perimeter. What choice do I have?"

"How many men are inside?" Jacko asked.

"Ten, including the master."

"Do you have a key?"

"On my key ring."

Jacko grabbed it from his belt, covered his mouth, and then slid his finger-knives into his throat, silencing him forever. He felt bad killing him, but knew that it was necessary if they were going to free Torhan. They dumped the guards' bodies down the stairs and made their way to the front. Surprisingly, there wasn't anyone posted outside of the door, and they walked up, unlocked it with the key, and entered.

Inside, the house was very quiet. There was a staircase on the right leading up to a long hallway straight ahead which ended in a T-junction, and a room on the right with tables and chairs. Katara was about to say something, when she heard footfalls approaching from somewhere down the hallway. She beckoned Jacko inside the room on the right and hid by the entrance with their weapons drawn. Whoever it was, hurriedly walked past their room and up the stairs.

Once the footsteps faded, they left the room and moved quickly down the hallway and stopped at the junction. To their right, the corridor went on beyond their sight and the one on the left ended at a closed door. They quietly followed the corridor to the right until it ended at an empty room and then went back the other way. Katara kept watch, while Jacko pressed his ear against the door and listened. After hearing a few voices inside, he held up three fingers indicating how many people there were. With their weapons ready, they threw open the door and surprised the unarmed men inside.

There were two men seated in chairs across the room, and another carrying a tray of food on his way over to them. All three men reacted differently; the portly man seated to the left was so surprised by them, he froze and stared up at them with his mouth open. The man seated next to him stumbled out of his chair and fell flat on his face, and the person with the tray dumped the food on the floor and held it like a weapon.

Katara and Jacko attacked. The first to fall was the guy holding the tray. After swinging and missing Katara, she smashed him across the face with her mace and then hit him on top of the head, splitting his skull apart. The next one to die was the guy who fell out of his chair. As he was getting to his feet, Jacko gave him an axe-kick on the top of his head and snapped his neck. The chubby man was so terrified by their ferocity; he was unable to do or say anything, and when Jacko swiftly plunged his finger-knives deep into his neck, he offered little resistance and died with a whimper.

Katara barred the door, while Jacko walked into the small room on the left and found two more doors. One led to an empty kitchen and the other led downstairs, which they took. No matter how carefully they navigated down the spiraling stairway, the steps creaked under their weight, causing them to pause on more than one occasion. After deeming it safe, they descended further and came to a closed door at the bottom. Jacko pressed his ear against it and listened. He held up two fingers. He was about to test the knob, when he heard a muffled voice getting closer. His facial expression told Katara everything she needed to know, and they retreated up several steps and waited.

The door opened, closed, and footsteps began climbing the stairs. Jacko crouched down and when the figure rounded the corner, he grabbed him by his garments, and Katara whacked him on the head with her mace, coating the walls with skull fragments, brain matter, and blood.

After placing the dead man's body on the stairs, they walked to the bottom of the stairs and opened the door. Peering inside the dimly lit room, they saw tables, empty cages, torture devices, a robed figure with his head down working on something towards the back, a couple of odd-looking creatures dressed in tattered clothes mulling about and a door at the far end.

Two unconscious figures were chained to the wall, with tubes protruding from their bodies. Jacko was pretty sure Torhan was one of them, and as he was about to rush in, Katara grabbed his arm and whispered.

"Hold on. Those are the creatures I told you about; the ones dressed in the shabby clothes."

Jacko reached into the backpack and took out three flasks; two of oil and the one of dissolving. "Whatever you do, don't get the liquid on yourself. It will melt whatever it comes in contact with." He said and handed it to her. "Ready?"

She nodded and they quietly entered the room.

The creatures and the cloaked figure, which still had his back turned toward them, did not hear them enter. Slowly and hunched down, they walked toward the front of the room, and by the time they were halfway to the front, the robed figure spoke without turning around.

"Gregor, did Fefantor give you more serum?"

Jacko lit both flasks from a nearby brazier. "Fefantor said to use this instead." He replied and threw them at him.

The glass container shattered against the wall, sprayed hot oil all over the table and the robed figure, setting them ablaze. The man screamed, dropped to the ground, and began rolling around.

The creatures turned, saw the intruders, and charged. Jacko threw the other flask directly at their feet and when it hit the ground it shattered, covered them with oil and set them on fire. The monsters continued advancing. Katara knew that they couldn't fight them without the risk of getting burned, so she waited until they were close enough and doused them, like a priest would do with holy water, with the contents from the flask of dissolving. The vile fluid landed on their face and began liquefying flesh, bones, and eventually their brains. It happened so fast that they fell over after taking one more step. Katara went over to Torhan and found him unconscious. His breathing was shallow, which gave her concern as she began removing the tubes.

Jacko searched the smoldering corpse until he found a key and walked over to Katara. "Is he going to be alright?" He asked.

"I don't know, look at his legs; they're turning black. It's usually a sign that the limbs are dying." Katara said and finished removing the tubing.

Jacko undid the locks and unfastened the chains. "What about the thief?"

"Leave him be; he has it coming to him." Katara responded coldly.

"It's cruel and we can't leave him like this. No one deserves to be turned into one of those things."

"He's killed many people, setup Torhan for murder, and would have killed us if it wasn't for Fefantor interfering."

Jacko looked at Molech, who raised his head and opened his eyes.

"Please stop the pain, it hurts really badly." Molech pleaded.

Jacko saw both of his legs were already green, and his stomach was starting to turn black. He decided to remove his tubes anyway.

Someone entered the room and said. "What do we have here?"

Startled, Jacko and Katara turned and saw a tall middle-aged man, wearing gray robes standing there.

"I'm assuming you are Fefantor." Jacko said and stepped away from Molech to face him.

"The one and only, and you are?" Fefantor replied arrogantly.

"What did you do to them?" Jacko barked, curling his fists.

"What did I do?" Fefantor giggled. "I didn't do anything. You see; they killed some of my children, and now they are in the process of repaying their debt."

"A debt? How so?"

"When I get finished with them, they will take their places."

Katara laid Torhan on the ground and faced Fefantor.

"Oh, I see you brought Katara with you. That's good, now I don't have to find her either."

"Your days are over and the only thing you're going to create is a home for bugs as they burrow through your flesh." Jacko stated.

Two tall, muscular, men came running down the stairs to join Fefantor. They wore robes and carried wooden staves.

"Sorry to end your fun, but I have other things to do." Fefantor said and reached over and pressed something in the wall.

Everything in the room, which was made of some sort of metal, began sliding toward the walls by an invisible force. Katara tried to resist, but her chainmail was too much, and she ended up against the wall along with her studded mace. Meanwhile, if Jacko wasn't standing so close to the wall, he might've had a chance to remove the finger-knives, but he too, ended up there with his back against it and his hands outstretched. Torhan slid over to the wall because of the metal cuffs that were still wrapped around his arms and legs.

Fefantor absolutely loved his little invention, and really enjoyed the expression on their faces as they struggled helplessly. "I would like to thank you both in advance for being my servants." He laughed insanely while playing with his long ponytail. "Tie them up." He ordered.

His men walked over to Katara, placed the leathery straps around her wrists and secured her arms to the metal rings on the walls.

"I'll kill you." She said and spit in the face of the closest guard, who then punched her in the stomach knocking the wind from her lungs.

"Leave her alone." Jacko said to them.

"You're next." The other guard said.

When they were finished securing Katara, they approached Jacko and began wrapping the leather restraints around his arms. Fefantor studied him with interest, and was about to say something, when Jacko took advantage of the wall's magnetic force for leverage and kicked the guard on his right in the left knee with a front kick, and then in the head with a crescent kick, sending him to the ground dazed.

The other guard took one step and was hit in the head by a powerful hook kick and knocked out. In a panic, Fefantor threw a dart at Jacko, but must've forgotten about the magnetic pull, because the dart flew against the wall. Jacko frantically wiggled his fingers out of his knives and once free; he kicked the stunned guard in the head and knocked him out.

After seeing Jacko moving freely, Fefantor disappeared up the stairs and locked the door behind him. Jacko followed and found the button he'd used and pressed it. The magnetic field deactivated, and everyone was free again. As soon as Jacko moved the door handle, he heard something click on the other side of the door, indicating that a trap was set.

"Let's get out of here." Katara said to him.

"I want to end his life. His magic walls can't stop me." Jacko said in frustration.

"I do too, but what if he has deadlier traps upstairs?"

"If we let him go, then he'll continue turning people into those creatures."

"I have a better idea. Let's burn the place down." Katara said.

Jacko grabbed his finger-knives, while Katara gathered Torhan's items from a nearby table and placed them into her pack. She didn't find the scabbard among them and figured Fefantor must've taken it with him.

"Release me." Molech whispered.

"Are we going to leave him like that?" Jacko asked Katara.

"I haven't changed my mind. I know it's cruel, but he's a trained assassin, and if he gets free, he might come after us. For Torhan's sake and mine, I can't risk it."

Jacko walked over to the door and discovered a few traps in place.

After several long minutes, Katara grew inpatient. "Can you disarm them?" She asked.

Jacko nodded.

"I can if you agree to set me free." Molech offered weakly.

"What do you think?" Jacko asked her.

"Don't do anything stupid." Katara warned the thief.

"Like what? Look at me."

Jacko freed Molech and as soon as he took one step, he fell flat on his face. He knew the fluid coursing through his body was irreversible, and he would never walk again. "Help me over there." Molech said.

Jacko carried him over to the door.

"Walk back to the far end while I'll get this opened." Molech said.

Jacko and Katara carried Torhan to the other end, while he went to work. The master thief skillfully removed several traps and before working on the last one, he paused to ponder his future. "What good would a thief be without his legs?" He said to himself and then took a deep breath. Instead of disarming the trap, he set it off and closed his eyes, knowing what was coming next.

A few loud clicks and the door exploded outwardly blowing the wooden frame apart along with the thief. The entire house shook, rumbled and knocked everyone to the ground. Daylight poured through the opening.

"I guess he couldn't disarm the last trap." Katara commented.

"I don't think he wanted to. Here use this on the ceiling." He said and handed her the last flask of oil. He then slung Torhan over his shoulder.

Katara lit the flask and threw it at the ceiling, setting the wood on fire, and then dumped the braziers over. With the fire burning out of control, they left the mansion and made their way up the hill.

Jacko and Katara walked for about a mile before finding a place to lay Torhan down and rest. Jacko walked around, making sure they were safe, while Katara tended to Torhan.

She poured red liquid down his throat and kept him warm. He stirred and regained consciousness a few minutes later. The first thing he saw was Katara's pretty smile and her long black hair dangling just above his face. He smiled at her, and she hugged him.

Jacko came over after he returned. "You're a hard man to find." He said.

Torhan looked over and was surprised to see him. "And you never showed up for our training."

Jacko chuckled.

Torhan tried getting up, but Katara placed a hand on his shoulder easing him to the ground.

"You're in no shape to get up." She said, interrupting their reunion. "I need you to drink these." She poured a few more vials of red liquid down his throat, and he made a face because they tasted foul. "What I am going to do next is really going to hurt, so you should bite down on this." She placed a small stick in his mouth. "Ready?"

He nodded.

She ordered Jacko to hold his arms and then smeared black paste up and down his legs. At first, the paste felt cool, so Torhan thought she was kidding, until his legs started burning like the fires of hell. The pain was so intense that he passed out several seconds later.

"We need to get him to Snowdrift if we want to save his legs." Katara said and rummaged through her pack until she found his bracers. "Wear these and they'll enhance your strength."

Jacko put them on and immediately felt a tingling sensation race up and down his body. "Where did you get them?"

"They're Torhan's. I think he found them in some cave."

Jacko wrapped Torhan in Katara's furs, picked him up, and they made haste to town.

The loud explosion was a bitter sweet sound for Fefantor. Yes, it ruined his basement, but at least the intruders died. After regaining his footing and walking to the window to assess the damage, he saw Katara and the others escaping up the hill and white smoke billowing from below, which angered him to no end. He vowed revenge on them and then when he smelled smoke, he left the room in a panic.

Back at the crypt, at the precise moment Molech died, Shoel's spirit finally found solace and disappeared from the mortal world for all of eternity.

Chapter 10: An Old Nemeses

Breen smiled when she saw Sun Chin open his eyes. "I'm glad you finally woke up." She said

"Where am I?"

"You're in Snowdrift at the healer's house." Sun tried rising, but the pain tore through his stomach, causing him to wince in discomfort. Breen placed her hands on his shoulders and eased him back down. "Take it easy, your wounds are fresh."

"Where's Jacko?"

"While you were asleep, we found out Torhan was taken prisoner, and Jacko went off to rescue him."

"What? By himself? Why didn't you go with him?" Sun replied angrily.

"Calm down. After we arrived, we met Katara, and they went after him."

"How long ago?"

"Last night."

Sun Chin slammed his fist down in frustration. "Where's the healer?"

"You're not going after them."

"Get me the healer." He demanded.

Breen did so, and the healer entered the room.

"What is it?" The healer asked.

"You need to give me something right away. I need to leave."

"That's impossible, your wounds are far too great and I don't have anything strong enough to deaden the pain. Plus..."

"I need to go after my friend. He's in danger." Sun snapped at him.

"And do what? The first time you get into a fight and get hit in the stomach, or turn the wrong way, you'll tear open your stitches and your guts will spill out. You'll need a few more days of rest before you can even walk."

"Do you have something that might speed up the healing process?"

"I don't, but the Botanist store does." The healer scribbled a few words onto a parchment and turned to Breen. "His store is down the street from here. Give him this and he'll give you what you need. It's pretty expensive."

Breen took the note and left the building.

Outside, snow flurries and the crisp morning air greeted Breen, as soon as she opened the door. She took a deep breath, letting the cool air settle into her lungs, and proceeded down the street. She was looking down at the note, when she nearly bumped into someone.

"Watch where you are walking human." The person snapped at her.

She looked up and came face-to-face with a fox creature wearing an eye patch over his left eye and carrying two short swords strapped across his back. Her face went pale and heart sank because she knew it had to be Slyantom.

"What is it human, haven't you ever seen a talking fox before?" Slyantom was amused by her reaction. "Maybe you'd like to see my skills in the bedroom. Would you like that human?" He laughed at her and walked away.

Breen stared at him and realized that he was heading directly towards the healer's house. She raced behind the buildings and entered through the back door ahead of the fox. Sun rose onto his elbow when he saw the look of fear on her face.

"What is it?" He asked.

Just then the front door opened, and she placed her finger on his lips and whispered. "Slyantom is here."

He moved her finger away. "What? Where?"

She pointed toward the front of the store. Sun Chin got off of the table, even though it caused him great pain, and walked up to the curtain that separated the rooms and listened. He couldn't hear them too well, so he moved the curtain aside slightly and saw the fox. He was about to rush out and confront him when Breen grabbed his arm.

"Don't do it, you're too wounded." She warned.

He looked at her and conceded. "Follow him and tell me where he goes." Sun said.

"I'm proud of you for your restraint." She whispered and left the building.

A few minutes later Slyantom left the healer's house and began walking back toward the direction from where he came. Breen waited until he passed and then followed him at a safe distance.

The fox entered the Inn of the Snorting Dragon, and two humans emerged from within and took up position on either side of the door. She was deciding on what to do next when someone spoke directly behind her.

"Why are you following me human?" A familiar voice asked.

Breen hesitated and then turned around. Slyantom was standing a few feet away. "I was curious that's all." She said.

"About what?" The fox asked.

"You were right I've never encountered your race before and wanted a chance to talk with you."

A sly and devious smiled crept across his furry face. "Care to have a drink?"

They entered the inn and walked to the back of the room. Of the many people sitting around eating and drinking, only one person paused long enough, from shoveling food into his mouth to stare at them as they passed. He was a tall, lean man wearing leather armor. Breen wondered if he was associated with the fox. Slyantom sat with his back to the wall, and Breen sat across from him. It made her feel uneasy, and the fox knew it as he watched her look around. He told her to relax and called the serving wench. She came over begrudgingly, after seeing him, because her last run-in with him had left a sour taste in her mouth. One she would never forget and also prompted her to carry a small hunting knife for protection.

"What can I get you?" She asked.

"Hello my dear, did you enjoy my last visit?" He smiled at her.

If Slyantom could read her thoughts, he'd know that all she was thinking of was taking out her knife and plunging it through his good eye.

Breen noticed that she had a fat lip and black eye.

The fox turned his attention back to Breen. "I do not even know your name my dear."

"My name is Elva." Breen answered.

"I'm Slyantom, would you like some ale?"

Breen nodded. The fox ordered two tankards and dismissed the serving girl like she was a child. For a brief moment, she almost pulled the knife out and acted on her desires, but decided against it because she had a better idea.

"Elva, were you raised in Snowdrift?" Slyantom asked.

"No, I'm not from around here. I grew up in Stonybrook. Where are you from?"

"A small village toward the north."

"What are you doing here?" Breen asked.

"My profession takes me all over the place."

"And what would that be?"

He was about to answer when the drinks promptly arrived. The serving wench carefully placed them in front of the couple and left without saying another word.

Slyantom picked up his beverage. "Let's just say that if someone needs something done, they hire me." He said proudly, which surprised her because he was so blatant about his profession, and he didn't even know her. "I like to make people pay for their stupidity." He paused. "And people, like humans, should take notice to my race and not mistake us for dumb animals like my un-evolved cousins." He paused again. "Here's to us and getting to know one another better."

She picked up her mug, clanked it with his, and took a long drink.

"How long are you staying in Snowdrift?" She asked.

"A few more days, I have to go to Mirkin to take care of a few things, if you get my drift." He bragged proudly, took a long swig and then ordered two more ales. He suddenly started feeling a bit strange. "Does your ale taste alright?"

She took another swig and said that it did. He emptied the rest of the contents just as his new tankard appeared, grabbed it from the wench and took another long gulp. "This tastes as bad as the last. There's something wrong with this ale." He yelled at her and threw the tankard on the ground. "Get me three more or I'll gut you where you stand." He demanded.

The serving wench raced away and brought back more.

Slyantom downed the first one and smiled. "This tastes better. Get out of here." He said to the girl and then looked back at Breen. "I was thinking, do you want to come to my room?" He asked her directly.

She noticed that he was swaying, but wasn't sure if he was drunk.

"Maybe another time, I have to go." She got up, and he grabbed her arm.

"Promise me that you will." His eyes narrowed.

She thought about whipping out her blade and slaying him on the spot, but knew that his men were among the patrons sitting nearby. "I promise." She said.

"Until we meet again." He said and then the room began spinning, and he let go of her arm.

On her way out the inn, Slyantom's guards snickered at her as she passed.

"Make sure you come back soon." One of them said.

"You can count on it." She replied and walked away.

After she was gone, Slyantom became dizzy and returned to his room.

She returned to the healer's house.

"Well where did he go?" Sun asked as soon as she entered.

"He's staying at the Inn of the Snorting Dragon. I think he has more enemies in town than he is aware of."

"What do you mean?"

"While we were drinking..."

"You had a drink with him?" Sun interrupted her.

"Yes, why, are you jealous?" She said and smiled at him.

"No, just concerned for your safety." He was clearly annoyed with her decision.

"I can handle myself in case you haven't noticed." She said. "Anyway, he is staying here for a few days and then leaving for Mirkin."

Sun Chin placed his hands on her shoulders and stared into her eyes. "I know you can handle yourself. I'm just concerned about your safety. He's very dangerous and—" He never finished his sentence, because Breen kissed him full on the mouth.

She pulled away. "As I was saying, I think there was something wrong with his drink, because he kept saying it tasted funny."

"How did yours taste?"

"Fine, but I told him it wasn't."

"Maybe he can't handle his ale."

"I don't think that's it, because he only had two."

"Maybe he was drugged." Sun said.

"You might have something there, because the serving girl seemed pretty scared of him."

"I will go there and talk to her." Sun got up from the table wincing. "What did she look like?"

"Are you sure you're okay?"

He nodded.

"Let me go instead." Breen offered.

"She already saw you with him, so she might not say anything to you. What does she look like?"

"Long red hair, wafer thin, and sporting a black eye."

Sun began placing his studded gloves on his hands.

"What if the fox sees you?"

"He doesn't know me." Sun said.

"Be careful, he has men with him."

"How many?"

"Two at the entrance and I think another one wearing leather inside of the inn. Be careful please."

"I'm not going to do anything stupid, so don't worry. Just be ready to leave when I get back." Sun said and left.

Sun Chin arrived at the inn, and Slyantom's men immediately stepped in front of him preventing him from entering.

"What do you want, slanted eyes?" The man on the left said.

"I want to have a drink."

"Go somewhere else. This inn doesn't serve your kind."

Sun's jaw tightened, and just as he was about to do something, a guard passing by took notice to them and stopped.

"What's going on?" He asked.

"We're just greeting every patron who enters." The man on the right said, and both men stepped aside to allow Sun to enter.

"You're lucky they arrived." Sun whispered to them as, he entered.

The guard waited for Sun to enter the inn before addressing Slyantom's men. "Any trouble from either of you and I'll throw you both in jail. This I promise." He said.

"No trouble from us." They answered together.

Satisfied, the guard walked away.

Sun sat down at a secluded table near the corner, spotted the serving girl with the black eye, and called her over.

"What can I get you sir?" She asked.

"I'll have roasted bird, a tankard of ale, and a few minutes of your time." He placed ten gold pieces on the table.

She looked at him, the money, and then leaned in. "What do you want?"

"I would like to talk to you about one of your patrons?"

She was growing suspicious. "Which one?"

"The one with the eye patch."

By the tone of his voice and the look on his face, she knew he wasn't a friend of the fox and abruptly said. "I'll be right back with your order."

Sun didn't stop her and hoped that she wasn't going to tell anyone.

A little while later, she came out of the kitchen with his food and ale and placed it in front of him. He was about to say something when she reached over, and slipped him a note and left. While he was eating, he opened the tiny parchment without anyone noticing and glanced at it. It had two words written on it. "Out back." Sun finished his meal, placed three gold pieces on the table and left.

As soon as he walked out the door, one of Slyantom's men spoke. "Hey slanted eyes, it would be wise for you not to return here again."

"Meet me at midnight at the north end of town, if you're brave enough." Sun said without turning around and walked away.

The man was about to draw his blade when his friend noticed the same guard from earlier walking in their direction. "Not now, the guard is coming. We'll get him later tonight." He whispered.

Sun walked further south until he was out of the sight of the men, circled back, and met the girl behind the inn.

He could tell she was nervous. "What do you want to know?" She asked.

"My name is Sun Chin, and it appears that we have a common enemy."

"I've never seen you before so why are you asking me?"

"My friend was having a drink with him earlier. She was the one with the long blond hair."

"Why would she drink with him?"

"She was gathering information about him. Believe me when I say he is going to die."

"Then why involve me? Just go upstairs and get it over with."

"I haven't decided on how I'm going to kill him, because he has men with him."

She started becoming uneasy. "I have to go."

"I need to know what you slipped into his ale."

"I don't know what you're talking about." She turned away, and he grabbed her arm.

"Please miss, don't you want to see him pay? He's a dangerous creature and killed one of my fellow classmates."

She looked at him, and it was something in his eyes that convinced her that he was telling the truth. "He violated me and my sister and because of it; I have poisoned him with a very slow acting poison."

"Won't he figure it out?"

"It will be too late by the time he does. At first, it mirrors you getting drunk, and you'll get real sleepy. When you wake you'll throw up. By tomorrow, he'll think he has a common cold and the following day; he'll begin throwing up violently, and then he'll be dead a few hours later."

"Take heart, he will not live that long, I promise. What's your name?"

She hesitated and then answered. "My name is Tyla."

"Tyla, thanks for your help." He handed her a small bag of coins. Sun was about to turn away when she reached out and stopped him.

"Take this." She handed him a key. "He's staying on the first floor in room six."

"He will pay, I promise." Sun reassured her again. "Is there another inn nearby?"

"The Snowdrift Inn is further down the road." She pointed toward the west.

He thanked her again and left.

Breen anxiously paced around the room, while waiting for Sun. She was worried about him and hoped that he didn't do anything unwise by fighting the fox. To occupy her time, she bought some healing supplies and wrote a note for Jacko, in case they were gone when he returned. It dawned on her that she hadn't thought about him since before her encounter with Slyantom and now this added to her stress level as well.

She was about to leave when Sun walked through the door. He told her they needed to leave right away and assured her that everything was okay. She gave him the note for Jacko, and he scribbled where they would be staying and handed it to the healers. He gave them specific instructions not to mention they were there to anyone else.

Outside, Sun told her they would be staying at the Snowdrift Inn and kept a safe distance from each other just to make sure they weren't being followed. As they passed the Inn of the Snorting Dragon, he was relieved that Slyantom's men weren't posted outside. After arriving at the Snowdrift Inn, they booked a small room on the top floor, and left a message for Jacko with the innkeeper.

****

A short while later, Jacko and Katara arrived at Snowdrift and took Torhan to the healers. He was still unconscious. When the healers saw his legs, they gathered everything they would need for their procedure. Katara insisted on helping them. Before they started, one of the healers handed Jacko the note and then asked to leave room.

"Tell me everything." Breen said as soon as Sun closed their room's door.

"The serving girl poisoned Slyantom, and that was why he must've said the ale tasted funny."

"What? She could have poisoned me just for being there. Is he dead?"

"No. She said it's a very slow acting poison that will take days for him to die, unless he gets help."

"Then you don't have to fight him?"

Sun smiled. "There's no guarantee he'll die."

"And there's no guaranteeing he won't." Breen added.

"I can't leave this to chance; this might be my only opportunity to kill him."

Breen looked down.

"Breen," he lifted her face by her chin with his left hand so that their eyes met, "when I joined my Order, I placed an oath, and I have to live by those codes; it's who I am."

"I just don't want you to get hurt or..." she was unable to finish her words.

"I'll be fine." He produced a key and showed it to her. "It's to his room."

"So what's your plan?"

"Since he did not engage my fellow classmate in a fair fight then he will be shown the same courtesy, and I will do whatever is necessary to kill him. If that means sneaking into his room while he is sleeping, I will do that."

"I am going with you." She firmly stated. He was about to object when she interrupted him. "Like you just said, you will do whatever it takes to end his life and so will I."

Sun shook his head in protest. "No. If Jacko returns, then you will stay here, and we will take care of him." He firmly said.

"What about your wounds? The healers said you will be in trouble if your stitches tear."

"There's no time for them to heal. Did you get the items they wrote on the paper?"

"I forgot all about them. I'll go get them now. If I return and you're gone, I'll rip your stitches out myself." She said grinning.

Someone knocked on their door.

Breen drew her weapon and stepped to the side of the door.

"Who is it?" Sun asked.

"It's me Jacko, open the door."

Sun opened the door, Breen sheathed her blade after seeing him, and he closed the door behind him.

"We rescued Torhan." Jacko said smiling.

"Where is he now?"

"In the care of the healers. He was injured."

"Where's Katara?" Breen asked.

"She is with him."

"Sit down brother, I have some news." Sun said.

After they were seated, Sun told him about Slyantom, where he was staying, his men, the key, and how he was poisoned.

Jacko was delighted by the news, and then he realized something. "If he's still alive that means either more of our brothers have died by his hand, or they haven't found him yet." He stated.

"I hope you're right about the latter." Sun replied.

"I will face him alone. You're too wounded."

"Thanks for your concern my friend, but despite being in my current condition, I can still fight better than you. We will fight him together."

"And me too." Breen said.

"We are not assassins we have standards to abide by." Jacko said.

"Not this time. He killed Teacher Ma like a coward, and we will not show him mercy and have a fair fight."

"So what's your plan?"

"I have a fight scheduled with one of his men tonight for insulting me when I went to the inn earlier. After I am finished with him, we will go to Slyantom's room and kill him while he's sleeping."

"I have a better idea." Breen said, and both men looked at her. "He took a liking to me earlier, so how about this. I go to his room, get him drunk and get his weapons away from him. After that, you enter and take care of the rest."

Jacko liked her idea, but Sun clearly did not.

"No it's too dangerous. He's a trained killer." Sun said.

"You said it yourself we need to take full advantage of every opportunity available."

"Sun she's right." Jacko said.

"Don't let your feelings for me sway your decision." Breen said.

"Feelings? When did that happen?" Jacko asked.

"Don't start." Sun's reaction brought a smile to Breen's face, which was followed by her chuckling.

"Will Torhan and Katara help?" Breen asked.

"Torhan won't be able to, but I'll ask Katara." Jacko said and turned his attention back to Sun. "I am going with you tonight just in case there will be more than one of his bodyguards." He got up.

"Where are you going?" Breen asked him.

"To see Katara, why?"

"If Slyantom sees you before tonight, our plan will fall apart. I'll go back and talk to her."

"She's right. We need to stay out of sight until this evening." Sun added.

They spent the next hour finalizing their plan and when they were through Breen got up, kissed Sun on the lips, and parted. After she left, Sun spoke. "I'm not putting her in any danger, so we need to go after Slyantom before—"

"Look," Jacko stopped his friend from continuing, "I know that you care for her, but if she manages to take him by surprise, we might be able to kill him. I've dealt with him before. He's clever and skilled with his blades." Sun was about to say something, but Jacko continued. "Teacher Ma died by his hand, and he was ranked higher than you."

Sun reflected on his words. "Alright you convinced me. I'm going down for some tea, did you want to come?"

Jacko nodded.

"After we have tea, let's train for a bit." Sun said on their way downstairs.

After Breen entered the healers, she went straight to the back room and saw Katara sitting next to Torhan. "How is he?" She said looking at Torhan, who was still unconscious.

"We won't know for a few days if he'll keep his legs."

"What happened to him?"

"That maniac in the house had him connected to a device that pumped greenish liquid into his body. I can only imagine what would've happened to him if we hadn't gotten there in time."

"We need your help." Breen simply said.

"In what way?"

Breen told her about their plan to kill Slyantom and how the fox was poisoned. Katara simply said no and stated that she was needed by Torhan's side.

"But Jacko is his friend. What do you think Torhan will say if something happens to him, and you could have prevented it?"

"Look, I don't feel any obligation to your cause. They can avoid him and let the poison do its work."

"No they can't. They need to make sure he dies, because he's going to Mirkin to kill someone else."

"I've been through enough. I can't support you on this." Katara went silent and turned her attention back to Torhan.

Breen got disgusted and left.

Jacko and Sun had just finished training when Breen returned and delivered the news about Katara.

"I don't blame her," Jacko began. "She has no ties to us."

"But Torhan is your friend and out of respect for him, she should help us." Breen stated.

"I'd rather she watch over him anyway."

"I still think she should help."

"You can't force someone." Sun said.

"She's been through enough." Said Jacko. "Who knows she might help if you give her time."

Breen handed Sun the healing supplies and spoke. "I'm hungry can I get you something from downstairs?"

They told her what they wanted, and she left.

Breen ate, while Sun continued preparing for his fight with Slyantom's man. He had to be careful of his wound, so he protected the area with extra bandages and had Jacko attack him, purposely aiming for the wound. When he felt ready, he sat down and ate.

"Make sure you protect your wound." Breen said.

"I will."

"What's your strategy?" Jacko asked.

"He's right handed, so once I disable his arm; he should be easy to beat. Plus he's a bit cocky, so I'll exploit that as well."

"How do you know that he's right handed?" Breen asked.

"That was easy to figure out. His weapon was sheathed on his left side."

When it was time, Sun put on his studded gloves, and hid a dagger somewhere on his body.

When they arrived at the area where Sun was supposed to meet his adversary, Jacko and Breen stayed just out of sight and checked the area for anyone else that might be there to help Sun's foe.

Meanwhile, Sun proceeded into the open and said he was there. A few seconds later, the man who insulted him stepped out of the shadows. His antagonist was armed with a long sword and wearing leather armor.

"I'm glad you showed slanted eyes." He said to Sun.

"Of course I did. I challenged you and now I am going to teach you a lesson."

"We'll see about that, crooked eyes." Slyantom's man belligerently said.

"Is this to the death or would you like a few broken bones?" Sun said confidently.

"You can do whatever you want. I only leave life-altering wounds."

"Good, that's very good. I'll let you pick. Would you like your arm or leg broken? Better yet, how about I pluck one of your eyes out or make you a mute, so you can finally shut up?"

"Your arrogance will be your downfall slanted eyes."

"And your racial slurs are just a cover up for your inability to control the situation."

"I hate your kind and you are nothing better than the smelly boar race."

"We all bleed red and now you will. I've decided that you're not even worthy to breathe any longer. So fight to the death you racist pig." Sun had had enough of his mouth and decided to end his life instead of teaching him a lesson.

"Where's your weapon?" Slyantom's man asked as he was unsheathing his sword.

"My hands and feet should suffice. Let's get this over with; I need a drink." Sun replied, and they began closing the distance.

Sun had a knack for determining an opponent's strength and weakness just by his posture and the way that he moved. He studied his opponent as he shifted his weight from his front leg to his back while walking up to him. When Slyantom's man was close enough, he placed all of his weight on his front leg and swept his blade downward and viciously at Sun's head. Sun recognized the attack and easily moved out of the way and then invited him to continue his assault by exposing his left leg.

The bodyguard, thinking he had an opening, attacked Sun's limb, and was surprised when he missed. Sun continued his muse with false openings, until he had an opening of his own and kicked him in the chest. The strike failed to hurt him, because his armor absorbed the blow, but it did, however, disrupt his next attack, and Sun kicked him in the head and sent him stumbling away. Sun advanced but his adversary recovered in time and swung his sword in a slicing motion, aiming for his chest. Sun leaned out of the way. His opponent whipped the blade in the other direction, and Sun stepped in and simultaneously blocked his attack with his right hand and punched him in the ribs with his left.

The powerful impact cracked his ribs, labored his breathing, and gave Sun another opportunity to attack. He then raked him across the face with the dragon technique. The deadly clawed hand ripped chunks of flesh away and sent him reeling off balance. Sun followed him and leapt into the air kicking him in the head and sending him to the ground.

Sun paused. "You're no match for me." He said.

Slyantom's man climbed to his feet and then spit blood on the ground. "Maybe you're right, but it's not me who will die this evening. Munder?" He shouted for his companion and when he didn't answer, Sun grinned.

"There's no help coming for you. You see; I had a feeling that you would have someone waiting for me, so I took the liberty of bringing some of my friends with me."

Jacko and Breen stepped out from the left, dragging a dead body.

"You already met the female and here is my other friend."

"You're the women who drank with my boss." Slyantom's man said.

Breen nodded while she and Jacko approached.

"You may kill me, but Slyantom will kill you all."

"I don't think so. You see we're in Snowdrift to kill him." Jacko said. "He killed one of our classmates about a month ago and will now atone for his crime."

"Plus, he's been poisoned as well so it's a foregone conclusion that he'll die." Sun added.

"You'll never get away with this." Slyantom's man said, but his tone was unconvincing.

"It's time for you to die." Jacko said.

Realizing his fate, Slyantom's man attacked Breen with a thrust. She easily parried his weapon away, while sidestepping and slicing his wrist with a draw cut. The wound severed his tendons, which resulted in him dropping his weapon. Jacko kicked him in the groin, and as he was doubling over, Sun executed a devastating axe-kick on the back of his head, which snapped his neck and killed him instantly.

"That's that." Sun said.

"It's almost time to deal with Slyantom." Jacko added, and they walked back to their room.

Slyantom awoke from his deep sleep, drenched in sweat. His fur was matted and disheveled, and he felt terrible. It was dark outside so had no idea what time it was, or for how long he had been asleep. He began to ponder what had happened to him and came to a swift conclusion that someone put something into his ale. The list of suspects included the cook, the serving girl, and Elva. After all she could've slipped something into his drink when he wasn't looking. His stomach abruptly tightened and churned. He reached over for a nearby bowl and vomited. Afterward, he tried to rise, found that he couldn't and fell back down reeling in pain.

Silently, he promised that whoever did this to him would pay for this with their lives. With a shaky hand, he drank the last vial of greenish liquid. The brew burned his throat on its way down. A few seconds later, he felt drowsy and then fell asleep.

****

"What are you proposing?" Sun said to Jacko.

"I'm going to climb down onto the ledge from the second floor and move over to his room. If he's asleep, I'll climb in and kill him. If he isn't, then I'll signal down to Breen for her to come up to his room while I wait outside on the ledge." Jacko said.

They looked at Breen.

"When Jacko signals me to come up, I'll drink with him until he passes out, and then we'll kill him." She said.

"How are you going to get past his guards?" Ask Jacko.

"Womanly charm." She replied, smiling.

"I'll make sure that she gets in and then return to the room above and wait for your signal after she enters." Sun said.

"What if he doesn't want to drink?" Jacko asked.

Sun looked at them in turn. "If he doesn't want to then don't do anything foolish, just talk to him. I'll be there shortly, disguised as an old man who thinks that's his room. I'll jiggle the handle and bang on the door. When Slyantom opens it, I'll continue to act like that's my room. My distraction should give you enough time to enter the room and hopefully, Breen, will be able to snatch his weapons away from him.

He'll grow tired of me and when he tries to force me out of the room, I'll attack him. Breen I want you to stay out of our way." He looked at her. "Jacko and I fought as a team before, and I'm afraid he might try to use as a shield."

"I just thought of something. How are we going to use the room on the second floor if it's already occupied?" Jacko asked.

"I have the answer to that." Breen said and produced a long instrument that looked like a metal finger. "I picked this up in Mirkin. It's called the Finger of Lock-picking, and it's supposed to pick any lock known to man."

"I'll take care of whoever is inside." Sun said and then went about dressing as an old man.

The inn was unusually crowded when Breen entered the establishment. People were scattered about the room making merry with their tankards raised high, and songs being sung. She looked for the fox, but he was nowhere in sight and motioned for Sun and Jacko to enter. Sun looked around for Tyla, but the serving wench wasn't there either, which made him wonder what befell her. They blended in with the patrons for a while until Jacko motioned that he was going upstairs and left without drawing too much attention.

After he went up the stairs, Breen went outside and stood on the side of the inn where the fox's room was. Jacko stopped when he reached the top landing, looked around to make sure no one saw him, and then disappeared down the corridor. When he rounded the corner, he saw two heavily armed men standing outside of a room at the far end. He was pretty sure that it was Slyantom's room and proceeded up the stairs on the left.

He picked a random room, knocked a few times to make sure no one was inside and used the tool Breen gave him. He then unlocked the door and stepped inside. He was relieved to find the dark room empty of occupants and after his eyes adjusted, he navigated his way over to the window, looked outside until he spotted a way down to the first floor, climbed down and then positioned himself to the side of Slyantom's window. Sun waited a few minutes after they were gone before going upstairs and taking up position near the room the two men guarded.

Outside on the ledge, Jacko looked through the window and saw Slyantom walking around. He signaled to Breen, who then walked back inside the inn and up the stairs. She stopped when she reached the old man.

"Ready?" Sun whispered.

"Wish me luck!" She replied.

"Be careful and wait for us once you're inside."

Breen took a deep breath and was gone before Sun could say anything further.

When the guards saw the cute girl with long blonde hair approaching them, they became a bit suspicious and the one on the right stepped forward. "What do you want?" He asked.

"I'm here to see Slyantom." Breen replied.

"For what?" The other guard asked.

"He invited me to his room."

The guard on the left smiled, running his gaze up and down her lithe form. "I'm sure he did." He commented.

"Are you going to let me in or what?" She pressed.

"What's your name?"

"Elva."

"Wait here." He said, opening the door using a key and entered.

"If the boss doesn't want you, how about you have a go with me?" The other said.

"Not on your life. You're just a hired hand."

The guard was seething and about to do something, when the door opened.

"He agreed to see you only if you get searched first."

"Don't bother." Breen said and handed him a dagger.

"Not good enough. Well?"

She agreed, and the other guard ran his hands up and down her body. Lucky for her, he did not find the dagger hidden in her boot. Satisfied, he stepped away and the other guard moved aside, allowing her to enter.

After the door closed, Sun knew that he couldn't leave her in there for a long period of time. His first order of business was to take care of the guards. He needed to be careful, because if he made too much noise, Slyantom might overhear him, realize it was a trap and turn on Breen. He was afraid for her, but needed to push aside those thoughts and take care of business. He inspected his gloves, tightened any of the loose studs and then hunched over and walked down the corridor.

When the guards saw an old man in tattered clothes, hunched over and limping his way towards them, they looked at each other.

"Now what?" The guard on the right whispered.

"Get out of here old man." The other guard sternly said.

Sun ignored him and continued walking.

When he was close enough, the guard on the right placed an arm out in front of him and blocked his passage. "We said to leave old man!"

"My room is over there." Sun replied in an elderly voice and pointed down the hallway to the right.

"Come back later."

Sun turned his head toward him and said in a weakened voice. "Please let me pass?"

"I SAID TO COME BACK LATER!" The guard said and shoved him backwards.

Sun did his best to appear to stumble away.

"Get out of here before we get angry." The other guard warned.

Sun ignored him and walked toward them again. The same guard who shoved him approached with his arms extended to push him once more. Sun quickly sidestepped to the right, wrapped his left arm around both of his arms, and punched him under the jaw, knocking him out.

The other guard's smile faded and he engaged the old man. Sun kicked him in the stomach and used the Eagle Claw technique to grab him by his throat and squeezed his fingers on his windpipe. The guard's eyes widened from both the excruciating pain and the fact that he couldn't he breathe.

"Know this before you die. Your boss is next." Sun whispered and yanked his hand away, taking his throat with him.

After breaking the other guard's neck, he propped their bodies up against the wall in a way that they appeared to have passed out. He ran upstairs, entered the room, and waited by the window for Jacko's signal. After Breen entered the room, she was asked to join her host at the round table in the center of the room. The chairs were positioned so that the window was on one side and the door on the other. After they were seated, Slyantom rolled up his sleeves and filled their goblets with wine. Breen glanced over his shoulder and saw his swords and armor near the bed.

"So you decided to come see me after all?" The fox said.

"Could you blame me for being attracted to you? You're smart, strong, and look to be cunning. That's everything that I look for in a person, regardless of their race."

Slyantom smiled. He loved having his ego stroked. "Drink up my dear."

She placed the goblet to her lips and took a small swig and found the wine to have a sweet delicate taste. The tasty swill beckoned her to drink more, and she couldn't pull her lips away until she emptied the goblet. The fox smiled.

"What is this?" She asked.

"A special wine that creates a magnificent experience for you, I call it 'delight'. Do you like it?"

"I've never tasted anything like this before."

Slyantom picked up his trick goblet and drank the imaginary wine.

"You never told me why you're in Snowdrift?" He asked.

"Just traveling and seeing the world."

"I'd be happy to show you around town before I leave." Slyantom refilled her goblet and Breen felt compelled to drink it, which she did in one gulp.

"This wine is so good. I can't get enough of it."

"I know. That happened to me the first time I drank it as well." He poured her another cup, and she hungrily downed that too despite knowing in the back of her mind that he was the one that was to get drunk.

She craved even more and the fox obliged her. By the time she finished it, her vision was blurred, and she was unable to think straight. Suddenly, her world closed in around her, and she fell over, unconscious.

Jacko watched things unfold and was shocked at how much Breen was drinking, knowing that if she got intoxicated things could go terribly wrong. He looked up, and motioned to Sun in a panic that he needed to get down there, and he disappeared from view in a hurry. When he turned his attention back, Slyantom was carrying Breen in his arms to the bed. It was then that Jacko noticed his swords near the nightstand. He was about to enter the room and make an attempt at getting them when the door opened, and an old man stepped in.

Slyantom stopped and said. "Now isn't this interesting. Who are you and how did you get past my men?"

When Sun saw Breen in his arms, he dropped the old man act. "Did you train them? It wasn't hard to get past them." Sun stated.

"Let me guess you're not an old man?" The fox cradled Breen in his arms. "Why would you go through all of this trouble of getting dressed up, kill my men, and enter my room, especially when I have business to attend to?" He glanced down at Breen and then back at Sun. "You must want to die."

"Not today fox, it's your turn. You killed one of my classmates and must atone for that."

"Oh? Which one? I've killed so many men in my lifetime."

"Does the name Ma sound familiar?"

"Hmm, a man named Ma let me think."

His words sounded as if they were mocking the name instead of trying to recall it, Jacko thought, and then he saw Slyantom inching his way toward the side of the bed closest to the window.

"I remember the name. He was from the Order of the Open Palm. He owed my boss some money or something like that." Slyantom said.

"You have it wrong. His father owed it to him, and you murdered an innocent man." Sun said.

"If I remember correctly it was a fair fight." Slyantom's mocking tone struck a nerve with Sun.

"Put the girl down and let's settle this."

"Was she part of your ruse?" Slyantom said, cradling her closer.

"No, I don't know who she is.

"Well I believe that she was, and it's too bad because she would have been a nice mate for the evening."

The reaction on Sun's face told Slyantom that his assumption was correct and in the next instant, he released the lower half of her body to the floor and had a knife against her throat. Jacko entered through the window; and the fox turned his head toward, him causing Jacko to stop.

"And who are you?" Slyantom asked.

"I'm with him." Jacko replied.

Slyantom studied Jacko for several long seconds and then pressed his blade tighter against Breen's throat. He suddenly realized that the new intruder was closer to his blades then he was. "You look familiar to me, have we met before?" He paused. "Wait a minute. I do remember you. You were the one with Ma on that day he died. Now I understand everything. You got away from my men and told your Order, and that's how you found me."

"Not exactly, but close enough." Jacko said.

"Let her go." Sun demanded.

Slyantom turned his gaze back to him while keeping a wary eye on Jacko. "Well, it appears that we have a standoff, so I'll make you a deal. Leave now and I'll release your friend. Otherwise, she dies; your friend dies, and I'll get my weapons and kill you too."

"What makes you think that you'll succeed?" Jacko asked.

"Boy I don't know how escaped my men, but know this; I will kill you and anyone else I choose. There's no need for you to die tonight. Your classmate's death was all about business."

"That's where you're wrong," said Sun, "you killed him unfairly and will pay with your life. Now put the girl down and let's settle this like two warriors."

Breen finally woke up and heard Sun's voice. She opened her eyes slightly, saw him by the door and a blade only inches away from her face. Despite her head spinning and her mind being clouded from the drug; she realized what was happening. If she didn't get away from the fox by the time Sun attacked him, then she would definitely get hurt. In one swift motion, she grabbed the knife hand, planted her feet firmly on the ground, and pushed herself backward, taking the fox with her to the ground. Breen's full body weight landed hard on his chest and knocked the air from his lungs.

The unexpected move caught Jacko and Sun by surprise, and they weren't sure what to do because Breen was in the way. Breen squirmed around, while holding his wrist firmly, until she was out from underneath his arm and rolled off of his body while twisting his wrist in an unnatural way. The pressure on his wrist forced Slyantom to drop his weapon. The fox squirmed and as he was getting to his feet, he punched Breen in the face so that she couldn't do anything else him.

Sun and Jacko moved in, with Jacko striking first. He stabbed at Slyantom's face with his finger-knives, but the fox grabbed his arm, flipped him over his shoulder, and into Sun, sending them both to the ground.

Slyantom's path to his precious swords was unimpeded, so with determination he made his way over to them. As soon as he wrapped his hands around their hilts, he was rewarded with a sharp burning pain in his right shoulder. He gritted his teeth and turned around to see his attacker standing there with another knife in hand and her two friends rising to their feet. Glancing over his shoulder, he saw the hilt of a small knife protruding from his shoulder blade and was pretty sure his arm was useless. He let go of the sword in his right hand.

"Not as easy as you thought." Jacko taunted Slyantom.

"The battle is far from over human. If it wasn't for her lucky throw, I would have killed you all by now." He said confidently.

"Let's finish this." Sun said to him, and they started spreading out to flank the fox.

Slyantom knew that if they managed to do so, he would be in trouble, but the room's large size was his ally, so he waited until they were close enough and then charged after what he believed to be the strongest of the three, the fool in the old man costume.

Sun wasn't all that surprised that he made an attempt to kill him first, and since he was ready, he easily blocked and evaded several attacks. What he failed to realize was that Slyantom was setting him up for a real strike, and he sliced effortlessly across Sun's stomach, ripping into clothes, stitches, flesh and sending him spiraling away. The fox had been in many fights and faced several opponents at once, so after he cut the old man, he quickly turned around and blocked Jacko's attack with his right arm and butted him in the head with the sword's hilt, knocking him out.

The fox was about to finish him off, when a dagger whizzed by his head and got his attention. He turned and saw the female with her arm extended. His eyes quickly shifted from Jacko and Sun and after seeing them still on the ground, he smiled and began confidently walking towards her.

"You see my dear, even with one blade I am more than a match for the three of you."

Sun tried to rise, but his wound was deep and he fell back down. Breen started backing away, and Slyantom took one last look at the two men on the ground and then turned his gaze on her again. What he didn't see was the open flask, cupped in her right hand that was down by her side.

"Please let us go." She pleaded.

"Go? It's too late for them, but you, maybe if you do your womanly duties and service my needs, I'll let you live."

Breen continued backing away and with each passing step, she could tell Slyantom was becoming more confident and relaxed.

Slyantom stopped. "Well this is your last chance. Do you want to come with me or die along with your friends?"

Breen realized that her friends were far enough away so they wouldn't get hit with the contents of the flask and then stopped. "Only if you let them go."

Sun did not know what Breen had in mind, but there was no way he was going to allow Slyantom to live, so he somehow found the strength to stand. He could feel blood flowing freely down his leg and gripped his stomach, trying to stem it. "I'd rather die than see that happen." He bravely said.

Slyantom glanced at him over his shoulder and said. "Regardless of her decision, you will."

The distraction was enough for Breen to throw the flask of dissolving at him. Out of the corner of his eye, Slyantom saw something coming in his direction and moved to the right, but not far enough to evade it entirely, and was hit in his left shoulder instead of being hit fully in the chest. The liquid rapidly ate through his clothes, fur, and flesh causing him to wail in pain and drop his sword. Seeing his opportunity, Sun took three steps and leapt off of his front leg, but his weakened state hampered his aim and instead of kicking him in the head, he managed to hit him with a glancing blow to his shoulder.

The impact sent them both to the ground in separate directions, with Sun holding his stomach in obvious pain and Slyantom reaching frantically for his sword. Everything slowed for Breen, until the fox held his sword and began to rise. She moved past him and grabbed his other sword and pointed it at his face. The fox could tell that her threat was more of a deterrent than anything else. He glanced at the fighter dressed as old man who was kneeling on one leg and poised to make one final attack, and the other human was awake and getting to his feet.

He quickly assessed his own strength; his left arm was useless, and his right was limited due to the dagger still embedded in his shoulder. He wasn't sure if he could even parry another attack if the girl decided to swing. He decided that he wanted to live to fight another day and backed away to the window, keeping his sword in front of him so that no one had any bright ideas of attacking.

When the fox reached the window, he said. "Next time we meet I will kill you." He climbed out and jumped down.

Jacko stumbled over and saw him running away, while Breen checked Sun's wound.

"You're bleeding pretty badly, so we need to get you to the healers." She said.

"Should I go after him?" Jacko asked.

"No." Sun answered.

"But he's wounded."

"We'll get him another time."

They helped Sun to his feet and left.

Chapter 11: Celthric -A Blade's Quest (Part II)

With a sense of pride and accomplishment for misleading the knights, the Presence rode on through the light snowfall and ever growing darkness. They were weak-minded and easily fooled. Now with their assistance, It was sure to reach Celthric by morning.

In the early morning hours, a voice whispered for It to change direction and go northwest through the forest. It listened with eagerness, guiding the horse around trees and through undergrowth for several miles until the forest parted and opened up in a circular shape. Bodies, from a battle long ago, littered the ground. Most of the broken skeletons were still wearing tattered armor and clutching various weapons of war in their bony hands. The Presence knew this was the place Celthric had described, so It called out for the entity.

"WHERE ARE YOU, CELTHRIC?" The Presence shouted.

"Come to the center," a voice responded seconds later, taking the Presence by surprise.

The Presence nudged the horse forward. It was amazed at the number of bodies that fought in this battle and wondered which side had won on that day. It was lost in thought when the horse suddenly reared up, bucked around, threw It from the saddle, and ran off in the opposite direction.

The Presence landed hard on the ground, crushing many bones under Its weight. It got up, brushed off many bone fragments, and removed the ones sticking out of Its host's arms and legs. Gingerly, It moved toward the center, avoiding sharp bones and weapons along the way. Halfway there, It saw a lone warrior hunched over with a large spear sticking straight through his body. The Presence smiled, knowing Its journey was coming to an end.

When It was only a few feet away from the warrior, It stopped abruptly to study him in his final moments. The armor, once a proud display of workmanship and design, was nothing more than a rusty piece of tarnished metal that looked like it could crumble at any second.

Arrows and bolts protruded throughout the hardened plate, and dents from heavy war hammers were visible. The Presence's gaze fell upon the rusty, two-handed sword held firmly in his gauntleted hands and buried several inches into the earth. *"Could that be Celthric?"* the Presence thought.

An answer ensued, "Yes. Take hold of the sword and all will be revealed."

Cautiously, the entity walked closer until the weapon was within reach and all It had to do was unclench the skeletal fingers and take it. It was about to do so when It heard horses behind him.

Turning around, It was surprised to see Chief Weis and the men from Solarce.

"How did they find me so fast?" the Presence thought.

"Hurry. You don't have much time. If they reach you, you will die and all will be lost," the voice warned.

Chief Weis shouted from his horse to give up.

"GRAB IT," the voice said.

The Presence wheeled about, unfolded the dead warrior's metal digits, and took hold of the hilt. In a blinding flash of light, the Presence was suddenly whisked deep inside the recesses of his host's mind, where he stood in a dark meadow, along with the old man and Norice.

"It's time for you to leave this host and be on your way. I will save Norice," Celthric said politely to the Presence.

"You said that we would rule together."

"You're a fool and a pawn. I only needed you because of what you did. I was merely afraid you would get him killed, otherwise I would've banished you a long time ago."

"You have tricked him as well, so don't be noble."

"I ask you again to release your hold."

The entity laughed. "That's the thing, Celthric. When I touched the sword, I discovered just how powerful the weapon is and your true nature."

"Really. And what do you think I am?"

"An entity living in this metal shell."

The old man grinned. "And how did you come to that determination?"

"I have abilities of my own and powers that you underestimated. So, I'm going to give you the same choice you gave me. Leave on your own accord or be destroyed."

"Are you sure this is what you want?" Celthric smirked.

"You don't have any power over me, especially within his mind."

"Oh, don't I?" Celthric paused, letting his words take effect. "Since you refuse to leave, you will now be subject to my horror."

"You can..."

The meadow suddenly transformed into a place surrounded by cold steel walls. The Presence's smile faded as It looked around, realizing that there was no escape, and maybe It made a grave error. Meanwhile, Norice realized the area had changed, became frightened and retreated to the far corner, cowering.

Celthric took on a disturbing look, and the Presence knew Its fate was all but sealed.

"I've reconsidered. You can have him, let me go," the Presence pleaded.

"To tell you the truth," the old man shook his head, smiling, "I was never going to allow you to leave."

Celthric suddenly morphed into a giant humanoid creature, standing nearly ten feet tall, with long arms ending with razor-sharp talons, and four inch fangs dripping with an unknown substance from his mouth. The Presence instantly became terrified and moved away until It bumped against one of the walls. Celthric laughed hideously. The Presence tried to escape Norice's mind, but Its actions were in vain.

"You almost cost me my host. Do you know how many centuries I've waited for someone to answer my call? He and I will rule, and you will cease to exist. Goodbye fool," Celthric boomed.

"Please let me go?"

"The time for you to leave should have been before you ever met me. Now you will exist no more," Celthric said, walking closer.

Celthric raised his talons and struck the entity repeatedly. Each blow ripped through Its shadowy form until the Presence dissolved away into nothingness. Satisfied when it was over, Celthric morphed back into the old man, and the walls gave way to the meadow.

"It felt good to kill again," Celthric thought and walked over to Norice, who was still cowering with his head between his knees. "Norice?" Celthric said, waiting for him to look up before continuing. "You now have your destiny to fulfill."

"Why did you destroy him?"

"If I hadn't, then he would have destroyed you, and I couldn't allow that to happen. You're far too important."

"Are you going to destroy me as well when you're finished?"

"I destroyed the creature because it tried to take possession of your body. If it wasn't for me, he would've succeeded and your family would have been left all alone to face the demon."

Norice stood up. "You still didn't answer my question. Are you going to destroy me after you're finished?"

Celthric shook his head. "No. I need you, and you need me."

"You're no better than that other creature."

Celthric smiled. "Unlike that entity, I will give you a choice. You can either allow me to flow through your body and take control, or deny my request and deal with the men that are here to murder you. We both know how this will end if you refuse me."

"If I'm so important to you, then why don't you force your will on me?"

"I cannot even though I've been waiting for a very long time. Choose swiftly, because you don't have much time."

Celthric was clever; while Norice was given two options, there was no way he was going to allow him to pick anything other than what was right for him. He just wanted his host to think he had a choice.

"If I do this, what will happen to me?"

Celthric smiled reassuringly. "Nothing, I will only control your limbs, and you will get to watch me destroy your enemies with my sword."

"And after they're dead?"

"We will travel to a place not too far from here and deal with your nightmares until they're all destroyed. You will have peace again and so will your family."

"And then?"

"I will also know peace, and we will separate."

"I don't understand."

"Once I do an act of unselfishness, I can leave this prison and rejoin my family in the afterlife."

"How did you become trapped?"

"It's a very long story and we don't have time. Are you ready?"

Norice nodded.

When they arrived, they saw the criminal standing as still as a statue. It was hard to tell what he was doing, because Norice was staring at the ground, holding a rusty two-handed sword. Weis knew there was no way in hell Norice was going to escape him this time. He was coming with them dead or alive, that he was sure of.

They dismounted and gathered close to the captain.

"Dead or alive," Weis instructed.

"We will give him a chance to surrender. There's a lot at stake, and my brother and I have questions for him as well," Hrist countered.

"Fine, but he's not escaping, so you better keep that in mind." Weis' tone told everyone present just how frustrated he was.

Timol and Granit loaded their crossbows; Hrist notched an arrow; Weis unsheathed his short sword with his left hand, and held his shield in his right. Tranter held his single-handed crossbow in his left and a dagger in his right; and Prol grasped his mighty two-handed ax with both hands. When they were ready, they advanced.

****

Norice's eyes snapped open, and he was standing on a battlefield. It took him several minutes to realize where he was and to take notice of the rusty sword in his hands. It felt strange because the last thing he remembered was being in the town, and now he was standing on a battlefield.

He saw men approaching from the south. He recognized Chief Weis and some of the others, but not the men in armor. Lost in thought, he didn't realize his left hand moved on its own and slid down the rusty edge of the weapon, cutting his palm deep enough to draw blood. He winced, looked downward, and watched his arm move up and down the blade, smearing blood all over the weapon. Like water washing away dirt, the rust began to disappear, and the sword began pulsing and vibrating as if it had a life of its own. In the next instant, the memories from creatures, both human and non-human that ever wielded the weapon, surged through Norice's mind. So vast they were that he was driven down to his knees, clutching his head in obvious pain.

His psyche was on the brink of being crushed when Celthric used his superior intellect to ease his mind, and then controlled the flow of thoughts being processed. After the experience ended, Norice knew everything and everyone that used the sword and more importantly, the truth about Celthric. He wasn't an entity, a demon, or even a ghost. He was nothing more than an evil, intelligent sword with the ability to read minds and manipulate others.

The metal alloy wrapped around Celthric, also had a purpose, and that was to kill. How the two became one, he didn't know. Norice felt an enticement to be one with the weapon and felt power like none he'd ever experienced before. He also knew that he could be something greater and become the stuff of legend.

"Norice," Celthric whispered in his mind, "you and I can rule the world. Let me take control of your body until you are ready. I will train you to be an incredible fighter like your predecessors. Do you want this?"

"Yes." Norice eagerly said.

"From this day forth, you will be known as Widowmaker."

"Widowmaker. I like that," Norice whispered.

"Let's kill those men who are here to kill you."

The Widowmaker stood erect and studied the intricate carvings on the sword while he waited for Weis and the others.

****

Chief Weis and the others were less than fifty feet away from Norice when they saw him drop to his knees, clutching his head.

"What is going on with him?" Prol asked.

"Careful, it could be a trick," Tranter responded.

"He's clever, so don't take any unnecessary chances," Weis warned.

They walked cautiously as a unit; Granit was to the far left, followed by Tranter, Weis, Prol, Hrist, and Timol. Hrist kept the bowstring slacked, while Tranter, Granit, and Timol held their crossbows trained on Norice with their fingers off the triggers. By the time they reached Norice, he was back on his feet, staring at the sword.

"Norice, drop your weapon and come quietly. We don't want this to end poorly for you," Weis said.

Norice didn't respond and continued staring at the mystical blade as the rust finally dissolved, exposing an alloy that was as shiny as freshly polished steel. The hunting party neared him and began to fan outward.

"Norice, I'll ask you again. Drop your weapon and come quietly, you have nowhere left to go."

The Widowmaker slowly turned his head toward them. "The man you seek is dead."

"Norice, you need help, and I promise to do everything I can."

"His voice sounds different, don't you think?" Prol whispered to Hrist.

"You're right. He does sound different."

"If you're not Norice, then who are you?" Tranter amusingly asked.

"Me? I'm the Widowmaker."

"Well, whoever you think you are, you're still coming with us," Weis said.

The Widowmaker raised the sword into a high guard, and the blade sparkled in the morning light.

"Trust in me and allow me to flow through your limbs," Celthric whispered reassuringly through Norice's mind. The farmer gave his will over to Celthric.

"I'll disarm him." Prol announced to the others and stepped forward, hefting his ax in front of his body. "Last chance, drop the weapon," he said to Norice.

Norice didn't reply and waited for him with a disturbing look etched across his face. Prol was a very experienced fighter and knew exactly how he was going to disarm the man. In fact, he knew it should only take him three moves at most to accomplish this feat.

When Prol was within striking distance, he swung his weapon toward the right side of Norice's head. The attack was only meant for him to block the weapon, which Norice did. As soon as the weapons clashed, Prol released his bottom hand from the weapon, stepped closer, and wrapped his left arm around Norice's arms, trapping them underneath.

Prol was in the process of punching him in the jaw with his free hand when Norice pushed his arms outward and created enough separation to move his left arm upward, and wrap it around Prol's right arm.

Prol punched Norice twice in the head with his free hand, but despite the steel gauntlet, it had no effect on his opponent. Norice squeezed Prol's trapped arm against his body and crushed both his arm and the steel armor as if it were made of tin. Prol's screams were interrupted when the Widowmaker wound the mystical blade around his head and cleanly chopped off Prol's head. Norice felt a rush of adrenaline after the man died and then crouched down in the Pflug guard to await their next attack. For Celthric, it was far too easy. He merely read his opponent's thoughts and knew exactly what he was going to do before he even moved.

Timol, Granit, and Tranter fired one after the other, while Hrist, still shocked over his brother's death, stood idle.

The Widowmaker easily evaded two of the bolts and parried a third. The men reloaded, fired again, and had similar results. Frustrated, Weis charged forward. Tranter unsheathed his short sword and followed, while Timol and Granit reloaded their weapons.

Hrist snapped out of his trance, knowing for the first time in his life what true hatred was. Intent on slaying this evil man with one well-placed shot, he carefully aimed his bow, and fired at Norice's head.

"A true shot," Hrist thought until the arrow was deflected away by the Widowmaker, who now possessed cat-like reflexes with Celthric in full control. Weis was upon him, and as he attacked his flank, Norice spun around and easily moved aside Weis' sword with his, then brought Celthric around with lightning speed. So fast was the move, Weis barely had enough time to raise his shield and block the attack.

The powerful impact broke Chief Weis' arm in several places and shattered the shield with a deafening sound, sending wooden fragments everywhere and hitting Chief Weis in the head, knocking him senseless. After the chief fell to the ground, a bolt and an arrow flew past Norice, and Tranter was in front of him, swinging at his head. The Widowmaker ducked under the attack, feigned a stab to draw Tranter's blade down, and with amazing speed, shifted his weight backward, and whipped Celthric around, cleaving the tracker in half at the waist. Hrist fired again, grazing Norice's right arm and catching the Widowmaker's full attention He then raised the ancient blade above his head and charged.

With the speed and agility of the fastest animal on the planet, the Widowmaker was on top of Hrist, whose only option was to use his bow to deflect the heavy two-handed sword. It was a move that saved his life before, but this time he lost his life when the thick ash snapped in two along with his skull. The Widowmaker attacked Timol next, who fired one last time, missed, and lost his head. Granit, sword in hand, charged Norice. As he was about to stab him, the Widowmaker sidestepped the attack, grabbed the hilt of Granit's sword with his right hand, turned the weapon around, and plunged the tip into his throat. He smirked at the dying man and then twisted the blade, separating his head from his body.

Weis finally regained his wits and couldn't believe what had happened. A lowly farmer, with no prior training, killed everyone. He thought about running for the horses, but knew his attempt would be futile.

The Widowmaker turned his attention toward him. "You should have let me go, Chief Weis."

Weis got to his feet, holding his sword. "You're a killer," he said and spat at the ground.

"I did what I had to do."

Chief Weis looked around at his dead companions. "Even if you kill me, there will be others."

The Widowmaker smiled. "No there won't. In time, they will forget about the person named Norice and just remember the Widowmaker."

"What about your family?"

The Widowmaker began walking toward Weis. "Celthric is part of my family now."

"Who?"

"You know what to do," Celthric said to Norice, loud enough for Weis to hear.

"Who said that?" Weis looked around.

"You heard him?" Norice asked. "That's my new friend. Take a look." The Widowmaker presented the sword proudly.

Chief Weis had heard stories about powerful weapons with the ability to possess an individual and speak, and now he realized what was going on. "Norice, that weapon is cursed. Get rid of it before it's too late."

"Cursed? Oh no, chief, it has given me purpose."

"Your family needs you."

"Family? Who do you think I am doing this for?"

"I don't understand."

"Nor would you."

"Then tell me, and I can help." Weis said.

"Do you promise to help me?"

"You have my word on it."

Norice relaxed his stance and lowered the weapon. "Okay. What do I need to do?"

"Give me the sword and come with me."

Norice nodded.

As soon as Weis was within striking distance, Norice brought the full weight of Celthric down upon him. It happened so fast, Chief Weis wasn't prepared, despite having been ready.

The sharp steel bit into his right shoulder and cleaved straight through his jerkin until the blade came out of his left hip, splitting Weis diagonally in half. The last thing he felt before everything went dark was searing pain. The Widowmaker, covered in blood and gore, stood tall, staring out at nothing. He was glad he freely gave himself over to the id of Celthric, because it made him feel powerful and invincible.

Celthric was also basking in the moment. The highly intelligent sword waited a very long time for someone to answer his call, and now he was ready to continue a journey that started more than a century ago. One that would fulfill his own desires and not the ones of whoever wielded him. He also pondered why he was drawn to his journey of finding a pool of water. Maybe during his creation he encountered these waters, and like an inborn calling, he needed to go there once again.

Turning his thoughts back to Norice, he knew the simple farmer was perfect for the task. He was inept with a blade and weak in both mind and spirit, so there was no chance he would take up his own quest. *"He just might make it this time,"* he thought, then commanded his new host onward.

For six days and nights, through two snowstorms, Norice traveled with very little sleep. Eventually, he came upon a large castle, bathed in gloomy shadows as the day faded into the night. The structure was nestled atop a sheer cliff with only one road leading up, and another one running parallel along the base about a hundred feet down. After describing the area to Celthric, the sword ordered him to stop and wait. Norice began thinking about the enormity of the task of breaking into someone's home and the physical danger that lay beyond it. He wasn't a very brave individual, so how was he going to survive if the owner had many guards? Celthric detected his fears and doubts.

"Norice," he whispered, "trust in me. Our dreams are within reach. You will see your family again."

"How? Even if I go back, I'm a wanted man."

"With me, no one can stand in your way. I promise"

Norice knew he was too far invested in this journey, so he really didn't have a choice but to see it through. "Is this where we are going?"

"Hold on." There was a long silence before Celthric spoke again. "Yes."

"What are we looking for?"

"What I'm looking for lies somewhere underneath the structure."

"And what is it?"

"For your protection I will tell you after we enter. I need to keep the information from you for now." Celthric could sense that his quest was finally ending, and he was exultant.

"So how do we get in? Do we just ride up to the gate and ask the lord for admittance?"

Celthric mentally scanned the area and detected several secret passages nearby. "There are a few ways in on the road running along the castle's base. I suggest we take one of them."

"How did you discover them?"

"I can detect them. Let's go and..." he suddenly went silent, because he felt someone of intellect trying to scan his mind.

"And what?" Norice asked impatiently.

"Think only of your family or all is lost," Celthric ordered and allowed his own mind to go blank.

Norice did as he was asked.

****

In his study, the Lord of the Mind detected a greater presence somewhere outside of his castle. The intense feelings interrupted his nightly studies, causing him to get up and walk over to the balcony. He scanned the thick darkness, looking east and then west, trying to pinpoint the source. He was about to lock into it when it suddenly stopped.

"What do we have here?" Repan said aloud. "An intelligent creature that rivals me. Interesting." Whoever was out there needed to be dealt with and Repan wasn't a fool because he never let strange findings go unanswered. He left his room and calmly walked down several flights of stairs, through the cold, empty hallway, until he entered the dojo, where he found his bodyguard training. Ying stopped what he was doing after Repan entered.

"What is it, my lord?" Ying asked.

"I've detected someone or something nearby that could be a threat to our home. Take Dojar and the skeletons, and let me know what you find."

"What am I looking for? A man, beast, giant?"

"I'm not sure, but this being has abilities, so be careful."

Ying bowed and then secured a two-by-four inch metal box on his wrist.

"Whatever it is, it won't escape my wrath," he said and turned around to face a wooden man ten feet away. He closed his fist, and an instant later, a long, spiked chain jutted forth from the box, and pierced the target. The chain spun around so fast it made a large circular hole in the middle of the target and then retracted back to its housing. "Do you like it? I just created it."

"You truly are an innovator. Happy hunting," Repan said and left the room.

Ying followed a few minutes later, walking briskly back to his room. He loved killing for and serving Repan because the man respected and paid him handsomely for his services, unlike the ungrateful Order to which he'd once belonged. After entering his quarters, he quickly dressed in his special leather armor and wrapped the Gauntlets of Strength tightly around his wrists. A few seconds later, he felt a tingling sensation racing up his arms, which made him believe he was unstoppable. As he was placing his sheathed sword inside of the leather belt, he heard a light knock on his door.

"Sir, may I enter?" Dojar asked from the other side.

"Come in."

The door opened and his bodyguard entered. He was already armed and dressed in his leather armor.

"Where are we going?" he asked upon seeing Ying ready for battle.

"The master detected an intruder outside. Let's go find him and make him wish he'd never set foot upon his kingdom," Ying replied and grabbed a green gem off his shelf.

"Is it that serious that we'll need the undead?"

"He doesn't want to take any chances. Go tell Kohter to wait here just in case."

They left the room with Dojar taking the left corridor and Ying walking straight out to the courtyard to animate six of the Skeletons of War.

****

After the being inside of the castle stopped probing his thoughts, Celthric ordered Norice to hide the horse and guided him to the secret entrance closest to them. Norice then began feeling the rocky surface until he discovered an outline of a door and began tracing around it with the hopes of discovering the mechanism to open it. He was a quarter of the way around, when the door slowly opened inward, followed by the sound of horses galloping toward him from the far end.

Celthric sensed that there were undead guardians among the riders and knew if they got close enough to Norice, he might cower and scream. He ordered him to retreat behind a nearby boulder, then quickly entered his mind and blocked the fearful sensation. After the horses thundered past their hiding spot, Norice peered around the rock, and caught a glimpse of eight cloaked, hooded riders, and was glad that they didn't see them.

"We don't have much time, so let's move quickly," Celthric warned.

Norice left the safety of his concealment and entered the tunnel. At the far end, he saw a faint light radiating off the walls.

He cautiously followed the corridor until it ended with a dozen empty stables and stairs leading upward. To his right, he saw an upright lever with a sign above it that read, "PULL UP TO OPEN THE DOOR." He pushed it down and heard the tunnel door rumble until it closed.

Back in his study, Repan sensed the trespasser as soon as he entered his fortification and quickly scanned the lower levels. He had just covered one of the three secret entrances when he lost their signal, then he picked up the intruder's thoughts again and could locate his exact position.

What puzzled him the most was that he could do so rather quickly this time, when the previous attempts were nearly impossible to get a fix on the location.

"You're mine now," he whispered and left the room.

In the stable area below, Celthric felt that same someone probing their thoughts again and quickly shielded his and Norice's minds. Once protected, he partitioned off a small portion of his mind and tricked the interloper into thinking he was reading his true thoughts. In reality, it was just an illusion while he read the other's mind. It was easy enough for him to do now that he was prepared. Celthric discovered many things about him. His true name, the title he went by, his darkest fears, details of his early life, the layout of the castle, the bodyguards in his service, and the undead creatures and how they were controlled. He even learned of his plans for ruling the world, the location of something called the Pool of Knowledge and the traps that surrounded it. The heavily guarded room must have been the source of Repan's powers, he surmised, and at some point in time, he too must've had some interaction with the water as well.

After Repan stopped probing, and Celthric was satisfied that the Lord of the Mind was tricked into thinking only Norice was in his home, he had his loyal subject enter through the eastern portion of the castle.

****

The Lord of the Mind moved down the hallway toward the area that housed the Skeletons of War. He was about to enter the room when Kohter came around the bend. Repan paused to address the young man.

"We have an intruder in the lower levels."

"Where, my lord?"

"I've detected him in the eastern entrance. I want you to go there now and capture him."

"Are you sure that's where he is?"

Repan gave him a look that made him feel foolish for asking.

"I'll go there right away, my lord," Kohter said and left.

Repan wasn't going to take any chances. He would take the skeletons with him and guard the pool just in case the intruder slipped past his man.

Something deep down inside nagged at him about the trespasser. How did he enter his castle if the entrances could only be opened from the inside? Was he here to assassinate him? That didn't make sense. Why would his rivals send just one man? They had to know about his bodyguards, Ying and Yang, and the others who protected him. "*Could he be here to drink from the Pool of Knowledge?*" That didn't make sense either, because no one alive, not even his men, knew of its existence. His fears began to get the better of him, and he entered the room in haste.

****

Norice navigated his way up the creaky wooden stairs. After reaching the top, Celthric told him to stop.

"What's wrong?" Norice asked.

"There's a door on your left."

Norice turned and faced a wall. "Where? I don't see anything, its solid earth."

"The wall is an illusion. Feel around until you trigger it open."

Norice painstakingly moved his hands all around the wall. He came to rest on a small hand-sized indent and pushed. The wall rumbled and slid open, revealing a dark corridor beyond.

"Let's go," Celthric ordered.

After stepping inside, Norice saw a lever and pushed it down, closing the hidden door and leaving him in total darkness.

"How much further?" he asked.

"I believe the room we are looking for is another level down."

"I can't see anything. How am I going to do this?"

"I'll guide you the rest of the way," Celthric reassured him.

****

Repan stood in front of six sets of bones, stuffed neatly in leather armor, and took the gem out of his pocket. After saying a few words, the gem glowed, and the bones began rattling and moving toward each other, until they formed six humanoid figures inside of the armor. The undead knights stood up, grabbed nearby weapons, and took up position in front of their master. With eyes glowing green, they radiated fear so powerful that if it wasn't for his superior intellect, Repan would've cowered down in front of them.

"Children, come with me," he commanded, and led his bony troops through a secret door.

The pitch-black corridor Celthric and Norice were in, narrowed and went on for a hundred feet, turned left, and began a steep descent for another hundred. Norice heard the tiny feet of animals scurrying somewhere ahead.

"We need to be careful. I can sense many traps ahead," Celthric warned.

"I can't see a damn thing. Are you sure this is where we want to go?" Norice said, clearly frustrated.

"Yes."

"What are we looking for?"

"Now that we are almost there I can tell you. I am looking for something called the Pool of Knowledge."

"A pool of what?"

"It's called the Pool of Knowledge, and it's very..."

"You made me come all this way for water? And how are you supposed to drink it?" Norice was livid.

"I'm not. You will dip me into the cool water."

"I've killed many people, and for what, so that I can dip you into water? Where's my reward?"

"The water will be yours as well. Just one mouthful and your intellect will grow beyond the average man. Think about it, you can rule over the weak-minded."

"Like you do? What about my family, was there ever a demon?"

"Norice, I needed to do what I had to, otherwise you wouldn't have answered my call or agreed to come with me. You are now the Widowmaker and will rule our vast kingdom."

"If you do not live up to your end of the bargain, I'll sell you for scrap," Norice warned.

His comment almost made Celthric laugh. "Agreed, let's go."

****

Ying, Dojar, and the six undead guardians had just finished walking through a thick part of the woods, looking for this mysterious intruder, when the undead warriors mounted their steeds and rode off in the direction of the castle.

"Where are they going?" Dojar asked.

Before he could respond, Repan contacted Ying through his thoughts and told him the intruder was somewhere inside the castle, and he needed him right away.

"The intruder got in somehow. Let's go." He said.

"How do you know?"

"The master contacted me." Ying quickly mounted his horse and sped off.

By the time they caught up to the skeletons, they were already in front of the door, trying to open it. Dojar thought it was somewhat comical as he watched them struggle with their bony fingers, trying to pry it open.

"For the love of the gods," Ying exclaimed. "How did the door close?" He jumped down from his horse and pushed his way past the skeletons.

Although mindless, they backed away from the bearer of the gem and studied him as he pulled and prodded the door. Ying finally grew annoyed and slammed his right fist against the door.

"Do you think the intruder entered after we left?" Dojar asked.

Ying turned his intense gaze upon him, and if looks could kill, Dojar would've been obliterated. Ying was seething and grabbed the closest skeleton by the head, ripped it off his shoulders in one motion, then tossed it at another skeleton. Dojar had seen him angry before but never this irate.

He was about to say something further, when Ying mounted his mare and galloped toward the main entrance. Dojar followed seconds later while the skeletons stared at them until they were gone, and then turned their attention back to the door.

****

"Be careful. There are steps leading down, so take your time." Celthric said.

Norice slowly descended, taking them one at a time until he reached the bottom.

"This is so frustrating not being able to see," Norice commented.

"Relax and allow me to be your eyes, okay?"

"Alright."

"Take it slow from here on out. I am detecting something down the passageway."

"A creature?"

"No. Maybe a trap."

The descending corridor went on for some time until Celthric detected a carefully placed trap and screamed into Norice's mind for him to stop.

Norice froze. "What is it?"

"There's a trap right in front of you. Back up."

Norice took a few steps. "Where is it?"

"There's a pit full of spikes a few feet in front of you."

"How do we get around it?"

"I need you to trust me on this. Take ten steps backward and allow me to control your limbs."

"Are you sure?"

"Yes, and whatever you do, clear your mind of everything. Think about your kids. Do you understand?"

"Yes."

Norice did as he was instructed, and when he was ready, Celthric controlled his legs and easily jumped over the trap by at least three feet. Norice was amazed.

"That was close," Celthric said and released his control.

"Can you teach me to control my body like that? I never jumped that far in my life, even as a child."

"Once you drink from the water you'll be able to do amazing things. Of course, I'll have to teach you."

They continued until Celthric discovered another trap and said. "Listen carefully. The walls ahead of us have holes in them filled with poisonous javelins. The pressure plates that will release them is in the center of the corridor."

"How do we get past them?"

"I want you to crawl on your stomach next to the wall on your left until I tell you to stop."

"Are you sure?"

"Very."

Norice did as he was instructed and once he was safely past the trap, he was on his feet again and heading down the narrowing passageway.

They had just rounded the bend when Celthric sensed the pool and suddenly became distracted. The interruption almost proved fatal when Norice stepped on a pressure plate, which was followed by the sound of something clicking into place. Lucky for Norice, his instincts kicked in, and he dropped to the ground just as arrows flew out of the wall on his left. After the barrage finally stopped, Norice was only slightly wounded in the left arm.

"What the hell happened? Didn't you sense that trap? You almost cost me my life," Norice barked at the darkness.

"Calm down. The pool is straight ahead, so stay focused."

"A lot of good it will do us if I die."

"It won't happen again. I promise."

Celthric kept his word. After getting by two more traps, they arrived at the large entrance to the room, and Celthric commanded him to stop.

"One more trap and we are home free," he said.

"Where is it?"

"There's a large pressure plate spanning the width of the entrance. I need you to run straight ahead as fast as you can, and once you hear a click, jump forward."

"By the time I hear a click I'll be dead. There is no way I can do this."

"You can. Without your vision your hearing will be more acute."

"Alright," Norice said.

He backed up a few feet, took a few deep breaths, and ran straight ahead. When he heard a loud click, he jumped forward as far as his legs would carry him and landed just as something very heavy crashed to the ground behind him. Once the noise stopped reverberating off the walls, he heard the sound of trickling water up ahead.

"I can hear water," he commented.

"Let's go take a drink," Celthric said in delight.

The Lord of the Mind was very close to the room with the water, when he stopped and began scanning the castle. He found Kohter near the eastern entrance, Ying and Dojar walking toward his study, but no sign of the trespasser until he heard someone's thoughts near the pool, and then it was gone.

"Now I've got you," he whispered.

He was perplexed as to how the intruder shielded his thoughts from him, knew exactly where the pool was, and was able to get past his traps. He knew there was no way, unless he had help. But who would betray him. Ying? Dojar? Or Kohter? To think he was betrayed angered him immensely. Then it dawned on him that maybe the intruder read his thoughts. The idea horrified him. He was done being made a fool of, and entered Ying's mind to show him exactly where the pool was and told him to hurry.

****

Norice followed the sound of trickling water until he bumped against a wall. He pressed his ear against the cold earth and listened. "I think it's behind here."

"Give me a minute." Celthric scanned the room until he detected something odd on a nearby wall. "Walk to the wall on your left. I'm pretty sure there's something that will release the one in front of you."

With his arms extended, Norice carefully moved across the room until he came to another wall. He began running his hands over the surface until he felt a small recess and pushed it down. A loud click ensued, which was followed by the wall on his right sliding upward.

Light from an unknown source illuminated a much larger area with a pool of running water at the far end.

"You did it," Celthric said in excitement.

"No, we did it," Norice added and made his way over.

He was about to step inside the room when someone off to his left spoke, "Well, well, what do we have here?"

Celthric detected undead guardians and quickly used his mind control to steady Norice, then instructed him to turn around and face the speaker. Standing directly in front of them was a middle-aged man, slightly taller than Norice, of slender build, and wearing black robes. His salt and pepper hair and goatee were manicured perfectly. In his right hand, he held a bone staff, in the other, a glowing gem. Two leather-clad large skeletons, armed with swords and wooden shields, moved past him and stopped a few feet away from their master. Four additional skeletons stayed behind him.

Celthric knew who he was and told Norice to repeat everything he was going to say to him.

"Who are you?" Repan demanded.

"Who I am isn't important."

"Cocky aren't you? Alright then, why are you here?"

"It's obvious. I wanted to drink from the water, and once I get my fill, I'll leave without further incident."

"I can't let you do that."

"Why not?"

"Because it's mine." Repan sneered at him.

"Is that the only reason?"

"Pretty much."

"How else was I supposed to get the water? Walk up to your door and ask?"

This entire situation still bothered Repan to no end. "Who told you about my pool? No one alive, not even my men, know about it." He demanded.

"How I came to know about your precious pool is my secret."

"I've had enough of you," Repan said, raising the gem.

The two skeletons in front responded and took a few steps closer.

"There's no need for violence," Norice said, lowering Celthric. "I'll leave peacefully if you allow me to take a drink. I promise."

There was no way Repan was going to allow him to do so. He decided that this man before him was fated to be his servant, just like Paven, and began plotting.

Celthric was reading Repan's thoughts and knew exactly what his intentions were. He was going to have the skeletons attack Norice and then crush his mind once he was engaged with them. Celthric knew this tactic would make it difficult to protect Norice. He would have to fight the skeletons, and fend off their fearful powers, while safeguarding Norice's thoughts from Repan's mind control.

Something had to give. It was either the skeletons or Repan. He made his decision and hoped his gamble would pay off. Norice raised the sword into a high guard and said, "I've decided that this water you so cherish isn't yours at all, and I'm going to drink from it, and there's nothing you can do about it."

"Oh, no?" The Lord of the Mind's eyes narrowed, and he grinned at the challenge before him. He commanded the two skeletons to attack with a mere thought, and they closed in.

Celthric devoted his full attention to defending his host and waited for the skeletons to strike. Their movements were both slow and predictable, and he easily brushed aside and parried the attacks. After the third melee, he baited Repan into entering Norice's mind. Seconds later, he did. While the Lord of the Mind probed Norice's thoughts, trying to discover everything about him, Celthric battled the skeletons. With the graceful and fluid movements of a master swordsman from long ago, he removed the head from the closest skeleton's shoulders and followed through with an overhead strike that split apart the skull of the other. With the threat neutralized, he quickly reentered Norice's mind, hoping it wasn't too late to stop the antagonist.

Repan had just found out who Norice was, the long journey to his castle, the men he killed along the way, the Presence and what befell the entity, and another being. He was about to discover the latter's identity when he suddenly appeared in a tranquil meadow, facing an old man in robes. The sudden change of the landscape startled him, and he knew something was wrong.

"Who are you?" he asked the old man.

"I'm the one who seeks your pool." The old man replied.

"What do you want with the water?"

"The same thing it gave you. Intellect."

"I sense that you aren't a part of Norice, so who are you?"

His confusion brought a smile to Celthric's weathered face. "My name is Celthric."

"What are you, then?"

"What I am isn't important. I could've been many things."

"How did you hide from me?"

"That was easy. You were so focused on finding a person that you didn't think an intellectual being could be anything else but human. Did you really believe you're the only one in the entire world with mental powers? A little presumptuous, don't you think?"

Repan needed to figure out what form this being took the shape of in the outside world and began asking him more questions. "So, tell me, how does a being like you come to exist? I mean you're not an entity or a ghost. Did someone create you?"

"Ah, the vast mysteries of the world that you'll never understand…"

"Tell me!" Repan demanded.

"To do so would fry your brain."

Repan was becoming annoyed with this being. "Can you at least tell me how you knew about my pool? Did someone tell you?"

"I don't see how it will hurt. Actually, I didn't know about your pool. I was drawn to it, so it was only a matter of time before I found the right person to bring me here."

"Drawn to it?"

"Yes, like an animal returning to its place of birth." The old man grinned.

"If you're an object, how does a farmer get past my men, enter my castle, and foil my traps?"

"That was easy. I merely guided him. Now to answer the question that's been bugging you since we entered your home. You were the one who told me where your pool was."

"How?"

"I read your thoughts."

"Impossible! There's no way."

"Everything is possible; you just need to use the right bait."

Repan's jaw tightened. "It appears you have made a grave error."

"Really? How so?"

"I figured out what you are, and after my skeletons kill your host, you will become useless. I will melt you down and sell you for scrap. I wonder what will happen to you or the pain you will feel burning away in my furnace? Did you think about that?"

"And that's where you're wrong again. I figured you would waste time discovering all you could about Norice, so I already defeated the two skeletons before pulling you into my domain. You should have commanded the other four to attack as well, but again, your arrogance will be your downfall."

"After I destroy you, I will turn him into a mindless servant like Paven," Repan stated.

"That won't be easy. My powers are far superior to yours."

"We'll see about that," Repan half-heartedly said.

"Yes, we w..."

Celthric was in mid-sentence when his foe went on the offense, trying to catch his opponent by surprise and end the encounter quickly.

The Lord of the Mind thought about needles. Suddenly, thousands of tiny, razor-sharp projectiles appeared out of thin air and charged at the old man. The attack took him by surprise, and the only defense he managed to throw up in time was a Mind Net. The defensive maneuver stopped half of the needles, while the rest tore through his upper torso, staggering the elderly man.

Repan continued his onslaught and projected a barrage of Mind Daggers. This time, Celthric was ready for the attack and projected Mind Fire. On contact, the daggers melted away. By the time the wall of fire dissipated, Repan was ready for him again and launched a Mind Blast. The wave radiated from his thoughts and crashed into Celthric, sending him flying backward, where he landed on his back several yards away.

Celthric staggered to his feet and was pelted with more needles that tore through virtually every part of his body, knocking him to the ground, where he remained motionless.

Repan grinned, thinking the fight was over. "I guess your powers weren't as superior as you thought, old man," he taunted.

When the area didn't change back to his castle, Repan realized Celthric was still alive, so he conjured up the dreaded Mind Drill with a mere thought, and sent it at him. The cone-shaped twister twirled around and around toward Celthric until it hit him in the stomach and began shredding his body.

Repan was so preoccupied with Celthric's demise that he failed to see someone else flanking his position, or the illusion of the old man shimmering and distorting as it was being minced apart. After positioning himself behind Repan, Celthric thought that his plan worked perfectly. He erected an illusion of himself shortly before pulling Repan inside of his mind, and now he waited until the Lord of the Mind was convinced of his victory before launching his entire arsenal.

The deadly combination of attacks took Repan by surprise. It began with a Mind Blast that left him confused; next the Mind Daggers ripped through his body and sent him to the ground; and finally Repan was hit with Mind Wind. The swirling tunnel lifted him high into the air and tossed him around like a leaf blowing in the wind. Eventually, Repan landed face first on the ground with a loud thud. Celthric hit him again with another Mind Blast that crippled him mentally and left him like a blathering idiot.

Shortly after Norice defeated the two skeletons, Repan was in the heated battle with Celthric and remained perfectly still, staring straight ahead. A few seconds later, the gem controlling the Skeletons of War fell from his limp hand and caused them to crumble to the ground.

Norice thought he was in some sort of trance and wondered if he should kill him or wait for Celthric to advise him. He'd just made up his mind when the Lord of the Mind screamed and fell to his knees, holding his head in obvious pain.

"Celthric must have defeated him," Norice delightfully thought and called out to him. When he failed to respond, he called his name again. After a third time of no reply, he grew concerned that something had happened to him.

Afraid that his indecision might cost him his life, Norice decided to kill Repan, but after taking a few steps, a pair of tough-looking men entered the room.

When Ying and Dojar entered the room, they saw their master on his knees, holding his head, and an intruder within striking distance. Ying instinctively raised his arm and closed his fist, firing his weapon. With deadly accuracy, the thin-spiked chain pierced through the right side of the intruder's body, burrowed into a few organs, and spun around so fast that they were torn to shreds in seconds. Blood spewed forth from Norice's mouth as he silently screamed.

Meanwhile, back inside of Celthric's cerebral domain, he was about to crush Repan's id further, when he felt Norice's pain and returned to his mind. In a fraction of a second, he shielded his companion by sending him to a place of sanctuary deep within the recesses of his mind, then took hold of the chain before it could retract. The friction from the chain stopping tore his flesh away from his hand. Ying never saw anything like it and tried to retract the chain, but the intruder held tight and wouldn't let go. This led to a tug of war, which Celthric knew Norice would eventually lose, so he commanded the right arm to swing the sword down hard on the chain. The blade severed the chain cleanly and sent both men to the ground. Norice's body violently coughed up blood.

Dojar was pretty sure the intruder wasn't going anywhere, so he helped Ying to his feet. "He's finished." He said.

Ying was so mad that his weapon was broken, he ripped it off and threw it to the ground in a fit of rage. "I don't care. My weapon is ruined." He spat on the ground and walked over to Norice, intent on beating him to death.

When he reached him, the man's eyes were vacant, letting him know that he would never get his satisfaction.

Dojar joined him a few seconds later and asked, looking around, "What is the room?"

"Who the hell knows?"

"I wonder what he's doing here."

"Search him." Ying said.

Free from Celthric's control, Repan returned to the present but no longer knew who or where he was. He saw two men standing over a body and thought that he was the next to die. He got up and ran for the nearest exit. The bodyguards turned and saw him running.

"Stay here. I'll get the master," Ying said and stormed away.

****

Norice suddenly appeared on a shoreline as the sun was setting. He gazed out at the crystal blue water and listened to it lap gently against the sand. The sound was both peaceful and soothing. The familiar old man appeared by his side.

"Where am I?" he asked Celthric.

"You're in a safe place. Free from danger."

"I feel tired and weak."

"It's natural, because it's part of the crossing."

"Crossing? I'm dying, aren't I?" Norice realized.

"I'm afraid so, my friend. I couldn't prevent it."

"But I don't want to die. I want to go home to see my family."

"I'm sorry, but it will have to wait. There's a bridge on your left. Walk across and wait for them on the other side. Your wait won't be long while you're here. I promise."

Norice smiled. "For what it's worth, I enjoyed our journey

together."

"You served me well, and I will always consider you my friend. Go now and be at peace."

Norice nodded and walked away.

While Celthric was helping his friend deal with his death, he remained vigilant and made Norice's body appear to be dead. When the bodyguard was close enough, Celthric stabbed him in the stomach. Dojar gasped in horror before falling over. In Norice's final moments, Celthric pulled himself free from Dojar's lifeless body and, with a mighty toss, was thrown into the pool, where he tumbled into the depths below, absorbing all the pool had to offer.

Ying finally caught up to the frightened Repan and grabbed his shoulder, stopping him from going any further.

"Master, what's wrong? Why are you running?" he asked.

"Let me go," Repan responded and tore free from him.

Ying grabbed him again and Repan turned around quickly, ramming a knife into his stomach several times.

Ying grunted and fell to his knees, clutching his wound. When he looked up again, his master was gone.

*Here ends the third installment of A Demon's Quest the Beginning of the End. Many more tales of adventure await the reader in **A Place Known as Other.***

ABOUT THE AUTHOR

Charles Carfagno Jr. is a native of Pennsylvania. He's been writing since 2003 and currently writes on nights and weekends in addition to his successful day job in the IT field. He is really excited to share his writing with the world and would love to hear from and interact with other authors and readers

ADQ Series:
A Demon's Quest The Beginning of the End Volume 1
A Demon's Quest The Beginning of the End Volume 2
A Demon's Quest The Beginning of the End Volume 3
A Place Called the Other
The Awakening
The Dawn of the Chosen One

Short Story:
The Wayward Knight

Standalone Novel:
Madness of My Dreams

Email:
cdcinkwell@gmail.com

Web Site:
https://demonsquest.com/

If you haven't signed up for my mailing list, you're missing out on exciting news, free stuff, and articles.